The HINDSIGHT PROJECT

THE HINDSIGHT PROJECT

A Travel in Time

Robert Connell

MILL CITY PRESS

Mill City Press, Inc.
2301 Lucien Way #415
Maitland, FL 32751
407.339.4217
www.millcitypress.net

Printed in the United States of America

ISBN-13: 9781545636817

CHAPTER

1

Either I've screwed up big time, or something momentous is about to happen.

Those prophetic words echo through Kyle O'Brien's head as he impatiently waits in line. He doesn't have a clue why he's been ordered to the Pentagon—but he knew this meeting would be the most important of his Marine Corps career, possibly even his life.

Finally he reaches the reception desk. "I have an appointment with the Secretary of Defense."

All five people behind the counter glance his way.

"Yes," the woman seated in front of him gave an indulgent smile and replied, "*And* with whom do you have an appointment in the Secretary's office?"

"My meeting is at 1400 with *the* Secretary . . . Henry Evans."

She hesitated. "Could I see your military identification card please?"

Kyle slid it across the counter.

She scrutinized his ID, and placed a call. "Yes, I have a Marine Corps Major, Kyle O'Brien, in the lobby." She glanced his way. "Says he has a two o'clock appointment with Secretary Evans." After listening for a moment, she gave him a curious look.

I know why she's giving me that look. Majors don't meet with the top gun in Defense.

1

She handed back his ID. "Have a seat. Someone will be with you shortly." She beamed a big smile, leaned forward and whispered, "I'm sorry about the questions. I've worked at the Pentagon for ten years and you're the first major to have a private conference with the Secretary."

Kyle smiled, thanked her, and took a seat in the reception area. Within minutes he hopped up, straightened his tie, adjusted his sharply creased, green service uniform, and began to pace.

How the hell do I prepare for something this important when I don't have a clue what it's about?

He couldn't stop thinking about the request he'd received two weeks before from the Commanding General of the Second Marine Corps Division. Kyle had been ordered to report to the Secretary of Defense. When he asked for additional information, they informed him the order came from the Commandant of the Marine Corps, at the request of the Chairman of the Joint Chiefs of Staff—no additional information provided.

In the meantime, every inch of Kyle's body had been probed, examined and stressed in the most complete physical of his life. Afterwards, a team of Navy psychiatrists had taken over for another three days of intensive testing and interviews.

And still not a hint as to why? He continued asking, but no one had an answer.

After checking his watch, Kyle glanced at the fifty or so people moving past him in a lobby the size of a large Hilton Hotel. About half were civilians. The other half wore uniforms from all branches of the U.S. military, plus a smattering of foreign uniforms.

He was just another Leatherneck in a sea of military uniforms. His height, at six feet just a little above average. His build, muscular but trim, and his light brown hair close cropped. Probably only his blue eyes gave any hint of his concern regarding this meeting.

He had visited the Pentagon only once before, as a junior in high school. The school-sponsored trip to Washington D.C. had included a two hour tour of the Pentagon.

Now some of that trivia percolated through his brain—data that seemed awe-inspiring at the time. The Pentagon—the world's largest office building—had five interlocking rings, starting with A in the center and moving out to E. The powerful "E Ring" held the larger offices, with windows for the high ranking officials. No doubt Secretary Evans would be located there.

Kyle continued pacing, finally giving in and rechecking his watch. Only ten minutes had passed.

Out of the corner of his eyes he spotted a general moving through internal security and entering the lobby. He wore three stars on each shoulder and looked like an actor in a war movie. Tall, slim, ramrod straight, he sported a perfectly tailored Army uniform, with rows of ribbons covering half his chest.

I don't think a Lieutenant General would be my escort.

The general stopped, scanned the lobby and headed in Kyle's direction.

Well I'll be damned, he just might.

"Major O'Brien?"

Kyle snapped to attention. "Yes, sir."

"I'm General Campbell, Senior Military Assistant for Secretary Evans." The general reached out and shook his hand. "Welcome to the Pentagon. I'll escort you over to the secretary's office." He handed Kyle a visitor's badge. "We've got tight security. Put this on for the checkpoints."

As they walked briskly through different corridors, Kyle remembered his high school tour guide telling the students about the more than seventeen miles of passageways and over twenty-three thousand people working in the building. She had jokingly mentioned people being lost for days in the maze of hallways.

They passed through three security checkpoints and entered D Ring. General Campbell moved through checkpoints the way Moses parted the Red Sea. With a simple wave of his hand, the U.S. Pentagon Police ushered them to the front of the line and around the X ray equipment, all accomplished without breaking stride.

"I'm glad you know where you're going," Kyle said.

Campbell smiled. "It gets confusing. Story has it, back in the days of Western Union, a messenger in a green uniform got lost in the Pentagon. He emerged three days later as a Lieutenant Colonel."

Kyle chuckled. "Maybe there's hope. I'm in a green uniform. Maybe I'll get lost and promoted to Lieutenant General."

"Who knows Major, stranger things have happened in this building. I personally don't believe it." He hesitated a moment. "In three days the most he could have made was major."

They continued the fast pace. As a high school student Kyle never imagined he would walk these halls as a Marine, and even now, never for a meeting with the Defense Secretary.

"Major, have you met Secretary Evans before?"

"No, sir."

"I almost never escort people in from the lobby," Campbell said. "Admiral Cary requested this . . . wanted you to have a little briefing before the meeting."

"That would be helpful, Sir."

They entered E ring and most of the corridor traffic disappeared.

Once through the checkpoint Campbell continued. "The secretary is a no bullshit kind of guy. Small talk will consist of hello and goodbye. Give him direct, concise answers, the shorter the better —no rambling. He hates that."

"And if I don't know the answer?"

"Just say so. Don't give him—what he calls military doubletalk. By the way, he'll probably stand up for most of the meeting—says he thinks better on his feet."

"Will you be in the meeting, General?"

"No. The secretary has asked Admiral Cary to join him."

Kyle let out a slight whistle. "The Chairman of the Joint Chiefs of Staff will be there?"

"Yeah, not many majors get to meet with their boss's, boss's, boss's, boss's, boss's, boss." The general gave a chuckle. "And I probably left out a few bosses. I've got to say, Major, you're in damn exclusive company. The secretary has plenty of short meetings ... slam bam, get to the point and out. But few like this."

Kyle asked, "Do you know what this is about, sir?"

"No, but to give you an idea of today's importance, in my one year as Secretary Evans's assistant, there have been few meetings scheduled for more than a half-hour. Four of them were with the President—only the President. The remaining handful all included staff, a weekly briefing with Admiral Cary, two with Senator Harris, who heads up the Senate Armed Services Committee, and one with the Director of the Central Intelligence Agency, and now, one with you—only you."

Kyle took a deep breath. *This might be even more important than I thought? But why me?*

The U.S. Pentagon building in Arlington County, Virginia, headquarters of the U.S. Department of Defense and the world's largest office building by floor area, with 6,500,500 Sq. feet. Approximately 26,000 military and civilian employees work in the Pentagon. Construction started in 1941 and was completed January 1943.

CHAPTER

2

$\mathcal{S}$ecretary of Defense Henry Evans hung up the phone, walked across his large, dark paneled office and stared out at the panoramic view of the Potomac. After a few moments Evans glanced over at Admiral Dennis Cary, who sat at a conference table and continued to thumb through a thick file.

"General Campbell and Major O'Brien will be here shortly," Evans said.

The admiral, dressed in his crisp, white summer uniform, with four-star shoulder boards and a chest full of ribbons, closed the folder and looked up. "I reviewed O'Brien's file a few days ago and liked what I read. This additional psychiatric report only confirms it."

"I agree," Evans said.

"Sir, when we narrowed down the list of candidates last week, you inquired about Major O'Brien's Navy Cross Medal. I have a copy of the citation—it's short, I can read it if you like?"

"Please do."

Cary pulled a file from his briefcase. "O'Brien received the medal four year ago." He looked down and started. "Captain Kyle O'Brien commanded a Force Reconnaissance unit attached to the First Reconnaissance Battalion, Second Marine Division in the vicinity of Asadabad, Afghanistan.

While leading an eight-man force with the mission of cap-turing a high level Taliban leader, Captain O'Brien's unit was ambushed in extremely rugged, enemy controlled territory. In the ensuing action, against an estimated force of forty to sixty fighters, all members of his team were wounded. Although shot twice and barely able to walk, Captain O'Brien . . ."

Evans interrupted, "So that's where he got the Purple Hearts. Where was he shot?

After a quick check, Cary answered. "In the thigh and the shoulder, both fortunately flesh wounds. The most impressive part comes after he's wounded."

"Go ahead, Admiral, I didn't mean to interrupt.

Cary glanced back at his notes. "Captain O'Brien fought his way to a high and commanding position overlooking the enemy. With rifle and grenades he continued the fight for an hour, causing the enemy to withdraw from their exposed posi-tion. The enemy retreat allowed additional support to arrive by helicopter. All eight members of the team were evacu-ated, although only four survived the attack. By his excep-tional leadership and immeasurable courage, Captain O'Brien upheld the highest traditions of the Marine Corps and the United States Military. He is recommended for our nation's second highest military award, the Navy Cross."

"That's impressive," Evans said. "After being shot twice, he climbs up a steep hill and keeps fighting to save his men."

Cary nodded and closed the folder. "He also led a mission in Iraq, where they targeted an important Iraqi general. On his third tour he received a Bronze Star with Valor, for a Pakistani operation that took out a Taliban commander. He's currently Executive Officer of the Second Force Reconnaissance Battalion. That's the elite of the Marine Corps. His skills fit perfectly for this mission."

"You know, Admiral, in my three years as secretary I've been involved in a number of life-and-death troop decisions. But it's always been at a macro level. This is different and much more difficult. I've never picked *the* person to go into harm's way."

The phone rang and Evans answered. "Yes. OK, give me a minute."

He sat next to the admiral and looked him in the eyes. "O'Brien's in the outer office with the General. So, we're in agreement. We approve this project, the CIA is in charge, and Major O'Brien is heading it up."

The admiral shrugged and nodded. "As we've already discussed, I don't feel comfortable with the CIA being in charge."

"Who does?" Evans said. "I don't trust the CIA any more than you do. But we've got no choice—they've got the contacts and the technology. Hell, we're lucky the President insisted the military supply the personnel for this operation. The CIA Director didn't like having this crammed down his throat." Evans paused. "Now, Admiral, let me ask again. Do we move ahead with Major O'Brien?"

"Sir, we're not going to find any better. O'Brien's my choice."

"I agree." Evans nodded. "Hell, he's your classic all American success story. He could be on those recruitment ads the Marines used. You know. . . . 'A few good men.'"

Evans looked down at the photo fastened to the top of O'Brien's file. "I know it's a dangerous mission. But I don't want to see this young man die."

CHAPTER

3

*K*yle **walked in with** General Campbell, who made the introductions and quickly exited.

Secretary Evans motioned to a chair at the conference table. "Please have a seat across from Admiral Cary. I'll stand for a while. Have you been to the Pentagon before, Major?"

Kyle sat and couldn't help but notice the size of the office. A half-court game of basketball could be played there with room to spare. One wall held photos of the Secretary with world leaders.

"This is my second visit, sir." Kyle considered telling them about the school trip, but remembered General Campbell's comment on small talk.

Evans walked over to a huge, ornate desk and leaned back on the edge.

Kyle had seen Evans in numerous TV interviews, but he had always been seated, or behind a lectern. Evans stood only about five-foot-six, and yet his deep, booming voice gave him a commanding presence. He wore a dark blue suit, a white, buttoned-down shirt, and a deep red power necktie

"I see you're admiring my desk." Evans placed a hand on the highly polished, dark wood surface, completely clear of paperwork. "It's got quite a history—originally built for the World War I commander, General 'Black Jack' Pershing. They moved it here after construction of the Pentagon in 1942."

Crossing his arms, Evans leaned back and continued. "Sometimes I sit and think of all the tough decisions that have been made around this desk—where to drop the first atomic bomb—the Inchon invasion of Korea—the naval blockade of Cuba, the response to the 9/11 attack on the World Trade Center and on this building. And now this decision."

This decision? How the hell does this decision rank up there with 9/11?

Evans suddenly sprang from the desk and vigorously rubbed his hands together. "Well, enough chit-chat. Do you have any idea why you're here?"

"No one's given me an explanation, sir. When my commanding officer told me about this appointment, he said, 'Either you've screwed up really big time, or something momentous is about to happen.'" Kyle grinned. "I'm hoping for momentous."

Both Evans and the admiral chuckled.

"Sir, I've given it a lot of thought. The only thing I came up with, it has something to do with my counterterrorist experience."

"You're right," Evans said, "but, it goes far beyond your combat experience. You've probably wondered why you were given such a battery of tests. We wanted to determine your adaptability. I call it your ability to think outside the box, or to make a paradigm shift. By the way, we tested a large group from across the military spectrum. You came out on top."

Evans strolled over and pulled a plaque off the wall. "I've hung this in every office I've occupied since college. Let me read you a couple of memorable quotes. 'The telephone has too many shortcomings to be seriously considered as a means of communication. The device has no value to us'—Western Union, 1876. 'Airplanes are interesting toys but of no military value'—Marshal Foch, French Army Commander, 1916. 'Everything that can be invented has been invented'—Charles Duell, Commissioner, U.S. Office of Patents, 1899."

10

After hanging the plague back on the wall, Evans chuckled. "Mr. Duell wanted to close the US Patent Office. There's more, but you get the idea."

Evans moved over and looked down at Kyle. "I mention these quotes because you're going to be assigned an operation that could have a far greater impact than the airplane, or man's first step on the moon. It's outside the box, and that's the reason you're here with the two highest officials in Defense."

More important than the moon walk? Enough talk, tell me about this crazy mission.

"Now," Evans pointed to Cary, "the Admiral will fill you in on the details."

"Thank you, Mr. Secretary." Cary pulled a sheet of paper out of his briefcase. "Major, before we get started, I have a form for you to sign. It's very basic. The project you're being assigned to is classified Top Secret. I might add it's probably the most highly secretive mission in the U.S. government today. You may discuss this assignment only with your immediate supervisor. You may not share this, or any part of it, with your fellow operatives, or any other official in the US government—and obviously, no one outside the government. If you violate this agreement, you will be prosecuted to the full extent of the law."

Cary handed him the one page agreement. "By the way, we're the only two people in Defense who know about this assignment. We both signed the form."

After a quick read, Kyle picked up the pen. *I've got plenty of doubts, but not about disclosing top secret information.* He signed and laid the paper on the table.

"Welcome aboard," Evans said, "One last little bit of paperwork. We think it should be led by an O5 pay grade. If you accept this assignment, you will be immediately promoted to Lieutenant Colonel."

"Mr. Secretary, is that possible? I'm not eligible for promotion for another year."

Cary gave him a sidelong glance. "If there's one thing I've learned about Secretary Evans, he generally gets what he asks for. If he wants you promoted—you'll be a Lieutenant Colonel. Now, let's get down to business. You won't work for Defense. You'll report to the CIA on this project. The CIA Officer in charge will be joining us after this meeting."

Kyle jolted up straight. "The CIA? I won't report to the Marine Corps or the Defense Department?"

"That's right," Cary said, "it's a combined operation. The CIA has the contacts in country, and they'll be providing a new technology."

Evans interjected, "I know you've got questions. We'll fill you in on this exciting technology shortly."

"So, we're providing the manpower," Cary continued, "and you'll be in charge of a small special ops unit. We want to keep this very tightly controlled. That's the reason you're meeting with just the two of us. I think you'll understand when you hear the details of the project."

Kyle considered probing a little deeper. *I'll be in charge, but I'll report to the CIA. I don't like the sound of that.* "Sir, maybe a little clarification would help. Who will I report to within the CIA?"

"Good question," Evans said. "It's a subject the CIA Director and I have . . ." he hesitated for a few seconds, "let's say we've had *meaningful discussions* about who you report to. They will provide you with detailed information and recommendations on the operation. But you're in charge. If pushed, you work for the Defense Department. If there is an unsolvable problem, you call my office. I guess you could say you report to me. Is that clear?"

It sounded surprisingly vague for such an important assignment. But Kyle at the moment didn't have a better solution. "Yes sir. If I run into problems I'll call you."

Evans nodded. "That's correct. Go ahead, Admiral."

"Yes, sir. The mission objective is to infiltrate and destroy an Iranian underground facility currently assembling nuclear warheads."

"Nuclear warheads! I didn't know they were that advanced. Isn't that against their agreement?"

"Yes. Damn right it is." Cary said. "We don't know the exact number of warheads, but over twenty-five. They will be transported out of the cave within three weeks to unknown locations in Iran, and to other of their allies in the Middle East."

Evans tensed. "They must be destroyed before that happens! You, Major are selected to lead this operation."

Kyle, in total shock, stared at the two men. *Nuclear warheads being distributed throughout the Arab world!*

Evans continued. "I might add that neither of us knows the full details of the assignment. We only know the overview. This operation will set back their efforts by at least eight years. But there's a second aspect to the mission that makes it even more confidential. You will be using an advanced technology."

After a quick glance at Cary, Evans continued. "Major, this is where you need to make that paradigm shift we discussed." He took a deep breath. "In this assignment, because of its importance, you will be using a new and somewhat untested technology—time travel."

"Time travel?" Kyle gave him a puzzled look. "Like in science fiction movies?"

"Major—I'm sorry." Evans gave him a grin. "Maybe I should be calling you Colonel. I'm not a scientist. I don't know all the technical details. Nor will the CIA give them to you, and for good reason. If by chance you're captured, the Iranians will torture you and probably get answers. This technology simply can't be revealed to the Iranians."

"I understand. But you must be able to tell me something, sir."

"OK." Evans stood and started pacing again. "You will use this technology, but not know all the details. Hell, I can relate to that. I use a computer, but I can't tell you how it works. You'll leave here and be transferred to a CIA facility."

"Where is this facility located?"

"They haven't told us where. The complex has a complete mock-up of the Iranian site. That's where you'll do mission training. But they have provided limited details on this time travel. In a nutshell, this is how it works—you will wear something called a relativity transponder. It's a type of device that has the ability to transport you back in time for fifteen minutes. They are currently working on expanding that window to hours instead of minutes."

Kyle found this confusing. It sounded kind of hocus-pogus to him. He needed details. "Can you explain *how* this helps in combat?"

"I'll give it a try." Evans continued to pace. "Let's say you are moving through the nuclear facility. After rounding a corner, a guard with a machine gun surprises you. You're wearing one of these transponders."

"Sir, wait a minute. How big is this thing?"

"It's small, the size of a wristwatch. You push a button and are transported back in time for fifteen minutes."

"Push a button?" Kyle asked, "So what do you mean *transported*? You just dissolve in air and reappear back where you were fifteen minutes before? Kind of like Star Trek?"

After a quick glance at Cary, Evans asked, "Can you help me out, Admiral?"

Cary cleared his throat. "I'll try. A CIA Officer will be here shortly and he can give you better answers. Did you ever see the movie *Groundhog Day*?"

"Yes sir. Quite a few times, it's a favorite."

"This may sound stupid," Cary said, "but it worked for me. It's like that movie. Remember, Bill Murray wakes up every morning in the same place—Groundhog Day in Pennsylvania. Each time he does something different, and no one else knows it's a remake. Finally he gets it right and continues on with life.

He just went to sleep. But, for you, it will be by disappearing and traveling through space."

Kyle could tell that neither of these men had a clue as to how this relativity thing really worked. But it was his body—no, make that his life—and he needed more information—which, unfortunately would have to come from the CIA. "Has this thing been tested on humans?"

"Yes. That was my first question. It's been tested on chimpanzees and then humans." Cary paused. "I'm going to be truthful with you, Major. The CIA had time travel scheduled for at least another year of testing. It's being released early because of the importance of this Iranian mission. But the CIA scientists on the project have assured us it is safe."

Evans stared intently at Kyle. "This technology will change modern warfare as we know it, and has the potential to save thousands of lives. It reminds me of the Apollo space missions. First they tested chimpanzees and then humans. And we successfully put a man on the moon."

And I think they lost three astronauts along the way.

Evans glanced at the form on the table. "You signed this Top Secret document and know the consequences. That doesn't mean you have to go through with this." Evans motioned to the ribbons on Kyle's uniform. "You have already risked your life—-more than once—-and served your country with honor. If you don't feel right about this, get up and walk out of this office right now, no questions asked. Nothing about this mission will ever appear on your record." Evans stood. "We're going to step out of the office and meet with the CIA Officer. Take your time and think it through. When you come to a decision, pick up the phone and let us know."

"Thank you, sir. It's considerate of you."

The two men left the room. Kyle stared at the wall. He'd never walked away from a fight in his whole life. On the other hand, he'd never come across an assignment with so many unanswered questions. Plus unknown risks.

15

To top off Kyle's concerns, he would be working with the CIA. His past experience with that organization while in Afghanistan had been terrible. But he could tell that issue had already been settled.

It's a CIA project.

Kyle stood and paced the length of the large office and considered his options. Deep down he knew this mission meant a career change. He would never again go back to regular Marine Corps duty and would probably stay in covert operations. And what about this time travel thing? It's one thing to face an enemy holding a rifle, quite another to be atomized and shot through space. He could walk out now—go back to Camp Lejeune and the life of a Fleet Marine Force Officer.

He stopped abruptly. A conversation with an instructor during his Marine Officer's training flashed through his mind. He remembered it well—an order from your superior officer must not be questioned—-if it puts you in harm's way, tough shit. The Marine Corps is not a debating society.

I can't walk away from something this important to me and the country. I would never forgive myself.

He stood for a moment. Then finally heaved a sigh and picked up the telephone. "Tell the Secretary I'm ready."

Cary and Evans reentered the office.

Evans looked Kyle in the eyes. "What's it going to be?"

"Mr. Secretary, Admiral, I'll take the mission. I've got hundreds of questions buzzing around in my head. Hopefully, the CIA can answer them—if not—can I change my mind?"

"Of course you can." Evans grasped his shoulder. "I meant what I said. You meet with the CIA, if by tomorrow you want to turn it down, I'll understand."

"Thank you. I know the consequences of this mission. We've got to stop the Iranians."

"Colonel O'Brien, you're correct about this mission— I have full confidence you will be successful."

The Admiral headed to the door. "I'll get the CIA officer."

Evans reached out and shook his hand. "With this assignment, you're now working with the CIA. I sense your concerns. They definitely look down their noses at the military. If you have any problems . . . call me—night or day."

The two locked eyes. Kyle nodded.

"Colonel," Evans said, "you've got exciting and perilous times ahead. On behalf of our nation, I thank you."

CHAPTER

4

*S*ecretary **Evans made the** introduction between Kyle and the Central Intelligence Agency's Stan Jackson. Within minutes the two of them left the secretary's office.

Kyle gave a quick glance at Jackson. He looked forty-plus, stood about five-seven, wore glasses and had a receding hairline. A slight paunch hung over his dark blue suit-pants.

I wonder what ever happened to all those James Bond secret agent types?

As they exited the building, Jackson also sized him up. "That's what I call a high powered meeting you had going in there."

Kyle nodded. "You're right. I was a little uptight, but it went okay."

"What's up?" Jackson pointed to Kyle's shoulder. "They introduced you as colonel. But your record lists you as major, and that's the rank you're wearing."

Kyle grinned, "Along with this assignment, I got another surprise—a promotion to lieutenant colonel."

"Congratulations." Jackson reached over and shook his hand. "It must have gone a hell of a lot better than okay if you walk out with this assignment plus a promotion. But I'm afraid you're not going to have much time to celebrate, Colonel."

"That's alright. I know this is important." Kyle paused. "Although Colonel sounds great, and still hard to believe, how about we do away with the formalities? I'm Kyle, and you're Stan."

"Sounds fine to me. The CIA's not big on military protocol."

Stan pointed ahead. "The car's right up here. I'm sure you're familiar with the Quantico Marine Base."

"You bet. That's where I went through Officers Candidate School. I've done Force Recon training there, and a few years back I attended a six month program at the War Fighting Laboratory."

"Good, that's where we're headed. We're having your gear from Camp Lejeune packed up and shipped ASAP."

They walked up to a green, two-year-old Chevy Malibu.

Kyle chuckled. "I thought you *Secret Agent Men* all drove fancy sports cars with machine guns mounted in the hood. I'm disappointed."

"Well, first off, my official title is Operations Officer, not Secret Agent. That's strictly Hollywood stuff. Regarding my car, this is only temporary. My Lamborghini Huracan is in the shop right now. The rear-mounted cannon's not working properly." Stan grinned. "Hop in, but don't touch the cigarette lighter. That activates the passenger ejection system."

They pulled out of the Pentagon, and headed south.

"When we get there," Stan said. "I'll introduce you to some of the people involved in this project. They're engineers and physicists, and some are CIA Officers with an inside knowledge of Iran. None of the technical types will have a last name, nor will they necessarily be using their real first names. We'll know a lot about you, and you'll know nothing about us." He shrugged. "Sorry, that's just the way it's got to be."

"Secretary Evans filled me in on that, but you told me your last name."

"Yeah. Do you really think my name is Stan Jackson? My real name is Rock Solid. I'm a six-foot-four, blue-eyed Adonis. This is all a disguise."

Kyle laughed. "Well Rock, it's nice to see you've got a sense of humor."

"The world would be a terrible place without it."

Stan drove for a while in silence. "Now, on a serious note, I will be your main contact. This project is as high up the flag pole as Top Secret gets. We've labeled it The Hindsight Project. I'm limited on the information you can receive."

"I'm glad you brought that up. I'm putting my life and those of the team selected on the line. I'll need additional information on time travel—the effects on the body—even more, on the mind. The Secretary of Defense didn't have many details. He said you would fill me in. I'll also need all the details regarding the operations side of the mission."

Stan gave him a quick glance. "To be truthful, the Director of the CIA is the one calling the shots. He's *really* limited the ops and technical information you'll receive to a need to know basis."

Kyle pointed to the I-95 Quantico exit ahead. "Once you're off the interstate, pull over. We've got to talk."

After exiting, Stan headed into a Kentucky Fried Chicken parking lot and cut the engine.

Kyle immediately faced him. "Stan, I don't want to be confrontational in our first hour of working together. However, I'm not going to be pushed into the corner with this *Need To Know* bullshit. The Secretary of Defense assured me I would be given full information on the mission, except for the technical details—no holding back."

"Calm down." Stan held up both hands. "You know we're two lucky guys. This is the most exciting new development to hit warfare in God knows how many years and we're in charge of it. Don't fuck it up."

"I don't see how my getting additional info fucks anything up," Kyle said. "Let me tell you a story—a sad but true story. I'm sure you've read my service records. Did you read my Navy Cross commendation?"

"You mean about the mission in Asadabad, Afghanistan. Yes I did."

"That commendation's not the whole story. The CIA authorized the mission—the only involvement I've ever had with your organization. Normally before a local mission I would gather all the details and study them carefully. This one started differently. Three haughty, pretentious CIA men showed up with orders from Central Command."

Stan stopped him. "Do you know their names?"

"Are you kidding me? The same crap you just pulled—first names only. And no background info provided. It was above *my need to know*"

"What was the mission?" Stan asked.

"The capture of a chief Taliban leader. Another anonymous Taliban official was providing the info. The CIA said they would vouch for his reliability. I complained, but to no avail."

Stan let out a sigh. "And you stepped into an ambush."

"You're damn right I did." Kyle hesitated. "It's hard to talk about. A CIA liaison was supposed to join us—he canceled at the last minute. They choppered us into the village and a complete disaster. Four good men died, the other four, including me, were seriously injured. All because I trusted the fucking CIA."

"I'm sorry," Stan said

"See this blue and white ribbon." Kyle pointed to his chest. "It's the Navy Cross. When I put it on this morning—I only wear it when required—I'm reminded of those four men going home to their families in coffins. "

"What happened to the three CIA men?"

"Never showed up, not a word. You're the first person I've talked to since *your agency* vouched for the mission— no apologies, no excuses, no condolences. I still have nightmares about it, and always will. Now you understand. Don't use that *need to know* bullshit on me."

"I get it loud and clear, Colonel." Stan rubbed his face. "For what it's worth, I would love to get my hands on those guys." He held up both hands and shrugged. "There's not a damn thing I can do about it, except show you that we're not all like that. Kyle, this mission is important. The most important mission I've ever been involved in—maybe ever will be. I'm sure the same for you. For this country, let's make this damn thing work."

Kyle stared at him. "I need that information or I call Secretary Evans."

Stan groaned. "This project is so important everybody wants a piece of the action. The CIA Director wanted to handle this Iranian time travel without any help. The Secretary of Defense gets wind of it and wants the same thing. So it ends up in the President's lap. Being the ultimate politician, he compromises and pisses off both sides. Now *The Secretary* and *The Director* can't stand each other."

With a shrug Kyle said, "How does that change my job?"

"Let's not get in the middle," Stan said. "Someone once told me, 'When two big, mean bulls get in a barnyard fight, whole bunches of little chickens get stomped on.' In case you don't know, we're the chickens. Give me a chance. I have the Scientific Director on time travel flying in day after tomorrow. Ask any question, I'll do my best to give you an answer. Regarding the mission facts, we meet tomorrow and the same goes. If you're still not satisfied, then we call in the bulls."

Stan gave him a hard look. "Deal?"

Kyle didn't want to be pushed around. But did he really want to call Evans with less than one day on the mission? The scenario reminded him of a little kid running to his daddy for help.

"It's a deal." Kyle held out his hand. "This mission is more important than interagency rivalries and big egos. I'll hold off. But, in a few days if I'm not satisfied, I make that call."

"I think we're going to do just fine." Stan grabbed his hand.

Kyle said. "By the way, that was a damn good analogy. I've never thought of myself as a chicken."

Stan started the engine. "Let's get to Quantico. I need a drink." He pointed to the KFC sign above them. "That reminds me. We're having steak, not chicken for dinner."

As they approached the Quantico base, Stan said, "My car has a special sticker. We're going around to a side gate where they'll wave us through. Our group is located in old abandoned warehouses out in the training area of the base. We wanted to keep a low profile. The area's fenced off, highly secured and isolated. We've got individual sleeping quarters and some mockups in the warehouses."

"I thought I'd be flying back to Lejeune tonight. I don't even have a toothbrush."

"I know," Stan said. "I've ordered three days of clean clothes and supplies for you. By then your gear should arrive from Camp Lejeune."

A Marine MP waved them through the side gate. They drove about ten miles into the base, where their ID's were scrutinized at a CIA checkpoint.

"By the way," Kyle said, "you pointed out the passenger ejection system. Where's the driver ejection system?"

"Good thing I didn't tell you. I'd be lying back there in the KFC parking lot." Stan turned onto a side road. "There're our buildings in front of us. This will be your home for at least the next three weeks. Looks like a Ritz Carlton or a Four Seasons Resort, doesn't it?"

Kyle checked out the buildings. "Yeah, real fancy— reminds me of Alcatraz, only no water and no San Francisco."

CHAPTER

5

Three large, corrugated metal warehouses loomed ahead of Kyle. Each appeared to be twenty to thirty thousand square feet and built in the 1940s. The buildings had no windows, but plenty of rust spots and dirt. They needed repair—lots of it.

"Well," Kyle said, "about the only nice thing I can say is, you've selected a beautiful location."

The warehouses stood alone in a small meadow, surrounded by a forest of northern red oaks and pine trees. A brook meandered through the green meadow.

Kyle studied the area. "In my three tours of duty at Quantico, I've never seen this part of the base. To use a Marine term, it's in the boondocks."

"It's perfect. We needed privacy." Stan pulled into a parking area. "Before we go in let's discuss tomorrow's schedule. We thought about giving you Iranian Farsi language classes. I noted you picked up a little Dari Persian during your tour in Afghanistan, which is similar to Farsi. We're under a tight deadline and our in-country operative is fluent in Farsi. So, we decided to drop the classes."

"That's fine. How much time do I have before the mission?"

"This really hit the President's hot button. It's a window of opportunity that we don't want to pass up. You're going to cram about four months' worth of preparation into three

24

weeks of intensive planning and training. Most of your days, nights and weekends will be spent in this lovely spot."

Kyle gave him a hard look. "But first thing tomorrow, I learn the mission details, correct?"

"Tomorrow morning I'll give you the ops files. They're detailed and should answer most of your questions. You'll have a couple of days to study them. Day after tomorrow, the scientific operations guy comes in to brief you on transponders and time travel."

They entered one of the warehouses and headed down a long corridor. Kyle noticed a couple of conference rooms and then numbered doors extending along both sides of the center hallway. Stan opened the door to number seven. "Welcome to your home for probably three weeks."

The roughly fourteen-by-eighteen-foot room had a concrete floor, a bunk bed and a small desk and chair. The Spartan quarters had neither windows nor a bathroom.

"This building was put back into use two weeks ago. The bathroom and showers are down the hall. Just a few luxuries— they installed air-conditioning and it's got a small safe. You'll be working with confidential reports. Each night make sure and lock them up. Pretty fancy, huh?"

Kyle smirked, "Yeah, kind of reminds me of a cell in the brig."

Stan pointed to the closet, which also had a small dresser. "You'll find three full sets of desert tan utilities hanging there, plus a pair of boots, extra socks and underwear. Hope I got the sizes right. I don't completely understand this belt thing with Marines. I know it has something to do with a Martial Arts program. The Marine I worked with said that, since you're Force Recon, you're probably a Black Belt."

Kyle smiled. "Thanks for arranging all this—and he's right, I am a black belt."

Stan checked his watch. "Dinner will be served in about an hour. They normally bring in food from main side, but it looks like a beautiful evening, so you'll be the guest of honor at cocktails and dinner. We'll BBQ steaks at the picnic tables behind the barracks and you'll get to meet some of the team. We've got twelve people here currently. It's split between the scientific team and my CIA ops guys. Very casual dress. See you there."

Once alone, Kyle took off his uniform jacket, loosened his tie and sat on the bed. It had been a whirlwind day—a meeting with the two top officials in Defense, a promotion, and an important assignment . . . one that's a cross between Mission Impossible and Star Trek.

His last two promotions had been celebrated at an Officers Club with a large group of friends, and many rounds of drinks. *Instead, here I sit, in an old warehouse in the middle of nowhere, with a group of scientists and CIA spooks I've never met.*

He reached into his pocket for his cell phone and punched in Jennifer's number. The phone rang four times and switched to voice mail. He left a message. "Hi, Jenn. Sorry I missed you. I mentioned last week that I would be heading up to Washington and the Pentagon for meetings. Well, I've got exciting news. I've been given a new assignment and also a promotion to Lieutenant Colonel. I'll call you back later and we can talk. I love you."

Their year old relationship had grown serious in the last six months with his driving most weekends from Camp Lejeune to her apartment in Atlanta. The word "love" was a recent addition. When he first expressed his feelings Jenn had smiled and said. "My God, I'm amazed—you just said the L word. I thought Marines only used F words."

Kyle leaned back on the bed and closed his eyes. They first met while he attended a Georgia Tech football game with two of his buddies. He spent most of the game admiring the auburn-haired, blue-eyed beauty sitting one row in front of him. By games end he had managed to strike up a conversation.

Jennifer Ryan had graduated from Georgia Tech with a degree in architecture and worked for a firm in Atlanta. The first date happened two weeks later.

His next conversation with her wouldn't be easy. Her cousin's wedding was in less than two weeks. As the Maid of Honor, Jenn had invited him to join her. It would be his first chance to meet her parents and extended family. They'd scheduled a whole weekend of activities: lunches, a rehearsal dinner, and a big, black-tie wedding. She would be very upset when he canceled.

Four years earlier, Kyle had been engaged to a girl he'd met while an undergrad at the University of Florida. A month after their engagement his unit had shipped out to Iraq for a year. Upon his return to the states she had given his ring back. After a year of separation, anxieties and loneliness, she had decided the life of a marine's wife wouldn't suit her.

I don't want this relationship to end the same way.

He picked up the phone and called his parents in his home-town of Ocala, Florida. At least this would be a happy call.

He heard his dad's familiar low southern drawl. "Hello. This is the O'Brien residence. Sorry we missed your call. Leave a message and we'll get back to you."

Kyle had exciting news and no one to tell. He decided to leave a short message. "Hi, Mom and Dad. I'm sorry I missed you. I've got great news—I've been promoted to Lieutenant Colonel. I'll give you a call later and fill you in."

Almost a year had passed since his last visit home. He'd planned on a quick trip over the Labor Day weekend. Now it looked like he might be in Iran at about that time. His dad, a butcher by trade, had retired a few years back. Now he put-tered around on their small farm, planting a few crops each year. The farm, located outside the city, had been in the family since the mid eighteen hundreds. He looked forward to going home again—if not Labor Day, then Thanksgiving, with Jenn joining him.

That is if I make it through this crazy Iranian mission.
He'd be glad to get the details of how this time travel stuff really worked.

Kyle rolled off the bed and started dressing. It had taken his parents a while to adjust to his choosing a career in the military. The 911 attack had happened right after he graduated from college, and greatly influenced his decision to join the Marine Corps. They would be pleased to hear he'd been promoted.

Dressed in his new utilities, Kyle headed down the warehouse hallway and into a small mess hall that seated twenty. A door led out to a grassy area with four picnic tables. Most of the twelve people were gathered around a makeshift bar, which had a cooler of beer and a few bottles of wine on a card table.

Stan motioned him over. "Glad to see you found the cocktail lounge of our fancy resort. It's turned out to be a great July evening."

Stan waved everyone over. "Could I have your attention for a moment? As you know, our project is now ready to move to an exciting new level. This is Kyle O'Brien. Kyle will be in charge of the tactical operations for our project. You'll note he is a Marine Corps Major. I might add, a highly decorated Marine."

Stan reached into his pocket and pulled out a small box. "This afternoon Kyle received a promotion. Fortunately, since we're on a Marine Base, I managed to round up the new, shiny silver insignias." He held up the two of them. "I have the honor of presenting these to, Lieutenant Colonel Kyle O'Brien." He grabbed Kyle's hand. "Congratulations, Colonel, we wish you success on this new vital mission."

"Thank you, Stan." Kyle looked over the group. "By the way, my first order as a Colonel was for the mosquitoes to clear out. It seems to have worked."

The group laughed, and then he continued. "I understand we've got a very busy few weeks ahead of us. I look forward to meeting and working with you on this exciting project."

During the next hour, all members of the team came round and said hello. As the party wound down, Stan joined him with a beer in hand. He scowled. "I just got a call from the Scientific Director on the project, the one who was heading down here."

Kyle gave a puzzled look. "Did I hear, *was* heading down?"

"That's right. The CIA Director called him this afternoon and canceled his visit. The Director told him not to release any time travel data to you."

Kyle shook his head. "So the shit starts already?"

CHAPTER

6

*A*t **0630 the next** morning, Kyle walked into the nearly empty warehouse mess hall. A Marine Corps PFC busily made coffee. He snapped to attention. "Good morning, Colonel."

"Good morning. You must be the cook."

"Well, sort of, sir. I pick up all the food from main side and bring it out every day. Today we have cereals, fruit, muffins, scrambled eggs, hash browns and bacon. I just got here . . . breakfast won't be ready for about fifteen minutes. But, Colonel, there's coffee."

The name Colonel had a nice ring to it. Kyle grabbed a cup of black coffee and headed outside. Light streaked across the Eastern sky, with sunrise moments away. About a hundred yards across the meadow, near the edge of the tree line, a large doe and her fawn grazed on the wild grass. Not a sound disturbed the setting.

Kyle sat at a picnic table, drank coffee and enjoyed the silence. It reminded him of his family's farm in Florida. He took a sip and considered the previous evening. It had been hectic for Stan. After more than three hours of phone calls with his boss and other CIA officials, Stan informed him the Scientific Director would arrive as originally planned, and he'd be ready to discuss all non-technical aspects of time travel.

Stan had smiled. "My bull just made a tactical retreat—*for the time being.*"

The Marine Corps Hymn interrupted the peaceful setting. Kyle reached in his pocket for his cell phone. It was Jennifer.

He smiled. "Good morning."

"Good morning to you, Colonel. You mentioned a visit to the pentagon, but nothing about a promotion."

"It surprised me, too. But, it came with bad news as well. I've been reassigned and over the next few months I'm going to be extremely busy."

"Oh Kyle, are you going to tell me you can't make the wedding next week?"

He took a deep breath. "I'm afraid so."

"This is a really big deal. All my old friends and relatives will be attending. My parents will be disappointed. I was counting on you." She paused. "You're not going to Afghanistan, are you?"

"No. It's a special assignment that I can't discuss." He hesitated. "Let me check. Maybe, just maybe, there's a chance I can get the weekend off."

"Kyle, if the President can take time off to play golf, at least you could take a weekend for a really important wedding."

He chuckled. "I'll mention that to the Pres if we happen to meet. I promise I'll give it my best and let you know by tomorrow."

After breakfast he headed to the conference room for his first meeting with Stan. The room was all Government issue, with a writing board mounted on the wall; an eight-foot-long laminated wood table, and eight straight-backed wood chairs. The unadorned white walls still had a slight aroma of fresh paint.

Stan entered the conference room holding a thick stack of folders. He dropped them on the table with a loud thud. "OK, let's get started. This is general information about the Iranian facility you'll be entering. As you can see, it's thick." He pushed the thickest file across the table.

Kyle fingered the file. It had to be at least a foot deep.

"Don't spend much time studying it now." Stan said. "In the two warehouses next door we've just finished the mockup of both buildings in Iran. We also have hundreds of enlarged photos of almost all the rooms in the facility. And to top it off, we have specifications for the security systems and structural drawings. You'll be spending a lot of time in those mockups."

"This is a hell of a lot of data you're shoving at me." Kyle gave a puzzled glanced at the thick file. "How the hell did you manage to get all this?"

With a confident grin, Stan pushed a second file across the table. "Sometimes you're lucky. Sometimes you're good. This time we're both. Our source is a top level nuclear scientist currently working in the facility. He's on the central council of the Islamic Society of Engineers, and has had numerous meetings with the Iranian President. He'll help you gain access to the facility and, if needed, help you escape. The file covers everything you need to know about him."

"Why's he doing this?"

"Good question. He received a PhD from MIT, and lived in Boston for eight years in the seventies. He knows, and more importantly, admires America. He started working for his country with good intentions—to develop nuclear power, and to make Iran respected in the world scientific community. Somehow that high scientific goal has morphed into his current job—development of nuclear warheads for guided missiles."

"That's a long way from peaceful uses of nuclear power."

"Yeah, you're right." Stan paused. "He's disillusioned with the antics of his government, fed up with the Ayatollahs, and maintains he wants out. Of course that also means with his wife and three children, a lot of money, and a new identity. Before leaving, he wants to destroy all development of nuclear weapons in Iran. In this file we have all the data regarding those programs and their locations inside the facility."

Kyle took a moment to inspect the file. "Wow, I see what you mean. It's really complete. An opportunity like this doesn't come along very often."

Stan held up the third file. "Now comes the frosting on the cake." He dropped it in front of Kyle. "We have another Iranian working for us in the same facility. He's second in command of all security services, has turned over the security codes, the locations of the guard posts, and all security cameras within the complex. As with our scientist, he has volunteered to help with your entry and exit into the compound. He's never been to the states, nor does he want to live here. He wants to move to the south of France, be a millionaire, buy a winery, and live with a big breasted French woman who can cook . . . his words not mine. We'll help him with that dream, but only after we're successful."

"Finding a big breasted French cook.' Kyle chuckled. "Sounds like the perfect job for the CIA. He'll fit right into the Western world. But can he be trusted?"

"No. He can't be trusted. But in many ways his goals are more credible than our scientist friend. Hell, we can't trust either one. But neither man has any knowledge that the other one exists. On more than one occasion we've requested detailed information on the same sensitive project. Every time they've come back with confirming, consistent data. We think they're both the real deal."

Stan placed his hand on the last file. "This is the most important folder. We've spent about a month researching all aspects of the mission: how to enter the country; how to do the same at the facility; how many troops we think are needed; how to destroy the facility and how to escape from Iran. In most cases we've given you multiple scenarios."

"This is a ton of information. How long do I have to study all this?"

"As Secretary Evans told you. Regrettably we're on a tight schedule. Both sources tell us the warheads leave the cave in four weeks. We've got to launch this mission in three weeks."

Stan patted the file. "Concentrate on this. You've got the rest of today and tonight to work on it. We meet tomorrow morning with the chief scientist on the project. How about we review this again tomorrow afternoon? At that meeting we'll decide the size of your team. We'll need them here for training as soon as possible. Also we need answers on getting you into Iran, and the date you plan to blow up the complex. The CIA will be responsible for sneaking the engineer's family out of the country a few days before the explosion. That way we're sure of his loyalty."

Stan stood up. "I'll leave you to it."

Kyle lifted the files. "I think it'll be a late night."

With a nod, Stan said, "Many long nights. By the way, these files are to stay with you. No one else is to see them. Make sure and lock them in the safe."

Stan headed to the door, hesitated, and then turned to Kyle. "I'm not authorized to tell you this, but I think it's important. This is not my first assignment in Iran. Do you remember that huge explosion at the Revolutionary Guard base near Tehran? They reported seventeen people were killed, including the founder of Iran's ballistic missile program."

"Yeah, I remember. The Iranian government called the blast an accident. I always suspected there was more to the story."

"Well, there is. I was in charge of that operation. It went perfectly. The Iranians know we did it. They just don't want the world to know. We can do it again. Only now we have time travel on our side. I'll see you tomorrow."

Kyle tilted his chair back, stretched, and checked the time . . . midnight. He had been at it for about twelve hours, and slowly it was coming together. He had to admit, the CIA had done an outstanding job on research and organization of the mission. The objective: destroy all assembly equipment and the warheads.

To protect the facility from detection and missiles, the Iranians built the compound within a cave hundreds of feet underground. Pressured by the government for a fast completion, it had been hastily constructed and reinforced. A minimum amount of strategically placed explosives could collapse the cave and bury the structures under tons of earth and rock—and forever.

From the four options offered by the CIA, Kyle chose the simplest. It would be a team of five. The CIA officer currently in contact with the two Iranian spies would be used, plus Kyle would select three men from military special ops units. He wanted men he had worked with on missions in the past and could be relied upon. One of these men would need to be an explosives expert. Kyle knew just the man for the task, a Navy SEAL: Petty Officer First Class, Carter Weston. They had worked together on two previous operations, and he was perfect for the job: smart, savvy, dependable and an explosives expert. Carter had returned from Afghanistan about eight months ago. Kyle didn't know his current assignment. He would have Stan check that tomorrow.

The other two men would be selected from a list he was compiling. It would be a simple plan, but it had its advantages. No choppers breaking down as had been the case many years before during the Iranian hostage crisis, and also during the Osama bin Laden raid. That had also been the start of problems in Somalia, and on more than one occasion in Afghanistan.

With a small team, his chances of detection were minimalized. The team would enter one at a time on false passports and through different routes into Teheran. The CIA would supply false passports from nonaligned countries. With his fluency in the language, Kyle would use a French passport, as that country still had Iranian diplomatic relations.

They would be met by the CIA officer in Teheran and travel by van to the Nuclear Weapons complex located about two hundred miles northeast of the city, in the lofty Elburz Mountains. The highly secret facility was well hidden in a narrow valley near the small village of Pasha Kola. All of the workers including their two contacts, lived in a camouflaged housing complex very near the entrance to the cave.

The Iranian security officer and scientist would only be disclosed to each other at the last moment. Then the team members, along with explosives, would travel into the complex hidden in the cars of the two men.

After setting the timed charges in predetermined locations, they would leave the complex and drive to the fishing village of Mahmoud Abad, located forty miles away on the Caspian Sea.

From there the five team members, plus both the scientist and the security officer, would travel about two hundred miles by fishing boat to Baku, the capitol city of Azerbaijan. They would be met by CIA agents and flown by private jet to Italy. The explosives would be electronically activated once they departed on the boat.

As an insurance policy, the CIA would have drones loaded with hellcat missiles circling over the Caspian Sea. If trouble developed, within minutes they could dart into Iran and provide air support.

Kyle knew it would take days to work out the exact details of the plan, and possibly after the review with Stan, many changes. But, he felt with the help of this time travel technology the mission stood an excellent chance of succeeding. He picked up the files, locked them in his room safe and sat on the bed.

Tomorrow morning he would meet with the team's Scientific Director and have his questions on time travel answered — if the CIA Director didn't screw it up again..

CHAPTER

7

*T*he next morning Kyle picked up his phone and punched in Jennifer's number. She answered immediately.

This should make her happy.

"Hi Jenn. I've got great news. I can make the wedding. I'll fly out of Ronald Reagan Airport Friday afternoon and back in on Sunday morning."

She took a quick excited breath. "That's fantastic. All my friends and relatives can't wait to meet the mysterious, handsome marine I've been telling them about."

"You mean the marine with the broken nose that twists to the right?"

She chuckled. "It's a cute nose, despite the slight angle. And, speaking of marines, I don't know for sure you *are* a marine. I've never seen you in uniform. Could you wear that fancy blue thing for the wedding?"

"Since it's a black tie affair, I could wear my dress blues."

"And the sword, don't forget to wear the sword."

He laughed. "No sword, that's for fighting pirates, not weddings."

"Why don't you make the flight back on Sunday as late as possible? My dad wants to set up a golf match with you."

Kyle wondered if this might be one of those, *'What are your intentions with my daughter?'* meetings. "Jenn, I told you, I'm not a good golfer, and I haven't played in months."

"That doesn't matter. My dad loves to win."

"OK. I'll check on flights and let you know."

"Kyle, this is important. Thank you for coming." She whispered, "I promise to make this worth your efforts."

"Wow, how can I pass up that offer." He glanced at his watch. "I'm sorry, I've got a meeting coming up. I'll call you later. Love you."

He rushed to the warehouse conference room and found Stan and another man sitting at the table.

"Good morning." Stan said, as they both stood to greet him. "Kyle, I'd like you to meet John. He's with the CIA's Directorate of Science and Technology and heads up the scientific operations on our project. As mentioned, we're leaving out last names of the team for security reasons. "

"It's nice to meet you." Kyle reached over, shook hands and laughed. "I guess that means we're immediately on a first name basis."

Stan spoke up. "Kyle, before we get started let me mention that John and his team know none of the details of your mission. They know you'll possibly use time travel and that's it.

In his early forties, John appeared a bit shorter than Kyle's six feet and weighed considerably less than his two hundred pounds. Hopefully his pale complexion testified to numerous hours spent slaving away in the lab. His short-sleeved white shirt and dark green tie seemed out-of-place in the rusty old warehouse.

John pushed his thick glasses backup on his nose before speaking. "Nice to meet you. I'll try to answer all your questions."

"Have a seat." Stan motioned to the table. "Normally I would start by running through John's qualifications, which are impressive. But again, due to security we'll skip that. Suffice to say he holds a number of degrees. We could call him Doctor John, and also professor. Probably, one of these days, when this goes public, he'll win a Nobel Prize." He glanced at Kyle. "I'll keep my mouth shut unless we stray too far into information that could compromise the project. Fire away."

"OK," Kyle said. "How many times have you *personally* used the relativity transponder?"

John fidgeted with the file in front of him.

He's nervous, I'm sure he's been given strict instructions from the CIA bosses on what can be said.

"Two times," John answered. "Everyone on my team has used the transponder." He held up both hands, smiled and pointed to his nose. "My nose is still in the right location. I've still got all my fingers. You're welcome to count my toes, and my eyesight was horrible long before this project."

"That's encouraging," Kyle grinned. "When they told me you just sort of disappeared, like when they beamed people aboard the Enterprise in Star Trek, I had my doubts."

"I'm sure you did. Having all the molecules in your body vanish into thin air is not something you want to do without some strong assurances that you'll reappear—in the same order. We've tested the transponder on humans for six months. Before that, we tested mice—then chimpanzees for three years. In all that testing we've *never* had a time travel accident."

"How many total trips have been taken?"

"I assume you mean by humans?" John asked.

Kyle nodded. "Yes. Well, maybe you could throw the chimpanzees into that number as well."

"Forty-six for humans." John checked his notes. "I don't have the exact chimp number, but well over three hundred. We've used chimpanzees for testing because we share 98% of the same DNA."

"Where is this research being done?"

With his hand in the air, Stan interrupted. "I'm sorry. I don't think you need to know the location. Most of the scientists and engineers on this project and all of the transponder equipment are located at a secure facility. You're seeing a very small portion of a large team that's backing you up. To give you some idea of the scope of the project, it includes a large test lab and a power generating plant that's completely off grid. Time travel currently requires a massive amount of electricity to operate." He glanced at Kyle. "OK, you can go ahead."

"Kyle, let me ask you a question," John interjected. "Have you by chance recently seen the news regarding the discovery of particles traveling faster than the speed of light?"

"Sure. That made a big splash in the newspapers. Didn't it happen in Europe, at that Swiss accelerator lab?"

John nodded. "That's right, a team of particle physicists at the CERN facility in Geneva. They fired a neutrino beam four hundred and fifty miles underground to another research facility in Italy. To their great surprise it traveled sixty nanoseconds or one billionth of a second faster than the speed of light."

"That doesn't surprise me," Kyle said. "Everybody in Italy drives fast."

They all laughed.

After pulling a newspaper article out of the file, John moved over to the wall. "Kyle, I'm sure you know this equation?" He picked up a marker and wrote $E = MC^2$ on the whiteboard.

"Of course, I'm not a scientist but I know Einstein's theory of relativity."

"It's now wrong. For over a hundred years we assumed that the speed of light was the absolute limit." John held up the newspaper article. "Let me read this from the *Los Angeles Times*. They're quoting a colleague of mine, Doctor Stephen Parke, a renowned physicist at Fermilab in Illinois. 'If you have particles traveling faster than the speed of light, you can, in principle, go back in time.'" John looked up from the paper. "The rest of the world is now discovering that Einstein's theory is wrong. We, meaning our team, came to that conclusion eight years ago."

"The government's never released this information?"

"That's right. Ironically, we discovered it almost a hundred years to the day after Einstein's announcement. For eight years we've dedicated a tremendous amount of manpower and resources to this. We haven't seen this kind of commitment since World War II and the Manhattan Project. And, it's also been done in total secrecy. Not a single leak."

"That's amazing."

"Yes." John took a deep breath and pushed the glasses back on his nose. "Now, let's get into the project details. You'll be traveling back in time for fifteen minutes. For some reason, which we've yet to determine, time travel only works in units of fifteen. Fifteen seconds, fifteen minutes, fifteen hours, and we're working on fifteen days. It's not logical, but that's how it works. Our next step will probably bring us to fifteen months, or maybe fifteen years. We're working up to that right now."

"That makes no sense. I'm not a math whiz but I know about arithmetic progression. Numbers move in sequence."

John nodded. "I know, I'm a math whiz. But this comes from outer space and I can't explain the logic."

"OK." Kyle shrugged. "That's cool. Fifteen minutes works for me."

"Good. Now, I've tried hard to come up with a simple description for an incredibly complicated subject. And one that will pass the CIA requirements."

Kyle gave Stan a quick glance. "I know what you're up against."

"I hope this works," John said. "We currently view everything in three dimensions—height, depth and width. Let me quote that *LA Times'* article and Doctor Parke again, 'Or, maybe the neutrinos were traveling through different dimensions, taking shortcuts from Geneva to Italy.'"

John pointed to the article. "Dr. Parke is absolutely correct. We have confirmed there is a fourth dimension, which is time. And, I might add we've found three more dimensions."

Suddenly, Stan's hand shot up again. "OK, OK, that's enough, he doesn't have a need to know about other dimensions."

"Sorry. I'll get back on track. What does this mean to you? Parke was correct, there are shortcuts that allow time travel. Scientists call them wormholes. You can enter a wormhole, travel at unheard of speeds that we haven't been able to measure, and out again at what we call a white hole. You have traveled so fast that you have gone back in time. Am I making sense?"

Kyle thought for a moment. "Where the hell are these wormholes?"

Rubbing his temples, John sighed. "This is going to be difficult because of our dimensional mindset. Wormholes aren't visible, but they are here, just in one of the other dimensions." He pointed to the ceiling. "Maybe up there or maybe down on the floor. They are all around us. But, you can't see them. The transponder is placing you in that dimension, into the nearest wormhole and out again. It happens much faster than a nanosecond, so fast it's immeasurable. To give you some idea, a nanosecond is one billionth of a second. Your brain can't even register that time, and you're going many times faster."

"Use the example you gave me," Stan said. "The race in Chicago."

"OK. We're using Chicago because it's my hometown. Let's say we're in a race from the top of the Sears Tower—I know it's not called that anymore—down one hundred and eight floors to the street and then a run across town to the Trump Towers. You're real fast and far ahead of the pack. You charge up ninety-two floors to the top. At the finish line you find the race is over, someone else beat you by over an hour. How can that be, you were far ahead? The reason is, the winner found a secret zip line running between the two buildings—he took a short cut. That's kind of the way a wormhole works."

Kyle leaned back in his chair and shook his head. "Quite honestly, that's really simplistic. You've got to be leaving out

43

one hell of a lot of information, because it's still not making sense. I'm assuming all of the team members who have time traveled knew the full details?"

"Yes. And, that's a good point. They are scientists or engineers with full knowledge of time travel . . . and they allowed themselves to *have all of their molecules disappear.* That should make you feel better."

Kyle rubbed his chin, *if well informed people have done this two times, maybe I'm being overcautious.* "I'm assuming you've tested it out in different locations?"

"Different locations, different altitudes, all sorts of variations."

"And no health or mental issues with time travel?" Kyle asked.

"None. Each person was given a complete body MRI before and after to determine if there has been any change to your body. Your team will receive the same."

Leaning back in his chair, John seemed to relax a bit. "I'm glad to hear you use the term *time travel.* This is about time, not space. We can't put you into a wormhole in Virginia and transport you to Japan, or Mars. We *can* put you in a hole in Virginia, and take you back in time. You will reappear at the same location you were in fifteen minutes before. You will then move forward with full knowledge of what will be happening for the next fifteen minutes and adapt accordingly."

"Let me add something," Stan said. He hesitated before speaking. "This project was originally scheduled for another year of testing. Because of the importance of The Hindsight Project it's been moved up. We feel confident it's working correctly, or we wouldn't have done it.

"Do you have one of these transponders?"

John reached for his briefcase. "Yes. I'll bet you've never worn a hundred million dollar watch before."

CHAPTER

8

*K*yle scrutinized the wristwatch John pulled from his briefcase. It was about the size, shape and look of a Rolex Submariner, with a metallic, dull grey finish.

"We've made it as unobtrusive as possible," John said. "It's the most expensive watch you'll ever hold. If you add in the R&D cost, probably more like a hundred and fifty million." John tossed it over to Kyle.

Kyle caught it with both hands and gave a surprised look. "Damn. Be careful."

"I might add," John chuckled, "You can throw it up against that wall, it's almost indestructible—water and fireproof."

Kyle weighed it in his hand. "It's light. Does it also keep time?"

"Of course," John said. "We added the time feature to make it as real as possible. It's made of titanium—light, and very strong. You've got four buttons on the transponder, a button located at 0300 on the face, one at 0600, 0900 and 1200. To activate the transponder you press the one at 3 first and then the 9. Hold that one down for three seconds. This transponder's inoperative. Put it on and give it a try."

Kyle placed it on his wrist, closed the double- clasp on the band, and pressed the 3 and 9 buttons. "Easy enough."

"Now take it off."

He pushed the clasp, but it wouldn't unlatch. He tried again. "How does it come off?"

Reaching over, John pressed the 12 button. "Push this three times and it unlocks. Each transponder has a special combination. This prevents it from being stolen off your arm, or accidently falling off. In case of an emergency, press the 6 button for three seconds, and you will return to real time."

"Now the big question," Kyle said. "How the hell does this thing operate, and please—no bullshit about security?"

John gave him a weak smile. "I'll try. It's similar to a GPS. When those two buttons on the transponder are pushed, it emits a signal via satellite to our operations center. The center generates a signal back through the satellite to the transponder. You will have a microchip implanted in each earlobe. Once activated you'll simply disappear, and reappear fifteen minutes back in time at the same location."

He says that so calmly. I get up in the morning, brush my teeth, eat breakfast, and then simply dissolve into thin air. A piece of cake.

"John, you say, '*You'll simply disappear*' so calmly, as if it's an everyday occurrence."

"It is. I've worked this project for eight years. I've gone through this many times before. Although, the first time someone used the transponder." John smiled. "They came back naked."

Kyle laughed. "Hopefully that's been corrected."

John grimaced. "Believe it or not, transporting apparel was a difficult assignment. Figuring out how to transport your weapons took even longer. We now transport anything that's in contact with living cells."

John pulled both earlobes. "You'll note you can't see my chips. They are tiny and painless."

"Any side effects? Do you feel disoriented after being transported or have a headache, jetlag or anything?"

"None."

"I think that covers it." Stan stood up. "I'm sure you'll think of more questions, and we'll try to answer them. But, as far as the technical aspects of the mission, this is about all we're going to be able to cover."

After examining the transponder for a moment, Kyle handed it back to John. "You're right. I'd like to know more about the technology. But, reluctantly, I accept the reasons."

Stan said. "So, that means no calls to bulls?"

"Bulls?" John looked puzzled.

Kyle laughed. "It's a private joke. No calls to the bulls. Let's go get a cup of coffee and walk outside. I've got to clear my head."

With coffee in hand they moved outdoors. They sat in the shade under an umbrella at one of the round tables.

"I do have one more non-technical question," Kyle said. "When we go back in time, even for fifteen minutes, we are altering history. Are there consequences?"

After adjusting his glasses, John let out a slight cough. "You've brought up two difficult subjects. The first is known at the lab as the butterfly effect. This states that the disturbance of the air by a single butterfly is enough to change the weather patterns all over the world. But, in reality it applies to all things, meaning small events can have huge effects. You miss a plane by a minute, it crashes . . . you're alive. That will change history.

"The second is called the grandfather paradox. You go back in time and kill your grandfather . . . then realistically you should no longer exist." He gave Kyle a curious glance, "Is that where you're headed?"

"Yes, that's it."

"I can't answer it, but not for security reasons. It's not been a problem over the past three years of testing. But then, we've been working in minutes not years. It's been discussed and argued back and forth by our team numerous times. I'm sorry to say, we don't know about consequences."

Stan spoke up. "I'll give you an example of what we've debated. Let's say you pick up a history book, it reads that John Kennedy was shot by Lee Harvey Oswald in 1963. You are then transported back to 1963 for one day. You kill Oswald before he shoots President Kennedy and are immediately transported back. Upon your return, you go back to that history book. It has to be changed, since Oswald no longer killed Kennedy. If it has, how is that possible?"

John smiled. "Now hopefully you see why I didn't give you an answer. We don't know the serious repercussions of time travel, or if there are any. We'll just have to see how it plays out."

"I was looking for a more definitive answer," Kyle said. " But, I understand. This is all new ground—I guess I'll just avoid my grandfather. Next question, when do I try out this time travel?"

Stan answered. "We need to move ASAP. You'll get that physical tomorrow. If all goes well, you'll time travel the next day."

"I'll leave you two and head back to work." John stood up. "Kyle, I'll be back for your first time travel."

Kyle shook hands with John and they watched him leave.

"Well," Stan paused, "how's it coming on selecting a team for Iran?"

Stan seemed uncomfortable with the question, but Kyle didn't know why. "It's going well. The team will consist of five men including myself. One will be your man in Iran, the one with the two contacts at the Iran nuclear facility. The other three will come from special operations military units here in the states. I have picked one so far. Maybe we could speed things up by having the CIA locate him. His name's Carter Weston, a Navy SEAL that I've worked with on two previous missions. He's a weapons and explosives expert . . . perfect for the job."

Stan took a deep breath and let out a sigh. "I need to talk to you about that. I got a call last night from my boss. He had just left a meeting with the CIA Director. The Director decided that you will be the only military man on this mission. All the others will be CIA, chosen by him."

Kyle looked Stan in the eye and took a sip of coffee. "Let's see if I can give the Director an answer that clearly states my position. *No fucking way!*"

CHAPTER

9

A **heavy knock sounded** on Kyle's door. He sat up in bed. "Who is it?"

"It's Stan. We need to talk. Could you meet me in the mess hall in half an hour?"

Kyle checked the time—0530. "Yeah. I'll be there."

At 0600, the aroma of coffee brewing hit Kyle as he headed down the hall.

With a cup in hand, Stan stood by the coffee maker. "It's ready. Want some?"

"Yes, thanks. What's up?" *As if I don't know.*

With two cups of coffee, Stan joined him at the table. "Have you called the Secretary of Defense yet?"

"No, I wanted to sleep on it."

"I'm glad you held off." Stan took a sip. "Remember that old saying about the bearer of bad news? I don't remember the exact ending. I think the messenger is killed."

Nodding, Kyle said nothing.

"Kyle, people like the Secretary of Defense and the CIA Director . . . they live in a parallel universe, or you might call it a big bubble. Something goes wrong and cadres of *yes men* rush out to satisfy them. If someone can't fix the problem, they're replaced. In their bubble, people don't rush in and say, 'I have a problem and you need to fix it.' Do you follow me?"

"Of course. I don't want to make that call any more than you do — I have no choice. I'm not going to be a *yes man* for the CIA."

"I want you to listen to something," Stan said. "I've come up with a compromise that might work."

Kyle held up a hand. "Stop right there. I'm not compromising with the CIA."

"Hold on for a minute, Kyle, the Director is still smarting from the Osama bin Laden raid. We busted our asses for years to find that maniac. The SEAL's are brought in for the attack and get all the press."

"I don't care who gets the headlines. I only care about this mission and nuclear warheads. And, that's what your Director should be worried about."

"OK. But just hear me out."

Kyle studied Stan. He seemed like a good man, no doubt about it—but could he be trusted? *Was the Director pulling the strings?* After a deep breath, Kyle looked him in the eye. "I'm listening. What's your compromise?"

"Thank you. I've had a busy night. I've located Carter Weston. He's stationed in Pensacola, Florida, and teaching a class on explosives. We could have him here by tomorrow."

"Good. I'm glad you found Weston. So, what about the other two men? We need at least five on this mission. And, I still need to be in charge."

"I think we've got something that's doable. The two of you train here and head into Iran as the leaders of the project. As you mentioned, we use our CIA agent that's dealing with the two spies. He's essential. The CIA also maintains four undercover paramilitary agents on the ground in Iran at all times. All four are highly trained, know the culture and speak the language perfectly. We use two of those men on the team."

Kyle leaned back in his chair and scratched his head. *I want to have at least three men on the team that I have worked with and can trust. I have no idea if these two paramilitary CIA types are trustworthy. I won't go down that road again.*

"No, can't do it. I want the team I select, which will be military. Stan, you are an honorable man, you just work for a fucking lousy organization."

"I've worked with two of those men," Stan said. "Both were used in my successful operation in Iran. *I will vouch for them*. You can review their files and have the final decision. What do you say?"

Kyle considered it. Weston was the key member. The other two weren't as important. Besides, having two additional men who knew the country and spoke the language would help.

"OK, here's the deal." Kyle said. "We go with your two men. But, when we arrive in Iran, I will thoroughly check them out. Any doubts—any at all, and they are off the team. I don't care how much *the Director* yells. By the way, what does *the Director* think of this?"

"You're kidding me? He knows nothing about this until you agree."

"If he accepts those conditions," Kyle said, "it's a deal. Of course, if you can't get Weston approved, then I'm on the phone to *the Secretary*."

Stan finished his coffee, stood, and smiled. "Great. I should work in the Diplomatic Corps instead of the CIA. I'm off to Langley. Hopefully I'll return with two files, a clear understanding that you're in charge, and a green light for Weston. He looks great. It'll be hard for the Director to turn him down."

Kyle said, "Let me fill you in a little more on Carter Weston. On our last mission together in Afghanistan, six of us set explosives in an empty Taliban headquarters. Westin being the expert left the compound last. Ten Taliban fighters showed up and caught him in the open. They immediately fired and hit him in the thigh."

"Where were you?"

"All five of us had taken cover behind some boulders a short distance away. We opened fire. I ran out, slung Weston over my shoulder and headed for cover with shots zinging all around me."

"Obviously you both made it back," Stan said.

"Yes. It ended well. While firing away at us, the Taliban dodged into their headquarters for cover—the one we'd just loaded the explosives in. We ignited the charges and blew them up. Two days later I visited Weston in the hospital. The only time we ever discussed the mission, he said, 'Thank you, Captain. I owe you a big one.'"

Kyle grinned. "That's who I want on my team, someone that's smart, brave, strong—and owes me a big one."

CHAPTER

10

*T*he next morning Kyle woke at his normal 0600, and decided to take a run. It would be his first physical exercise since arriving. His clothes had been delivered from Camp Lejeune, and he now had running shoes and gear. He tied his laces and headed out the door for his usual six miles.

Even at 0615 he could feel the heat—by mid-day it would be hot and sticky. The run took him past the meadow and he noticed the doe and fawn had returned. She saw him, but didn't seem to mind.

Yesterday had been hectic. It had started early with a meeting with Stan, then a medical checkup, which he passed easily. Later, another doctor painlessly installed a microchip in each earlobe. He was good to go for the time travel journey.

Kyle considered that for a moment. Maybe it shouldn't be called a journey—possibly a mission, a flight or an adventure? He smiled. What had they called it in Star Trek? All he remembered was the phrase 'Beam me up, Scotty.'

The CIA had also approved Carter Weston. He would be transferred to their team as soon as possible.

Yesterday he met with Stan and they worked out the details of the upcoming operation. Stan gave him the files on the two CIA agents currently in Iran. Kyle still felt uncomfortable using CIA men, but they both were qualified, and it made sense.

During the last mile of his run, he cranked up the speed. It felt good to work off the tension of his upcoming travel in time. He chuckled. It sounded like something out of Superman. *Today I'll travel faster than a speeding bullet, hell I'll travel faster than a speeding beam of light. It's hard to believe.*

He lengthened his stride and headed for the warehouse.

After the run Kyle checked his cell phone. Carter Weston had called. He punched in the number and Carter answered.

"Hi Weston, this is Kyle O'Brien."

"Hello, Colonel. They told me about your promotion. Congratulations. They also gave me your cell number. Hope you don't mind me calling?"

"Not at all. It's good to hear from you. So, you've heard about your change of duty."

"Damn right I've heard." Carter laughed. "Yesterday afternoon my Commanding Officer called me in a panic. He'd received calls from the Commanding Officer of the Pensacola Naval Station, a Marine Colonel attached to the Commandant of the Marine Corps, a Navy Captain on Admiral Cary's staff, and the Assistant CIA Director. All of them wanted me transferred to the Quantico Marine Base ASAP, and to report to a Lieutenant Colonel Kyle O'Brien. All other details — top secret. You've got some high powered juice behind you, Colonel."

Kyle laughed. "At least you didn't get a call from the President."

"That's funny, my Commanding Officer said, 'Next I'll probably have the President calling.'"

"That should give you some idea about the importance of the assignment. I can't tell you anything over the phone. How soon can you be in Quantico?"

"I've never seen personnel move so fast. They cut my orders this morning. I'm checked out and ready to leave. A CIA guy called me early today. They're flying down a Learjet 45 to pick me up. Would you believe — my own private jet!

It's a nine passenger plane. I'm hoping for a steak dinner and free booze, served by a gorgeous blonde."

Kyle laughed. "That's great. It'll be nice working with you again."

"I'll be there around 1800. I can't wait to find out what this is all about. It's got to be huge."

With the phone back in his pocket, Kyle headed over to the warehouse. After a restless night's sleep he wanted this first trip under his belt.

Stan and John met him in the conference room.

Kyle let Stan know about Carter Weston's arrival.

"That's good news. I must have impressed somebody at Langley if they sent a jet down for him. We can fill him in on the mission tomorrow morning, and then get him in for a physical in the afternoon."

"Seems kind of crazy," Kyle said. "A trained SEAL's in better shape than 99.9 percent of the population—and we require a physical."

"Yeah, you're right." Stan said. "But remember, that establishes a baseline for his second physical, which happens immediately after time travel."

John reached into his pocket and pulled out a transponder. "Are you ready to travel?"

"I'm apprehensive—but ready."

"I know the feeling." John handed him the transponder. "Go ahead and put it on, and then we'll go through some of the precautions."

Kyle slid the transponder on his left arm and snapped it shut.

"Press the 0300 button," John said.

He reached down and hit the button. "It's vibrating."

"That's to caution you that the transponder's activated. If you hit it by mistake, just press the same button again to deactivate it. If someone else is traveling with you, their transponder will also vibrate. That notifies them that you are preparing to time travel. Press the 0900 button and you start the time travel process."

Stan spoke up. "Don't let the following conversation alarm you. Remember, we've never had a problem with time travel, and we're not going to now. But, we'll still cover all the bases before your first trip."

"As we discussed," John said. "You should have no side effects from time travel. If you do, let us know immediately and we'll have you checked out. Don't hold back or think you'll just try to work through the pain. This first trip is really important. If you're going to have a problem, it'll probably be now."

"We've got an ambulance standing by." Stan added. "Don't worry—they do this for everyone the first time."

"Now I'm really nervous. An ambulance? Are you sure no one's had a problem?"

"It's just a precaution." John shrugged. "Now, there are a couple of other things to consider. You'll press the two buttons on the transponder and travel back in time fifteen minutes. It happens with the blink of an eye. The first time, you may find it a little disconcerting or confusing. Different things happen to people. Possibly a ringing in your ears, but don't worry, that's normal.

"The ringing goes away?"

"Yes, immediately," John said. "Now, let's say you open your eyes and you're not where you should be. You're somewhere else." John held up his hands. "Or, you're where you should be, but at a different time, not the fifteen minutes we've programed. Don't panic. You can press the 0600 button on your transponder and it will bring you back to the present."

Kyle scowled. "Has that ever happened?"

"No. But we've planned for all the contingencies. Let's move along on this scenario: you've pressed the button, and you aren't transported back. Again, don't panic. Just remember, you're being monitored. The minute something goes wrong, we'll override the system and start working on bringing you back. It may take some time, but it will happen."

"*How much time*, and what do you mean, override the system?"

After glancing at Stan, John answered. "Let's see if I can explain this . . . without going too far. You are going to be traveling on what we call CTC's through the wormholes."

"Hold it." Kyle held up his hand. "What the hell's a CTC?"

With a sigh, John continued. "I'm sorry. A CTC is a closed time-like curve. This will ultimately bring you back on a closed loop and will cross present time at some point. That's when we pull you out."

"I'm not completely following your explanation."

"Kyle,' Stan shook his head. "We've told you much more than we should have. You've just got to trust us. We're not going to leave you spinning around in space."

Kyle stared at him. He doubted if Stan had a clue as to what a CTC was either. "OK, but at least tell me how long I could be stuck back in time."

John shook his head. "I'd tell you if I knew. We just don't know—at least a day or two. The maximum time for a CTC to loop back is estimated at probably four days."

"Would I need to stay in the same location and just wait for it to happen?"

"No," John answered. "You could move around. Distance wouldn't be a problem. As long as you stay in the Northern Hemisphere so our satellite can track you down. Let me stress, *this has never happened*."

Stan stood up. "Since you'll be using time travel under combat conditions we've decided to make this as realistic as possible. A CIA weapon's expert is waiting for us over in the next warehouse. For training purposes you'll need a weapon, and he's got a room full of them to choose from." He slapped his hands together. "OK, let's go fly through time."

CHAPTER

11

*K*yle and Stan entered the warehouse through a side door that opened on to a narrow room about twenty feet long. Neatly stacked in racks along both walls were an assortment of weapons and explosive devices.

A man in his mid-sixties sat in the center of the room with his feet propped up on a workbench. He jumped up as they entered. What remained of his gray hair was cut into a close-cropped, perfect flat top. He towered over Kyle's six-foot frame by at least five inches.

"Hello, Colonel." His deep Southern drawl rumbled across the room. "I'm Gunny Boyer. Welcome to my make-shift armory."

He reached for a shake with a right hand the size of a base-ball catchers mitt. Kyle noted a USMC with globe and anchor tattooed on his huge forearm.

"You're a Marine."

"Yes, sir. Semper Fi. I retired twelve years ago as a Gunnery Sergeant. Now I got the terrible task of tryin' to teach CIA types how to fire a weapon without killin' themselves. It ain't easy. Hell, most of them can't hit the side of an outhouse with a shotgun loaded with birdshot."

Gunny Boyer reminded Kyle of the first Gunnery Sergeant he had served with in the Corps. The crusty old-timer had let the green second lieutenant know in a big hurry who was the *real boss* in the platoon. "Well, Gunny, it looks like you've got me for at least three weeks. I hope I'll do better than the CIA."

"It'll be a pleasure, Colonel." Gunny gave Stan a quick glance. "Mr. Jackson filled me in on your background: Navy Cross and Bronze Star with valor, two Purple Hearts, and special ops tours in Iraq and Afghanistan. You've done some shootin' in your time. I understand you got a Marine explosives expert coming in tomorrow."

"He's Navy, not Marine."

"Navy? *Navy*? What the hell you doing with a Navy guy?"

"You'll like him, Gunny. He's a SEAL, a Petty Officer First Class with more combat experience and more ribbons than I have."

"A SEAL . . . well that's different. At least he knows which end of a rifle to hold . . . but, he still wears one of them funky little white hats."

Stan spoke up. "Gunny, why don't you give Kyle a rundown on the training you've designed?"

"OK, sir." Gunny lumbered over to a large diagram hanging on the wall. "From the CIA asset, we know the exact layout of the engineering department at the Iranian underground nuclear base and how many security guards they have on patrol. It's too fucking bad, but the source says the guards don't patrol in a set pattern. You'll probably find yourself in some trouble."

"Hopefully, I'll have a chance to use this." Kyle pointed to the transponder on his wrist.

"You'll get a chance," Stan nodded. "By the end of training you'll know every inch of the two buildings. And you'll be very familiar with time travel. And remember—don't wait till the last second to use the transponder. You can't push a button if you're dead." He started for the door. "We've got cameras throughout the warehouse. I'm heading over to watch you on video. Any problems, you let us know right away. Good luck."

"Thanks, Stan." Kyle glanced over at the rack of weapons. "Do I get one of those?"

With a big smile, Gunny proudly patted one of the rifles. "You bet. I've got a hell of a selection for you. An M4A1 assault rifle with a hybrid sight, M16A1, AK-47, MP25 sub-machine gun, an AKM, a SR25, a TR-15—hell, I even got a Heckler and Koch M27. On the table is a whole fuckin' assortment of night vision goggles. Along with the NVGs, I also got thermal weapon sights and noise suppressors."

"I'm impressed." Kyle examined the table, picked up some NVGs and smiled. "You've got a real arsenal here."

"That ain't all." Gunny hustled across the room. "Over here I've got six pistols for you to choose from. Against the back wall is an assortment of grenades--from flash bangs to frags, smoke and concussion. And finally, a flack vest and helmet, both Marine Corps issue—of course. If none of this stuff suits your fancy, let me know what you want and I'll have it here ASAP."

Gunny spread both mammoth arms, grinned and scanned the room. "All this, courtesy of your friendly neighborhood CIA."

"How the hell are we supposed to get all this equipment into Iran?"

"Don't worry about that. Them CIA guys don't shoot straight, but they sure as hell know how to smuggle stuff in and out of countries . . . everything from tanks to dead bodies."

Kyle inspected the row of rifles and picked up the M4A1. "I'll take this."

"Ha . . . I told them a Marine would go for the M4. It didn't make any sense bringing in all this extra shit."

"Good guess, Gunny." Kyle put the weapon to his shoulder and aimed down the sight. "This mission's all close quarters— perfect for the M4." He put it down on the workbench, walked over and studied the pistols for a moment. "I'll take the 45."

Gunny slapped his thigh. "Hell, I'm two for fuckin two. Good choice. At close range that thing'll knock an elephant flat on its big ass."

"Are we using blanks for the training?"

"No. I'll set your weapons up with a laser sight. You aim, pull the trigger and a laser beam will light up the target." Gunny strolled back to the map. "This is how the course works. Your objective is to hide an explosives charge near the engineering files along that wall. You'll enter the building through this door."

Kyle studied the warehouse. "What type of explosives?"

"C-4, Sir." Gunny walked over, picked up a large backpack. "Here's the pack, same size and weight as two M112 blocks of C-4. That's enough to make confetti outa them files, and maybe bring the whole fuckin' mountain down. There are at least three security guards patrolling the building. Try to avoid them, but if necessary, aim and fire. It should take you about an hour on your first try. Remember, the objective is to plant the explosives and leave the building without being detected. By the time you leave here in a few weeks you'll be doing this blindfolded. Any questions?"

"Let me study this layout for a few more minutes."

"No problem." Gunny picked up the two weapons. "That'll give me a chance to install the lasers."

Kyle pulled a chair over to the layout and sat down. It looked straightforward enough. He would enter the building and sneak down a corridor with individual glass fronted offices on either side. At the end of the corridor a hallway led to a large open room, probably a hundred-feet-across, and filled with office cubicles. The far wall of the room held a long row of five-foot-high filing cabinets that contained engineering documents on the nuclear missile project. He would place the explosives under a desk near the cabinets, activate the timer and exit through a door at the far corner of the building.

"Gunny, do I need NVGs?"

"Yes sir, it'll be dark in there." Gunny aimed the M4 at the wall and pulled the trigger. A bright red dot of infrared appeared on the wall. He handed Kyle the rifle. "Let's go get the rest of your gear."

The helmet, NVGs, flak jacket, and explosives pack, loaded Kyle down.

"Colonel, I'm also going to hook you up with a throat mike and headset. That way if there are any problems you can communicate with us."

"Do the guards know about Iran?"

Gunny started wiring him up, "No. By the way, I hired the guards—all retired marines—and my drinking buddies. If you find yourself in a situation where hand-to-hand combat is required, tap the guard on the shoulder to let him know he's been killed. The same applies if you get tapped on the shoulder." Gunny gave him a big grin. "Those guards would like nothing better than to catch a whippersnapper lieutenant colonel fuckin' up. Now, go play 'cowboy and injuns.'"

"Thanks for the help, Gunny." Kyle exited the building and stepped into heat and bright sunshine. He hurried over to the second warehouse, located a short distance away. Inside the semi-darkened building, he waited for his eyes to adjust, and took a few deep breaths. Even though this was only an exercise, an adrenalin rush hit him. He hadn't felt this way since Afghanistan.

Once adjusted, he lowered the four-tubed night vision goggles, crawled over to an open door and entered the first office on his right. The NVGs cast the room in an iridescent green glow, but definitely helped his vision. All the individual offices were the same size, each about a ten-foot-square space, with a desk and chair—plus an additional chair or two in front of each desk.

Probably, during the day, the Iranian building would be loaded with mechanical, electrical and nuclear engineers and scientists. He peeked around the corner and down the seventy-foot hallway. He doubted if any of the guards would be in an individual office, but who knew, possibly one of them had his feet propped up on a desk, taking a break.

Kyle stayed low and moved down the hallway, checking out the offices on both sides. At the end of the hall, a door opened and loud footsteps echoed off the concrete floor. He darted into an office, quietly slid the chair back and slipped under the desk.

The footsteps grew closer, and he saw flashes of light. The guard must be shining a flashlight into each office. The light flashed on the wall in front of him and the guard moved on. After checking all the offices, the guard retraced his steps and exited through the door at the end of the hall.

With the guard gone, Kyle moved out of the office and cautiously made his way down the hallway. Upon reaching the door the guard had used, he halted. The next step would be difficult. He would open the door, check for guards, and dash into one of the office cubicles in the next room.

He gripped the handle, gradually pulled the door toward him, and took a quick look.

A guard stood right by the door.

"Who's there?" the guard yelled.

Kyle put his shoulder into the door and slammed it shut. The guard pounded. "Open up, open up!"

Now he could use the transponder.

Here goes. With both fingers he pressed the buttons on the watch.

Immediately a piercing ring sounded in his ears. Kyle turned to run, but his legs wouldn't move. The floor had turned into a black, sticky mud, which oozed around his ankles. He struggled to pull his legs out, but now the quagmire had reached his knees.

Something's gone wrong.

The guard yelled and banged against the door.

The mud extended to Kyle's waist. He twisted and turned, fighting to free himself. Wildly he jabbed at the transponder buttons again. He had to stop this thing. In seconds it would be over his head!

The ringing grew louder. The mud pressed against his ribs and then seeped around his neck. The banging continued at the door.

When it touched his chin he took a deep breath and tilted his head up.

I'm going to drown!

The ringing ceased. Amazed, he realized the mud had disappeared.

He glanced around.

Gunny Boyer stood next to him with a big grin. "Colonel, those guards would like nothing better than to catch a whipper-snapper lieutenant colonel fuckin' up. Now go play 'cowboy and injuns.'"

I've heard that line before. I'm in the armory. I've traveled back in time.

It took Kyle a moment to compose himself—then he repeated. "Thanks for the help, Gunny."

He exited the building into the same heat and bright sun-shine, and darted across to the second warehouse. Once inside the warehouse he dropped to the floor and leaned against the wall.

It works. The Gunny had no idea that we were echoing our conversations. The guard that's going to walk down this hall in a few minutes won't know either.

He moved up behind the door and waited.

It didn't take long. The guard opened the door and entered the room. Kyle reached over, tapped him on the shoulder and whispered. "You're out of action."

A voice came through on his earphone. "Kyle, this is Stan. I'm assuming you're on your second run and you've had a successful time travel?"

"Yes, and other than nearly drowning in mud, I feel great. Why don't we keep going?"

Stan chuckled, "So you had some mud. Let's call it a day and have you checked out. We'll meet you outside the building."

Kyle spotted Stan and John as soon as he left the building.

"Congratulations, great job." Stan smiled and held out his hand. "You're now part of the most exclusive group in the world--time travelers. Any problems?"

"Hell yeah. You didn't warn me about the ringing in my ears and getting stuck in mud. It's like being trapped in quick-sand. That scared the shit out of me."

"There's a reason why we didn't warn you," John said. "It's different with everyone. Only about half the time travelers experience a ringing in the ears. Getting stuck in mud only happens to about twenty percent of them. Most are enveloped in a thick cloud of mist, or everything just fades into darkness. We wanted to see how you handled it."

"Remember," Stan said. "We did say we wanted you to be alone for your first time travel. That's because it's so disorienting."

"Disorienting?" Kyle said. "It caught me completely by surprise. I figured you'd just close your eyes for a second, and when you opened them, you'd be back in time . . . no bell ringing, no mud. Will I experience the same thing every time?"

John nodded. "In most cases you continue to experience the same phenomenon. Don't worry, you'll adjust real fast. Someone described it as similar to bungee jumping. The first time scares the shit out of you, but by the third time you're bored."

"Kyle," Stan said. "Let's get you down to the hospital for that physical."

"I feel fine. Do we have to go through this every time?"

"Probably. We want to make sure everything's back where it should be. Come on, I'll give you a ride to the hospital."

On the ride over, Stan asked, "So, other than being surprised, what do you think of time travel?"

Kyle gave it a moment's thought. "It's amazing. If I'd had a transponder in Afghanistan I could have saved the lives of at least ten men. Right before I came home we lost two men to a roadside blast. With time travel we would have disarmed the IED and they'd be alive today."

"We'll start exploring some of those opportunities in our meeting tomorrow," Stan said. "There is something else scheduled for you this afternoon at four o'clock. You'll be meeting with a CIA psychiatrist."

Kyle frowned. "I went through a whole battery of tests a week ago with Navy psychiatrists."

"This will be different. You may remember some years ago the CIA had all kinds of problems with turncoats and spies. Well, now our personnel go through regular testing by a team of psychiatrists. Doctor Madelyn Hurst heads up that program. She requested a meeting with you right after your first time travel. Be careful—she can be a real pain-in-the-ass. Consider it like a trip to the dentist—a little agonizing, but necessary."

"Has she met with any of the time travelers in the past?"

"No. As far as I know, you're the first."

Why me and not the others? Could this be another attempt to get the military off the mission?

CHAPTER

12

*A*fter a morning run and breakfast, Kyle headed for the conference room. He would spend two hours with Stan concentrating on the mission. He also needed to discuss his meeting with the CIA psychiatrist. When it came to the CIA bureaucracy, it seemed to be a never ending battle.

Stan sat at the conference table leafing through a file. He looked up. "Good morning. How did your physical go at the hospital yesterday?"

"Great. The doctor said nothing had changed from two days ago. He was puzzled as to why I required another physical, especially an MRI after only two days, but let it pass. More importantly, aren't you going to ask me about my interview with that crazy psychiatrist?"

Tilting back in his chair Stan gave a concerned glance. "It didn't go well?"

"Stan, you've got to be naïve if you're surprised. There's no doubt she's trying to railroad me out of this mission. We talked for almost two hours. Hell, I'd probably still be talking to her if I hadn't stormed out."

"You walked out on her?" Stan grimaced. "That's not good. I'm sure her report will end up on the Director's desk."

Kyle sat across from him. "I don't give a shit what *the Director* thinks. As part of the selection process for this assignment, I had a battery of psychiatric tests by Navy doctors. They gave me high ratings. She'll have a tough time discounting those interviews."

"OK, that's good to know. By the way, don't feel singled out, Hurst hates everybody. I'm sure you noticed, the tougher the question, the softer she speaks and the greater her look of anguish."

"Of course I noticed. She questioned my family, my love life, even my *sex life*. I told her to go to hell and stamped out when she asked if I missed killing people now that I'm out of combat. She spoke so softly I had her repeat the question three times. Each time she appeared to be in mortal pain. You should get rid of that bitch."

"I know." Stan nodded in agreement. "But we're stuck with her. I'll call my boss and give him a heads-up on your meeting. And, yes I knew what would happen. That's the reason I warned you."

Kyle stared at Stan a moment and took a deep breath. "OK, I'm not going to worry about all that bullshit. We've still got a mission . . . let's get down to some real business." He looked over at the file. "Not another stack of papers for me to dig through?"

"I'm afraid so. This one brings new challenges." Reaching over, Stan dug into the pile. "This is a report from our in-country agent. He got word from our mole that they moved the schedule up. The nuclear warheads will be shipped out of the cave in two weeks."

"Two weeks?" Kyle gasped.

"Yeah. He notes they are really beefing up security at the site. The perimeter fences have been strengthened and would now require explosives to break through. The guard force is being replaced by the Ansor-Ul-Mahdi Brigade—which means followers of Imam Mehdi. It's an elite, fanatical military unit of the Revolutionary Guard."

"What happened to our security guy?"

"He's been shuffled off to a minor security function and is very nervous. He wants us to act fast and get him out of the country. He's afraid he'll lose that dream of France, wine, and a big breasted woman. Our plan to drive through the gate in the trunk of his car might not be possible."

Kyle grimaced, "Damn, I don't want to use choppers or blast our way into the compound. We'd need a large force for that. Stealth is the only answer. Are they checking all vehicles entering the compound?"

"I don't know. He mentions that in here somewhere." Stan searched through the report. "Here it is. In addition to checking all IDs, they randomly search about half the cars, including undercarriage, trunks and interiors."

"Stan, I still think we can make it work. But we need to move fast."

"Are you crazy? You want to roll the dice and hope you're in the fifty percent not checked?"

Kyle thought a moment. Eventually, he gave a positive nod. "I've got the perfect solution. We've been looking at time travel as a defensive tool. Something happens and we react. Let's turn that around. We pull up in the cars knowing they may check. If they do, we hit the buttons on the transponder, go back and start over. We keep doing that until we make it through the gate."

"That makes sense. I like it much better than swooping down in choppers. I'll pass it to Langley and get back to you later today."

"I'm starting to feel confident that if we make a mistake in Iran, all we need do is press a button and correct it. Time travel will be invaluable—despite the mud."

Stan checked his watch. "We've got over an hour before Weston shows up. Let's start digging and see where we can cut the schedule."

"What if we arrange for Carter's physical immediately, and then take the rest of the day and evening filling him in on the mission and time travel? Tomorrow we can both go through training together. I don't think it will be that confusing for him. It cuts another day off the schedule."

"OK." Stan studied his notes. "We'll plan on the mission starting in ten days. That means we'll have to move immediately to get you passports and visas for Iran. The visas aren't easy. It could be a major hang up."

"The CIA must be able to get us passports from other countries?"

Stan gave him a slight grin. "That's the easy part. As the Gunny said, we may not shoot straight, but we do know how to move people. The details for passports and visas have already been worked out. We just need to speed it up."

"Is it still set for me to get a French passport?" Kyle asked.

"Yes, but we've changed Carter's from Canada to New Zealand. The Iranian visa office is rejecting about forty percent of Canadian visa requests. New Zealand citizens have a one hundred percent approval rate."

Kyle frowned. "I don't know, Carter's got a heavy southern twang—that's a long way from a kiwi accent."

"Accents are hard to spot unless English is your first language. If he can answer a few simple questions without throwing a ya'll at them, we'll be OK. We've run people into Iran on a regular basis using different country passports. We've yet to have an Iranian agent detect accents. Your passports will be slightly dog-eared and show both of you as experienced international travelers--but never to the U.S."

"Can you get an Iranian visa in ten days?"

"That's the problem," Stan said. "We can't fake a visa. I've checked with our documents section. They will apply for a fifteen day tourist visa. Approval time for students and teachers is the fastest, at around eight days. You'll both sign up for a seven day sightseeing tour as teachers, and we'll use the tour company to help expedite the visas."

"How do we fly into Iran?"

"You'll fly through Paris, and Carter to Rome, using your passports. From there you'll fly direct to Tehran with the new passports and a round trip ticket. You arrive a few days ahead of the tour. That's pretty common for tourists. By the time the tour company notifies the government that you're a no-show, you should be out of the country."

Kyle gave him a half-smile. "I'm impressed. You've been busy."

"Thanks, it's what I do for a living."

Kyle and Stan met with Carter Weston in the conference room. It had been two years since they had worked together. He looked in great shape. At five-eight and over two hundred pounds of solid muscle, his stocky build reminded Kyle of a fire hydrant with arms—very muscular arms. His close crop red hair and wide grin made him look much younger than his twenty-nine-years.

"Colonel O'Brien, it's great to see you." Carter's Alabama drawl came across in almost every word.

Kyle held out his hand. "Carter, before we start, no more Colonel stuff, we're working as a team of two. From now on it's Kyle."

"OK, but that's not easy." Carter hesitated. "Now, *Kyle*, you caused quite a ruckus down in Pensacola. I'm dying to know what the hell this operation is all about."

Kyle pointed to Stan. "This is the man who'll fill you in on the details, Special Officer Stan Jackson, from the CIA."

With the mention of the CIA, Carter gave Kyle a puzzled glance. "Mr. Jackson, nice to meet you."

Stan shook his hand. "That name stuff goes for me too. It's Stan. I look forward to working with you."

"Thank you, Sir. The Colonel" . . . Carter glanced over. "*Kyle,* saved my life in Afghanistan. There's no one I'd rather go into combat with, and I'm pretty sure a combat mission is why I'm here."

"You're right," Kyle said. "This will be the most important mission you've ever been on." He gave a fleeting look at Stan. "And, the most unusual."

Stan reached in his briefcase. "That reminds me." He pulled out a sheet of paper and handed it to Kyle. "This is that top secret form like the one you signed in the Secretary's office. Explain it to Carter and get his signature. I'm driving up to Langley to tell the bosses about the mission changes. You brief Carter on the Iranian mission and our new technology. I'll also get going on passports and an appointment for Carter's physical and ear implants. "

Stan headed out the door with a wave. "I'll see you guys around six."

Carter frowned. "What's this about passports and ear rings?"

"You've got an interesting day ahead. Regarding ear implants, I've got them." Kyle held an earlobe. "It's painless and not noticeable."

"What's this Stan like? I worked with a CIA guy on one of my missions. You could never get a straight answer, and you couldn't trust him."

Kyle shrugged, "So far so good. He's not your combat type. He's done a hell of a job of organizing this mission. He's CIA, so he has a certain amount of self-importance. We'll just have to see how he handles problems. Regarding the passport, you're about to become a citizen of New Zealand. How's your kiwi accent?"

Carter snorted. "Are you shittin' me? It's about as good as my British, New York and New England accents. They all got a southern twang." He gave Kyle a big smile. "And smooth as fine bourbon."

Kyle chuckled. "Once I give you the details of the new technology we'll be using—you'll need a tall glass of that whiskey."

CHAPTER

13

*K*yle walked onto the patio and spotted Carter. "Good morning, how'd you sleep last night?"

"Horrible." Carter sat at a picnic table. He checked to see if anyone was nearby and then dropped his voice. "All night long I woke up to thoughts of blowing up an entire Iranian cave complex. And, when I wasn't thinking about the cave, this time travel shit kept me awake. You mentioned traveling zillions of miles in space and going through worm holes, whatever the hell they are . . . it's enough to keep you tossing and turning all night."

Kyle leaned in closer. "I know what you mean. I'm still having trouble getting my head around this time travel shit."

"Between you and me, Kyle, it's creepy. When they implanted those microchips in my earlobes yesterday and you described how my molecules would take shortcuts through space, it scared the shit out of me. What happens if those particles get mixed up along the way? I come back with my foot hanging out of my ass or something."

"Yeah." Kyle nodded. "But remember, we're not the first to try this out. Those scientists, as well as the CIA guys, have all been doing time travel for a couple of years. Just think of what that first guy must have felt like. Look at me." Kyle spread out both arms. "I did it two days ago. Everything's in the right place." He sniggered and glanced behind him. "Nothing hanging out of my ass."

Carter cracked a smile. "Very funny."

"Discovery is not easy," Kyle said. "Think of living in the eighteen hundreds and someone loads you aboard a Boeing 777 jetliner with four hundred other people. Once inside, you're told it will take off, fly half-way around the world at thirty-thousand feet and at faster than five-hundred miles an hour. You'd say they're crazy. We'll get used to this time travel, just like we did boarding airplanes."

"Well, I'll do it," Carter said. "I'm just glad we're doing it together." He smiled. "And that you did it first—without anything hanging out of your ass." He took a gulp of coffee and set the cup down. "Now, what's the schedule today?"

"We work with Stan and start planning how many packs of explosives you're going to need and their placement. After lunch you meet with a retired marine, Gunny Boyer, and select weapons and equipment for the mission. By the way, Gunny doesn't like sailors."

"I'll be damned, a marine who doesn't like sailors, what a surprise."

"Since you're a SEAL, he's giving you some slack."

"Well," Carter snickered, "that's most high-minded and righteous of him."

"At 1400 I join you and Gunny and we head over to the warehouse for, as he describes it, 'some fuckin' cowboy and injuns.' Gunny tends to throw a fuck into just about every sentence."

Carter laughed quietly. "I remember one of our instructors in SEAL training managed to cram four fucks into a single sentence. That's probably a record."

"Four?"

"Yeah, it had something to do with describing the enemy. You've got to admit, that's creative use of the language."

They both laughed.

"So, it's after the meeting with Gunny," Kyle said, "that we'll time travel and you get to checkout those worm holes."

Carter gave him a concerned look. "Kyle, on a serious note, you mentioned those worm holes. I need a little more info about this time travel shit."

"OK, they wanted you to do this by yourself. They said it was less confusing. We're doing it together because it saves a few days in training. Did they caution you about mud?"

"No."

"I will," Kyle said. "When I pressed the transponder button, I heard a loud ringing in my ears. Then I looked down. Mud was coming up around my ankles—and it continued to rise."

"Mud?"

"Yeah, mud. I started to panic, and then bam! I looked around and I was fifteen minutes back in time—standing in the armory talking to Gunny again. He had no idea it was a redo. It frightened me, but only for a few seconds. You may experience something other than mud, maybe, a fog or mist—but remember, it's over fast."

"Thanks for warning me." Carter let out a sigh. "If you and all those other people made it, I guess I can."

Kyle nodded. "You will. Look on the bright side. This will change modern warfare and save lives. We're really on to something with time travel." He stood up and downed his coffee. "Let's grab some chow."

After lunch Kyle joined Carter and Gunny in the armory. Carter's selection of weapons and equipment lay on the workbench in front of them.

With a big smile on his face, Gunny said, "You picked a good fucking man, Colonel. Hell, he could even be a marine."

Kyle glanced over at Carter, who rolled his eyes, but said nothing. "Thank you, Gunny. I knew you'd like him. What's our exercise this afternoon?"

"Before we get started," Gunny held up two transponders, "let's talk about these things. You'll be working as a team, so you need to coordinate when you want to time travel." He handed a transponder to each of them. "Put them on and let's run through a drill."

They both slipped a transponder on their left arms.

"Colonel, would you press the 0300 button, please?"

Kyle pressed his. "It's vibrating."

Carter raised his left arm. "Mine too."

"Good." Gunny said. "They're both working. If either of you presses the 0300 button both units will vibrate. This signals the other person to press his button and start the time travel process."

"Do we have to go back at the same time?" Carter asked.

"No, it just alerts the other person that you're preparing to activate the second button. However, I think most of the time you'd want to go back together."

"Are we using the same warehouse I went into the other day?"

Gunny shook his head. "No sir. As you know, them fucking Iranians are changing that warehouse. We're going to move to the next warehouse. They're assembling all the electronic components for the missile guidance systems in that building. It's the last building you'll be setting charges in before you leave the cave and head to the coast."

Walking over to the wall, Carter studied a map of the entire complex. "The explosives consultant is arriving tomorrow and we'll be reviewing the maps and photos and make a final decision then. I think we'll place the charges near that large assembly machine in the middle of the building."

Pointing at a small room off a hallway on the layout, Kyle asked, "Is that the guard room?"

Gunny checked. "Yeah, there are two guards on duty in this building. One stays in that little guard room about fifteen feet from the only entrance. The other roams at will through the building. Every hour they switch posts. That gives the other guard a chance to sit on his ass for a while. Not bad duty."

Kyle pointed to the hallway leading from the entrance and past the guard room. "Is it possible to sneak past this guard?"

"It'd be tricky," Gunny said. "It's more like a cubical than a room. There's a four-foot- high counter along most of the open space. I guess you could stay low and get past him. But, remember you've got to exit back the same way."

"I vote we take out both guards," Carter said. "Since it's the last building we'll set charges in, it'll be blown sky high before the guards are discovered. Let's face it, if we don't kill them they'll probably die when the explosives go off."

Kyle nodded. "I agree. You sneak up to the counter. I'll bang on the entrance door. The guard will rush out into the hallway to see who's making the noise, and you take him out. Since the other guard is in the assembly area, we'll locate him once we move inside."

After staring at the map for a moment, Gunny said, "I think it'll work." He reached over and grabbed the headsets and communications equipment sitting on the bench. "I'm wiring you up for sound. That way you can communicate with each other, and with us. We'll be watching your every move from the video room."

Putting on his flak jacket, Kyle said, "Thanks for the suggestions, Gunny."

"No problem." Gunny moved over and helped Carter with his headphone.

They both put on helmets. Kyle glanced over at Carter. "We're ready."

Gunny walked with them to the door. "I'll see you in a little while. Now go play some fuckin' cowboy and injuns."

Kyle and Carter opened the door and squeezed into the dimly lit hallway, with barely enough light to recognize the counter of the guardroom ahead of them. Kyle motioned to Carter and they both pulled their NVGs into place. The room lit up a bright green.

Whispering into the mike, Kyle said. "Work your way down the hall and signal me when you're in place." He heard Carter's acknowledgement signal, a click on the mic. The second click would mean he was in place and ready.

Carter moved quietly down the hallway and up against the counter.

Once Kyle heard the two clicks on his earpiece, he made a fist and banged noisily on the door behind him.

A shout came from the room as the guard rushed out from behind the counter and looked down the hallway. As the guard opened his mouth to speak, Carter reached up and tapped his shoulder. "You're dead."

The door at the end of the hall burst open and the other guard appeared in the doorway. He took a quick look. Before Kyle could raise his weapon, the guard turned, rushed into the warehouse and slammed the door.

He's getting away, I'll use the transponder. Kyle reached down and pressed the button. It started vibrating. He waited a few seconds and pressed the second button.

Immediately the ringing started in his ears. He felt pressure on his legs and looked down to see the pitch-black mud creeping up to his knees. *At least I know what's going on this time.* Over the ringing he heard a scream coming from Carter.

The mud now reached his chest and he felt the pressure on his ribs. *Any second now I should be jerked back.*

The mud continued to rise. *I don't remember it coming this high!* He took a deep breath as it reached his chin.

CHAPTER

14

*T*he sudden intense green glare of the blazing sun blinded Kyle. He yanked his helmet and NVGs off. *What the hell just happened?*

Carter stood beside him. He flung his helmet to the ground. "Shit, I can't see anything. Where are we?"

"I don't know." Kyle rubbed his eyes and searched the area. "We aren't back in the armory, that's for damn sure."

"Kyle, you said mud. But you didn't tell me it was going to go over my head. I thought I would drown!"

"So you had mud, too?"

"Yeah." Carter spun around. "Are we still at Quantico?"

"I don't know." Kyle peered at his transponder. "Something's gone wrong with this thing. I expected mud, but this is a new twist."

"Should we press the button and go back?"

Kyle didn't recognize anything. They were in a grassy meadow, surrounded by tall pines and in the distance, oak trees. Nearby a small stream twisted through the meadow. No warehouses, no cars and no people were in sight.

"This is not where we're supposed to be." He motioned to Carter. "Let's press the button. Remember, you push the 1200 button for six seconds."

Carter reached down to push. "Wait a minute. Are we going back into that mud again?"

"How the hell do I know? This didn't happen to me the last time. OK, push."

They pressed the button.

Nothing happened.

"Let's try once more," Kyle said.

Again nothing.

"Colonel, I think we've got a malfunction."

Kyle took a deep breath. "You're right." He remembered it had been discussed during the checkout. "John mentioned this—if you discovered you're not in the correct time, press the buttons on the transponder and it transports you back to current time."

"We did that."

"Yeah, he also said we would be monitored if something went wrong. That they'd override the system and bring us back."

"I remember." Carter frowned. "He also said it could possibly take days for them to retrieve us . . . then he assured me it would never happen."

Kyle motioned toward the trees. "Let's get out of this hot sun and take off our gear."

They walked about a hundred yards, waded across a small stream, and entered the cool shade in a grove of large pines.

Kyle propped his rifle against a tree, and took off his flak jacket and helmet. He remembered the conversation about traveling through time and not distance. That meant they should be at the same spot, but at a different time. He recalled a stream behind the warehouse. The terrain looked different—still, he thought, this could be the same stream.

Carter dropped to the ground. "Where do you think we are?"

"I think we're at the same location—but somewhere back in time."

"It's sure as hell not fifteen minutes back in time." Carter looked around. "There aren't any warehouses. I'll bet they were built during the Second World War. If the warehouses aren't here, it must be the early 1940's or before. How can we check that?"

Kyle shook his head. *All this bullshit about never any problems and here we sit—to hell and gone back in time. I should have known better than to trust the CIA.* He stood. "I guess we start walking until we run into someone or something."

With a wry smile, Carter said, "And if we run into a dinosaur?"

"Very funny. And besides, if we saw a dinosaur, we couldn't shoot it." Kyle pointed to his rifle. "These weapons are rigged with lasers and we've got no ammo."

Carter kicked his helmet. "I don't see any reason for taking K-pots and this other gear, but I don't want to leave my weapons."

"OK. We might find ammo, but I doubt it."

They hid most of the equipment in the brush. Carter looked back pensively. "Think we'll come back for our gear?"

"Yeah, we won't go far."

They located a small animal trail that headed east, the direction of the Quantico Marine Base. A half-hour later they crested a hill.

Kyle pointed to a nearby pine tree. "Why don't you put that SEAL training to good use? Climb up that tree and check our location."

After a quick check of the tree, Carter gave Kyle a grin. "You've got to be Spiderman, not a frogman to climb that tree. But I'll give it a try."

He easily scrambled up the tree and scanned the horizon. "Not a building, a road, an airplane, or a human—nothing. I do see a river off in the distance, but no boats. And no fucking dinosaurs."

As Carter climbed down, Kyle added, "The river's probably the Potomac. If the Marine base were here, we would've run into something or someone by now. It was constructed to train Marines in the First World War. That means 1917."

"You're kidding me." Carter gave him an amazed look. "We're back in time almost a hundred years?"

"At least," Kyle said. "It could be a hell of a lot earlier than that. Maybe Columbus hasn't even discovered America yet!"

Carter looked around. "Man, this is bad shit. So what now?"

"I say we just wait it out and hope they yank us back."

"How about we head back to that meadow?" Carter said. "There's water there—and our gear."

"Good idea. It's where we started this mess."

They followed the trail back. Kyle rested under the pines while Carter went over to the stream and got a drink.

"How does it taste?" Kyle yelled.

"Great. At least we've got good water. So how long are we going to wait here?"

Kyle checked his watch. "It's 1800. We've got about two more hours of daylight. Let's sleep here tonight. If we haven't been transported back by tomorrow morning, we'll work on another plan."

"I'm hungry. You didn't happen to bring any food?"

"We were only going for an hour." Kyle said. "What do you think, I've got a sliced ham in my back pocket?" He pointed toward the weapons. "Why don't you grab a rifle. You can shoot one of those dinosaurs with a laser beam."

"Now who's being a wise ass?"

"Looking for food isn't a bad idea." Kyle stood up. "We've both been through survival training, we should be able to find food. Maybe there are some wild fruits, fish in the stream, or small game. Let's scout around. I'll head upstream, you head down, and we'll meet back here before dark."

Kyle headed over and checked the stream. It was only about three feet across and no more than a foot or two deep. He spotted a few minnows but no fish. He then moved upstream to an area of oak trees. Earlier on their walk he had noticed a deer print, but he hadn't seen any large animals. He checked the trees and spotted a bird. He didn't know the first thing

84

about birds, but it looked small, harmless and familiar . . . at least it wasn't some prehistoric creature waiting to swoop down on him.

On up the trail he saw a large patch of what looked to be berries. He picked one and rolled it around in his hand. It had the same dark texture and small seeds as a blackberry. He took a small bite. It tasted sweet, juicy and delicious.

Definitely a blackberry.

After picking a handful, Kyle headed back. By the time he reached camp, the blackberries were eaten. He grabbed a helmet and headed back for more.

When he returned to camp with a helmet full of berries, Carter sat under the tree.

He looked up at Kyle. "I didn't find anything. I saw some deer tracks and signs of small game, but nothing for tonight. What's in the kpot?"

"Blackberries. We may not have dinner but we have dessert."

They ate berries and talked for a while, primarily about the upcoming mission in Iran and how this problem might set back the schedule. Then the conversation turned to their current situation.

Carter asked, "Did John or Stan talk to you about what they called the grandfather paradox, and also about the butterfly effect?"

"You mean about altering history? Yes they did, although John didn't give me a real definitive answer. I don't think they know. I think my grandfather was born around 1915. If we're pre-1917, it's possible I could meet him." Kyle chuckled. "But I don't think he'd be old enough to talk."

"Damn, this is mind-blowing," Carter said. "When you described the mission it sounded exciting. We'd go back in time fifteen minutes and correct our mistakes. I never really considered it *real* time travel. Now, sitting here knowing we're at least ninety-five years back in time. Hell, with this crazy fifteen digit thing, we could be fifteen thousand years back in time—I don't like it."

"Yeah, you got that right." Kyle leaned back against the tree. "We need to think through our every action." He pointed to an ant on the ground. "Do we change history if I smash an ant? I don't think so. That's taking the butterfly thing to the extreme. But, we have to be careful."

"What are our chances of getting out of here?"

"We won't get out tonight. It'll take them a while to figure this out. But they'll do it. We've probably got the best scientific minds in the world working on this project. They'll figure it out all right. I'd say by tomorrow afternoon."

Kyle stood up and stretched. "Do you think we need a fire?"

"Nah. Certainly not for protection or warmth. The biggest things I've seen are tiny fish and small birds . . . air conditioning would be nicer than a fire." Carter slapped the ground next to him. "We could gather up some pine needles. By tomorrow morning this ground could get real hard."

They both made beds out of needles and settled in for the night.

Kyle stretched out. "Well, just think if this had been January. We would have frozen our asses off."

"Yeah. You know, we were so busy when I arrived at Quantico that I didn't even have a chance to call my girlfriend and tell her I'd been transferred."

"Where does she live?"

"In my hometown, Troy, Alabama. I was going to drive over from Pensacola this weekend. She's expecting me."

"Hopefully, sometime during the night, we'll hear a ringing in our ears and end up back in the warehouse. You can call her tomorrow."

"Goodnight, Kyle. Never thought I'd be looking forward to a pea-green mud bath."

Kyle laughed. "By the way, my mud's pitch black. I'm glad—never liked pea soup."

On a warm evening with a bright moon just rising, Kyle tried to sleep. His mind wandered, first to what if it rained, then of the year they had landed in. After tossing around for a few minutes he considered how this would set the Iranian mission behind schedule. As he drifted into sleep, he thought of Jennifer and the upcoming wedding he just might miss. She would really be upset.

The next thought jolted him wide awake.

What if we never get back?

CHAPTER

15

*T*his **would be the** most important meeting of Stan Jackson's CIA career. In his ten years with the agency he had met with the Director of the CIA on only two occasions, both times as an assistant, with someone else doing the talking. This time he'd be in charge. The meeting would include the Director, the Deputy Director, the agency's Director of Science and Technology, and Stan's boss, the Director of National Clandestine Services.

Stan made good use of his drive time from Quantico to the CIA headquarters in Langley, Virginia by practicing his presentation. The plans for The Hindsight Project still weren't complete, but they wanted an update anyway.

His boss, Jim Hightower, had told him, "This project is about as high up the flagpole as you can get. The Director of Central Intelligence, the Secretary of Defense, and the President have all inquired more than once about your progress. This time travel thing, plus eliminating Iran's nuclear capacity, has piqued everyone's interest. You'd best get your ass in gear and don't screw anything up."

Today Stan would present a program evaluation and review, with a complete timeline, which ended with the destruction of the Iranian nuclear facility. Stan walked the corridor of the George Bush Center for Intelligence and checked his watch . . . just enough time to again review his presentation.

When he entered the conference room he spotted Hightower's young assistant.

"Mr. Jackson, it's nice to see you again. I've got everything set up for you."

The room—standard Government Issue, with the exception of all the state-of-the-art electronic jamming equipment—would hold about twenty in a classroom setting. Stan headed to the small table at the front, quickly plugged in his laptop, and checked the large screen mounted on the wall.

He nodded approval. "Thanks, Doug. Looks great. Is everyone still attending?"

"Yes, plus two Assistant Directors. You must be popular—it's a full house." Doug headed for the door. "If you need anything, I'm just four doors down on the left. Good luck."

A few minutes later, Jim Hightower walked through the door. At six foot-four and well over two hundred-and-fifty pounds, the former Notre Dame linebacker filled the entire frame. The seasoned veteran of the CIA had been his boss for over two years.

Hightower held out his hand. "Good afternoon, Stan. I reviewed your presentation this morning. You shouldn't have any problems today. If anyone objects to moving up the dates, just stand your ground. You know better than anyone how much time you need. And remember . . .

Stan knew what was coming next.

"And remember," Hightower repeated, "we don't want to screw this up."

Stan nodded in agreement. Hightower was big on not screwing things up.

Most of the attendees arrived on time or a few minutes ahead of the nine o'clock start. At ten after the hour, Hightower came over and whispered in Stan's ear. "Hold off starting the meeting until the Director arrives. He's always late for meetings, but gets really pissed if you start without him.

At quarter after the hour, Director of the CIA, Richard Adams arrived and took a seat in the back row. Adams reminded Stan of the most boring professor he'd ever had in college. Adams appeared meek, talked in monotones and rarely looked you in the eyes. Stan had never experienced one of Adams' legendary temper tantrums and hopefully wouldn't today.

Hightower opened the meeting. "Good afternoon. We've had more inquiries about this Hindsight Project than any other since the Osama Bin Laden raid. I finally came to the conclusion we needed this meeting to bring all departments up to date." He motioned to Stan. "Before I turn this over to Stan, let me fill you in on his qualifications for the assignment. He joined the agency ten years ago, after receiving his Masters from Georgetown in International Relations. Stan has concentrated on Iran for most of his career, with three years spent in-country on covert operations. He speaks Farsi, understands their politics and culture. This'll be the third mission Stan's headed up in Iran. His last—the highly successful explosion of the Iranian Revolutionary Guard base."

Hightower motioned to Stan with his hand. "It's all yours."

Stan stood and moved to the table. "Thank you, Jim. I'll start with the background information on the team we have selected. We have five members: a Marine Lieutenant Colonel with Special Ops, Force Recon training, and a Navy SEAL with extensive training in explosives and field operations. Both are currently in Quantico. The other three are paramilitary CIA officers already positioned inside Iran. The Iranian facility will be destroyed by these five men on August first— just ten days from now."

Stan heard a few surprised mumbles from the audience and knew he would be challenged on the time schedule. "I might add that's just two days before the scheduled removal of the warheads from the cave." He pressed the remote. "This is the leader of the team, Lieutenant Colonel Kyle O'Brien, a highly trained and decorated Marine."

From outside the room someone knocked on the door. It cracked open and Doug stuck his head in. "I'm sorry to interrupt." He glanced at Hightower. "Sir, the head of the technology team down in Quantico is insisting I interrupt. He needs to talk to Mr. Jackson. I told him this was a very important meeting, but he was adamant."

Hightower gave Stan a sharp look. "OK, Stan, why don't you take the call and get back here as fast as possible. I'll start to fill them in on the rest of the team's background."

Stan hurried down the hall with Doug and rushed into the office.

Doug pointed to the phone. "It's a secure line. I'll be right outside."

He picked it up. "Hello. This is Stan Jackson."

"This is John. I know you're in a big meeting, but this is really serious. We've had an accident."

Stan interrupted. "Did you say accident? It's hard to hear you, there's static on the line. Are you on a secure phone?"

"No, I'm on my cell phone."

"Shit, we can't talk on your cell phone!"

"Stan, you don't understand . . . two people have disappeared."

"Stop right there! Call me on a secure line. There's one over in my office. Get back to me immediately." His mind raced as he paced up and down the small office. *I know Kyle and Carter are in a time travel exercise. Shit, shit, something must have gone wrong.*

Stan continued to pace, loosened his tie, and checked his watch. *Ten minutes. Where the hell is he?*

The phone rang. He grabbed it. "Stan here."

"It's John. I'm on the secure line."

"What the hell's going on? Who's disappeared?"

"Kyle and Carter were in the warehouse about two hours ago. They pressed their transponders and went back in time. They haven't returned."

"Two hours?" Stan took a deep breath. "You've tried to retrieve them?"

"Of course I've tried. We've tried everything. Our lab in Illinois is urgently working on the problem. It will take time."

"How much time?"

"I don't know. This has never happened before." His voice rose in pitch with each word.

In a steady voice, Stan said, "John, calm down. You pulled me out of a meeting with the top officials in the CIA, including the Director. This will probably be in front of the President within half an hour of my report. I need answers. And, *I don't know,* is not going to cut it."

"Stan, remember, I told you about CTC's, those closed, time-like curves going through the wormholes, and how ultimately we could bring them back as that loop closes. That's probably what we'll have to do."

"So that means it could take four days to retrieve them?"

"Possibly," John said.

"*Possibly*? Don't give me that bullshit. I need answers. I can't tell the Director of the CIA that his agency just might *possibly* retrieve men whose particles are spinning somewhere out in the universe."

Stan's phone went silent for over ten seconds. "Are you still there, John?"

"I'm here. Tell them it will take four days. That gives me time to figure out what's going on. I'll get back later with a solution."

"OK. I'll be back at Quantico in three or four hours. You get your facts together, and we need to talk—immediately."

Stan slammed down the phone and rubbed his forehead. He had to go back in there and break the news.

Hightower will be horrified. Not because we're missing two men, but because I've managed to screw this up. What the hell am I going to tell them?

Stan let out a long sigh, readjusted his tie, and feeling like a condemned man, headed down the hallway. He knew an Adams temper tantrum was headed his way.

CHAPTER

16

*S*ix staff members of the CIA Directorate of Science and Technology sat around the conference table at the Quantico facility.

As Stan Jackson walked in, only one set of eyes met his. Stan sat down and stared at John. "I never, ever, want to have another meeting like the one I just left at Langley."

John nodded. "I know what you must have gone through."

"You don't know shit. I had to tell the Director and senior staff of the CIA that two highly decorated war heroes had literally disappeared into thin air. As I left, an extremely pissed off Director was placing calls to both the Secretary of Defense and the President to inform them about what happened."

John buried his face in his hands. "The President."

Stan scanned the group. "All of you look at me. Don't stare down at your notes. We're going to get these men back. Now, what progress have we made?"

"None," John said. "We keep detailed records of all time travel. We need to figure out what made this trip different. We have this staff, plus over three hundred back at project headquarters in Illinois working every angle. We'll get an answer. I just don't know how soon."

"Could it be the location?" Stan wondered.

"No. We've tested locations all around the world. And, before you ask, we've also transported up to six people at one time, with no problems."

"How about the equipment?"

"We're checking out all the equipment." John held up a transponder. "We've just finished checking all the transponders and microchips . . . no problems."

John turned to one of his team. "Rick, you're the astrophysicist, fill Stan in on the flares."

A man in his late-twenties nodded and looked down at his notes. "Today we experienced some powerful solar flares. These are caused by intense magnetic activity. In 1989 we had a geomagnetic storm so large it collapsed the Quebec electric transmission grid. Some satellites in polar orbit also lost control for several hours. It's possible this type of storm could have an impact on time travel. No one on our team can answer that question, so we're going outside the agency to find an expert. It'll take at least two days."

John spoke up. "We're also looking at this fifteen digit phenomenon. Recently in testing we sent someone back fifteen days and successfully brought him back. It had no effect on the man, but maybe it did on the equipment. We've also been experimenting with moving out to the next level. We're not sure if that's fifteen months or fifteen years. Nor do we know why this phenomenon even happens. It makes no sense. But maybe it's causing the problem."

"OK." Stan stood up. "Tomorrow morning at 0900 I have a conference call with the CIA Director. I want those two men back as soon as possible. Now get going!"

The next morning, Jim Hightower called Stan. "Have you got any answers yet?"

"No. And I probably won't for at least four days."

"Four days. Stan, you've really screwed this thing up." Hightower's voice grew louder. "This Hindsight mission is the most important I've ever worked on. What am I going to tell the Director?"

Stan thought for a moment. "Tell him that *his* Tech Team has no answers and probably won't for at least four days."

"O.K." Hightower's voice lowered. "Maybe we can dump this in the Tech Department's lap. They screwed it up."

CHAPTER

17

At first light, Kyle awoke from a fitful sleep. He rolled over, sat up and glanced around. Carter had disappeared.

Kyle jumped up and rubbed the sleep from his eyes. He was still back in time at the same spot. He yelled for Carter—with no reply.

Am I alone? Has Carter been transported back during the night? Or, has he been hauled away by an animal?

Kyle ran out of the trees and desperately searched the meadow.

No sign of him. Is something wrong with my transponder?

He pressed the transponder button and it started to vibrate. He yelled again.

Carter came running out of the trees fifty feet away. "My transponder's vibrating," He shouted. "Are we about to be transported?"

Think God he's still here.

Kyle yelled. "No, I pushed the button. You scared the shit out of me. I thought I was stuck here by myself."

Carter headed back. "I'm sorry. He held his helmet in front of him. "I was rounding up breakfast. The woods are loaded with blackberries." He approached with a sheepish grin. "I can see how it would shake you up." He held up the helmet. "How about some chow?"

Kyle reached over, took a blackberry and popped it in his mouth. "Hell, some animal could have grabbed you. Next time, wake me up if you decide to go grocery shopping."

They sat and ate berries. "What's our plan for today?" Carter asked.

"We can stay here. There's water and signs of animal life. With our survival skills we could probably live off the land, at least until winter." Kyle glanced at Carter. "What do you think?"

Carter gave a quick look around. "It's not a bad spot. But, I'm curious, how far back in time are we? Maybe we check this area and see if there's any civilization around here. And, what happens if we do run into people?"

"Well, for sure we don't tell them the truth. If we do, they'll lock us up in an insane asylum or burn us at the stake."

"Should we take our weapons?" Carter asked.

Kyle shook his head. "No. We know we're at least a hundred years back in time. This gear would be a dead giveaway that we're from the future. The ammo for all our weapons hasn't even been invented yet. And besides, with these weapons we could change history. They get left here."

"Man, I hate leaving my weapons. How about keeping the KaBars?"

"Yeah, they did have knives." Kyle nodded. We'll keep the KaBars. And, we'll hide the weapons. We can always come back for them."

Carter pulled at his uniform. "How about these?"

"You want to take them off and run around in our skivvies?" Kyle laughed, "Or, we could go nude? Either way we'd be more noticeable."

"Good point. We stay in our trousers and just wear t-shirts. How far should we go? We could be transported back at any time."

"They said that wasn't a problem," Kyle said. "As long as we stay in the Northern Hemisphere the satellite can locate us."

Kyle slapped his hands together and stood up. "Ok, let's make sure the gear is well hidden, and then we take off. It's going to be interesting to find out how far back in time we've traveled."

For three hours they walked through a heavy forest of cedars and pine trees, at times on animal trails, and often through heavy underbrush. The terrain then flattened, and thinned out. Small streams, willow trees and marshes became more prevalent.

Other than a deer, which they flushed out of the undergrowth, a few squirrels, and numerous birds, they saw no living creatures.

Kyle checked the watch on the transponder. "It's almost noon and we still haven't seen any signs of civilization. Those jokes about dinosaurs aren't funny anymore. Maybe we're way, way back in time."

Finally, after another hour, they crossed a well-worn path.

Kyle examined it closely. "I'll be damned, we've found evidence of civilization. These are horse prints, and they've been shod."

"You're right," Carter said. "Horses came over with the Europeans. So we're looking at least the Sixteen Hundreds, and up to probably the Eighteen Hundreds." Carter pointed to the edge of the path. "That's a footprint, also wearing a shoe. At least we don't have to worry about those damn dinosaurs."

"This is good news. We'll probably find people who speak English and won't try to kill us."

As they traveled along the path, Kyle noticed more bushes loaded with blackberries. They rested and ate a few.

In the distance Kyle heard a rumbling noise. "Hear that? It sounds like thunder. We might be in for some rain."

Carter listened intently. "I don't think so. Too consistent for thunder, I think it's artillery, maybe three or four different guns firing."

"Well, it's not coming from Quantico. You're the munitions expert . . . how far away?"

"A long way, maybe ten to twenty miles depending on the wind. Should we head for the noise?"

"Let's stay on this." Kyle motioned up the trail. "Sooner or later we've got to run into people."

After another half hour, Kyle pointed to the sky. "Is that smoke up ahead ?"

"I think it is, probably no more than a half-mile in front of us."

They continued up the trail. Through the trees a log cabin came into view.

Kyle stopped and viewed the cabin. "Well, civilization at last. Let's hope they're friendly. What year do you think we're in?"

Carter shook his head. "I don't know. Hell, people today are still living in log cabins. It looks pretty primitive and small. It's got no electrical wires running to it and an outhouse. A wild guess would be Seventeen to late Eighteen Hundreds."

"The fire is burning over by that shed," Kyle said. "Someone's probably nearby. I'll check it out. You stay out of sight and cover me."

"Cover you with what? My knife?"

Cautiously, Kyle moved down a path that opened onto a hard-packed dirt yard. Two tall pines provided shade to the small front porch of the cabin. An empty corral, probably for a horse or cow, was on the left. He thought he saw movement in one of the little windows on either side of the front door.

Kyle moved between the two pines and yelled. "Hello. Anybody home?"

A loud shot rang out.

Bark flew off the trunk of the tree about five feet to his right. He lunged left, hit the ground and rolled in behind the other tree.

A female voice yelled. "Next shot's tween the eyes. What do you want?"

Kyle shouted from behind the tree. "I need some directions. We're lost."

"Are ya'll Yankee soldiers?"

He leaned around the tree and took a quick look. The woman peeked out through the edge of the cabin window.

Kyle yelled, "No. I don't know anything about Yankees. Please don't shoot. Can I stand up and come out?"

"Yes, but keep your hands in the air. Tell your friend to join you. Both of ya'll move up next to the porch so's I can see you."

Kyle stood up with hands in the air. He spotted some movement at the other window. It looked like one or two small children peering out. He yelled back to Carter. "Come up and join me."

Carter moved up and whispered. "What's going on?"

"She thinks we're Yankee soldiers."

"*Yankees*?"

"Yeah, that's what she said. We must be in the Civil War era."

"Quit yapping and move forward before I shoot," she yelled.

Carter whispered, "You want me to move around behind the cabin?"

"No. She's protecting some small kids. Let's move forward and show her we don't have weapons."

With their hands up, they walked to within twenty feet of the front porch. The door to the cabin opened slowly. A small woman, in a loose tattered dress, with scraggly brown hair and no shoes, squeezed through. She had a gun pointed at them.

"I ain't never seen clothes like them before. They some kind of fancy Yankee uniforms?"

"It's for work, not an army uniform," Kyle said.

She held a flintlock, smooth bore musket. The hammer was cocked and ready to fire. It had to be from the early 1800's. The woman glared. "Yankees come through here yesterday and stole my pig and three chickens."

Kyle said again, "Trust me, we're not Yankees. Are you alone?"

She pointed to the cabin. "I got three youngn's in there. My husband went off to war two months ago." She aimed the musket at them. "But, I ain't alone, I got this gun and I shoot real good."

"We're not here to cause you any trouble nor steal anything." Kyle knew the answer to the next question, but had to ask. "You mentioned your husband went off to war. What war?"

She stared at him. "Where you been, mister, in a cave? We ceded from them Yankees bout' four or five months ago."

After he thought a moment, Kyle asked, "So this is the summer of 1861 and we're in Northern Virginia?"

"Course it is. July 1861, Prince William County, Virginia. I know it's a Thursday, but don't rightly know the exact date." She frowned at him. "You crazy or somethin'?"

He whispered to Carter. "Well, now we know the time." Kyle turned to the woman. "We're not crazy, we just need directions to the nearest town, and some food."

"Yankee money ain't no good here."

"She noticed our uniforms immediately," Carter murmured. "We stand out like a sore thumb."

"You're right. Let's see if she can help." Kyle turned to the woman. "Can we trade our clothes for some food and some of your husband's old things?"

"I got little use for them clothes. Show me that knife you got on your hip?"

Kyle pulled out his KaBar and held it up.

She peered at Carter. "Give me yours too."

"No, just one," Kyle said. He pitched it on the porch.

She bent over and cautiously picked up the knife with one hand, while holding the musket with the other. "That's a fine knife." She put the knife down, lifted the musket and aimed it at Carter. "I want both knives."

After a quick glance at Kyle, Carter removed his knife and threw it on the porch.

She scooped up both knives. "Don't move. I'll be right back."

Turning, she raced into the cabin and returned with a pair of old shoes. "I'll give you these shoes, some of my husband's clothes and food. But, I want them fancy shoes." She pointed to Kyle's boots.

She threw the shoes to Kyle. "Them's perfectly good brogans."

He picked up the shoes and looked at Carter.

"Don't look at me, Kyle. I may be short, but I wear a size twelve, my big toe wouldn't fit."

Kyle sat down and unlaced his boots. The shoes were worn, stiff, moldy and smelled, but still had a little leather on the soles. He slid his foot into the hard leather. They sort of fit, but sure weren't comfortable. What the hell, he only needed them for a little while.

Kyle threw his boots on the porch. "Food, information, clothes and some money. In exchange for my boots, our clothes, and both knives."

A big smile emerged on her face. "It's a deal. Cept I ain't got no Yankee money. I only got Confederate." She examined one of the boots. "I ain't never seen shoes this fine."

"They're French." Carter said.

She giggled. "Them Frenchie's is pretty fancy."

"OK. You drive a hard bargain," Kyle said.

With the deal concluded, she relaxed and took the boots inside. In a few minutes she returned with three little girls, but still held the musket. The girls appeared to be about two, four and six. All three peered out from behind their mother. "I piled a bunch of Myron's clothes on the floor. You're welcome to go in and try them on. I'll go around to the cook shed and fix ya'll something. Remember, only one shirt and britches each. Leave them funny uniforms on the floor."

Most of the clothes in the pile were well worn, made of coarse cotton, and hand stitched.

Kyle picked up a shirt. "It smells like Myron didn't wash very often." He took a deep breath and slipped it on—it was slightly small.

Carter tried both shirt and pants, both bulged at the seams. He looked down. "I'll have to be careful. I stand a good chance of busting out of these pants if I bend over."

Both chose long sleeved, light weight shirts, which hid their transponders.

Carter held up a small Swiss Army Knife and put it in his pocket. "I still got this."

"Right," Kyle chuckled. "That three inch blade looks deadly. I'm starving. I hope she cooks as well as she bargains."

Supper consisted of a slab of salt pork heated in a skillet, a sliced potato fried in grease, and a fresh tomato from her garden. The three young girls intently watched as they ate, but remained behind their mother.

The distant, deep boom of artillery interrupted the meal. Kyle asked, "What's that noise?"

She answered, "My husband come home two weeks ago and told me the war was bout' to start. I think that's the noise from them big guns. It started up early this afternoon."

"Where did your husband think the battle would be fought?"

"Somewheres' round Manassas Junction. It's where them two railroads hook together. Myron's been soldierin' at Centreville for the last month. Diggin' trenches and stuff. That's up north of Bull Run."

She bit her lip. "I sure hope he got cross the run before them Yankees showed up."

Kyle took a bite of the chewy pork and looked at the three young girls. Life would be tough for the next four years. Hopefully, their father would survive.

"Armies tend to move slowly. I'll bet he managed to make it across," Kyle said. "If we were going to Washington DC, would we need to pass through Centreville?"

She pointed to the trail in front of the house. "Turn right . . . stay on it till ya'll come to Sullivan's Ford on Bull Run. Cross over and after a mile or so, ya'll will come to a fork in the road, turn right for Alexandria and Washington, go left to Centreville. Ain't nothing but Yankees up that way. Ya'll should go out front and take a left. That's the way to Richmond. Myron told me that's the new Capitol of our country. I ain't been there, but it's supposed to be real nice."

They both stood up and Kyle said. "Thank you for the meal . . . and the hospitality."

She picked up a package, wrapped in old newspaper. "This here's some cornbread. Not part of the deal, but ya'll got a long trip, whichever way ya'll choose."

Kyle smiled. "Thank you. We wish you and your family the best."

They strolled down to the trail in front of the cabin. The woman and three girls waved good-bye. The sound of artillery had finally stopped.

Kyle stopped at the path. "So now we know . . . July, 1861. The civil war is about to start with the battle of Bull Run."

"You know that fifteen seconds, fifteen minutes, fifteen hours shit they told us about," Carter said. "I just did some arithmetic. It's working. We're back in time one hundred and fifty years. Can you fucking believe that? And caught in the middle of a Civil War battle to boot."

Kyle took a deep breath. "There's not a damn thing we can do about it. We just wait and survive. I do know quite a bit about Bull Run. I was stationed at Quantico in July, 2006. I went over to the Manassas Battlefield National Park and watched a reenactment of the battle and took a three hour tour. It really caught my interest, and I read a couple of books on Bull Run. Today was probably the opening skirmish. The real action starts in three days, on Sunday, the twenty-first. Never in my wildest dreams did I image being here for the actual battle."

Carter looked left and right. "What now, Colonel?"

"We find ourselves at a major decision," Kyle said, "When I was a company commander in Afghanistan I would use a quote from Abraham Lincoln. 'Some see opportunity in every obstacle, while others see obstacles in every opportunity.' I think we're looking at one of those opportunities."

Carter gave a chuckle. "Colonel, you're blowing my mind. You just quoted someone who's alive and living less than a hundred miles from here-- to top it off he probably hasn't even made that quote yet."

"Yeah, but, it's still an opportunity. Is it North or South?"

"Sir, I think those scientists really screwed up. We may be stuck here for a while—hell, we could be here forever. I've served ten years defending my country . . . the United States of America. I want to go North. How about you?"

"I agree. No reason to get caught up in this war. Let's skirt around the battle and head to Washington D.C. Hell, we may even see Honest Abe."

Typical log cabin, Virginia 1861.

CHAPTER

18

Brigadier General Daniel Tyler, Commander of the First Division of the U.S. Army of Northeastern Virginia, rode alongside the horse drawn artillery team, his black gelding gave a nervous quiver. The twelve horses on the team strained as they struggled to haul the heavy cannon up the steep hill. Tyler leaned forward and patted the long graceful neck of his mount. "Easy boy, easy."

His aide, Lieutenant Nash, a young man from his home town in Connecticut, moved next to him. "General, that cannon's huge."

"It's a Parrot rifled cannon. It can fire a thirty pound shell over four miles. It's the biggest we've got. The rebels can't match it. But, it's damned hard to haul on these roads."

They crested the hill and entered the small hamlet of Centreville. It consisted of one dirt street, lined with about twenty modest houses, two churches and a few taverns and stores. The largest house in the village, a brick, two-story, which had seen better days, had a large number of horses and wagons surrounding it.

A squad of cavalry rode past them. The captain saluted. "Good evening, General."

Tyler gave him a snappy salute. The sixty-three-year-old Brigadier General prided himself on his military bearing, tall, slim, erect, and with a well-groomed, full grey beard and hair.

Lieutenant Nash pointed to the house. "That must be the general's headquarters. Do you think he's still upset about this afternoon's skirmish at Blackburn's Ford?"

"I don't know why he ordered me here, but if he talks to me like he did this afternoon, it'll be a short meeting. I'll rip the stars off my shoulders, and stick them up his ass. Then I'll get on my horse and ride home to Connecticut. I haven't been *scolded* like that since my West Point days, and that was over forty years ago."

They rode up to the house and Tyler dismounted off his horse. "Guess we'll find out real soon what our young commander wants."

An aide ushered them into the dining room. Brigadier General Irvin McDowell, Tyler's Commanding Officer, sat at a table cluttered with dirty dishes. A staff of three gathered around him.

McDowell motioned to the empty chairs. "Take a seat, gentleman. Would you like coffee?"

One of his men held up a bottle. "Or maybe some of this fine Tennessee bourbon? It's compliments of the owner of the house. He made a fast exit about an hour before our troops entered town this morning."

"No, thanks," Tyler said. "We're fine. How can I help you, General?"

McDowell stood up, his unbuttoned uniform revealing a large, protruding belly. The press had described him as stout and ungainly. Tyler, in private, liked to call him fat, ugly and uninspiring.

McDowell motioned to one of his staff. "Get this table cleared and bring in that map of Northern Virginia."

With the map spread on the table, McDowell moved in beside Tyler. "General, I need your advice. I've been told you quit the army in thirty-four and went to work for a railroad."

"That's true. I was hired as chief engineer on the Susquehanna Railroad. Later I became president of the railroad."

McDowell pointed to Centreville on the map. "Here's where we are. North of that small stream called Bull Run." He moved his finger down the map. "And, here on the South side of Bull Run, about eight miles away, is the railroad junction that connects the Manassas Gap Railroad and the Orange and Alexandria Railroad. The Manassas line heads west to Woodstock in the Shenandoah Valley. It's about a fifty mile run."

Tyler nodded. "I know that territory well. Last I heard General Patterson is facing off against General Johnston near the end of the railroad line."

"That's right." McDowell agreed. "Patterson sent us information that Johnston has an army of over twenty thousand men. He assures us that he has engaged the rebels, and they will stay in the Shenandoah. I seriously doubt he can do that."

McDowell pointed to the road connecting Washington DC and Alexandria to Centreville. "We're running behind schedule and won't have all our equipment and supplies in Centreville until late afternoon on the twentieth. We will attack on the morning of the twenty-first."

After running his finger along the Manassas Gap rail line located on the map, McDowell said, "General Tyler, I need to know how long it would take the rebels to move their men by rail along this line and into Manassas."

Tyler studied the map. "I know old Joe Johnston, he's a cautious general, but he's damn organized. Given the chance, he will efficiently move those troops. I recommend we attack as soon as possible, either tomorrow afternoon or the morning of the twentieth. Then we don't have to worry about Johnston's army."

"General." McDowell frowned. "I asked you how long it would take for the rebels to move their men, not your advice on when to attack."

Tyler glared back. "General. If Johnston started right away, and left most of the *supplies and equipment* behind, which is what we should do, it could be done in two and a half days.

They would finish the morning of the twenty-first. Anything else I can help you with . . . Sir?"

"Yes, there is," McDowell said. "We need to confirm that Johnston's troops haven't already shifted to Manassas. You have Colonel Richardson's brigade on the left flank. Have him send some cavalry units to Union Mills Ford and a little further over at Sullivan's Ford. It's the perfect place for those rebels to try and sneak some spies into our lines. Catch a few and see if you can squeeze some information out of them about Johnston's army. Find out if they are expected in Manassas."

"I'll do that right away, General."

"You remind Richardson not to get in another skirmish like he did at Blackburn's Ford today. Having his troops run back across Bull Run with their tails between their legs is bad for moral." McDowell stood. "We'll have a staff meeting on the twentieth to review our plan of assault. The attack will be on the twenty-first. Good evening."

Tyler started to say something, and then changed his mind. The two men walked back to their horses.

Nash mounted his horse, and turned to Tyler. "Sir, I don't think the General likes you."

Tyler gave a deep laugh. "He doesn't like anybody to question his authority. He's forty-two years old, was a major six months ago, and got this job by being friends with the politicians. He's way over his head and he knows it."

After climbing back on his horse, Tyler said. "The best thing we've got going for us is the Confederate's commander, Brigadier General Pierre – Gustave –Toutant – Beauregard. I know him well, he served under me years back. Amazingly, both McDowell and Beauregard graduated the same year from West Point. But the comparison stops there. Beauregard is dashing, arrogant, flamboyant — thinks he's the next Napoleon, and to top it off . . . really stupid."

They turned and headed down the road. Tyler snickered. "This will be an interesting battle. The winner could be the Commanding General who screws up the least."

Brigadier General Daniel P. Tyler, (1799-1882) A graduate of the U.S. Military Academy who served in the U.S. Army from 1861 to 1864. Tyler remained steadfast in blaming General McDowell for the Union defeat at the First Battle of Bull Run. Tyler's granddaughter, Edith Carow, would marry Theodore Roosevelt and become First Lady of the U.S. from 1901 to 1909.

Major General Irvin McDowell, (1818—1885). Would be replaced as Commander of the U.S. Army of Northeastern Virginia immediately after the First Battle of Bull Run. McDowell would continue to blame the loss of the First Battle of Bull Run on General Tyler.

CHAPTER

19

For over an hour Kyle and Carter walked the dusty, deeply rutted road in silence. They passed two small farms and covered close to three miles, but spotted neither humans nor farm animals. Kyle suspected the farmers had rounded up the livestock and headed further south to escape hostile troops.

Kyle's thoughts, and he assumed Carter's also, focused on their current predicament . . . how in the hell had they ended up a hundred and fifty years back in time? More importantly, what could they do about it? Somehow they were flung back to the most tragic time in U.S. history. He didn't remember the exact numbers, but during the next four years, over 600,000 troops, from both the Union and Confederacy would die. This horrible fight would involve over three million men—and here they were.

Very soon they would probably meet some of those troops—hopefully Union forces who could help them head north.

"I've been thinking," Kyle said.

"Yeah, me too," Carter interrupted. "How the hell do we get out of this mess? It's making our mission in Iran look simple."

"Sooner or later," Kyle said. "We'll be stopped and questioned before we reach the Potomac River and Washington, hopefully by Union and not Confederate troops. We can't tell them the truth."

"You're damn right. Telling them we dropped in for a visit from the 21st century is not an option."

"How's this sound?" Kyle said. "We were traveling in Europe when the South seceded from the Union. We sailed home from France on a ship scheduled for Norfolk, but we found the Virginia ports blockaded by Union gun boats. Since we flew the US flag, the ship changed course and headed up the Chesapeake Bay for Baltimore, Maryland. A Confederate gunboat chased us up on rocks somewhere near the Rappahannock River. With the ship sinking, we swam away, leaving all our belongings on board. A fishing boat picked us up and dropped us on the Virginia shore. We've been trying to make it north ever since."

"Hey, why France?" Carter asked.

"I speak the language and spent six months there as a student. I know Paris real well."

"What about me? I've never been there and don't speak any foreign languages. "

Kyle thought for a moment. "Let's keep it simple. Just say you traveled by yourself around Europe for about a year, but don't get specific. Remember, some of those countries didn't even exist back then, stick to Spain, France and England. Probably no one we run into has ever been to Europe. We'll tell them we first met aboard ship on the passage home. That way we don't have to coordinate our stories. How does that sound?"

"I can't think of a better way to explain why we're showing up without anything but the clothes on our back, and no money or identification."

"OK. That's what we'll say. Just don't get fancy."

The sun had set and darkness closed in around them. Bright, early evening stars lit up the sky . . . no street lights, car lights, airplanes, or city lights to contend with.

They could still make out the wagon ruts in the road and decided to continue on for a few more hours until they cleared the Bull Run area.

Carter held up an arm and pointed to the transponder. "Do you want to try this thing again?"

"OK. One more try. Ready . . . one, two, three."

They pushed both buttons. Nothing happened.

"Shit." Kyle shook his head. "So much for our brilliant team of scientists."

"Yeah. I've been thinking about that. Hell, maybe we *never hear from them again*."

They walked in silence for a while. The road started down a slight grade and, in the dim light, Kyle spotted what appeared to be a stream.

He spoke softly. "She mentioned we'd cross Sullivan's Ford on Bull Run, so this must be it. The battlefield's probably ten miles upstream. Let's move carefully. It could be guarded by Union or Confederate troops . . . or both."

Cautiously, they approached the water's edge. The combat gear they had hidden in the brush at Quantico would have come in handy right now, especially the night vision goggles.

Kyle tapped Carter's shoulder and pointed out the run. He could barely make out the other side—about fifty feet away. Step by step they waded out to the middle of the ford. The current flowed at a lazy pace and the waist-deep cool water felt good on his tired legs and sore feet.

Kyle checked the far bank for guards, but didn't see any movement. This would probably be their last chance to drink water for quite a while. He whispered, "We have to hydrate."

"You think it's safe to drink?" Carter asked.

"It might not be, but we don't have a choice. A purification pill would be great right now."

"Yeah, and so would a cold beer."

Kyle cupped his hands in the stream and brought the water up to his lips. "Here goes."

They took a number of big gulps, then headed for the other side. Once ashore, they carefully climbed the slippery bank and back onto the road.

"I'm surprised this ford's not guarded," Kyle said.

Near the top of the grade they reached a fork in the road.

Carter tapped him on the shoulder. "We're in luck, this is where we head right and out of the combat zone."

On the horizon a small dot of orange light appeared low in the sky.

Carter pointed. "What the hell's that?" He chuckled, "Maybe it's a light from an airplane or chopper."

"Well it's sure as hell not a street light." Kyle stared as the light grew larger and brighter. Finally, he snickered, "It's not a light . . . That's a full moon rising over the hill."

"You're right. But, a chopper swooping down for extraction would have been great."

With the increased moonlight, they could travel a little faster. After a short distance they entered a heavily wooded area. The road narrowed and the underbrush and overhanging trees closed in around them, blocking out most of the light.

Suddenly, on both sides of them, rustling noises came from the underbrush. On Kyle's right he heard a metallic click.

"Halt!" A voice shouted, "Who goes there?"

Kyle considered running, but didn't know how many men there were, or their locations. "We're civilians! We don't have any weapons!"

Someone yelled, "Get face down on the ground or we'll shoot!"

They dropped to the road and Kyle shouted, "We're down. Don't fire!"

A shadowy figure rushed up and kicked Kyle's knee. Pain shot up his right leg.

The man yelled, "One move and I'll smash your head in."

Another figure rushed to Carter and pressed a pistol to his head. "Put your hands behind you. We're gonna tie you up."

Someone grabbed Kyle's arms, while another tied his hands. They lifted him off the ground and shoved him along the road. His knee hurt like hell, but he managed to limp along and stay on his feet.

"Faster, keep moving." A man jammed a rifle butt in his back.

The forest thinned and the moon reappeared. Kyle spotted Carter ahead of him with his hands also tied. About ten men surrounded them, all in uniform and armed with rifles.

In the dim light Kyle couldn't make out the insignia. "Are you Union or Confederate?"

"Shut up. I'll tell you when to talk."

A soldier with a sword strapped to his waist joined them. "Colonel Richardson wants to talk to any rebs we catch. Take them to the 12th New York Regimental Headquarters. It's just south of Centreville on the Mitchell's Ford road. Be careful and make damn sure they are tied securely."

"Sir, we're not rebels." Kyle cried out. "We're civilians just trying to make our way north."

He moved closer and Kyle noticed a lieutenant's bar on his collar.

The lieutenant snapped back. "I don't give a shit. Tell your story to the Colonel." He turned to the other men. "Lift them up on the horse and get moving."

They helped Kyle up into the saddle, and then Carter behind him.

A soldier grabbed Kyles horse's reins and climbed on his mount. "There could be reb's out there. You two keep your mouths shut."

A second rider moved in behind them, and they headed down the road—back toward the field of battle.

For the first few miles they rode in silence. Kyle couldn't believe it, two highly trained seasoned Special Operations guys, being brought down by soldiers with probably only a few weeks' worth of training. He considered escaping. With only two men guarding them, they could easily overpower them, but possibly it would only make the situation worse.

Sooner or later they would be questioned, better now than later as fugitives. At least they were captured by Union troops. They would have a chance to tell their story to the Colonel, and be sent on their way north.

The soldier riding behind them spoke up, "Hold up, I got to take a piss." He dismounted and moved over to the side of the road.

Kyle asked the man holding their reins. "What's the date today?"

"It's the eighteenth of July. Now shut up, Reb. You can talk when we get to camp."

"We're not rebels." Kyle said. "We're trying to get away from the South."

The other solider buttoned up his fly and climbed back in the saddle. "Then you must be deserters."

"No, we're civilians."

"You keep your fucking mouth shut or you'll be dead civilians."

They traveled about six miles, twice passing through road-blocks. Each time a guard yelled out, "Halt, who goes there?"

The man in the lead yelled back, "Friends with the countersign."

"Advance forward."

Once in front of the guard, the front man whispered, "Minneapolis." Then they passed through.

They crested a hill and looked out over a wide valley. Kyle gasped. "Wow, look at this."

The encamped Union Army of Northeastern Virginia spread out before them. The full moon cast a bright glow that reflected off the white canvas tents, which stretched for miles. The added flicker of thousands of campfires lit the horizon. Men sat around the fires eating and talking. Laughter, songs, and music from banjos and guitars filled the air.

Carter whispered, "There's got to be more than twenty thousand men camped here."

"Yeah, you're right. It's sad . . . war to them is still a big celebration." Kyle checked to make sure the guards didn't hear him. "In three days over three thousand men, on both sides, will die, be wounded or captured in this battle. The army here tonight will be in a panicked, disorganized, full retreat. Look at this setting, it's like watching a war movie."

They rode through the camp for another half-hour, finally arriving in front of an old, abandoned farmhouse. The guard dismounted and ran inside. A few minutes later they were yanked off the horse and dragged into a small front room of the house. Kyle's knee had stiffened up, but he could still hobble on it.

A lantern glowed in the corner, and the only furniture consisted of a table and four chairs. They were pushed to the floor, their backs against the wall, hands still tied behind them.

"Are you OK?" Carter asked.

Kyle nodded. "My knee hurts, but I'll make it."

A sergeant and young lieutenant entered the room. The sergeant strolled over and glared down at them. His ragged uniform coat hung half open, exposing a dirty white shirt and a barrel chest. Gray appeared around the edges of his full brown mustache and unkempt beard. He ogled Carter's boots. "Put your foot out, I want to see them shoes you got on."

Kyle watched him bend down, admire the light brown boots, and stroke the top of the roughed-out, full grained, suede leather.

"Those shoes are from France," Carter said. "That's where we just came from."

The sergeant shook his head. "That's real soft leather." He rubbed the polyurethane molded plastic sole, looked down at his stiff leather shoes, and gave Carter an accusing stare. "I ain't never seen no shoe like this before."

Kyle gave Carter a fleeting look.

"Yeah," Carter said. "Those French are real smart."

The young lieutenant, clean shaven, with bright, shiny brass buttons down the front of his dark blue uniform, moved next to the sergeant. A sword and scabbard hung from around his waist. "Forget the shoes, Sergeant. I'll take over." He glared at Kyle. "What's your name, rank and military unit?"

Kyle answered. "We're not in the military. We're civilians."

The lieutenant laughed. "You were caught on the first day of a major battle trying to spy behind our lines. The only thing civilian about you are those ill-fitting clothes."

Kyle shook his head. "No, we aren't spies, and we're not farmers. We were heading north to get away from the Confederacy."

The lieutenant glanced across at the sergeant and smiled. "They wanted to join us. That's the reason they did it in the dark of night. For some strange reason they didn't want to be seen."

"I can explain what happened," Kyle said. "We were returning from . . ."

The lieutenant pointed at Kyle. "Stop . . . I'll do the talking. I have one question and I demand an answer. Have any of the forces of General Joseph Johnston moved from the Shenandoah Valley to Manassas Junction?"

Kyle shook his head and took a quick glimpse at Carter. "I don't know about that."

The sergeant stepped up, smiled, and gave Kyle a vicious kick to the ribcage. "Enough of this bullshit, answer the Lieutenant."

Kyle doubled up and rolled on the floor, groaning in pain.

The lieutenant pulled his sword out of the scabbard and pointed it at Kyle's throat.

"Answer my question or I'll run you through."

Kyle gasped in agony. "I know nothing about Confederate troops."

The lieutenant sighed, "You're lucky." He placed the sword back into the scabbard. "I don't have the authority to kill you, but Colonel Richardson does. I'm going to get him. You talk this over with your friend. The colonel's got a hot temper and no patience. If you don't give him the information, you'll both be dead men."

They left the room and Kyle grimaced in pain as he struggled back up against the wall. Now both his knee and his ribs throbbed. "I think he broke one of my ribs."

"This is not going as we planned," Carter said. "I don't think he's bluffing. Maybe we should give him some information."

Kyle checked the door to make sure no one eavesdropped. "I won't answer his question. Johnson's troops play a major part in the Southern victory. Most of them arrive early morning on the twenty-first. If the Union attacks a day ahead, on the twentieth, they will probably win instead of lose the Battle of Bull Run. Our information could change the course of history."

"But, I don't understand. It won't change the final results. The North still wins the war."

"Who knows?" Kyle said, "If the North had won at Bull Run, maybe they would have gotten cocky. What if, due to complacency they lose at Gettysburg? What if they become disillusioned and negotiate? Carter, there's too many what ifs. I'm not going to play God."

Carter thought a moment. "All right, I understand, but I don't want to die. Let's give them some cockamamie story, just so we can stay alive until these damn transponders kick in."

"We'll play it by ear. If it looks like they're going to shoot us right away, we give them a story. If it looks like they're going to imprison us, we stick to our original story and wait on the transponders."

Carter nodded. "OK. You do the talking."

About half an hour later, the sergeant returned. He walked over and kicked Carter's boot. "Stick your foot out again."

He placed his shoe alongside Carter's, and gave him a big grin. His teeth, what few he had, were heavily stained a deep brown. He appeared to have a plug of tobacco in the corner of his cheek. "We got near the same size foot. Them shoes are mine."

The sergeant sat down and started to unlace Carter's boot. "They sure look nice."

Voices came from the next room. The door opened, the sergeant jumped up, snapped to attention and saluted. "Good evening, Colonel."

A tall man, well over six feet, ducked his head through the doorway. He wore a white shirt with no coat, the sleeves rolled up and suspenders hanging down on his hips. The young lieutenant trailed behind him.

The Colonel sat in one of the chairs, and leaned back with his arms folded across his chest. "Sergeant, pick these men up and put them in a chair. I like to look a man in the eyes when I'm talking."

With their hands still tied, the sergeant moved each of them into a chair.

The colonel studied them for a moment. He was not only tall, but also large, with a full head of long, dark hair and a neatly trimmed mustache.

"I'm Colonel Richardson." He eyed Kyle. "They tell me you've been doing all the talking, so you must be in charge?"

Kyle shook his head. "No, I'm not in charge of anything. We were in Europe . . ."

Richardson held up his hand. "Hold it. We caught you spying. You're two healthy young men, and they tell me you're both well spoken. You may be dressed like some hick farmer, but I don't believe it."

Richardson rubbed his chin, which had a three-day stubble. "I think you're well educated and at least a captain, maybe a major in the reb army. No doubt you're a spy."

Kyle shook his head in frustration. "Colonel, listen to me. Let me tell you what happened. We don't know anything about the rebels. We just arrived back in the country from France."

"Shut up!" Richardson jumped up and stretched his shoulders. "Major, or whatever the hell you are, I've had a long and very bad day. Nineteen of my men are dead, thirty-eight seriously wounded and twenty-six taken prisoner." He moved right up to Kyle's face. "I'm in no mood to play fucking games with you. You've got one chance. Where is General Johnston's army? How many troops have moved over from the Shenandoah? "

Kyle shrugged and looked him in the eyes. "I give up. Believe what you want. I have no idea where the rebel troops are." The Colonel sighed, took a step back, turned and headed for the door. He grabbed the handle, and looked back. "You're lying. Tomorrow morning you will be shot as spies. May God have mercy on your souls."

Major General Israel B. Richardson. (1815-1862) After the First Battle of Bull Run, Richardson was promoted to Brigadier and later Major General in the U.S. Army. He played an important role in the Battle of Antietam, (September, 1862), where he was injured and would die from his wound.

A typical Union army camp during the Civil War.

CHAPTER

20

*A*fter **Colonel Richardson slammed** the door, the room turned silent.

Kyle glanced at Carter, who stared straight ahead, an astonished look on his face.

I don't believe this is happening! Our own government is about to shoot us as spies.

"Sergeant," The lieutenant said. "Let's get moving. We'll keep a special watch on these men. I saw a shack behind the house. I'll check it out."

A few minutes later the lieutenant returned. "It's sturdy. It'll hold them, at least till tomorrow morning. I'll round up some additional guards."

The sergeant sat across from them with a Springfield rifle on his lap. He gave them a chuckle, spit out a stream of tobacco juice, and looked at Carter's boots. "When they shoot you, I'll be wearin' them fancy boots. A few minutes ago, when I pulled you up on the chair for the colonel, I noticed you had some kind of bracelet on your arm. I want to see it. "

"It's not a bracelet, it's a wristwatch."

The sergeant tilted his head and gave him a frown. "A what?"

"A watch, but it's not working."

The sergeant cautiously moved in behind Carter. "Lean over so's I can see this watch."

Carter bent over in the chair.

The sergeant lifted Carter's sleeve with the rifle barrel. "You mean like one of them fancy gold pocket watches? I never seen one on the arm before."

"It's new," Carter said. "I got it in France."

The sergeant tapped it with the barrel. "What's it made of?" *I know they didn't have titanium in 1861.*

"It's a new kind of metal," Kyle said. "I'm not sure what it's called."

"How do you get it off?"

"The clasp is broken. It won't come off."

"When them guards show up we'll have to take a close look at this frenchie watch." The sergeant patted his bayonet scabbard and smirked. "It'll slide down real easy, if I cut your hand off."

Kyle stared at the sergeant. *This guy is dangerous. He'll follow up on those threats. We've got to get out of here—as fast as possible.*

The lieutenant came back into the house with two young privates. He picked up the lantern. "Let's go out to the shed. It needs to be cleared out."

They all headed out the backdoor. Kyle gave the shed a hard look. It stood in an open field, was about ten foot square, and constructed of large pine logs, with a single door and no windows—escape wouldn't be easy.

The sergeant held up a lantern and checked inside. "You men clean this junk outa here."

It took the two privates only a few minutes to remove the rusty old farm implements.

After a fast inspection, the sergeant moved out of the shed and checked the door. "Lieutenant, the door's missing a lock, but we can move one of those big logs in front of it."

"That should work." The lieutenant addressed the three men. "Sergeant, you're in charge. I want somebody on guard at all times. I'll arrange for a detail to relieve you. Be careful, it's your ass if they escape."

"Yes sir." The sergeant turned to the privates. "Throw them in the shed."

With the butt of his rifle a soldier shoved them through the door.

From the light of the lantern, the shed looked sturdy, with a hard-packed dirt floor and thick logs for both the walls and roof.

Kyle sat on the dirt, with his back against the wall and his hands tied behind him. Carter sat next to him. Given enough time, and the use of their hands . . . they might be able to dig out. But, they didn't have either time or free hands.

Kyle yelled, "Lieutenant, since we'll be in here all night, could you untie our hands? They're starting to hurt."

"That's not a good idea, Sir," the sergeant said.

The lieutenant grabbed the lantern and looked down at them. "No, I won't untie you. I warned you not to mess with the colonel. Now he's decided shooting spies is good for troop morale . . . you're dead men." The door closed and Kyle heard the log slid in place. Voices filtered through the cracks in the wall.

"Sergeant, your relief will be here at two. Tell them I'll be back at dawn. The execution will be by firing squad at seven in front of the entire battalion. Don't hurt these men. I want them alive and standing before that squad."

Carter whispered, "We need to get the hell out of here."

"First things first," Kyle said. "Let's get untied."

It took a moment for Kyle's eyes to adjust to the darkness. A small amount of lantern light filtered through cracks between the logs. He scooted over to the largest crack and peeked out. The sergeant sat on a log about thirty feet away, while the two guards gathered wood.

"They're building a fire. While they're busy, let's see if we can untie our hands. You try first."

They moved back to back, and Kyle felt Carter's hands on his wrist.

Carter whispered, "This is not going to be easy. They've got it tied in some kind of a double knot. And, I can't see what I'm doing."

"Work fast," Kyle said. "That asshole's going to show up before long, steal your boots and try to take the transponder. Then he'll find mine. Without the transponders we're screwed." After about ten minutes, Carter said, "I've made no progress. I don't think I can get it untied."

Kyle moved over and checked the crack again. "The fire's started and the sergeant and one of the guards are sitting on the log talking. The other man looks to be asleep on the ground."

After moving back, Kyle reached up and felt the knot on Carter's wrist. "I see the problem. It's such an awkward position you can't get any leverage on the knot. But, I'll keep trying."

"Wait a minute," Carter said. "They didn't search us. I've still got that little Swiss army knife in my pocket. Let's see if we can get it out."

"Great idea. If we can get it out."

Carter moved around and placed his thigh next to Kyle's hands. "Can you feel it?"

With his fingers, Kyle felt for the knife.

Carter jerked back. "Whoa, that wasn't a knife you grabbed."

Kyle chuckled. "This is no time for jokes. Get over here." With his fingers, he slowly worked the knife up to the lip of Carter's pants pocket.

With a sigh, Kyle leaned against the wall. "Damn, my hands are starting to cramp. I've got to rest."

"Make it fast. That asshole's going to show up anytime now."

After a few minutes, Kyle moved back in position. This time he managed to grab the knife with his index fingers. "Got it."

It took another ten minutes for Carter to help pry the small blade open. He whispered, "It's open, be careful, I sharpened it about a month ago. Don't cut my wrist."

Kyle carefully sawed back and forth. It took about half an hour, but he finally managed to cut Carter free.

"Damn, that feels good." Carter rubbed his wrist, cut Kyle loose and held up the knife. "No more wise cracks about my three inch blade."

After massaging his wrist and hands, Kyle lay on his back, put both his feet up against the log wall, and pushed hard. The wall didn't budge. "Forget knocking a log loose. We could try digging . . . Our only tool is that little knife. This ground's hard, it'll take all night."

Carter moved over to the crack and peered at the guards. "Only the sergeant's awake. Maybe we can lure him over by using my boots and watch as bait."

"It's worth the risk. Let's call him and hope we don't wake the other guards. You sit back against the wall with your hands behind you. I'll hide next to the door. Once he opens it, you lure him inside. I'll take him down."

Carter nodded. "OK. How are your ribs? You sure you're up to it?"

Kyle took a deep breath. "They feel better. I think it's just a bruise."

"What happens after he's down? We still have two guards and twenty thousand troops out there."

Kyle checked his watch. "It's about midnight. We've got a couple of hours before the relief shows up. Since the other guards are asleep, we'll take them one at a time—tie and gag them, and leave them in the shed. We'll put on their uniform jackets and try to sneak back across Bull Run. Then go south."

Carter nodded. "We don't have a choice. They'll never believe we're not spies. If we're caught up north, they'll sure as hell shoot us."

"If possible try not to kill him." Kyle moved into position. "Are you ready?"

Carter nodded and took a deep breath and called out. "Sergeant, Sergeant!"

Through a crack, Kyle could see the sergeant stand up. "He's coming—looks like the others didn't wake up."

The sergeant strolled to the shed door. "Yeah, what you want?"

"Could we have some water?" Carter asked.

"You don't need no water." The sergeant laughed. "You'll be dead in a few hours."

Carter said, "We're really thirsty. I'll give you my watch."

"I thought you said the watch was broken and you couldn't get it off?"

"I lied. I'll show you how to get it off. And you can have my boots. Just give us water, please."

The sergeant hesitated for a moment. "I'll get you water, but you better give me that watch or you'll suffer." He turned and headed away.

"Sit against the wall," Kyle said. "That way he can see you when the door opens. Remember keep him distracted."

A few minutes later the sergeant reappeared.

"We're in luck," Kyle said. "He didn't wake the guards. Probably doesn't want to share his loot."

The sergeant set down the canteen and rifle, then pushed the log aside. "OK, get back from the door. I'm coming in." He picked up the rifle before giving the door a hard pull. The door flew open and he glared inside.

Carter sat against the wall with his hands behind him. "You fucking idiot, I'm not giving you the watch."

"You sonabitch, you'll pay for this." The sergeant held the rifle at port arms and charged forward.

In one quick movement Kyle slipped behind and caught him in a headlock, with a hand over his mouth.

The sergeant let out a muffled cry, dropped the rifle, and slammed his elbow viciously into Kyle's ribcage.

Pain shot through Kyle's side. The blow caught him right on the cracked rib. It took all his will power not to scream. He rolled to the ground, with the sergeant struggling in his grasp.

In the same motion he gave a vicious twist of the man's head to the side.

The sergeant quivered, made a slight whimper . . . and went limp.

Carter rushed to the wall and checked. "The guards are still asleep."

Kyle felt the sergeant's wrist. No pulse. "He's dead." He looked at Carter.

"It was necessary," Carter said. "Shake it off. Change into his uniform jacket and cap. I'll keep an eye on the guards."

It didn't take long for Kyle to change. "Damn, this jacket smells horrible—it's been years since this guy took a bath." He checked the sergeant's feet. "I'm going to see if his shoes fit. My feet are killing me." He quickly slipped the shoes off. "My God, his feet smell worse than his jacket. But they fit."

Carter glared at the dead sergeant's bare feet and shook his head. "Just think, a few moments ago this guy wanted my boots—and my hand."

"Yeah," Kyle said. "And by killing him I just changed history."

"You didn't have a choice. A yell and the other guards are awake."

"Let's move," Kyle said. "We'll take the guards out one at a time. My ribs really hurt. You do the work. I'll shove a gag in the guy's mouth, and you pin him down. We'll bring him over here, tie him up, and go back for the next one. Try not to kill them. We don't want to screw with any more butterfly wings."

Kyle tore a piece of cloth off the sergeant's shirt for the gag. "Let's go."

Both guards lay near the fire, about eight feet apart and sound asleep. One guard snored loudly.

Kyle motioned to the snoring guard, and bent in front of him. Carter moved up and straddled the man. Kyle shoved a gag in his mouth, while Carter dropped on top of the soldier, pinning him to the ground. They hauled the man over to shed and finished tying him.

Carter changed into the uniform jacket. "It almost fits. Let's go get the other one."

They easily surprised the other guard, tied him up and moved him into the shed. After double checking knots and gags, they closed the door, and slid the log in place.

"Good job." Kyle checked his watch. "It's a quarter to one. We've still got over an hour before that relief shows up. Riding in tonight, I noticed some woods further down the road. Let's hide in there and start working our way down to Bull Run."

Carter picked up a rifle, and threw it to Kyle. "It's loaded. Have you ever fired one of these?"

"Hell no." Kyle slung the rifle over his shoulder and checked out Carter's uniform. "Let's get moving, Private. We've got 20,000 troops to stroll past."

CHAPTER

21

*O*n the first half-mile of their escape, Kyle and Carter passed a number of campsites and hundreds of soldiers. The campfires had died to embers and most of the troops had crawled into their tents for what Kyle knew would be a restless night's sleep. Only an occasional laugh, subdued conversations and the snort of horses broke the silence.

Kyle thought back to March, 2003, before his first combat mission. As a First Lieutenant, he'd joined his platoon beside a campfire near the Rumaila oil fields of southern Iraq. They waited for the bombing of Bagdad, which signaled their assault across the desert to begin. Finally that night he went to bed, only to toss and turn. The next seventeen days he spent with little sleep and continuous combat. His platoon raced through Iraq, finally halting in the northern Iraqi city of Tikrit, along the way having lost two of his men.

Probably the troops sitting around these camp fires tonight were discussing the same things as his men did in Iraq . . . their families, girlfriends, and what they would do when they returned home. Always evading the obvious . . . maybe, just maybe, you wouldn't make it home. Perhaps even the Roman Centurions had discussed the same subjects around their campfires.

Suddenly Carter mumbled, "We've got four horsemen coming at us."

As they drew closer Kyle recognized one of the riders. "Oh shit, it's Colonel Richardson." He checked the surroundings. A grove of pines stood about twenty feet off the road. "They'll run us down before we reach the trees. Pull your cap down, salute and hope he doesn't recognize us."

The colonel drew alongside, reined in his horse and stared at them. "Where are you men headed?"

Kyle anxiously searched for an answer. "We're going to relieve the guards up ahead, Sir."

"What's the password?"

Kyle remembered the guards had uttered a password when they entered the camp. *Would it be the same?*

He took a deep breath. "Minneapolis, Sir."

The colonel nodded. "Make sure and use it. Those men on the frontlines are trigger happy."

"Yes, Sir." Kyle and Carter both saluted.

The colonel gave them a casual salute, turned, then hesitated and gave Kyle a second look. "What's your name and outfit, Sergeant?"

"O'Brien, Sir. 12th New York."

The full moon cast enough light to see the puzzled look on the colonel's face. *Can he see me clearly? Does he recognize me?*

Kyle glanced at the nearby woods and then at Carter, who watched him intently. We could fire our rifles and kill two of them. But that still leaves two more, plus the whole damn Union Army. *Should I make a break for the trees?*

It took a few seconds before the colonel responded. "Have we met before, Sergeant?"

"No, Sir."

The colonel leaned over in the saddle and gave him a closer look. He heaved a sigh. "Okay. You men keep a sharp lookout for the rebs." He spurred his horse and the four men rode away.

"Shit, that was too close," Carter said. "I was all set to haul ass for the trees."

"Yeah, I was sure he recognized me. This full moon's not helping. I see the outline of the forest ahead on the left. We'll get off this road and head into the trees."

They had almost made it into the woods when a shout rang out from the side of the road.

"Halt, who goes there?" someone yelled.

"Two friends with a countersign," Kyle yelled.

They gave the guard the password

The young guard smiled weakly. "What are you guys doing way out here? I thought you was rebs."

Kyle shrugged. "Colonel Richardson sent us out on patrol. We're to check out Bull Run and see if the rebels have any pickets on this side of the run."

The guard lowered the rifle to his side and relaxed. "My sergeant told me they have at least four or five men on our side."

"We need to confirm that," Kyle said. "Any more of our men down this road?"

"Yeah, there's some pickets about a half mile farther down with about a squad of men on duty. After that you're in rebel country."

They thanked him and continued on.

"I think we stay on the road." Carter suggested. "We know the password. We can make better time walking the road instead of heading into the thick brush."

"You're right. When we get to the next roadblock we tell them the same thing. It sure helps being in a Union uniform."

"At least for the next half mile," Carter said, "after that we're going to need a costume change."

The next guard challenged them. They answered with the password and walked up to a sergeant and two privates.

The sergeant spotted the stripes on Kyle's sleeves. "You lost, Sarg? There ain't nothing but rebs up ahead."

Kyle answered, "Colonel Richardson wants us to find out what's happening alongside the run."

"Hell, he was here a short while ago. What outfit you with?"

"The Twelfth New York. How about you?"

"The Chelsea Volunteers, First Massachusetts." The man had a heavy New England accent. "There's at least a brigade of rebs up ahead, maybe two. We had six men killed and twenty wounded today trying to push them back. If you go much farther . . . you'll get your ass shot."

Kyle nodded. "We'll move into the woods and head off to the right until we reach the run."

"Good idea." The sergeant said. "The brush will give you cover. That's much better than strolling down this road. On the left there's another stream not too far over called Little Rock Run. It feeds into Bull Run. The forest is real thick. You'll have a tough time getting through at night. Then it opens up and there's a railroad bridge across the run. I'll bet the rebs are guarding that bridge."

"Thanks, we'll follow your advice and go right."

They moved into the woods on the right side of the road.

Kyle whispered, "Once we get out of sight we'll cross the road and head down the run. If they come looking for us this should throw them off."

About a hundred yards down the hill, they crossed over the road. Immediately they hit the thick growth the sergeant had mentioned. For more than an hour they clawed their way through a dense spruce forest, with thick underbrush and an occasional patch of blackberries. Finally they reached a small clearing.

"I'm exhausted." Kyle collapsed. "Even this hard ground feels good."

"Me too," Carter said. "It's been a long day."

"We've traveled over twenty-five miles, been shot at, captured, beaten up, sentenced to death, killed a man, and escaped."

"Yeah." Carter dropped to the ground and grinned. "Just a normal day in a SEAL's life. At least we're not packing ninety pounds of gear."

"I forgot, you guys start the day eating nails for breakfast." Kyle stretched out. "Let's call it a night. We can start again at daybreak."

"How are you feeling?"

"Terrible." Kyle felt his knee. "My knee and ribs are killing me. That guy really caught me with his elbow. Let's get some sleep." He closed his eyes and sighed. "In the morning I'm supposed to fly to Atlanta and join my girlfriend for her cousin's wedding. It's a really big deal. She's going to be pissed."

"When we get back, just tell her you traveled back in time to the battle of Bull Run." Carter let out a chuckle. "I'm sure she'll understand."

Kyle starred at the full moon. What is going to happen tomorrow, he thought. The Confederates might not believe us either.

At 0600 Kyle checked his watch. Still here—another day in this nightmare. Jennifer hasn't heard from me now in three days, he thought. I'm sure she's tried my cell phone numerous times and is starting to panic. She'll probably try calling the Marine Corps to find out what was happening. But, they don't have a clue, nobody knows, only the CIA. For the next three days she'll have to make up excuses as to why I stood her up.

Kyle rolled over on the hard ground and slowly got to his feet. He ached everywhere, especially his ribcage. "Carter, wake up. We've got enough light to make our way out of this underbrush."

Carter cracked his eye open. "Damn, I was hoping for Quantico. I was in the middle of a dream about a nice hot shower, a cup of coffee, and a big plate of bacon and eggs."

"You're making my mouth water. What happened to nails for breakfast?"

Kyle extended his hand down to Carter and helped him to his feet. "Before we stumble out of these woods, let's come up with a plan. We made a mistake yesterday. The lieutenant that interrogated us last night was right. We acted like spies. We should have stayed at that woman's cabin until this morning, and then marched down that road in broad daylight. When we saw someone, we should have thrown our hands into the air and waved a white flag. Then I think they might have believed our story, or at least given us a chance to explain."

"Yes, but with that dead sergeant back at camp, we're not going to get a second chance."

"That's right, maybe we can try it with the Southerners. Hopefully they'll let us through the line. If we get to Richmond or Atlanta we can blend in." Kyle put a hand to his side and winced.

"How bad is it?"

Kyle lifted his leg. "My knee is stiff, but no real damage. My ribs hurt, big time . . . I'll bet at least one is cracked. But I can travel."

"Now that we're heading south what's our story? It's got to change."

"We don't have to change much. Our ship still runs up on the rocks and sinks, but now we're found by fisherman from Maryland and dropped over there. We're heading south, to our homes in Florida and Alabama."

Kyle started to take off the sergeant's jacket. "I guess we can shed the uniforms."

"What about the rifles?"

"Sooner or later, probably sooner, we're going to run into Confederate troops. How do you explain away two military rifles? They'll think we're soldiers and we'll be in trouble again. Leave them here."

"I don't feel good about this." Carter leaned the rifle against a tree. "It's the second weapon in two days I've given up."

"Carter, I'll give you another reason. If we start shooting people, we'll change history. We've already killed the sergeant—no more."

They both removed the coats and caps, then worked their way down to the run. In the dim light of dawn it looked about sixty feet across, and thickly forested on both sides.

Carter cautiously moved to the bank. "There's cover on both sides. This is a good spot to cross." He waded out a few feet. "Something's in the water out there. It looks like a body."

Kyle checked. A bloated man dressed in a Union uniform slowly drifted, face up in the water. *What a hell of a burial. I hope someone will drag him ashore.*

"It's a Union soldier," Kyle said, "from yesterday's engagement at Blackburn's Ford."

Carter took a few steps into the run. "It drops off fast. I think we'll have to swim across."

A shot rang out and a bullet buzzed over Kyle's head. He dove behind a tree. Carter rushed back toward shore. Another shot sounded; the bullet ricocheted across the water next to Carter. He dove underwater, reappeared further downstream, and crawled ashore.

A voice boomed from across the stream. "You Yank's better get your asses back up north. If you don't, you'll end up like your friend out there—just floatin' down the run."

The sound of laughter rang up and down the stream. Kyle worked his way back into the brush and headed toward Carter.

"That second shot damn near got me," Carter said.

"Did you hear them laugh? That side of the run is loaded with troops."

"This is for shit," Carter said. "Now we've got both sides trying to kill us. Let's keep moving until we get the hell out of this battle."

They moved away from shore and headed cautiously downstream.

"OK," Kyle said. "We keep moving. I guess it doesn't matter that we're not in uniform. If we're on this side of the run, they assume we're Yankees."

It took them another hour before they finally broke out of the brush. They were about a hundred yards from the run and could easily spot the railroad ahead of them, it led up to the stone abutments of the rail bridge.

Carter climbed a tree and checked out the structure. "The tracks are ripped out all along the railroad bed. The Confederates must have done that in the last few days to keep Union trains from crossing."

"Do you see troops on either side of the bridge?"

"No, I don't. The bridge sits on a little hill. It looks like the abutments are more than thirty feet above the water. It's still intact, but barricaded. "

Carter climbed back down. "Do we try crossing here?"

"No, it's too open. Stay on this side of the run, and keep heading downstream. My only concern is the hundred yards or so of open space before we reach the woods on the other side of the railroad."

They moved down near the edge of the clearing. Kyle sat under a tree and propped his leg up on a log. "Let's rest and see if there's any movement along the tracks."

Carter checked the brush, found some blackberries and brought Kyle a handful.

"Thanks. I wonder how long you can survive eating nothing but blackberries?" Kyle popped a few. "Even MRE rations would taste great right now."

"Are you kidding me? My favorite, beef shredded in barbecue sauce, would be fantastic."

They waited ten minutes, and Carter climbed another tree. "I don't see anybody. Do we make a mad dash across the tracks?"

"I don't think I can run that far. My knee's stiffened up. It looks like there's a small ditch alongside the rail track. I can make it that far . . . then I give my knee a rest."

Carter climbed back down. "I'm ready."

"OK, let's hit it." Kyle stood up and stretched his leg.

They headed across the open space at a trot, with Kyle favoring his right leg. They dropped into a shallow ditch. The forest about seventy yards in front of Kyle looked clear. Then he heard the sound of hoofs.

Carter yelled. "It's union cavalry! Where do we go?"

Ten men on horseback raced along the railroad bed toward them.

After a quick check of the forest and the bridge, Kyle yelled. "The bridge, it's closer!"

He glanced back as they raced down the rail bed. The cavalry appeared no more than a hundred yards behind them and gaining fast—it would be close. Carter pulled away, reached the bridge abutment first and leaped off the bridge into the water.

Despite the knee, Kyle ran at close to full speed. A shot whined over his head. Two more rang out. He reached the edge of the abutment with little strength left. In full stride he leaped the thirty feet to the water below.

He hit feet first, went underwater and popped back to the surface. After a deep breath he swam hard for the opposite bank. Shots continued, now from both sides of the run.

After reaching shore, he staggered up the slippery bank. Something buzzed around his head—it sounded like a swarm of angry bees. His forehead burned with pain—maybe he'd been stung. He reached up to swat it away and noticed the blood covering his hand. A ringing sounded in his ears.

Bull Run 1861

CHAPTER

22

*K*yle awoke to screams. He tried to sit up—someone grabbed his shoulder and pushed him back down. His head pulsed with pain.

"You've been shot," a male voice said. "Take it easy. Stay calm—take this pill and the pain will go away."

"Where's my cellphone?" Kyle yelled. "I'm late for the wedding!"

Someone shoved a bitter tasting pill into his mouth. He closed his eyes and floated back to sleep.

The same screams and moans jolted Kyle out of a deep sleep. *Where the hell am I?*

He cracked his eyes open. Carter sat in a chair beside him.

"You're back," Carter said. "It's early evening. You slept for over twelve hours."

"What is the place?"

"You're in a barn that's been converted into a field hospital. How's your head?"

Kyle felt the bandage above his right ear. "It hurts." He tried to sit up, clutched his mid-section and collapsed on the cot. "So do my ribs."

"You were lucky. The bullet just grazed your scalp. Another inch and you'd be a dead man."

"I was shot?"

"Yes. You jumped off the bridge, swam to the other bank, and climbed out. That's when they shot you."

"Who shot me?"

"The cavalry. Remember, they chased us to the bridge. A squad of rebs" . . . Carter glanced around . . . "A squad of Confederates were hiding on the other side. They saw us being chased and fired back at the Union cavalry" . . . He checked again . . . "At the Yankees. A Confederate soldier pulled you from the water. You bled like hell. I thought you were dying."

Kyle nodded. "I remembered running for the bridge. The rest seems fuzzy." He looked around the room. Wounded soldiers filled beds all around him. The man on his right had a bandage around his head and appeared to be asleep. On his left, a man missing an arm moaned and cried.

"Are we prisoners?" Kyle asked.

Carter checked to see if anyone listened. "They don't know what to call us. They questioned me for about two hours. Then, thank God, they gave me something to eat."

"So you told them our story."

"Yes. I think they believed me. They told me we'd be kept as guests until after the battle. They want to make sure we don't head back across the frontline with information."

Some of the details started to come back. Kyle recalled being a Union prisoner and trying to convince the colonel of their story. "Well, I guess getting shot in the head makes my story more credible." He rubbed his forehead. "I'm really woozy."

"No shit. They gave you a couple of opium pills." Carter laughed quietly. "You kept demanding a cellphone. You wanted to call Jennifer. Of course they didn't have a clue as to what you were talking about."

A man, probably in his early thirties, walked over. He had long tousled blond hair, thick glasses and a bloody white coat.

"Kyle, this is Doctor Daniels. He's the one who bandaged your head."

Kyle smiled. "Thank you, Doctor."

"Don't thank me. Thank the man who fired the rifle—he missed your brain by an inch."

Doctor Daniels glanced around the room. "You're coming around nicely. I wish I could say that about most of the wounded. Yesterday was just a little skirmish. We had fifteen killed and fifty-three wounded. Thirty-two still here in this ward. Hopefully it's going to be a short war."

"Doctor, do you think it's possible to get something to eat?"

Carter jumped up from the chair. "Earlier I had some beef and rice. It was fantastic. Of course after three days of mostly blackberries, almost anything would taste great. I'll see if they have any left."

The doctor sat in the chair. "Beside the head wound, you probably have a broken rib. Nothing I can do about that, it'll heal in time. Your knee is swollen and probably hurts, but just bruised. Those Yanks didn't treat you well."

Kyle remembered the sergeant and the kick to his ribs. "No, not at all. Thanks for your help. When do you think I can leave?"

"You can leave the hospital tomorrow morning. The Sixth Brigade Commander, Colonel Early, wants to talk to both of you. It's up to him when you leave the camp."

"What's Colonel Early's first name?"

"Jubal. Do you know him?"

"No. I have a friend named Early, but not Jubal."

"He should be here any time now."

The doctor reached over and patted Kyle's shoulder. His fingers were encrusted in what looked like dried blood and dirt. "You're a lucky man. We had five men here with head wounds." He pointed to the man in the next bed. "The two of you are the only ones still alive. There's nothing more I can do for him. Hopefully, like you, he'll wake up."

The doctor left, and for the first time Kyle gave the room a close look. The thirty-two patients filled the barn to capacity. A light layer of straw topped the dirt floor. Farm implements hung from the bare wood planked walls, and the smell of farm animals remained. About half of the patients appeared to be asleep or unconscious. The rest seemed to be missing either an arm or leg and were in severe pain. The sounds and smells were ghastly, he needed out of this place.

Carter returned with a bowl of steaming rice. "There's not much meat in here, but it's hot and filling."

Kyle gobbled the food down. "Better than another handful of berries."

Carter spoke softly. "I've got to get you out of here. I've read about civil war conditions, but this is unbelievable. Right outside the barn they left a pile of amputated arms and legs. It's loaded with buzzing flies, and stinks. You saw that doctor. He dressed your wound with those bloody hands. This place is nothing but a walking infection factory."

"The doctor said I've got a head wound. I guess that means concussion. Now that I've had something to eat, I feel much better. He also said a Jubal Early will be here tonight. It's his call on when we can leave."

"I've heard that name before."

Kyle finished eating, and handed the bowl to Carter. "Yeah. I can't believe we're about to meet him. He plays a big role here at Bull Run. Later he gets promoted to Lieutenant General, and if I remember right, was one of the most eccentric generals in the war. In 1864, he tries an end-run around Grant and makes it to the outskirts of Washington D. C."

"So what do we tell him?"

"Stick to our story. We're both heading home from Europe to our homes in Florida and Alabama."

"Oh, I almost forgot. When the doctor examined you he noticed your two previous bullet wounds. I told him you were injured doing farm work, but I didn't know how. If he asks, be prepared to fill him in. Now, try to get some sleep. I'll wake you if the colonel shows up."

Carter shook his shoulder "Kyle, wakeup. There are two men here to see you."

Kyle sat up. He felt stronger but still light-headed.

"Mr. O'Brien, my name is Jubal Early. Sorry to interrupt your rest."

Early appeared much older than Kyle expected, probably in his early sixties, with a full grey beard and receding, rumpled grey hair. His dirty, wrinkled grey coat had stains all down the front, and no military markings.

"No, not at all, General," Kyle said. "Have a seat."

Early gave him an indulgent chuckle, "Actually that's colonel. Looks like you were a little mistreated by our former friends from the north."

Damn, this opium is screwing with my brain. I knew he was a Colonel. I've got to be more careful.

Early pulled out a packet of tobacco and shoved a plug in the corner of his mouth. "This is my aide, Captain Edwards. From what he tells me you had quite a boat trip from France, and a run-in with that asshole, Richardson."

Kyle couldn't help but note Early's high-pitched voice, spoken with a slight lisp. Not the voice of confidence you'd expect of a future Confederate hero and three-star general. "Colonel Richardson thought we were spies."

"I can understand that. You're both young and healthy. You look like you belong in the military. Why were you trying to sneak through the Union lines?"

"We just stumbled into this battle. It wasn't by choice. We tried to tell Colonel Richardson we didn't know anything, but he wasn't listening."

Early spat a stream of tobacco juice out of the corner of his mouth and onto the ground. "Good old fightin' Dick , that's what we called Richardson, even though his first name was Israel. I've known him over twenty years. He's got shit for brains, but a big set of balls."

Early wiped his mouth with a brown-stained sleeve and eyed Kyle. "They tell me you're a Florida boy. What part of the state?"

"A little village in the center called Ocala."

"I fought the Seminoles down there in thirty-nine. You ever heard of a place called Fort King?"

I think he's testing me? Kyle knew a little about Fort King. During the Seminole Indian Wars, in the mid-eighteen hundreds, the army had built a log fort near Ocala to house the troops and protect the settlers from the Indians. Kyle had visited the site. Currently only an historical sign marked the spot.

"Yes, Sir. It was an army fort near town, but I think it burned down. My family's farm is just off Fort King Road."

"That's right. I heard it burned down." Early grinned and rubbed his chin. "I had some good times at that fort, went there as a Second Lieutenant right out of West Point." He took another spit. "So, now that the war's started, what are your plans?"

"I've been in Europe for about three years. I plan on visiting my family in Florida and then maybe join the army."

"Which army, ours or the Yankee's?

"I'm a Southerner, Sir."

"That's good to hear. Maybe you can help us out. Tell me what you saw last night when they brought you into their camp."

Kyle and Carter exchanged glances. "In the darkness we could see hundreds—maybe thousands of camp fires, and thousands upon thousands of troops. That's a huge army they've got over there."

"What questions did they ask you?"

"They wanted to know if General Johnston's troops had arrived from the Shenandoah Valley."

Early glanced at the captain standing next to him. "And what did you tell them?"

"I told them the truth. I don't know anything about that."

Early stared at him for a moment. "We think they are massing troops in front of Mitchell's Ford. They plan on attacking us there tomorrow morning. Can you confirm that?"

From his knowledge of the Battle of Bull Run, Kyle knew it wouldn't start for another two days, and that the Union Army would try a flanking movement across Sudley Springs Ford, about eight miles further west. He would tell them enough to gain confidence, but not enough to alter history.

"Colonel, when we escaped last night we walked down the road near Mitchell's Ford. We saw some guards posted, but no troops massing. It didn't look like they were getting ready to attack. That's about all I know."

Early stood up. "We're going to let you men go, but just in case, not until after the battle is fought. We'll move you into one of the tents. Don't try to leave without Captain Edwards's permission. Have a safe journey south."

The two officers started to leave, then Early hesitated and turned back. "Did you go anywhere else in Europe besides France?"

Is this another test, or is he really interested?

"Yes," Kyle said. "I also visited Madrid, Florence and Venice. I love history."

"A couple of years ago the French and Austrians fought some battles in the Lombardy Region. Have you heard of them?"

Kyle had studied the battles while attending a war strategies course a few years back. "The Battles of Magenta and Soferino. Yes I'm familiar with them."

"Not many people over here have heard of them. If we aren't attacked tomorrow, as you suggest, possibly we'll have a chance to discuss those battles."

Early turned and headed out the door.

Lieutenant General Jubal A. Early (1816-1894). By the Civil War's end in 1865, General Early had fought in eleven major battles including Antietam and Gettysburg. He is considered by historians as one of the most eccentric leaders of the Civil War. At war's end in 1865 he fled to Mexico, then Cuba and Canada. In 1869 he was pardoned and returned to his home in Virginia. Robert E. Lee referred to Early as 'my mean old man', even though he was nine years younger than Lee. Early remained an unrepentant rebel until his death at 78.

CHAPTER

23

*G*eneral Daniel Tyler leaned back in his chair and studied the men sitting at the table. They commanded the four brigades in his First Division of the Union Army, comprising over 13,000 Union soldiers. They had just finished breakfast. All that remained on the table were coffee cups, and a detailed map of the Bull Run area, taken off a dead Confederate captain the day before.

After a quick sip of coffee, Tyler said. "General McDowell will probably request a divisional meeting sometime later today and present his plans for our attack. Hopefully the battle will start early tomorrow. I've called you here this morning to discuss what you have discovered about our enemy in the last two days."

Tyler motioned to Colonel Israel Richardson, the Fourth Brigade Commander. "Your troops have had the most contact with the rebels. You start."

Richardson studied the map for a moment. "My brigade is located here." He pointed to a fork in the road, about a mile from Mitchell's Ford on Bull Run. "It's no more than three miles from the Manassas Junction train depot . . . close enough to hear trains entering the station, especially at night. The rebels have been hauling supplies in on a regular basis. At about two this morning I woke up to train whistles and loud cheering. It lasted over an hour. Very possibly they were celebrating the first arrival of Johnston's reinforcements from the Shenandoah Valley. I can't think of another reason for carousing around so early in the morning."

"I agree," Tyler nodded. "The timing is about right. If they started loading troops on railcars right after our attack started two days ago, the first load could have arrived at Manassas last night. But, our leader, General McDowell, says that we have received assurances from Washington that Union troops have the Confederates pinned down in the Shenandoah. We won't know that for sure until the battles over. In the meantime, we formulate the best attack plan possible."

Tyler turned back to Richardson. "How many men do you estimate they have around Mitchell's Ford?"

"On Thursday, during our skirmish at Blackburn's Ford, we captured soldiers from four different brigades. They told us Early's got a brigade there also. That's over fifteen thousand men hunkered down in one location, plus we've been told Beauregard's headquarters is there as well."

Colonel William T. Sherman rubbed his dark red, well-trimmed beard and gave Richardson a quick look. "I understand you also captured a couple of spies."

Richardson glared at Sherman. "Yeah, but they escaped before I got any information."

"Spies?" General Tyler frowned. "What's this about?"

"Well, Sir," Richardson gave Sherman another dirty look. "We caught them sneaking across Bull Run the other night. I interrogated them but didn't get any useful information. I was going to question them again before we shot them, but they escaped."

"How did that happen?" Tyler said.

"They overpowered two guards and killed a sergeant. I questioned the lieutenant in charge. He didn't know how they managed to get loose. Said they were tied and locked in a shed when he left. "

Tyler shook his head. "That's too bad. Did they sneak back across the lines?

"We almost caught them, Sir," Richardson said. "One of our cavalry units spotted them heading for the railroad bridge at Union Mills. We shot one of them in the head? The other one made it across the run."

"Well, one less rebel anyway." Tyler turned to Sherman. "You reconnoitered along our lines late yesterday. Where do you think the rebels are expecting our attack?"

"I rode east from the railroad bridge all the way up to Sudley Springs Ford. That's probably eight to ten miles." He grinned, "I got shot at twice and chased by the reb cavalry once. They can't shoot and are even worse riders."

All the commanders, with the exception of Richardson chuckled. Sherman took a deep draw on his small cigar and exhaled. "Just like Richardson said, they are all concentrated along two miles of the run, from Blackburn's Ford to Mitchell's Ford."

Sherman moved his finger further upstream on the map. "They have a small force at both Island Ford and Ball's Ford, maybe a brigade guarding the stone bridge at Lewis Ford, and nothing further upstream. Either they think we're attacking at Mitchell's Ford, or they got tired of waiting and they're going to attack us there."

Tyler shook his head and pointed to the stone bridge on the map. "I don't understand . . . the ideal place for us to attack is here. Why wouldn't they guard that bridge with at least two, maybe three brigades?"

After another drag on his cigar, a smirk came across Sherman's face. "You're asking me to second-guess Pierre *G. T.* Beauregard? Hell, that cocky little son of a bitch has never been known for his intellect. I have no idea why he would leave the only usable bridge so lightly guarded."

The First Brigade's Commander, Colonel Keyes, spoke up. "Maybe he's smarter than we think. He lures us across the bridge, and before we have a full force across, he attacks with a couple of brigade's hidden in reserve. Or, possibly he's got it mined and blows it up before the full force crosses."

Sherman shook his head. "No, you don't know Beauregard. I spent many a night listening to him expound on the strategies of his hero Napoleon Bonaparte. Nothing devious about the prim and proper little general—It's always attack, attack, attack."

The other four men all laughed, and then Sherman continued. "Besides, I sent a couple of men across the run last night. There are no brigades hidden back behind Matthews Hill. As crazy as it may sound, I think he's gathering all his troops for an attack at either Blackburn's or Mitchell's Ford. It may happen tomorrow morning."

An aide walked into the tent and handed Tyler a message. After reading it, he said, "Gentlemen, McDowell has called a meeting for 1700 this afternoon, and all of us are invited. I'm going to end our chat and go take a look at this stone bridge. It could play a major part in our plans."

"Be careful, Sir," Sherman said. "There are lots of rebels running around on this side of the run. They would love nothing better than to catch a general."

General William T. Sherman, (1820-1891) Sherman would retire from military service in 1883 as a five star general and Commander of the U.S. Army. He is best known for the scorched earth strategy used on his 'march through Georgia.'

The Stone Bridge at Bull Run. One of the most important landmarks
of the First Battle of Bull Run.

CHAPTER

24

*G*eneral Tyler chose Lieutenant Nash to join him on the inspection of the stone bridge. With Sherman's comment about rebels in mind, both Nash and Tyler changed into private's uniforms. They also selected a sergeant and a corporal familiar with the area to join them.

The ride out of Centreville led them down the gentle grade of the Warrenton Turnpike. In the distance they could see Bull Run, the cultivated fields beyond, and Matthews Hill rising far in the distance. Once outside the Union picket line, and on the suggestion of the sergeant, they moved off the exposed turnpike and headed through the woods on the right side of the road. They stopped on a small hill less than a quarter mile from the run and within sight of the bridge.

Tyler pulled a new pair of field glasses from his saddle bag. The expensive binoculars, a recent European invention, were from Lemaire Paris, and a present from his wife.

"I can see some troops milling around the bridge," Tyler said. "It looks in good condition. I'm surprised they haven't blown it up. It's wide, sturdy and would allow our artillery to reach the battle much faster than wading across the fords."

He passed the field glasses to Nash, who scanned the area surrounding the bridge. "General, further upstream I see some men out bathing in the run. It looks to be shallow, they're near the middle and only about knee deep." Nash removed the binoculars and admired them. "General, these things are amazing. Those men looked to be right in front of me."

Tyler took the binoculars back. "You're right. Field glasses are going to make a big difference in this war. That could be a good spot to cross the run and flank the troops protecting the bridge. Sherman's right, there is probably less than a regiment camped in the fields behind the bridge. This is the spot to start our flanking action." He scanned back to the bridge. "I do believe we're being observed. There's some cavalry near the bridge and one of them is watching us with his own field glasses."

A shot buzzed over their heads, and then a second.

The sergeant reined in his horse. "That's from the bridge. We're an easy target. Let's get the hell out of here."

Tyler saw about ten horsemen charge across the bridge. "They're coming after us."

All four of them wheeled around and headed up the hill through the trees. Another Minie ball buzzed by. The sergeant screamed and fell from his horse.

Nash yelled, "General, I'll pick him up. You get out of here."

Tyler and the corporal raced through the trees, leaving the other two men behind. They reached a meadow and dashed across. As they reached the tree line, another shot rang out. Tyler glanced back — the cavalry had just reached the clearing. He put his head down, held tightly to the horses neck, and charged ahead, letting the horse find its way through the thick growth. Behind him he heard the rebels charge into the woods.

A half-hour later, Tyler rode into camp alone. An aide rushed up and grasped the reins. "General, what happened? Where are the others?"

Tyler wiped blood from a brush scratch on the side of his face. "They shot Sergeant Gaines. Nash may have been captured by rebel cavalry, and I'm not sure about the corporal. We got separated in the thick woods."

After dismounting, Tyler grabbed his knee.

"Are you all right, Sir?

"My leg got caught between the horse and a tree."

"Have a seat, Sir. I'll get you some water."

"Before you do that, round up some men and go find out what happened to Nash and the other two men."

Tyler collapsed into a chair. It had been a close call. The cavalry had chased him through the woods until he'd finally managed to cross through a Union picket line. He checked his pocket watch. He had two hours to get his thoughts together before the meeting with McDowell. The stone bridge must be the central point for a flank attack on the enemy.

At exactly 1700 hours, Tyler and his four brigade commanders rode up to General McDowell's command tent. The other four Division Commanders: Generals Hunter, Heintzelman, Runyon and Miles, plus their staff were milling around in the shade of a large tent. The sides had been rolled up to allow a little breeze under the warm canvas roof.

Tyler limped up to the group.

"What the hell happened to you?" General David Hunter asked.

"I rode down to Bull Run for an inspection. I had to cut through brush to outrun some rebs. My knee got caught on a tree trunk and I scratched my face."

Hunter, about Tyler's age, chuckled. "You're getting too old to ride a horse. We'll have to get you a carriage. Did you see anything worth a bad knee?"

Tyler dropped into a chair. "I think so. That crazy little Beauregard's only got a brigade or less guarding the stone bridge."

Hunter smiled. "Well, I'm sure little Beau didn't get any smarter with his promotion to General, only more arrogant. McDowell's had an engineer scouting out that section of the run for two days. He probably has that noted in his report."

Tyler pulled out his watch. "Speaking of McDowell, he's late."

General Samuel Heintzelman reached for a cigar, bit off the end and started chewing on it. "It's our young general's way of showing he's in charge. Give him another half-hour."

Half-an-hour later, General Irvin McDowell rushed into the meeting.

His aide yelled, "Attention."

A makeshift podium had been set up in front of the men. On such a hot, humid day, all of the men had removed or unbuttoned their uniform jackets.

McDowell stood before them in his completely buttoned, dark blue uniform.

Tyler noticed sweat rolling down McDowell's face and soaking the front of his coat.

I don't believe it — hot as hell and McDowell shows up with his collar fastened tight.

"Gentleman," McDowell said, "Please take your seats. I have just left a meeting with our Chief Engineer, Major John Barnard, who has for two days been exploring the terrain around Bull Run. We've come up with a very concise order of battle. We will attack early tomorrow morning."

McDowell flipped opened a thick folder. Pulled out a handkerchief and wiped his face. "Since we have just finished the plans, copies are not available, so take notes and leave the questions until the end."

He read the plan aloud, starting with the role that each Division would play. His detailed, nonstop presentation took close to an hour. It covered all details of the plan, including troop preparation, the 0200 march to battle positions and, finally, the attack commencing at 0600.

Tyler couldn't believe what he heard. His division would become a mere decoy. Richardson's Brigade would create a diversion on the far left at Blackburn's Ford. Sherman and Schenck's Brigades would be placed at the stone bridge, and used only as a distracting force. The main thrust would be Hunter and Heintzelmans Divisions attacking on the far right flank at Sudley Springs Ford. The rebels, now caught completely by surprise and in disarray, would retreat back to Fredericksburg and the protection of the Rappahannock River, allowing McDowell to capture the Manassas Junction Station. Tyler's Division would cross over the stone bridge only after the area had been cleared, and would remain in reserve if needed for support of the other two Divisions.

Tyler shook his head in disbelief. That asshole was punishing him for the battle at Blackburn's Ford on Thursday.

McDowell finished the presentation and then stared at Tyler. "We are not here today to discuss the merits of this plan. They have been discussed and decided upon. Now is the time for action. If you would like some clarification regarding timing, or the position of troops, I will be happy to answer those questions."

This further astonished Tyler. He would have no opportunity for input. *The main thrust must be made by my troops at the stone bridge, not six miles further upstream and across Sudley Ford.*

The group asked a few questions regarding timing of the attack and the order of march.

Then Tyler raised his hand. "What force, General, do you think we have to contend with tomorrow?"

Disdain spread across McDowell's face. "You know as well as I do what the force is, General."

Tyler stood up so that he could be heard, and put his hands on his hips. "General, I am as sure as there is a God in Heaven that you will have to fight Joe Johnston's Army at Manassas tomorrow."

The tent grew silent. McDowell scanned the faces, ignoring Tyler. "I will join General Hunter on his march tomorrow morning. A field headquarters will be established at Sudley Springs. If no further questions, this meeting is adjourned. On to Richmond, gentleman."

The men stood and hurried from the tent.

Tyler remained standing. McDowell glanced his way, then reassembled his papers and turned to leave. "General McDowell. I have additional information that you are not aware of."

McDowell turned his way. "General, now is the time to fight, not debate."

"Hear me out," Tyler said, "I have just returned from reconnaissance at the stone bridge. It is lightly guarded and we have discovered another ford close by. That is where the battle must be launched. It saves us at least six miles of marching to Sudley Springs, and allows a rapid advance across Bull Run. We can flank the enemy and the war will be over by noon."

McDowell hesitated. "Tyler, do you think we're idiots? We considered the stone bridge in our review. It's obviously the spot they think we will attack, thus the need for your deception. On this plan discussions are over."

"General, they have only a brigade at that bridge." Tyler's voice rose. "That is the place to attack!"

McDowell pointed a finger at Tyler. "Let me remind you, your assignment tomorrow is to engage the enemy and *feint* an attack — which is what you were ordered to do at Blackburn's Ford on Thursday. Under no circumstances does your division cross Bull Run tomorrow until I order it." He wheeled around and marched away.

CHAPTER

25

*O*n **Saturday morning voices** woke Kyle. Two young soldiers holding a stretcher were moving the man with the head wound.

"Where're you taking him?" Kyle asked.

The soldiers hesitated. "He died last night," one said. "We're taking his body over to Manassas Junction."

Kyle sat up in the cot. "He looks so young."

"He's seventeen . . . from Gladstone, Virginia, my hometown."

"I'm sorry."

The soldier looked a few years older. A tear formed and his chin quivered. "I know his mama. She's going to be real upset." He lowered his head and they carried the body out of the barn.

Vividly Kyle remembered the first dead man he had seen in combat, a young man in his platoon in Iraq . . . eighteen years old . . . in his first day of combat. Kyle had written the private's parents a letter. He closed his eyes—how difficult that letter had been. The weapons of war had advanced, but the grief of a mother for a lost soldier remained unchanged. His thoughts flashed to his parents. What kind of crazy tale would the CIA invent to explain away his disappearance? His mother and father would be devastated if he never returned.

160

Kyle opened his eyes, Doctor Daniels stood at the foot of his bed.

"How do you feel this morning?" Daniels said.

"I'm fine and ready to get out of here."

"I think that can be arranged. I've heard the battle may start today or tomorrow. We're regrettably going to need this bed."

"Then we can leave Bull Run?"

"The colonel's aide, Captain Edwards, stopped by this morning and inquired about your condition. He said you could move into a tent over by mine. Your friend's over there now. You'll stay in camp until Early gives you permission to leave, which will be after the battle."

Kyle stood, but immediately dropped back to the bed. "Wow, I feel dizzy."

"Take it easy for a few days and you'll be all right."

"I'm sorry to see that young man didn't make it." Kyle pointed to the cot next to his.

"No he didn't, and I suspect we're going to see many more like him. I just left a medical meeting. We're preparing for at least five hundred wounded and possibly two hundred dead in the upcoming battle."

The exact number eluded him, but Kyle knew there would be more than two thousand men wounded or killed on the Southern side. For the North, even higher numbers, close to three thousand.

"Doctor, while in Europe I had the opportunity to meet some French Army Officers who were involved in a recent war with Austria. Today's firearms are more accurate than in the past. Possibly you should prepare for more than five hundred wounded—quite a few more. If you win the battle, you may even be responsible for wounded Union soldiers left on the field."

"I can't imagine handling more than five hundred. We're not equipped for that, but I'll pass along the information. The medical commander for the Brigade will be meeting with Old Jubilee this evening."

"Old Jubilee?"

Daniels chuckled. "That's what the men call Colonel Early, but not to his face."

"He does look old to still be in the army."

Daniels hooted. "I thought the same thing until I found out he's only in his mid-forties. They say he's got health issues. But, I'm told he can outdrink and out cuss any man in the army."

Kyle stood again, and felt steadier this time. "Can you give me some directions to my tent?"

"I'm headed that way, I'll show you."

They moved out of the barn. Kyle walked with a slight limp and his ribs ached, but it felt good to breath fresh air. The building stood on a knoll and looked down across gently rolling hills. Pastures and cornfields extended for over a mile down to Bull Run.

Daniels pointed to an attractive two-story farmhouse, sitting higher up the hill. "That's the McLean house."

"Is the family still living there?"

"No, they left and General Beauregard's moved his headquarters there."

"What happened to the roof?"

"Day before yesterday, during that little battle at Blackburn's Ford, one of the Union artillery units got up close and fired a round right down the chimney and into the kitchen fireplace. Nobody was hurt, but it did a little damage and heaven forbid, destroyed General Beauregard's dinner. Damn good shooting on their part."

On Kyle's tour of Bull Run, he remembered the Forest Ranger mentioning the Wilmer McLean family. After the Second Battle of Bull Run they would move out of harm's way, to Appomattox Courthouse, Virginia, a small village about two hundred miles to the southwest. Four years later, the

McLean house in Appomattox would be selected by General Robert E. Lee as the location for his surrender to General Grant. The war would start and end on a McLean farm.

Kyle scanned the cultivated fields. A few days before there had been rows upon rows of green corn stalks. Now only a few remained, the rest stomped into the ground by thousands of Confederate soldiers and horses. For miles around the farm most of the Brigades of the First Corps of the Southern Army were bivouacked. They had stripped the picket fences for firewood and all of the orchard trees of fruit. No wonder the McLean's would move to Appomattox.

Openmouthed, Kyle looked out over the scenery. "Wow, this is really some sight."

"Yeah, yesterday I heard General Longstreet say it's the largest gathering of troops on either American Continent. If you counted both sides, he estimated over fifty to sixty thousand men."

Kyle considered Longstreet's comment. It would still hold true. The Civil War remained the largest war ever fought on both American Continents.

They passed near a group of about ten wooden huts, now used for storage.

"I understand the slaves lived here until a few days ago," Daniels said. "They probably left with the family."

Ahead of them were about thirty canvas tents with two cots in each. Daniels motioned to them. "Most of the headquarters and medical staff are camped here. The big tent over there is the kitchen. Food's pretty basic, but better than eating hardtack and salt pork, like the troops. Check with the corporal over there, he'll direct you to the tent."

Daniels reached out and shook his hand. "Nice meeting you, Kyle. Since you can't leave, you might consider helping us once the battle starts. If you're right, we'll need all the help we can get."

The corporal pointed out his tent. As Kyle walked through the camp, he remembered his last visit to the area back in 2006, or should he say *forward* to 2006. They had a reenactment camp set up. It was loaded with civil war tents, participants all decked out in uniforms and 1860's war paraphernalia. The reenactment camp sure looked a lot nicer than the real thing, he thought, and smelled a hell of a lot better.

I still have a difficult time accepting where I am, and even more so, that I might never leave!

Their six-foot-high tent had just enough room for the two cots and a narrow walkway between. The morning sun had already made the tent hot and sticky.

Carter sat on the edge of the cot. "Kyle, nice to see you up and about. How's the head?"

The large bandage on Kyle's head had been replaced with a smaller one. "The side of my head is still sensitive to the touch, but everything's working OK. Where's the guard we're supposed to have?"

"I don't know about the guard. They told me to hang around the camp. The Colonel's aide stopped by and said you're to go to Sixth Brigade Headquarters and report to Colonel Early at noon. I guess it's about those Italian battles."

"Yeah, I've considered it. I'll say I ran into some French Officers at a bar in Paris and we discussed the Second Italian War for Independance. I joined them for drinks at least three or four times and talked about the battles for hours. Are you familiar with the battles of Magenta and Solferine?"

Carter stood up. "No. I've heard of the color magenta. Only the French would name a battle after a color."

"Actually it's the opposite . . . Magenta was a village in Italy. A Frenchman named the color he had created in honor of the battle."

"Even so, a engagements should't have the name of a color. Well maybe a few colors, like the battle of red or maybe black, but never magenta." Carter wiped the sweat from his brow.

"Enough with colors. Let's get the hell out of this damn tent and find a shade tree with a little breeze."

They picked an oak tree near the McLean house. Below them they could see Confederate troops in the corn fields, drilling their skirmish formations.

Carter shook his head in amazement. "I don't believe this, it's like a dream, or maybe a nightmare. When do you think we're going to wake up and go home?"

Kyle leaned back against the tree and groaned. "How the hell do I know? I've thought about it a lot. I remember the conversation well. John said it could take up to four days to complete a closed loop and get us out. We went back at noon on Wednesday. Now it's almost noon on Saturday. We're entering our fourth day. It could happen at any time."

"And, if by tomorrow night we're still here, what then?"

"I have to believe if those guys were smart enough to get us here, they can also summon the smarts to bring us back. Until then, we take it one day at a time and try to stay alive."

"You got it, boss. My only concern is this transponder." Carter pulled up his sleeve and pointed to his. "We damn near lost it to that sergeant. Without it we're screwed."

"Yeah." Kyle checked his transponder. "And speaking of time, I'll catch you later." He smirked, "I'm going to lunch with a civil war colonel, who's soon to be a hero and general."

They met at Sixth Brigade Headquarters, located in a large pasture about a half-mile behind the McLean House. Colonel Early sat at a table under a pine tree waiting for Kyle. Early wore the same grey coat, even though the temperature had to be in the high eighties.

Early held out his hand. "Welcome. It's nice to see you up and healthy. Have a seat."

"Thank you, Colonel. I'm still a little wobbly, a chair would be nice."

Early pointed toward the Northern lines. "You were right. I haven't heard a single cannon fired this morning. I guess the battle won't happen today. I'm glad, it gives us a chance to talk." He motioned to a small, gray-haired, old black man, standing nearby. "This is Isaiah, he's cooked for my family for over fifty years. He just grilled us a chicken. He can work miracles. I'll bet this is probably the last chicken left among all these thousands of hungry men."

The meal was basic, half of a small chicken each, still warm from the open fire, some sort of beans, and two freshly baked biscuits.

Early held up a large tin cup. "How about some whiskey? I have a cup at noon every day, it helps settle my stomach."

"No thank you, sir." Kyle took a deep breath. "But I can't wait to taste the food, it smells wonderful." He picked up a chicken leg, sighed and bit in. "Delicious."

They continued to talk as they ate. At first they covered Early's experiences in Florida during the Seminole Indian War, and his travels through Central Florida.

Then the subject turned to France. "I was surprised when you mentioned yesterday that you were familiar with the Battles of Magenta and Soferine. We've received some information, but not a written analysis of the battles. You're the first person I've met, other than professional soldiers, that's even heard of them."

Kyle finished the chicken and wiped up the grease with the last bit of biscuit. "Colonel, I love history, especially military history. While in a bar in France, I met a group of French Army Officers. They had fought in the Battle of Soferine. We spent many hours discussing the battle."

For the next hour they discussed details of both engagements. Of major concern to Early were the effects of rifled weapons, including artillery and muskets.

"Colonel," Kyle said. "I don't remember the exact number of deaths and casualties, but the numbers were staggering. For the French and Italian, around 3,000 dead and 13,000 wounded. For the Austrians, 4,000 dead and 15,000 wounded—much, much higher than earlier wars fought by Napoleon Bonaparte. Both leaders, Napoleon III and Franz Joseph of Austria, were so shocked at the numbers that they sued for peace within a week."

Early pulled out a cigar and lit it. "We knew the battles were damn significant, but not the details. News travels very slowly now that a naval blockade has been established around the South. Thank you for the information. Are you familiar with our commander, General Beauregard?"

Kyle decided to play dumb. "No I'm not."

"Beauregard is from Louisiana, is of French descent, and Napoleon Bonaparte is his idol. His strategies are quoted by Beauregard on a daily basis. I fear that we may be making some of the same mistakes as the French and Austrians. I would like for you to meet General Beauregard."

Kyle realized he may have given out too much information. Possibly he could affect the outcome. "Colonel, why should he listen to me? I have no military background."

Early gave him a big smile. "I left the army in the forties, became an attorney—served as the Prosecutor for Franklin County, Virginia. I was a damn good prosecutor." He took a big draw on the cigar, and exhaled a cloud of smoke. "Shit, I'm not modest. I was a great prosecutor. I never lost a case. I won because I read people real well. When someone lied . . . I felt it in my gut."

The servant walked over with the bottle of whiskey and topped off Early's cup.

Early took a drink. "Aaaah, that's good." He pointed his cigar at Kyle. "I got that feeling in my gut right now. There's something strange about you. I can't figure it out—but I will. You're not from the backwoods of Florida. You're well educated. You don't talk like a Southerner. Hell, you don't talk like a Yankee either. You act military. You weren't in the US Army before this war—it's a small exclusive club. I don't think you're a spy, but I'll be damned if I know what you are."

He stared at Kyle. "So, what's your story?"

Kyle shook his head. "Sir, I have no story. I'm here by accident, not design. I don't want to cause you any trouble."

After another sip, Early said, "The doctor tells me that during your examination he spotted two bullet wounds— One in your thigh and another in your shoulder. He said that both had perfect entry and exit marks. Someone shot you Mr. O'Brien. I think you've been in a battle before."

Kyle didn't know what to say. Two bullet wounds were hard to explain away. *This guy's no fool. Maybe I should just keep my mouth shut. I would love to tell him the truth. I would tell him to go back home to Franklin and be a damn good prosecutor.*

"Sir, it was a hunting accident. Please, I just want to go home."

Early gave him a stern look. "You know, I could hold you here and press you into service, but I'm not going to do that. I'd like for you to meet General Beauregard, if for no other reason than he loves to talk about France. I have a meeting with him this afternoon. I'll get back to you. In the meantime don't stray far from camp."

Springfield model 1855. A rifled musket used by both armies during the Civil War. It was replaced by the Springfield model 1861. Both models had a rifled barrel and a Minie ball which increased the effective firing range from fifty to about 400 yards. The weapon weight is 9 pounds, and a rate of fire of 2 or possibly 3 rounds per minute.

M4A1 Carbine. Current weapon used by most U.S. combat forces. The weapon weight is 6.5 pounds and a rate of fire of 700 to 950 rounds per minute. Is magazine loaded and fired in semi-automatic and fully automatic modes. The M203 grenade launcher, a noise suppressor and telescope can be mounted to the weapon. It has an effective firing range of 500 to 600 yards.

CHAPTER

26

*K*yle rode slowly as he headed back to the Sixth Brigade encampment. The conversation with Jubal Early remained on his mind. That man was no ignorant old fool. He suspected something and he would continue asking questions. It's no wonder he had been a successful prosecuting attorney.

I should have kept my mouth shut. We have to get away from Bull Run, Colonel Early and the Confederate Army. And, where the hell is the CIA anyway? They should have rescued us by now.

A sudden thought hit him like a sledge hammer. Was this the CIA's plan all along. Drop us back in time a hundred and fifty years and replace us with an all-CIA team on the Iranian mission?

It's damn hard contacting the Secretary of Defense when the telephone has yet to be invented.

Kyle looked up to see Captain Edwards approaching. He'd have to work all this out later.

"Good afternoon," Edwards said. "How did your meeting go with Colonel Early?"

"Primarily we discussed the new rifled muskets and artillery now being used in Europe."

"Did he mention the Springfield 1855 musket?" Edwards asked.

"No, mostly it was about the changes in battle strategies. I really don't know that much about rifles."

Edwards pointed to an infantry company marching past. "See these men, they still have the old Springfield 1842. It's a smoothbore musket. That's true for most of our troops. With the naval blockade we probably aren't going to get rifled muskets from Europe for a while. Guess we'll just have to take them off the Yankees. I hear over half their troops have the new rifles."

They passed another company of infantrymen in an encampment. Edwards motioned to the weapons stacked in the camp. "Notice those muskets. They are 55's. When our troops took over the Federal Armory at Harper's Ferry we managed to confiscate a few thousand of them. We also managed to grab thousands out of other Federal Armories in the south. Have you ever fired one?"

Kyle remembered a demonstration of the 55 and the newer model 61 during his visit to Bull Run in 2006. "No. In Florida all my family had was an old smooth bore, flintlock musket."

Edwards dismounted. "I'll show you one of these new ones. Weapons development has come a long way."

If I could only show you my M4A1. Would you be surprised.

They moved over to a group of young soldiers sitting on logs around the ashes of a burnt-out campfire.

Edwards approached one of the men. "Private, is your weapon over in that stack?"

A red-headed teen, with a mass of freckles, jumped to his feet and awkwardly saluted. "Yes, sir. Them's my squad's muskets."

"Go get it for me."

The private rushed to the weapons, grabbed his musket and, in his haste, knocked the stack to the ground. The other men laughed and then moved over to help him reset the rifles. He hurried back to Edwards. "Sorry 'bout that, sir."

After making sure it was unloaded, Edwards handed Kyle the rifle. "Your family's smooth bore is probably accurate to about fifty yards, if you're a good shot."

Kyle nodded. "My Dad can knock a squirrel out of a tree at fifty yards."

"This weapon is accurate to about three hundred yards, possibly even four hundred--if you're aiming for a man or his horse."

Kyle balanced the rifle with both hands. It felt heavy. "How much does it weigh?"

Edwards grinned. "Real light . . . about nine and a half pounds. It's also shorter at about four and a half feet long. After some training, you can load and fire two, possibly three rounds in a little over a minute. That's a hell of an improvement."

Kyle looked down at the rifle and mentally compared it to his M4A1—which weighed six and a half pounds, was half the length, fired at the rate of 900 rounds a minute and accurate to over five-hundred yards. It could also be equipped with a noise suppressor, telescope and grenade launcher. "Can I fire it?"

"Sure." Edwards turned to the private. "Show the gentleman how you load the musket."

"Yes sir." The private reached down to his side. "This here's my ammo pouch." His hand shook as he clumsily pulled a paper cartridge from the box and dropped it to the ground. The cartridge resembled a hand rolled cigarette, with both ends tightly twisted off.

The private gave them a nervous laugh, picked up the cartridge, bit one end off and then spit it out. "This here paper and gun powder tastes like shit."

He grinned, showing the remains of black powder on his lips and teeth. "Now I pour in the powder and then squeeze this here Minie' ball out of the cartridge and into the barrel."

After finishing, he wadded up the empty paper cartridge and shoved it in also. Next he pulled the ramrod out from beneath the barrel and placed it into the muzzle. "I ram it home, and then take a cap out of this here box."

The private reached down and opened a small leather pouch attached to his belt. The percussion firing cap looked like a small brass thimble. "I place it on top of this here firing chamber and pull back on the hammer." He gave them a big smile. "And now it's ready to fire."

Edwards took the musket from him. "You forgot something didn't you private?" He pulled the ramrod out of the muzzle and put it back into the slot under the barrel.

The private put his head down. "I always put the rammer back in place. Guess I got a little nervous."

Edwards pointed at the black smudges around the private's lips and face. "The other day, after the battle at Blackburn's Ford, we could easily spot the men that had fired their muskets. All their faces were covered with black powder from loading the weapons. We also found quite a few muskets with the ramrod left in the barrel. The troops are in such a hurry to reload they just forget to pull it back out. It can cause the barrel to explode, injuring the man and destroying the weapon."

Edwards held the musket out to Kyle. "You want to fire it?"

"Sure." Kyle looked around and found a slight rise a couple of hundred yards away. "How about I aim for that little hill over there? My target will be the middle of that big rock."

He sighted down the barrel and squeezed the trigger. The loud noise surprised him, the recoil jolted him back two steps, and smoke filled the air.

"You shot high. I saw dirt fly up just above the rock. That's not unusual." Edwards chuckled. "We tell the troops to aim for the balls, not the head."

Kyle handed the musket back to the soldier. "Thank you. Are you a good shot?"

"I'm a good shot with my daddy's flintlock musket," the private said. "I ain't had much practice with this here new fancy one. I only been in the army two months. I fired my musket bout eight times."

Kyle noticed he not only had black on his face but also on his teeth and tongue.

He gave Kyle a big grin. "I hit the target twice. We hear them Yankees mostly all city boys and ain't never fired muskets before. We's gonna show em how to shoot."

By then the five other soldiers had crowded around. They were dressed in a wide assortment of clothing. Most had homespun, long-sleeved cotton shirts, whose color had turned from white to a dull gray or brown. Their trousers were of a cotton wool blend, with colors varying from grey to dark blue and brown. The only signs of a uniform were their floppy, brown leather, wide-brimmed hats and brown canvased canteens. The round-shaped, tin canteens held about three pints of water and had a shoulder strap.

"Where are you men from?" Kyle asked.

A corporal, with stripes roughly hand stitched onto his shirt, answered. "We're with the Seventh Louisiana. We come up here on the train. It took bout a week. First time we ever rode a train."

One of the other boys grinned. "Yeah. We passed through a bunch of towns with all the people lined up wavin' and cheerin' for us. Lots of pretty girls. It was fun."

Six farm boys from the south, away from home for the first time and all excited about their grand adventure. I wonder how many will survive the next four years of disease and war.

Kyle patted the redhead on the shoulder. "You men be careful out there tomorrow."

He gave Kyle a big smile. "We'll show them Yankees. In a few days this'll be over and we'll be headin' for home."

The corporal nodded in agreement. "Them Yanks don't know how to fight."

Kyle and the captain turned and headed for the headquarters camp. "Captain, I heard a lot of cheering coming from the train station. Is it OK if I find my friend and we hike over to Manassas Junction?"

"The colonel told me you have free run of the camp, so I guess it's all right. Just don't jump on one of those trains and head out of here. Trust me, you don't want Colonel Early as an enemy."

CHAPTER

27

*I*n **Northern Illinois, summer** had arrived with a vengeance. A blanket of hot, humid air greeted Stan Jackson and John Anders as they emerged from Chicago's O'Hare International Airport. They made a mad sprint for the CIA's black limo and the comfort of air conditioning. Once inside, they settled in for a forty-five minute ride to the Department of Energy's Fermilab complex, located northwest of Chicago in Batavia, Illinois.

Stan closed his eyes and relaxed. It had been a rough two days since Kyle O'Brien and Carter Weston disappeared from Quantico. Most of that time spent trying to explain to the upper echelon of the CIA and Defense Department what had happened—or since they had no idea—explaining what might have happened to the two men. Finally they were being summoned to the team's research center at Fermilab for an explanation . . . and hopefully a solution to their problems.

Though they had a closed window between them and the driver, Stan didn't want to discuss details of the project. "How long have you worked at Fermilab?"

"Since I got my PhD from MIT about ten years ago. It's an exciting place to work."

"Tell me more about the lab."

"Even with your high security clearance, there are things I can't disclose. But, I can give you a fairly good background.

About two thousand people work here, mostly physicists, engineers and computer professionals. About the same number visit each year from universities throughout the world. It's named after Enrico Fermi, an Italian physicist who won the Nobel Prize in physics. He led the way in creating the world's first nuclear reactor during World War II."

"Sounds like a college campus rather than a government facility."

"It is. Fermilab's located on about seven thousand acres. Hell, it's even got a herd of American bison roaming around the property. The labs's made some significant discoveries over the years, including the bottom quark in 1977, the top quark in 95, and the tau neutrino in 2000."

Stan held up his hand. "Hold it right there. You're talking to someone who struggled through high school chemistry. I'm not even going to ask what a quark or a tau neutrino is."

John chuckled. "That's great, because it would take longer than this ride to explain them. The lab's been here about forty years and most of our knowledge on matter, energy, and how the universe began was discovered here. I should also add that in 2007, I helped identify that supermassive black holes are the most likely source of high energy cosmic rays."

Stan grinned. "John, I hope you don't use that line to pick up girls. So, who will we be meeting with today?"

"With my boss, Evan Chao, and the team leaders — probably about six or seven people. The project is so secret it doesn't even have an official name. We've nicknamed it project T, because we're isolated at the only facility inside the Tevatron particle collider ring. All of the Fermilab employees call us the spook group. We're underground and completely removed from the rest of the complex. We have roughly three hundred working there. You may be the first visitor to ever enter our compound."

"I wish it were under better circumstances. You can't imagine the pressure I've been under the past few days. You guys damn well better have some answers for me. I'm not going to face the firing squad alone."

"I understand. Our team has quite literally been working night and day to find an answer. They wouldn't be calling this meeting if they didn't have a solution."

The limo turned off Interstate 88 at the Kirk Road exit, and headed straight for Fermilab. At the main gate, they pulled into a special lane and breezed into the complex. It resembled a modern university campus, with green belts, futuristic high-rise office buildings and housing for the visiting researchers. The limo wheeled into an underground parking structure, passed through a security checkpoint, and up to a nondescript double door. They exited the car and stood in front of the doors.

A voice from a small speaker located in the wall asked. "Good morning. Could I have your name please?"

They both answered.

The voice requested, "For confirmation please place your right hand against the screen in front of you, and your right eye into the opening above."

They each complied and, a moment later, the door opened. A security guard escorted them into the building and onto a long motorized beltway that extended at least the length of a football field. At the other end they entered a large cement tunnel that ended at an elevator.

The door slid open and a man stood before them. "Mr. Jackson, I'm Evan Chao. Welcome to Fermilabs." Chao, who looked to be in his early forties, wore jeans, a polo shirt and loafers.

Stan shook his hand. "It's nice to meet you."

Chao punched the down button. "I've got my team assembled. Are you ready to get started?"

"Yes, I'm very anxious to hear what you've found out."

They ultimately ended up at an underground conference room with brightly painted walls and cheerful artwork, but no windows.

A group of five men and one woman greeted them; all wore casual clothes similar to Chao's. Stan had imagined all the workers would be wearing typical lab coats.

Chao introduced Stan, but did not offer the names of the team. All appeared to be in their thirties, or possibly younger.

Once seated, Chao opened the meeting. "Mr. Jackson, let me start by saying that all of us in this group work for the CIA's Director of Science and Technology, and not the Department of Energy. We operate out of this facility because of our need for Fermilab's powerful electromagnets."

"It's an impressive facility." Stan said.

"Yes it is," Chao said. "The Pierre Auger Observatory is also located here, which we use to identify the wormholes necessary for time travel transportation. So like you, we work for the CIA and have received the same pressure you have. I take full responsibility for this problem."

Stan held up his hand. "Hold it right there. You don't even know what pressure is. I've had the Director of the CIA breathing down my neck. I presume he has the Secretary of Defense and the President breathing down his. That's pressure. Hopefully we can rectify the problem."

With a sigh, Chao placed his hands palms down on the table. "I agree. Let's see what we can do to fix it."

He motioned to the young woman on his left.

She spoke up. "Mr. Jackson. I head up the team researching the wormholes that were used for the transportation of the missing men. We can't be sure, but we suspect that a combination of three different events caused their disappearance.

"Number one: During their time travel the sun experienced unusually large solar flares, causing powerful bursts of x-ray and ultraviolet radiation. This distorted the transponder signals.

"Number two: The flares also altered our satellites. We use a system similar to the Global Positioning Satellites and suspect that communications to our time travel satellites was interrupted during their mission.

"Number three: While your men were activating their transponders – Unknowingly we were testing for fifteen days of time travel. The combination of all three of these actions may have caused a perfect storm scenario, which whirled them somewhere back in time."

The woman nodded to Chao and closed the file in front of her.

"OK. Thank you," Chao said, and turned to Stan. "Now to our real concern-—what's going to happen to your two men? We've had a team working continuously on this problem. They've come up with an inventive, but simple solution."

Chao nodded to the young man next to him. "Explain to Mr. Jackson what your team's developed."

The young scientist cleared his throat. "Yes, sir. We know one important piece of information—-the location of your men. They have gone back in time, but have not changed locations. They were instructed to stay within the Northern Hemisphere, and we assume they have. But we don't know what year they're in, or as we call it, their current timeline. If we did, our satellites and transponders could be readjusted to bring the men back to the present."

Stan glanced at all six of them, "How do we locate this timeline?"

"Our current technology is limited. We can send humans back in time, plus any inert objects attached to them. But we can't transmit any items without a human."

"Yeah, I remember," Stan said. "We had discussions about the difficulty of sending clothes, shoes, weapons and military gear back in time."

The man nodded. "Correct. We do have the equipment that can locate them. For example, we can send an instrument back to their suspected timeline and, if they are present, it will lock on to their transponder signal. Unfortunately this requires sending a human back as well. We have people who have volunteered, but it's far too risky. We don't want to lose anyone else."

"Let me correct one thing." Chao interrupted. "We can't send the instrument back in time unless it's attached to a *living* species. But, it doesn't necessarily have to be a human being. We share ninety-eight percent of our DNA with the chimpanzee. We are proposing sending a chimpanzee back with the instrument."

Stan frowned. "You can do that?"

"Yes," Chao answered. "As you know, we've used them successfully in the past. Our first series of time travel tests were performed by chimps and we've had no problems. We have one available—-his name is Elvis, and he's trained and reliable. We can send Elvis back with the instrument."

"Can he turn it on?" Stan asked.

"Elvis is smart. He can turn it on and off. We've even taught him to play a guitar and swivel his hips." Chao gave a quick grin and then continued. "Once back in time, after Elvis has turned it on, our instrument collects the data, then we transport him back to current time. Start to finish would be about twenty minutes. If the results are negative, we move to a new timeline. We keep doing this until we lock in on your men's transponders."

"Hold it a minute," Stan said. "Before this problem, these two men were training for a vital national security assignment. I can't disclose the operation, but it's directed from the very top. And you're telling me, we're going to rely on a *chimpanzee* to find them? This is what the Director of the CIA is going to tell the President. You've got to be kidding me."

"No, I'm not," Chao said. "We've determined it will take at least a year of research to send inert objects back in time, and that's our next best solution. Do we have a year?"

"Hell no."

"Then we go with the chimp," Chao said, "and start as soon as possible. Remember this fifteen digit phenomenon. We start by going out fifteen days, and keep working our way back. Who knows, we may get lucky and hit a fast lock-on."

"What's the time frame you're looking at?" Stan said. "How far back could they be in time?"

Chao took a quick glance at his group and a deep breath. "We've had long discussions on that subject. It's a time span of no more than 300,000 years."

Stan gave them a shocked look, too dumbfounded to speak.

"Hold it. That's not much," Chao said. "Remember, Earth's over four billion years old."

Stan jumped to his feet. "My God! Three hundred thousand years. Hell, they could be eaten by pre-historic animals, or freeze to death in an Ice Age. They have already been there two days. They could be dead right now."

"Please calm down," Chao said. "We're working as fast as possible. We're training more chimps as we speak."

"When do we get started?" Stan asked. "I want those men back—-and fast."

"We'll start transporting Elvis back by this evening."

Stan rubbed his temples. *I don't believe it. I've got to tell the CIA Director that the life of those two men now depends on a fucking chimpanzee. I'll leave out the dancing Elvis part.*

CHAPTER

28

*K*yle found Carter sitting at a table in the mess tent with a group of men.

Carter motioned him over. "Kyle, these men are in the artillery and assigned to Colonel Early's Sixth Brigade. I was telling them about our escape from the Yankees."

All four of the men wore lieutenant's insignia and looked to be in their mid-twenties. A dark haired man with a neatly trimmed mustache stood up and held out his hand. "I'm Charles Squires." He looked at the wound on Kyle's head. "Ya'll just lucked out, them yanks such terrible shots. Have a seat, we got coffee brewing."

Kyle sat down next to Squires. "No thanks, it's too hot for coffee. Where are you men from?"

Squires motioned to the man next to him. "We're from Louisiana. Those two are from Mississippi. This Brigade's got a mix of Louisiana, Mississippi and Virginia units. Our outfit is the Fourth Company, Washington Artillery, out of Baton Rouge. It's not much, just four old smooth bore six-pounders and two three-pound rifled cannons."

"Have you seen any action yet?"

"Yep." Squires proudly nodded. "We were right in the middle of it at Blackburn's Ford. Fired three hundred and ten rounds during the action, and helped chase them yanks back into Centreville. General Longstreet told our commander we did a great job." He smiled, "Our Company had only one horse killed and five men wounded. Not a bad day's work."

One of the other lieutenants gave Kyle a hard look. "You men look strong. We need replacements, you want to join us?"

"No thanks," Carter said. "I just returned from over two years in Europe. We're both going home for a short visit before joining the army, but I've always been interested in artillery and explosives. Could you show me your cannons?"

Kyle pointed to the East, where loud cheers could be heard. "Maybe you can do that later. I thought we'd hike over and see what's going on at Manassas Junction."

Squires groaned. "Hell, that started last night . . . woke me up about four times. It's our troops arriving from the Shenandoah Valley. If you want to go over there you can use a couple of our horses. That road's well trampled. If you try walking, you'll be eating dust the whole trip."

Twenty minutes later they mounted two large, slow horses, probably farm animals before the war, but certainly better than walking. The ride took them past the McLean's farm and continued on for another two miles to Manassas Junction, where the Orange and Alexandria Railroad and the Manassas Gap Railroad connected.

"How did your meeting go with Early?" Carter asked.

"I don't feel good about it. He's smart and suspects something. He called it a feeling in his gut. Hopefully we're going to get yanked out of here before he gets too inquisitive."

"And if we don't?"

"Then we run like hell before we end up fighting in the Confederate Army. We'll stay here until the battle's over, and then we decide what to do."

They crested a slight hill and looked across the cultivated fields. Kyle chuckled. "I've been in this area two or three times before while stationed at Quantico. It's loaded with fast food restaurants and shopping centers. Hell, even the McLean house is gone. There's just a plaque in a parking lot marking the spot."

Thousands of troops, horse drawn wagons and artillery, arriving from both the Shenandoah valley and Richmond, jammed the roads, all headed for bivouacs in the fields along the Southern slope of Bull Run. They stirred up a dust cloud that extended for miles around the junction.

"Damn." Carter rubbed his eyes. "This dust is terrible. I'm thinking about those sunglasses I left on my bunk at Quantico."

Trains arrived and men rushed about removing the cargo. Once empty they were turned and rushed back for more troops and supplies. Wooden crates and barrels, loaded with food and war materials lay stacked in the fields, awaiting transfer to Bull Run. Troops wandered around, or sat on the ground, waiting for orders.

Just as Kyle and Carter rode up, a train arrived from the Shenandoah, every boxcar crammed with troops. The men in the fields rushed over and cheered, as the new arrivals jumped from the hot cars and eagerly joined in the celebration.

Kyle thought he recognized one of the officers directing the troops into marching formations. "Carter, look at that tall guy over there. I'm sure that's General Thomas Jackson."

Carter stared at him. "I've seen pictures of Stonewall Jackson, but it's hard to tell. Hell, everyone on that train, except for the kids too young to shave, have heavy beards, mustaches, and long uncombed hair. They all look the same."

"He's got a star on each collar, so that's him." Kyle looked around to see if anyone was listening. "Remember, don't call him Stonewall. He gets that nickname tomorrow afternoon at Henry Hill."

Jackson continued yelling and directing the troops into ranks.

Carter said, "You want to go up and ask for an autograph?"

Kyle laughed. "Look at him, he's got them jumping. That's what you call a command presence." They watched for a moment. "I still can't get over it. We're watching one of the legendary leaders of the Civil War at a vital moment in history."

Carter asked, "Have we got enough time this afternoon to visit tomorrow's battleground?"

"I think so, the main battle takes place on the Henry Farm, which is only about six miles from here. If we kick these old plow horses in the ass we can make it. It sits just off Sudley Road. Hopefully I can find it without the National Park and street signs." Kyle grinned. "I remember eating at a Wendy's that's less than a half mile away. You want a hamburger?"

"Don't joke around about burgers. That would hit the spot right now."

They headed away from the busy train junction. The road north turned back into a small country lane with scattered farms. Kyle located the Henry Farm with no problems.

Wheat fields surrounded the small, four-roomed, two-story, wood framed house. In the distance, fields of corn surrounded another small, white farm house.

"That house in the distance is on Mathews Hill."

They sat on their horses and Kyle pointed to the Henry house about a quarter-mile away. "It looks remarkably the same . . . maybe fewer trees around the area, but the house, which was rebuilt shortly after the war, hasn't changed. The National Park Headquarters and Museum is about where we are now, and right behind the Henry House is a monument to the soldiers who died here. On my last visit in 2006, I got a four-hour tour of Henry Hill by a Park Ranger. Later I bought a couple of books on the battle at the museum."

Kyle motioned toward Sudley Road that led to the North. "The battle will start over on Mathews Hill. That stone house you see next to the road between the two hills will be used by sharpshooters and later as a hospital."

"How many men were involved?"

"It started with the Union troops having a big advantage. General Burnside's Brigade arrived first, with maybe three thousand men."

Carter chuckled. "Oh yeah, I remember him. The guy with the fancy whiskers. They named sideburns after him didn't they?"

"That's right. Another brigade joined him, making about six thousand men bearing down on nine hundred Confederates. For over two hours that small force did an excellent job of stalling the advance of the Union. It gave the Confederates time to send in about eight thousand additional troops. All morning long, men from both sides forced marched to Henry Hill. Like one of those black holes in space, the Henry House will suck in over fifteen thousand men by this time tomorrow afternoon."

Kyle pointed out the field in front of them. "A large bronze statue of General Stonewall Jackson will be placed right over there. When we finally get transported back, we'll have to revisit this site."

"You mean *if* we get transported back."

A man walked out of the Henry House, looked their way and waved.

Kyle waved back. "I'll bet he's wondering who the hell we are. That's probably the son of Judith Henry. She's in her eighties and bedridden in that house. Tomorrow she'll be killed by Union artillery that will be located right where we are now. During the middle of the battle rebel sharpshooters move into the top floor of the house and start picking off the artillerymen located here. They turn their cannons on the house and punch it full of holes."

Carter sighed. "And we can't even go over and move her out of there."

"No, we can't, and we both know why. Her grave will sit in front of the house with a nice picket fence around it."

Kyle reined his horse to the right. "General Jackson's First Brigade moved in near that tree line over there. Or I guess I should say he *will* move in tomorrow. Supposedly he says, 'This is the spot for a battle.' He has his men lie down, and mounts his dozen or so artillery pieces in front of them, right on that hill. He will just wait for the battle to move to his strategic position. He placed his cannons perfectly, just on the back side of the hill so the Union troops couldn't see them. When the enemy got in close range, he rolled the cannons up on the lip of the hill and blasted away. The recoil of firing would roll the cannon back down the hill a few feet and out of the line of fire. They would reload and roll it back up again. They kept this up most of the afternoon."

"This is where he gets the name Stonewall?"

"Not exactly. A little later in the day, the remains of the Fourth Alabama Battalion, which had retreated off Mathews Hill, was in disarray. The commanding officer, General Barnard Bee, rallied the troops and pointed to General Jackson on his horse directing the defense of Henry Hill. Bee yelled 'There is Jackson standing like a stone wall. Follow me.' It's disputed if those were his exact words, but we'll never know for sure."

Kyle pointed to the Henry house. "Early tomorrow afternoon there will about ten Union cannons blasting away near the home, and another six down by the stone house. The artillery barrage lasted for over two hours."

Carter looked out over the field. "I can see it now. This whole hill will be completely covered in smoke from the cannon and rifle fire. Probably all you'll be able to see through the heavy smoke will be flames leaping out of cannon barrels."

"That's right, plus the Confederate troops are going to charge across the field and capture the Union artillery pieces on three different occasions. Each time, Union troops will take them back. The battle seesaws back and forth for hours, with both sides firing thousands of musket rounds."

"When does the Union start their retreat?" Carter asked.

"At about four in the afternoon." Kyle checked his watch. "Right about now. My new friend, Colonel Early, arrives with his Brigade and plays a key role in the battle. Just by chance they charge on the enemy's right flank as Howard's Union brigade starts their attack. Howard's men are caught completely off guard and retreat. The other troops see this, hysteria sets in and the troops leave everything behind: cannons, rifles, explosives, supplies, and the wounded. Close to a thousand men and three hundred horses will die on or near this hill tomorrow. Another three thousand men will be injured or captured in the battle."

Carter looked out over the empty field. "Hopefully we'll be long gone by the time that happens."

"We better be." Kyle said. "I sure as hell don't want to die here. In the past and in somebody else's war. We've got to get out of here!"

CHAPTER

29

Kyle remained silent on the ride with Carter back to the encampment. The image of close to a thousand dead men scattered across the battlefield haunted him. Finally he spoke. "We need to make plans for our escape. Anticipating the carnage that will take place here tomorrow is driving me crazy."

"I agree." Carter said. "So, what do we do?"

"Good question. We may be stuck here for years. Hell, it could be forever. This needs to be a joint decision."

"OK," Carter said, "I'll give you my thoughts. After killing that sergeant we can't go north, at least not until after this war's over. We talked about going south to Atlanta or some other major city and blending in, but remember, Atlanta will be burned to the ground by Sherman in a few years. The rest of the South will go through holy hell. There's a good chance we'll be sucked up in this war. Why be a part of that?"

Kyle nodded. "I agree. How about this. We go to Europe until the South surrenders, or maybe we head out West? We'll be OK if we stay in the Northern Hemisphere."

"West . . . I hadn't considered that." Carter snickered, "As a kid, I always wanted to be a cowboy. Maybe this is my chance."

"Or all the way to the West Coast. San Francisco was booming in the mid-eighteen hundreds. We'd be in the U.S. but far enough away that we won't be noticed."

Carter gave it some thought. "It's going to be difficult getting to Europe, what with the blockade in place. I vote for the West Coast. But just how are we supposed to get there without money?"

"Didn't you bring credit cards?"

Carter snorted, "Yeah, in the bag with my iPhone and laptop."

Kyle laughed, "I think we do it the way they did back then. Find work where we can and keep moving. Tomorrow night the Union Army will be in full retreat. During the confusion we'll grab a couple of good saddlehorses and head west. Once we cross the Mississippi River and out of the Deep South we should be in the clear."

They arrived back at camp, returned the horses, and were invited to join four of the artillery officers for supper. All six of them sat around a table set up outside the mess tent. The four men had taken off their uniform coats, and rolled up the sleeves on their white cotton shirts. For miles around, the smoke of thousands of campfires drifted into the sky, as the troops settled in for the night.

Charles Squires leaned back in his chair and put his hands behind his head. "It was too damn hot to eat inside the tent. I had Jacob set up the table out here. I'm glad you could join us. My grandfather was from France. I'd love to go there after this damn war. Maybe you could tell us about it?"

Kyle smiled. "Of course, I would be happy to, and thank you for the hospitality."

A black man placed a glass in front of Kyle and Carter without looking at either of them.

Squires motioned to him. "This is Jacob."

The man, in his early fifties, gave them a quick look, nodded and went back to the tent.

"He's a house servant on my father's plantation in Louisiana," Squires said. "A fantastic cook, and spends most of his day rounding us up something besides beans, salted pork and biscuits. That's about all our army seems to provide."

"He's a slave?" Kyle asked.

Squires gave Kyle a quizzical look. "Of course. Our plantation has about four hundred slaves. We grow sugarcane. It takes a lot of labor. With the Mississippi River blockaded, we're going to have tough times in Louisiana. Does your family have slaves?"

"No. It's a small farm." Kyle remembered reading in his Civil War books that a number of Confederate soldiers, mostly officers, had brought slaves to war with them. Typically they were used for menial tasks such as washing, cooking, setting up tents or digging fortifications. They were not allowed to carry weapons nor fight—and later in the war, after Lincoln's Emancipation Proclamation, the practice mostly stopped as slaves started fleeing across to the Union lines.

Squires lifted up a bottle. "Let's celebrate to our upcoming victory. We managed to pick up four bottles of fine Tennessee bourbon while we traveled through that state a few weeks ago. We regretfully have only two left. Would you care for some?"

They both quickly held out their glasses and he poured a generous shot into each.

"Thank you," Carter said. "I love good bourbon."

"Yes, I guess it's not available in Europe." Squires held up his glass. "To victory!"

They all took a sip. The bourbon tasted smooth.

Squires finished his in one gulp and poured another. "Who knows, this could be the last night of our lives. Let's finish this bottle."

One of the other men smiled. "How about both bottles? I would hate to go to heaven or hell knowing I'd left a bottle of excellent bourbon on the table."

They laughed, and Carter held up his glass. "To long life . . . and more bourbon."

They all cheered and emptied their glasses.

Kyle looked up to see Captain Edwards ride up to the campsite.

He dismounted and strolled over. "Gentleman, it looks like you're celebrating early." He looked over at Kyle. "Mr. O'Brien, could I have a word with you?"

Kyle stood and joined him.

"There's a reception at Army headquarters tonight. Colonel Early has discussed your travels with General Beauregard. He's very interested in your observations on the battles in Europe. The General would like to meet you."

Kyle considered the offer. He should have kept his mouth shut and not talked to Early about Europe. He looked down at his clothes. "I'm not exactly dressed for a party. This is all I've got."

Edwards stepped back and gave him a look. "We're close to the same size. I have civilian attire in my tent. I'll be happy to give you some clothes."

"Thank you. I would like to meet General Beauregard." Kyle couldn't resist. "Will General Robert E. Lee be there tonight?" Who could pass up the chance to meet one of the most famous generals in American history?

"I don't think so. General Lee is still in Richmond. I'll be right back with the clothes. The function starts in an hour."

Kyle returned to the table, informed Carter, and turned to Squires. "I'm sorry, we'll have to discuss France another evening. Would you mind if I borrow that horse again?"

Edwards returned with a pair of trousers and a white cotton shirt. The fit was close and Kyle felt great to get out of the dirty clothes he had traded for three days ago. Now if only he could have a hot shower.

On the trip over, Edwards filled him in on the reception. "Some of the Generals and Colonels will be there tonight and a few civilians. General Beauregard is quite the host—there will be plenty to eat and drink."

Kyle pointed to the McLean house off in the distance. "Aren't we going there?"

Edwards chuckled, "It *was* the general's headquarters, but once the Yankees landed that cannonball right down the chimney they decided it was a little too close to the enemy. General Beauregard moved it to the Weir's plantation. It's a bigger house, and another mile or so away from the battlefront."

"What's the General like?"

Edwards hesitated. "I'll leave that for you to decide. He's well educated, a graduate of the U.S. Military Academy . . . finished second in his class. By the way, the Union Commander, McDowell—he graduated twenty-third in the same class."

"What rank did General Beauregard hold in the Union Army?"

"I don't know. His last assignment was Superintendent of West Point. I'm guessing maybe a Colonel. Since you were in Europe you might not know this, but General Beauregard was in charge when we captured Fort Sumter down in South Carolina. He's a hero now."

Edwards cleared his throat. "You didn't hear this from me. Some people call him the little Napoleon. He's always spouting off quotes from that Frenchman. When we arrive I'll be turning you over to his aide, Colonel James Chesnut."

Edwards cleared his throat even deeper and louder. "Be careful of Chesnut."

"Why?"

"He's nothing but a conniving politician. The US Senator from South Carolina till the war started. Goes back to South Carolina and hooks up with Beauregard. A few months later, he's a Colonel, strutting around like he owns the place, even though he knows nothing about the military. He just got back from briefing President Davis down in Richmond."

In the dusk, the stately front columns of the Weir home came into view. They rode along a circular brick carriageway and up to the front porch of the large, two story red brick home.

Edwards pointed out the two men standing on the front porch. "The tall one is Chesnut." Once again he cleared his throat, only louder, and whispered, "Watch that cockroach."

Edwards made the introductions and immediately turned and left.

James Chesnut could have played the movie role of the genteel Southern Senator, with a well-groomed mustache and goatee, plus flowing, wavy brown hair. Down the front of his perfectly tailored, grey colonel's uniform were two rows of eight shiny brass buttons.

Chesnut held out a hand. "Mr. O'Brien, such a pleasure to meet you. Colonel Early has filled me in on your European travels. Your shipwreck and recent escape from Union troops sounds quite exciting. Welcome back to the Confederate States of America."

His southern accent flowed as smoothly as the Tennessee bourbon Kyle had just downed.

Chesnut turned to a short, baldheaded man, with thick wire-rimmed glasses. His civilian clothes were disheveled, his tie stained. "This is Major Thomas. He has just joined the Signal Corps of our army, and is responsible for gathering information about our Union enemies. Before the war he worked up North for the Pinkerton Detective Agency. Can we ask you a few questions before we proceed in to meet General Beauregard?"

Kyle nodded. "Yes, I'll be happy to answer your questions." *So this must be the Confederate equivalent to the FBI. I'll need to be careful.*

With a big smile, Chesnut said, "That's very nice of you. Colonel Early mentioned you are from Florida and grew up on a farm. Tell us a little more about yourself."

"Yes, from Ocala, a small village in the middle of the state. After schooling, I worked on the farm with my father and then traveled to Jacksonville, where I caught a steamship to England and then France."

Thomas looked over the top of his glasses and stepped in closer. "You have a different accent than most Southerners. Why is that, sir?"

Kyle quickly considered an answer. "Perhaps because of my over two years spent in Europe, and the influence of my mother who was originally from England." *Should I mention his accent's straight out of New Jersey?*

Thomas nodded. "And also, you are well spoken for a farm boy."

"That also comes from my mother, who was well educated. She had me reading at an early age and stressed education."

"I see," Thomas said. "Colonel Early mentioned you hoped to travel to Florida when you leave here, and your friend to Alabama. Is that correct?"

"Yes."

"Not tomorrow, I hope?" Thomas said.

"No. When Colonel Early tells us we can leave."

Thomas moved in closer and inspected Kyle's forehead. "You're a lucky man, a few more inches and you'd be dead."

The front door of the house opened, and a short man came charging out. His swagger reminded Kyle of the proud rooster that ruled the henhouse in his father's farmyard. He wore a perfectly tailored, light gray uniform, buttons down the front and a star on each shoulder. Kyle immediately recognized him from Civil War photos. His dark complexion sported a well-groomed mustache and goatee, and black curly hair.

Chesnut motioned in Kyle's direction. "General Beauregard, this is Mr. Kyle O'Brien. Colonel Early mentioned him this afternoon."

"*Ah Oui.*" Beauregard held out his hand. "*Bonjour, parlez-vous Francais?*"

Kyle frantically searched for the correct words. "*Oui. Enchante, General.*"

Beauregard smiled and motioned to Thomas. "His French is good." He pointed to the door. *"Monsieur O'Brien, sil vous plait joinder a mor."*

Beauregard opened the door and strolled inside. Thomas held the door open and Chesnut followed the general.

Kyle started to move into the doorway and Thomas blocked his way. "Mr. O'Brien, I have one more question. Colonel Early told us about your unfortunate shipwreck out in the Chesapeake. If you would be so kind, what was the name of your ship?"

This guy is going to cause me big trouble. I'll give him the name of a French port city.

"*Calais*, Major. It was named after the French city, Calais."

Thomas smiled as he whipped out a note pad and pencil. "I'm afraid my French is not as good as yours and the General's. Would you spell that for me, please?"

Liberia Plantation House. Owned by William Weir on 1,660 acres near Manassas. The plantation produced grains and vegetables and had 90 slaves in 1861. It was used as headquarters of the Confederate Army during the First Battle of Bull Run and again as headquarters for the U.S. Army during the Second Battle of Bull Run. The House has been restored and is currently owned by the city of Manassas.

General Pierre G. T. Beauregard (1818-1893). He began the Civil War as the Hero of Fort Sumter and the Commander of the CSA Army during the First Battle of Bull Run. Due to Beauregard's conflicts with other senior officers and President Jefferson Davis, his influence decreased as the war progressed. He surrendered to U.S. General William T. Sherman at war's end and returned to his home in Louisiana.

Brigadier General Barnard E. Bee Jr. (1824-1861) Bee was the first general from either side to be killed during civil war combat. Bee observed General Thomas Jackson's brigade holding the line during numerous charges by Union troops at Henry Hill, and gave Jackson the nickname "Stonewall." Bee was 37 years old when he died while leading an attack on Union troops near Henry Hill.

CHAPTER

30

*T*he front door of the Weir mansion opened to an over-sized hallway that extended the length of the house. Near the middle of the hall a wide stairway led up to the second floor. To Kyle's right, a doorway lead into a large parlor, and on the left stood a dining room with an enormous table that would easily seat twenty. The centerpiece, a candelabrum, burned brightly and cast light onto a table laden with food.

Kyle took a deep breath and inhaled the mouthwatering aroma wafting up from the table. It smelled of his family's Thanksgiving, with roasted turkey, baked ham, yams, corn, sliced tomatoes and fresh baked breads.

Next to the table stood Colonel Early, holding a plate heaped high with food. "Ah, O'Brien, welcome. I'm glad Edwards found you. General Beauregard insists on a meeting with you."

Motioning to the table, Early said, "Please, help yourself."

"Thank you, Colonel." Kyle picked up a plate and glanced around the table. "It looks delicious."

Early checked around to determine if anyone was listening. "Yes, our Napoleon loves to entertain. I see Chesnut and Thomas stopped you on the way in. Don't worry, Thomas has recently joined the Confederacy. He's trying to impress our little general by looking for spies under every rock." Early tilted his head and gave Kyle a wry smile. "But, you have nothing to fear . . . do you, sir?"

Kyle attempted to speak, but Early held up an open hand.

"O'Brien. Don't give me any more of that—you're here by accident balderdash."

"It's the truth, sir."

"We've got a big battle tomorrow. Let's just enjoy the evening. Join me in the parlor after you have made your selections." Early strolled across the hallway and into the parlor.

Kyle watched him leave. *What the hell am I getting into? I should have kept my mouth shut about those battles in Europe. Now that snooping major is breathing down my neck, and the commanding general wants to question me. I've got to be more careful.*

Moving around the table, Kyle loaded his plate with a little of each. It could be days, hell it could be weeks, before he had another meal like this. He felt a twinge of guilt as he thought about Carter's probable meal of beans and salt pork.

Kyle headed across to the large parlor, which extended to the back of the house. He stood and gazed in awe. The setting could have been a scene straight out of, *Gone With The Wind*. A great marbled fireplace stood against the sidewall. The candles situated along the mantel and about the room cast a mellow glow on the occupants. The room hummed with conversation, as thirty to forty people had separated into smaller groups. Despite the warm night, most of the men wore Confederate uniforms — all of them high-ranking officers. All six women in the room had floor-length dresses with long sleeves.

Early sat at a small table near the fireplace with another officer and two ladies, he stood and waved Kyle over. Still wearing the same grey, ill-fitting, crumpled coat, with no insignia on the sleeve or collar, he looked out of place in the fine setting.

"O'Brien, this is an old friend of mine, Barnard Bee. As a young whippersnapper he served under my command in the Mexican War."

Holding out his hand, Bee stood and greeted Kyle. He was tall, well over six feet, distinguished looking, with long, wavy dark hair, and a groomed mustache and goatee. His grey uniform looked new, as did the gold star on each shoulder, and the gold sash with sword hanging from his hip. He appeared to be in his late thirties —young to be a general.

"Please join us," Bee said. "Jubal told us about your travels in Europe and the boat experiences upon your return."

A shiver went through Kyle as he shook his hand. "It's a pleasure to meet you, General."

Early laughed. "I'm still surprised when someone calls Bee a general. He received the promotion a few weeks ago and now outranks me. It couldn't happen to a more competent solider. That young man has a bright future with the Confederacy."

Kyle stared at Bee. *Little does Early know. I'm looking at a dead man. General Barnard Bee will be mortally wounded tomorrow on Henry Hill – the highest ranking officer to die in this battle.*

With his arm held out, Early motioned toward the two women. "May I present Mrs. Linda Collins and her daughter, Miss Mary Beth Collins. They live in Charlottesville and have established a hospital for our soldiers. After the battle, the two of them will help transport the wounded by train back to their city. Mrs. Collins' husband is a surgeon and an old friend of mine."

Kyle did a slight bow. "Ladies, it is a pleasure to meet you. You are to be commended for your efforts."

The mother appeared to be in her mid-forties and the daughter, who had a striking resemblance to her mother, in her early twenties.

Mary Beth had curly golden-brown hair, and a few freckles on the bridge of her nose. She held out her hand and gave him a gorgeous smile, showing deep dimples. "*Enchante' de vous renconter*. How long were you in Paris?"

"*Bonjour, Mademoiselle*." What a beautiful girl, a real Southern belle, Kyle thought. With her looks and that dress and hair, she could have played the role of Scarlett O'Hara in *Gone With the Wind*.

"I was in Europe for almost three years." He answered. "But in Paris regretfully for only a year. I love the city."

Her pale blue, light summer dress set off her deep blue eyes. She closed them and sighed. "Me too, my favorite city. I lived in Paris for a year, while I trained in medicine. That was two years ago. Where did you live in the city?"

Kyle glanced over at Early. *Did he set me up?* He searched for names of the different districts of Paris. "In the Left Bank, very near the Latin Quarter." *Had it been called the Left Bank in the mid-eighteen hundreds?*

She smiled. "I should have guessed . . . *the rive gauche*. That's where all the students and artists live."

"Yes. At least the poor ones like me." How true. He had actually stayed in the West Bank—just well over a century later.

"Colonel Early mentioned you arrived with a friend?" Mary Beth asked.

"Yes, Carter Weston. We met aboard ship during our return from Europe. He's back at camp."

"Did you study in France, Mr. O'Brien?"

"No." Kyle chuckled. "I was just there for a good time. You mentioned attending medical school in Paris. You're a doctor?"

With a frown, Early answered, "Of course not, in this country women are not allowed to be doctors. Surely you must know that, O'Brien."

He needed a fast comeback. "In my village in Florida, we didn't have a doctor, but we had a midwife who also set broken bones tended to fevers. I guess it never occurred to me that women weren't allowed to be doctors."

Mrs. Collins spoke up. "Well sir, you are partially right. Although women doctors are not allowed, Mary Beth helps my husband with his surgery and patients, especially the care of wounds after surgery. She will be of great assistance as a nurse for our seriously wounded soldiers."

"I fear you'll have busy days ahead of you," Kyle said.

"Hopefully tomorrow will be the end of this nasty business," Bee added. "We expect a major victory and a short war. The Yanks will go home with their tails between their legs."

"I wish for that as well, General."

A servant appeared and asked if they would like something to drink. Early and Bee ordered whiskey, and the two women . . . lemonade.

"General Beauregard is famous for his fine whiskey." Early held up his glass to the servant. "Bring the same for our guest."

After the servant left, Kyle looked around the room. "This home is beautiful."

"Yes, it's lovely," Mrs. Collins replied. "As a young, single girl, I attended parties here on many occasions." She briefly closed her eyes. "This plantation brings back such fond memories. I fear those happy days are over for the South. It's sad my daughter must visit for the first time under such unpleasant circumstances."

"Are the owners here tonight?"

"No. I'm afraid not," Mrs. Collins said. "The plantation is named Liberia and it's owned by Mr. William Weir and his wife, Harriett. I understand it has been General Beauregard's headquarters since early July. It's quite large, over two thousand acres, with about ninety slaves. I think the Weirs and their slaves have fled to the south side of the Rappahannock River, at Culpepper."

"Do you plan on being near the battlefield tomorrow, Miss Collins?" Kyle asked.

"Probably not. We'll remain at Manassas Junction and primarily handle the seriously wounded as they arrive from the battlefield. That is, unless the battle's worse than expected. Once we have a full train we'll transport them to my father's hospital in Charlottesville. We can handle possibly two hundred or so patients."

"And if there are more?" Kyle asked. *And for damn sure there will be more.*

"We hope not," Mary Beth said. "But if so, hospitals in Richmond and Hanover Junction are prepared for the wounded."

"There'll be less," Bee said. "I hear McDowell's troops turned and hightailed it back across Blackburn's Ford a few days ago. We had just a few casualties. I think it'll happen again tomorrow. Yanks don't have the will to fight."

Kyle noticed General Beauregard had just entered the parlor. He sauntered around, greeted some of the guests and then headed to their table.

"*Monsieur* O'Brien, I see you have found the most *belle femme* in the room." He bowed and kissed Mary Beth's hand.

"I agree, General, she is beautiful and also speaks excellent French." Kyle glanced over at Mary Beth, whose fair complexion revealed a blush.

Beauregard turned to Mrs. Collins, bowed and also kissed her hand. "I hope you take no offense that I called your daughter the most belle in the room. Since you look like her twin, it applies to both of you."

They all laughed.

During Kyle's visit to the Bull Run Battlefield in 2008, his Park Service Guide had described General Beauregard as cocky, with the social and political shrewdness of an expert, and the slapdash battle skills of a rank amateur. So far the guide had been right on target.

"General," Mrs. Collins said, "you're such a charmer . . . you could be a politician instead of a general."

Beauregard beamed and rubbed his hands. "Sometimes, madam, they intertwine."

Turning back to Kyle, Beauregard said, "Mr. O'Brien, this evening I had planned on having an interesting discussion with you regarding French war strategies. But, my plans have changed. General Joe Johnston has arrived from the Shenandoah Valley. We must meet to prepare for the battle. Regrettably, I have no time."

"I understand, General."

"Colonel Early has been impressed with your military knowledge. How did you gain all this information?"

"By reading and asking questions during my three years in Europe. Also, I was fortunate to be able to spend time with some of the French Army Officers who fought against Austria."

"Would you consider joining my staff—at least temporarily?" Beauregard asked.

"Sir, I have been away from home for almost three years. I wish to visit my family in Florida."

Beauregard scowled. "The Confederate States of America needs men dedicated to our cause. Surely you'll stay at least a few more days. That will give us a chance to have that conversation."

Kyle needed to back off. "Yes, Sir. It will be my pleasure to meet with you in a few days — after the victory." *And after I'm long gone from this place.*

"Ah, yes — victory." Beauregard beamed. "And, speaking of victory, I have battle orders to prepare." With hands clasped behind his back, he faced the ladies and bowed. "Please excuse me, ladies and gentlemen." He turned and strutted away.

Their group remained for another hour and chatted.

During one of the lulls in conversations, Kyle pulled Mary Beth aside.

"Miss Collins, I had a friend in London, who had also studied medicine. He mentioned new procedures were being developed to fight infection in wounds."

She gave him a puzzled look. "Infection, I'm not familiar with that word."

When you perform surgery on a patient and later the wound does not heal, it turns . . ."

"Ah, you mean sepsis. Yes it is a major problem in over fifty percent of our patients. Many die from sepsis. I know what you refer to. It comes from an English doctor named Lister."

"Yes, Yes. That's the name," Kyle said.

"His research was fiercely debated in one of my Paris classes. Lister suggests that if you thoroughly wash your hands and equipment before every operation, and also change gowns, you will reduce the cases of sepsis."

"Do you believe this, Miss Collins?"

"My professor in Paris, and also my father—who has been a surgeon for over twenty-five years—both adamantly disagree. They say it's caused by a virus within the wound and has nothing to do with the conditions of the room, nor of the hands. My father says the preparation time would slow down surgery and many more would die. I agree."

"My friend," Kyle said, "mentioned that Lister has experimented and found that good sanitation can save thousands of lives."

She gave him a startled look. "Thousands? There won't be that many wounded. Are you a doctor, Mr. O'Brien?"

"No – just a curious person."

"I will talk to my father."

Kyle grabbed her hand. "Please. Promise me you'll try it."

She gave him a warm smile. "I will, Sir."

What a nice girl. Kyle thought. Hopefully she makes it through this mess and does become a doctor.

Standing up, Bee stretched his arms. "I had a long train ride from the Shenandoah over the last two days and little sleep. It's time I retire. I suspect we'll have a busy day tomorrow."

He was joined by Early, who had consumed three large whiskeys, and staggered to his feet. "I'll join you, Bumble."

Bee grinned and turned to the women. "That was my nickname at West Point—Bumble Bee. I can't seem to get rid of it." He chuckled. "Would you follow a General Bumble Bee into battle?"

They all laughed. As they prepared to leave, Bee turned to Mary Beth. "It was nice meeting you, Miss Collins. Possibly I could visit your hospital in the near future . . . to see how our troops are cared for."

She gave him a big smile. "I would be honored, Sir."

"How about you, O'Brien?" Early asked, "You want to ride with us?"

"Yes Sir, if you don't mind."

They said their goodbyes and walked toward the door.

Thomas jumped up from his chair across the room and motioned Kyle over. "Could I have a word with you, Mr. O'Brien?"

"Yes, how can I help you?"

"I wanted to inform you. We have posted a guard near your quarters. As mentioned, please don't leave until you receive permission from *me* — not from Colonel Early. Have a nice evening."

"I will, sir," Kyle said. "When do you think I will be allowed to leave?"

Thomas smirked. "We shall see what tomorrow brings and then decide, sir."

The ride back to camp was peaceful and quiet. It had cooled off, with a bright moon and thousands of camp fires lighting the horizon.

Kyle kept glancing over at Bee. *I like him. He's a nice guy. We could be good friends,* Kyle thought. Tomorrow he'll yell to his men, 'There stands Jackson like a stone wall!" He'll wave that sword he has around his waist and lead his troops in a senseless charge across an open battlefield. Within seconds, he'll be shot from his horse and die, along with many of his men.

"General, do you have a family?" Kyle asked.

"No. My last posting, before I resigned my Union commission, was at Fort Laramie, in the Dakota Territory. Not many women that far west." He smiled. "But now that I'm back, I'm on the lookout."

"Bumble," Early said. "That was a lame excuse for a visit you gave Mary Beth. What did you think of her?"

Bee chuckled. "As General Beauregard said, a beautiful young lady . . . and smart. Possibly after the battle I might just head down for that visit."

I wish I could warn him, or just suggest that he not lead the charge. No, I can't do that, it would make those damn butterfly wings flap too hard.

They reached the first camp.

"This is my brigade," Bee said.

Early gave him a intent look. "Good night. My friend, you be careful out there tomorrow."

"You too, Jubal. Nice meeting you Mr. O'Brien."

Kyle took a deep breath. "And you too, Sir. As the colonel said, 'Be careful tomorrow'."

Bee waved and rode into the campsite.

They continued in silence past Bee's encampment, and then General Thomas Jackson's . . . soon, forever in time, to be called Stonewall Jackson. Early had started to nod off, but managed to hang on to the saddle.

In the far distance, beyond Bull Run, the glow of Union campfires caught Kyle's eye. They would also be preparing for battle. The Union would start its flanking action well before dawn. By tomorrow morning the attack would begin on the extreme left flank. In the far distance he could hear music playing. He could hum the tune, but didn't remember the name of the song.

Kyle decided to wake the Colonel before he fell off his horse. "Any chance the Yankees will attack tomorrow, Sir?"

Early's eyes popped open, he sat up straight and spat out a stream of tobacco juice. "That's what I was just thinking. Yes, a damn good chance. I'm surprised them Yankees haven't already attacked. But then, they got an idiot for a commander. McDowell's the best thing we got going for us." He glanced at Kyle. "How about you? Will the Yankees attack tomorrow?"

How much do I tell him? "I agree, Colonel. They will attack."

They pulled up in front of Early's encampment, and the colonel brought his horse to a halt. He looked at Kyle and frowned. "I still can't figure you out."

"Colonel, there's nothing to figure."

Early held up his hand again. "I know, a good old farm boy just trying to get home."

He took another spit and gave Kyle a hard look. "Give me time. I'll work it out. Stay close tomorrow. I don't want you disappearing on me. Good night, O'Brien."

"Good night, Colonel."

Early wheeled his horse and rode off.

Saturday, July 20, 1861
Dispatch to the NEW YORK TIMES
Reported by Henry J. Raymond

After the terrible heat of this afternoon, a cool breeze has descended upon Northern Virginia. This is one of the most beautiful nights the imagination can conceive. The sky is perfectly clear—the moon full and bright.

I have just returned from General Irvin McDowell's headquarters near Centreville. There is anxiety in the air. Tomorrow a major battle will ensue, the first and hopefully last of this conflict. During the return ride, I crested a hill and caught a view of the scene in front of me. It seemed a picture of enchantment. The bright moon cast the woods that bound the field into deep shadows, through which campfires shed a clear and brilliant glow.

The Marine Corps band has just concluded an evening concert, heard across this vast field of battle by thousands of troops -- both North and South. They played many of the favorites, including *The Girl I Left Behind*, *Annie Laurie*, and finished with *Home Sweet Home*.

Everything is quiet, save the sounds of an occasional shout or laugh from a soldier, or the lowing of the cattle, whose dark forms spot the broad meadow in the rear.

The soldiers are preparing for sleep, if that is possible. I am sure their thoughts are of home and family on the eve of this great battle.

CHAPTER

31

*K*yle left his horse in the Brigade's corral and headed for his tent. While passing the mess area he heard laughter coming from a group of soldiers sitting around a campfire. He walked up and noticed Lieutenant Squires, and Carter in the group of ten men.

"Gentlemen, sounds like you're having a good time," Kyle said.

Carter waved him over. "Join us for a drink."

Most of the men Kyle had met earlier with Carter. "Yes. Thanks for the offer." He took a seat on one of the logs placed round the fire.

Squires passed over a bottle. "Sorry 'bout the bottle . . . we're a little short on glasses."

Kyle took a big swig. It burned going down—really burned. He inhaled deeply. "Wow, that's strong stuff!"

The group laughed.

"Yes," Carter nodded. "We started with two bottles of smooth Tennessee whiskey—fine tasting stuff. We finished that real fast, and then found three more bottles of, shall we say, a less desirable, local brew, but with one hell of a kick. That bottle's all we got left. It's startin' to taste pretty damn good."

Another big laugh burst from the group. Carter's slurred speech indicated he had downed his share. The men around the fire all looked younger than Kyle, probably in their early to late twenties—three of them Lieutenants, and the rest Sergeants. He had spent many a night around a campfire in Afghanistan with marines that looked and acted just like these men. Warriors haven't changed much over the last hundred and fifty years—just the ability to kill, which had increased at least a thousand fold. Tomorrow this artillery unit would probably play a major role in the battle, and take heavy losses. Most likely some of these men will die. And, it's all for nothing,

After four years, tremendous suffering and the loss of well over a half a million men—some of these men here tonight, will hopefully go home and once again be citizens of the United States.

Squires staggered to his feet. "Gentleman, it's been a fine evening. Tomorrow we'll have a great victory for the Confederacy. I say we drink up and go get some sleep."

A cheer went up.

Kyle helped Carter to his feet.

Carter staggered "Thank you, Colonel." Immediately he realized the mistake.

Kyle quickly checked the group. No one had noticed. "Let's go to bed."

They headed toward their tent. Most of the men also headed for bed, with the exception of a few who stayed to finish off the bottle.

"I'm sorry about that . . . Kyle. I guess I'm a little drunk."

"You're way beyond a little, but no harm done, no one noticed. From now on remember, it's Kyle—no more colonel."

"You got it. How did the evening go with the big brass?" Carter asked.

"The food was great." Kyle reached into his pocket and pulled out a large slice of ham and a roll wrapped in a napkin. "I managed to slip this out for you. Sorry it's all I could manage."

Carter took the food in both hands and starred in amazement. "Oh man, this is fantastic." He took a big bite.

I briefly met General Beauregard, " Kyle said as they continued walking. "He wants to meet me again in a few days."

"We'll hopefully be long gone by then." Carter mumbled with his mouth full.

"I agree. I did meet an unpleasant little guy who's just joined the Confederacy. He seems to be in charge of finding spies. He suspects something and has assigned someone to guard us . . . just one more reason to get the hell out of here after the battle."

They reached the tent and Kyle checked around. "I don't see a guard anywhere."

They went in and sat down on the cots.

Stretching out, Carter put his hands behind his head. "My heads spinning, that's some potent stuff." He closed his eyes, but kept talking. "That's a damn good group of guys out there. Hell, I could have been talking to a group of SEALs. Damn funny isn't?" He snickered. "Hard to believe they're all over a hundred and seventy years old. None of em' looked a day over a hundred." He let out a little snort.

Kyle peeked outside the tent. No one was eavesdropping.

"I feel so sorry for them," Carter said. "They don't have a clue what they're in for."

With his eyes closed Kyle tried to sleep. We have to get out of here by tomorrow, before they either throw us in prison, or draft us into the Confederate Army. Those scientists should have figured out what the hell the problem is by now. Probably they've informed the Defense Secretary and the President. That takes it out of the hands of the CIA and should kick this thing into high gear.

"You know," Kyle said. "I should be at a country club in Atlanta right now. In my dress blues, dancing with a pretty girl and having a great time. I'll bet she's really upset—and her father's really pissed."

Carter didn't respond. Kyle glanced over, he lay fast asleep and snoring.

It's now the fourth day. The day they said we would probably be transported back. I'm going to sleep. When I wake up we'll be back in the warehouse.

CHAPTER

32

Stan slumped at his desk in the Quantico warehouse and took a sip from the mug. Coffee, donuts and cheese sandwiches had sustained him for the last three days. Each afternoon he had the dreaded task of calling the CIA Director. Stan would give him the same old story—we're working hard, we had problems transporting the chimp back more than fifteen years, and the engineers are working hard to resolve the problem.

Doctor Chao had left for the Fermi Labs early this morning to try to kick the software guys in the butt, but as of two hours ago, still no luck. Stan checked his watch and sighed, six o'clock—time to call.

He headed back into his room and the secure telephone.

The Director of the CIA answered on the first ring. "Hello, Stan. What have you got for me."

"Nothing new, sir. We still can't get the chimp past fifteen years." He knew what the next question would be.

"What's wrong with those guys? Tell them to get off their asses and make it happen!"

"Chao flew back to Chicago and the lab this morning to see if he could find an answer, but nothing yet." Again Stan knew the next line.

"I've got to call the God damn Secretary of Defense and the President. What am I supposed to tell them?"

After a deep breath, Stan answered. "Tell them we're covering new ground. It's going to take time, Sir."

"That's the same fucking thing you told me yesterday."

Stan took another deep breath. *Well, just maybe because you asked me the same question every time, asshole.* "I know, Sir. I'll get back to you as soon as we have an answer."

"Stan, I think it's time we cut our losses. Do you know what I mean?"

This sounded new. "No, Sir. I don't know what you mean."

"I mean it's time to move on with the Hindsight Project. We've got three CIA agents all set over in Iran. If the mission needs five men, as you've recommended, then get two new men moving ASAP. We've got to have a mission leader and explosives expert somewhere in our operations. What do you say?"

Stan had never considered dumping Kyle and Carter. "What do you think the Secretary of Defense will think of that idea, Sir?"

There was silence on the phone for a moment. "Start looking for two CIA agents to fill their spots on the mission. When it's time I'll inform Secretary Evans. Now get moving."

Stan put down the phone and stared at the wall. *Well I'll be damned. Am I just a pawn in this game? Did the CIA intentionally dump those men back in time?*

CHAPTER

33

*G*eneral Daniel Tyler stood up in the stirrups of his saddle and swept his arm forward. "Come on men, pull, pull."

A loud groan swelled from over a hundred men, who along with ten horses, strained on the ropes attached to the carriage. The wheels mounted to the gigantic six thousand pound, rifled cannon, creaked as they inched up the steep embankment of Cub Run.

Tyler charged up and down the line bellowing, "Keep pulling! The entire Union Army is relying on you. Don't let them down!"

Finally, a cheer erupted as the cannon reached the crest and rolled onto the road.

Glancing to the East, Tyler noticed pale pink stripes low on the horizon. Dawn would greet them shortly. He pulled out his pocket watch and flipped it open. In the dim light he could just make out the time . . . almost five o'clock. *Damn, this third-rate little bridge has cost me over an hour of valuable time.*

A major from McDowell's staff galloped up beside him. "Sir, General McDowell requests that you keep moving. We are hours behind schedule."

With a harsh look, Tyler yelled. "You go tell the General I am moving as fast as possible on this damn goat path of a road he selected. Inform the General I'm making a temporary headquarters at the blacksmith's shop near the Sudley turnoff. I need to talk to him as soon as possible."

"General McDowell is not feeling well, Sir. He ate something that has disagreed with him."

"He's not feeling well. This is the most important battle since the Revolutionary War, and he's got an upset tummy. Tell the general he is needed for a major decision!"

The major hesitated. "You wish me to repeat all of that to your Commander, Sir?"

"Yes, and get moving!"

After a snappy salute, the major spun his horse around and galloped away.

It had been a hellish night for Tyler. He rousted his men awake at two o'clock. Due to darkness and the confusion of his inexperienced troops, it had taken an hour to form the march. The skirmishers advancing ahead of his troops had also caused numerous delays. And, now this damn little creek and bridge—no one had warned him about that.

The army's flanking action required the element of surprise; Hunter's Division must arrive at Sudley Ford before full light. That would no longer be possible. Hunter had at least another two to three hours of hard marching ahead of him.

I told that idiot, McDowell, that Sudley Ford was too far. We still have time to change. Now maybe he'll agree to move across at the Stone Bridge.

An aide greeted Tyler as he approached the blacksmith shop. "General, the skirmishers have encountered rebel cavalry in front of the Stone Bridge. General Schenck has stopped his advance to reconnoiter the situation."

Tyler climbed off his horse and sighed. "If we halt every time the rebs fire at us, it'll take days to reach Manassas Junction. Tell Schenck to keep moving, he is backed by an army of thirty thousand men. Don't let a few rebs stop him."

Two officers joined Tyler at a small table setup on the porch of the shop.

"Would you like some coffee, General?"

"Yes please. It's been a bad morning. Coffee will help."

As the coffee arrived, Colonel William T. Sherman rode up to the porch and dismounted. He brushed the dust off his uniform and approached Tyler. "General, good morning. My brigade is moving into place above the bridge. This should be completed by six o'clock. We await your orders, sir."

Tyler took a sip of coffee. "That's the first good news I've had all morning. Would you care for coffee?"

"No Sir." Sherman held up an unlit, half-smoked cigar. "But, I will light one of these." He lit the stub and blew out a stream of smoke. "Ah, that tastes good. General, I've just returned from that ford you mentioned yesterday. As I arrived two Confederate cavalrymen crossed Bull Run right in front of me. To my amazement there are no troops on guard along the other side. With artillery protection and surprise I think we could cross that ford, rush the bridge and capture it intact."

"I agree," Tyler said. "Hopefully, our commander will be here before long and I can show him what we have found. I will do everything I can to convince him. In the meantime I want you to do as McDowell has ordered. We will approach the Stone Bridge and feint an attack."

Popping his watch open, Tyler said, "It is now five-thirty. That monstrosity of a cannon will be in place by six o'clock. At that time I will fire three rounds, as ordered, and signal the start of the first, and hopefully the last battle of this war. You may see action this morning. I'll notify you as soon as I hear from McDowell."

Sherman headed back to his troops and Tyler remained on the porch, watching Hunter's division trail past, heading for Sudley Springs.

Minutes later, Tyler spotted a group of three mounted horseman approaching, he recognized the large bulk of General McDowell on one of the horses. He stood up and walked to the edge of the porch.

McDowell, the major that Tyler had talked to earlier, and a captain rode up to the porch. McDowell appeared gray and in pain.

"Good morning, General," Tyler said. "I hope you're feeling better."

McDowell ignored the comment. "What are you doing here? You should be with your troops."

"My division is now in position and ready for action," Tyler said. "Colonel Sherman has just reported that the Stone Bridge is not heavily guarded this morning. Possibly we could ride down to the bridge so I can show you an alternate battle plan."

McDowell held his stomach and a look of pain crossed his face. "Tyler you should see the confusion and chaos of both Hunter's and Heintzelman's troops. It extends for miles behind us. This is your fault. You should have cleared the turnpike by four this morning. You will be held responsible for this. Your orders remain the same as last night. You will fire the cannon at six this morning and will continue artillery fire for the next few hours to feint an attack across the bridge. This will distract the enemy and allow us to flank him. Those are your orders and your only orders."

Wheeling his horse around, McDowell galloped off.

The major Tyler had spoken to earlier, gave him a sneer. "As you can tell, I passed along your message. Good day, Sir." He gave an indifferent salute and rode away.

The aide to Tyler walked over to him. "Sir, I think you just pissed off the General."

Heading for his horse, Tyler stopped and turned. "I don't give a shit, but we'll follow his orders. Mount up, we're going to the hill above the Stone Bridge and fake an attack. Then let's hope our troops at Sudley are not too exhausted to fight."

General Tyler and Lieutenant Peter C. Hains stood beside the Parrott cannon. It had been loaded with a thirty pound projectile capable of traveling up to almost 4 miles. They targeted a large white house on a hill over three miles away. Hopefully they might catch some important rebel commander sleeping in.

Hains glanced back at him. "Are we ready to fire, Sir?"

Tyler took a final check of his watch. Ten minutes after six, it didn't matter that he was ten minutes late. The person he was signaling, General Hunter, was still hours behind. The planned 0600 surprise crossing at Sudley Spring would not happen until at least 0930. He had been ordered to fire three rounds as a signal, and that he would do.

"Fire three rounds at will!" Tyler yelled.

A loud boom echoed across the battleground. Once the three rounds were fired, the remaining artillery would start their bombardment.

The first major battle of the Civil War had begun.

CHAPTER

34

*OOOOM.*

A deep rumble reverberated across the camp.

Kyle jolted awake. *Damn, we're still here.*

The first echo had just cleared, when the second roared through.

BOOOOM.

Carter lifted his legs over the side of the cot and rubbed sleep out of his eyes. "My head is killing me."

Kyle checked the time, 0612. "I think the battle's starting early."

BOOOOM.

"That a big cannon firing," Carter said. "It must be coming from the Union side."

Immediately following the third blast, a cascade of smaller cannons sounded all along the Union line, some only a few miles away. Shouts and chatter rose from around their tent.

"Time to get moving." Kyle stood and grabbed his trousers. "Sleep's out of the question. If I remember right, the battle starts over by Sudley Springs. That's got to be seven or eight miles away. Things don't start to heat up until about ten."

Carter rubbed his forehead with both hands. "That noise is not helping my head."

"No shit," Kyle said. "Last night you consumed some of the worst tasting booze I've ever come across. What's worse, you declared it tasted 'damn good.'"

Carter curled back on the cot. "Well I'm paying for it now."

"Come on. Rise and shine. They'll probably be moving the army out soon."

Carter sighed and swung his feet back to the ground. "We're staying with Early's Brigade?"

"Damned if I know. I wish I remembered more about the battle. I know this brigade plays a major role by making a forced march for Henry Hill around noon. But, I don't know what they do this morning." Kyle slipped into his shoes. "Let's go grab some coffee."

Carter stood up, moaned, and immediately collapsed back on the cot. "I need some food in my stomach."

Kyle moved out of the tent and spotted, despite all the cannon fire, a man asleep on the ground next to them. He wore a ragged, dirty white shirt and ripped dark grey trousers. Next to him lay a wide-brimmed grey hat and a leather belt, with bayonet and cartridge box attached. His right arm loosely held a smoothbore musket.

Kyle's instincts kicked in. He bent down, grabbed the musket, and hit the soldier's foot. "Wake up. Are you our guard?"

The soldier lurched up, gave him a shocked look, and jumped to his feet. He gaped at the musket Kyle held in both hands.

"Yes Sir. Private Samuel Jones, Sir."

"How long were you asleep?"

The private rubbed his eyes. "Don't rightly know. We just got off the train from Richmond late yesterday. I was real tired from all the marchin' and stuff. Figured I could guard this here tent sittin' down . . . must've dozed off. Are you an officer?"

The boy, in his mid-to-late teens, had long, brown, tangled hair. His attempt at growing a beard had proven unsuccessful, with scraggly patches of fuzz and hair on his youthful face.

Kyle handed his musket back. "No. Fortunately for you I'm a civilian, or you'd be in big trouble. Don't ever let anyone take your weapon."

"Yes, Sir." He held the musket in his left hand and gave an awkward salute with his right. "I won't let it happen again."

"You don't have to salute or call me sir. Is someone supposed to relieve you?"

He slowly shook his head. "I don't rightly know, Sir."

Carter came out of the tent. "Let's get some food before I die." He looked over at the private. "What's with him?"

"He's been assigned to guard us. I guess we'll let him do his job." Kyle turned to the private. "How long have you been in the army?"

"Bout a month, Sir."

"Let's go get something to eat, and remember, *don't call me sir.*"

They turned and headed for the mess tent with the private trailing behind. The camp hummed with activity. Troops rushed about, with officers shouting orders and rousting the men awake. Some of the men had small pup tents, but most slept on the ground, with only a blanket and ground cloth for cover.

Mounted on his horse, Squires rushed up, halted and shouted at his men. "Get moving. We got a battle to fight. Let's go!" He glanced down at Carter and smiled. "You look horrible."

Carter glumly nodded. "I feel much worse than that. Can we talk you out of a cup of coffee and some food?"

"Sure. I was just informed we're mounting up. Looks like we're getting ready to cross Bull Run and attack."

Carter reached up and shook Squires hand. "You be careful and keep your head down."

"Thank you. I think we'll kick some Yankee ass."

Squires turned, yelled at one of the soldiers, and rode out of camp.

The three of them moved into the mess tent. Squire's slave, Jacob, stood at the table. "I was about to close the kitchen. We still got Johnnie cake, coffee, and a little bit of bacon left."

They sat down at a table and Jacob brought over what looked like corn meal fried in a pan of bacon grease, a slab of salted bacon and coffee.

The private devoured the corn meal and bacon in seconds, and then glanced across the tent at Jacob.

Jacob smiled. "Would you like some more?"

"I ain't ate much in the last few days." He smiled. "Sure was good. My Mama serves this for breakfast every morning, cept with some molasses on top."

"Where are you from?" Jacob brought over a second helping and set it on the table.

"Near Hattiesburg, Mississippi. It's just called Jones Corner. Only bout eight homes there and everybody's named Jones." The private took a bite of the thick, chewy bacon. "I joined the army with my cousin, Billy Ray Jones. He's also my best friend."

As they ate, Edwards rode up and dismounted. "That coffee smells good. Mind if I join you?"

"Not at all. Good morning, Captain," Kyle said. "Sounds like the warm up for battle has started."

"You're right, Mr. O'Brien. I just notified all the battalion commanders to join Colonel Early for a meeting. We're going to back up General Longstreet's and General Jones' Brigades. We'll rush in at either Mitchell's or Blackburn's Fords if needed. The attack should start soon."

"What's Colonel Early think about those orders?" Kyle asked.

Frowning, Edwards took a gulp of coffee. "He's pissed. He wanted to lead the attack. Figures he's been left out. I'm waiting for him to calm down before I go back. That man's got a mean temper—and a foul mouth."

"What are we supposed to do?"

"Last I heard, the Colonel said for you to stay close. Quite frankly, I don't think anyone's worried about you, except for that Pinkerton man. We got a battle about to start." He looked over at the private, who had just gulped down his second helping. "Who's this?"

"This is Private Jones. He's guarding us," Carter said.

"Oh yeah, the Colonel told me the Pinkerton guy assigned you a guard." Edwards looked over at the private. "What outfit are you with?"

The private bolted to his feet and stood rigidly at attention. "The 13th Mississippi, Sir."

"I never heard of the 13th Mississippi," Edwards said.

With a nervous quiver in his voice, the private answered. "The Battalion just formed up bout two months ago, Sir. We got to Richmond five days ago, and we been marchin' and train riddin' to get here for the last two."

"You're not attached to Early's Brigade?"

"I don't rightly know, sir. Last night my Sergeant marched me over here and said to guard that tent over yonder."

Bouncing up, Edwards took a hurried final sip. "I've got to get back." He gave the private a quick glance. "You can send him back to his unit. We're going to need every man for this fight." He headed for his horse and glanced back. "By the way, the army's posted guards all around the area to keep soldiers from deserting during the battle. Don't stray far. I would stay close to Early's Brigade till the battle's over. "

"Thanks for the information." Kyle turned to the private. "You hear that. You've been ordered back to your unit."

Private Jones stood up. "Thank you. Sorry 'bout goin' to sleep last night."

Jacob came over with two cakes wrapped in paper and handed them to the private. "You take these Johnny cakes to your cousin."

The private put them in the cloth haversack hanging off his shoulder. "Thank you. They sure were good." He gave them a quick smile, put on the wide-brimmed slouch hat, picked up his musket and headed for the door.

They watched him go. Jacob shook his head. "Lord have mercy on that poor boy. He's too young for all this war stuff."

"You're right." Kyle said.

"Well, you heard Edwards," Carter said. "They've got guards posted around the perimeter. We're stuck here until the fighting's over."

In the distance, artillery fire started up. "That's close," Carter said. "It could be Squire's Battery. Let's head over there. It would be interesting to watch an artillery unit in action."

Kyle nodded. "It looks like they're up on the bluffs and out of the line of fire."

As they moved onto the road, Carter checked the sky. "Not a cloud in sight and no breeze. It's going to be a scorcher today."

"Yeah, one thing that hasn't changed in a hundred and fifty years — summers in Virginia are hot as hell."

Over the last four days, tens of thousands of shoes, hoofs and wagon wheels had pulverized the dirt on the road into dust. A reddish gray haze rose high above the road, covering them in a fine powder. It entered Kyle's nostrils and mouth with every breath.

Troops on horseback from Longstreet's Brigade rushed past them, kicking up even more dust. All were headed for the anticipated battle at Blackburn's Ford. The men, in good spirits, yelled and joked with one another as they rode past.

Kyle glanced at Carter. He resembled an old man, his black hair covered in a fine coat of grey. "Let's get off this road before we suffocate."

They headed into a cornfield and toward the battery firing from the ridge top about a quarter-mile away. The going was difficult, but better than inhaling dust.

As they crested the bluff, Squires rode over to greet them. All six of his cannons were in a line off to the side of the road, and aimed across Bull Run.

Squires waved. "Glad you could make it. You just missed some excitement. We chased off a Yankee artillery company. I guess they got tired of eatin' our cannonballs." He pointed to the two cannons next to him. "We're firing these Napoleon twelve pounders into those woods across Bull Run. That's where those yanks hightailed it. "

They watched as the teams loaded and fired the cannons. Every man had an assignment. After firing, the twelve pound cannonball exploded from the barrel in a large cloud of blinding white smoke, and a loud boom. The two-wheeled gun carriage violently recoiled back about five feet. Three men then rushed forward and struggled to haul the heavy piece back into position. Once repositioned, two men worked on the cannon simultaneously. One cleaned out the firing vent and then placed a gloved thumb over the vent to insure no air entered the chamber. A second man rammed a cork screw rod into the bore, removed any debris left from the firing, and then repeated the action, this time with a damp sponge pole.

Meanwhile, the sergeant determined the range and type of round to be fired, and yelled back instructions to a man standing at the ammunition chests about twenty-five feet behind the cannon.

As the man rushed forward with a ball and bag of powder, a corporal adjusted the sight and aimed the gun. With the gun powder and ball safely in the muzzle, a man would insert the primer and lanyard into the vent and yell "Ready to Fire." The sergeant would make a quick visual check, to insure all eight members were clear of the piece, and yell "fire."

Kyle timed the operation. It took a little less than a minute to complete. With all six cannons firing at will, he wondered how the sergeant managed to see through the smoke and direct the firing.

Below them the slope trailed about a mile down to Bull Run, with both Blackburn's and then Mitchell's Ford off in the distance. Confederate troops had lined up on the Southern side of both fords. Men from the lead companies had started wading across.

"That's Longstreet's Brigade crossing down below." Squires pointed to Mitchell's Ford. "Looks like he's going across without any resistance. Hell, this battle could be over before noon."

Kyle remembered some of the details of the battle. Both armies had planned a flanking attack, which would start this morning. The Union Army would launch a surprise attack around their right flank. The Confederates had also planned a flanking attack, around their own right flank. Both armies would attack at opposite ends of the battlefront, at roughly the same time. Due to miscommunication on the part of General Beauregard both generals leading the attack—Longstreet and Jones, would never receive the order to advance beyond the run.

"Tell me what's going on?" Carter whispered. "I thought you said the battle will be fought in the Henry Hill area."

"You're right," Kyle said. "Some of the first sounds of the Union attack should be coming from near Sudley Springs, about nine miles upstream from here." He checked his watch. "It's 0930. We should hear the cannons any time now. This will cause General Beauregard to drop his attack plan, and start rushing troops to Henry Hill."

"What happens to Longstreet and Squires?"

"Longstreet sets up a perimeter on the other side of the run, and pretty much sits on his ass for the rest of the day. I have no idea what happens to Squires. He might do the same."

The Union artillery that had retreated into the woods rushed out one cannon and fired. Kyle easily spotted the location by the grey smoke rising above the pine trees.

The cannon ball hurtled above the smoke and in their direction. It landed thirty feet away and took two skips across the hill top. The twelve pound ball slammed into one of the artillery horses that had been tethered behind the troops. The ball cleanly decapitated a horse, which immediately dropped to the ground. The ball continued another twenty feet before coming to a halt.

"Let's get the hell out of here before that happens to us," Kyle yelled.

They ran down the back side of the hill. Once out of firing range they stopped and caught their breath.

"So much for being out of the action," Carter said, "that must have been a misfire. It never exploded, but still was a deadly weapon."

Kyle pointed in the direction they had just traveled. "Let's go back to Early's Brigade. At least they know who we are and won't think we're deserters or spies."

They headed down the hill. About halfway back, the sound of cannon and musket fire came roaring in from the west.

Kyle stopped and listened. "I'd say the battle of Bull Run has finally started."

It took thirty minutes to reach the edge of Early's encampment. As they did a battery of artillery galloped past. Both Kyle and Carter put their arms up to their faces to keep the dust out of their eyes and mouth.

Kyle heard a voice and looked up through the dust.

Squires sat on his horse looking down at him. "Do you want to join us? We can squeeze both of you up on horses."

"Where are you headed?" Carter shouted.

"We've been reassigned. We were told to head towards the cannon fire and to search for General Jackson. The Yankee's are attacking on our flank and he'll tell us where to set up."

"We've been instructed to stay with Colonel Early," Carter said.

Squires tipped his hat. "We'll see yall this evening and celebrate the victory." He smiled. "I've still got a bottle of that local whiskey stashed away."

He turned his horse and galloped off.

"With Jackson he'll be in the thick of the battle," Kyle said. "I hope he makes it through the day."

I hope we make it through the day." Carter noted the time. "In a few hours we'll be into our fifth day. That's not good news."

"I don'know what that means for us. But, whatever happens it will be a hell of interesting afternoon."

CHAPTER

35

"**What do you see?**" General Daniel Tyler yelled.

The sergeant, twenty-five feet up a pine tree, yelled down. "Not much, General. The bridge is empty. There is a battery of four cannons located on a rise a quarter of a mile back from the bridge. They are supported by maybe a company of men. Off in the distance I can see smoke and rebel troops rushing in that direction. It looks like the battle is no more than maybe a mile away."

Tyler paced back and forth with his hands behind his back. He had sent the man up the tree at about 1015, when he had first heard the sound of muskets and cannon firing. Now over an hour later he feared the attack had stalled out.

"Damn it." Tyler turned to Colonel Sherman standing next to him. "I have no idea what's happening. We've sat on our asses for four hours waiting for orders—not one message from McDowell—nothing."

"I could have been across hours ago, sir." Sherman shrugged his shoulders. "That ford we found upstream from the bridge is still not guarded."

"You heard McDowell at the meeting. My orders are to feint an attack. Crossing over the run was how I got into trouble three days ago at Blackburn's Ford."

Both men looked up to see a horseman galloping toward them.

"Well I'll be damned. It looks like Lieutenant Kingsbury from McDowell's staff." Tyler said.

The Lieutenant charged up and saluted. "Sir, I bring orders from General McDowell."

"It's about time." Tyler ignored the salute. "What's happening on the other side of the run?"

The Lieutenant climbed down off his horse. "I don't know, sir. General McDowell's headquarters is near Sudley Ford and the fighting is further in from the run. The General told me to inform you to press the attack, sir."

"Press the attack." Tyler held up both hands. "What the hell does that mean? My original orders were to cross Bull Run when General Hunter had cleared the enemy from the other side." Tyler pointed to the man up the tree. "That man just informed me the enemy is still there and there's no sign of any Union troops."

"Sir, I gave you the message exactly as it was given to me. *General McDowell said*, 'Order General Tyler to press the attack.'"

Tyler shook his head. "He gave me very explicit, detailed orders yesterday on how not to attack. And now he gives me some vague order . . . press the attack. How the hell do I interpret it? Does it mean to attack with all four of my Brigades? Where am I to attack? I don't even know where the enemy is."

Sherman stepped forward. "Sir, why don't I push my regiment across at that ford and move forward to determine our situation?"

"Good idea," Tyler said. "We should have done that three hours ago." He turned to the Lieutenant. "Kingsbury, you ride like hell, find McDowell and tell him I interpret his order to mean moving Sherman's Third Brigade across and secure the Stonebridge. Then the brigade will advance forward to hook up with General Hunter's Division. I will remain here with the other two brigades until I receive *clear instructions* from McDowell. Repeat that back to me."

The lieutenant repeated it word for word, including the emphasis on clear instructions. He mounted his horse.

Tyler slapped the horse's backside. "Get moving."

CHAPTER

36

*T*he secure cellphone rang on the night stand next to Stan Jackson's bed. He grabbed it immediately. After a quick glance at his still sleeping wife, he raced into the bathroom and gently closed the door. "Hello, this is Stan."

"Stan, it's Evan Chao. We found your men!"

Stan let out a big sigh. "That's fantastic. Are they OK?"

"We don't know, this is only the first step. Elvis came through like a real champ." Chao chuckled. "I guess you could say, like a chimp champ. When we sent him back to 1861, a hundred and fifty years ago, he turned on the transponder tracking device, and bingo — we got a hit."

"From both of them?" Stan asked.

"Yes, two transponders. They are together and about twenty miles away from Quantico, near Manassas, Virginia. But let me caution you, I don't know if they are alive. We are only tracking the transponders. The units could have been removed from their arms. But it's showing them moving around, so someone or something has possession of the transponders."

Stan thought a moment. "Well, at least they aren't freezing their asses off in the Ice Age or being eaten by a T-Rex. They shouldn't have many problems going back a mere hundred and fifty years."

Chao hesitated. "I hope you're right. It would be difficult for someone to take off the transponders. So, we have to assume that they are still wearing them."

"Yeah, I agree," Stan said. "Then the only question is—when do we pull them out?"

"Let me think this through." Chao waited a moment. "It will take at least eight hours to recalibrate the equipment, and then maybe another two hours to test it out. Meanwhile, we start searching for a convenient wormhole."

"How long does it take to find one of those holes?"

"I don't know. We've never done this before. Maybe another twelve hours."

"Damn, get moving," Stan said, "that means midnight tomorrow."

"Slow down, slow down," Chao said. "Once we find the perfect wormhole, you'll be the first to know."

CHAPTER

37

*K*yle and Carter arrived back at the 6ᵗʰ Brigade to the rumbles of cannon fire in the distance. Most of the troops were sprawled on the ground in the scorching sunshine. Kyle noted the time—1230 hours. He remembered reading that Early would receive his marching orders about now. It should take the regiment at least three hours or more to march the eight miles to Henry Hill.

Up ahead, Kyle spotted Captain Edwards riding into camp. Maybe he had the marching orders with him.

Kyle waved Edwards over. "Captain, I'm surprised your brigade is still here. I figured from the sounds of battle, you'd be moving west."

Edwards nodded. "I agree. But we haven't received any orders. We've spent most of the morning marching down to Bull Run, and then back up again. I just returned from General Longstreet's headquarters. He hasn't received orders to advance on Centreville, nor to head further west. It's been hours since anyone's heard from General Beauregard."

"What does Colonel Early think?"

"He's pissed. He wanted to be in the middle of this battle, and from the sounds, it's started without him. If I were you I'd stay away from headquarters."

Edwards rode away and Kyle glanced at Carter. "This is not going the way it's supposed to. General Beauregard should have ordered the 6th Brigade to Henry Hill by now."

Carter gave him a concerned look. "You sure about that? Possibly the brigade doesn't go to Henry Hill."

"They have to go there. Without Early's support of about 1,500 men, who show up at exactly the right time and place, the Union forces will probably turn the Confederate's left flank. That could change this whole battle. The Union might win."

"What do we do?" Carter grinned. "Do we go tell Early we know what's going to happen —get off his ass and go make history?"

Kyle nodded. "You're being facetious, but you might be right. Who the hell knows, maybe *we're a part* of this history."

"What do you mean? We tell Early what to do?"

"That's right. We could be the reason Early shows up just in time and at the right place."

"I don't know about this," Carter said, "all this time you've been talking about not messing with history—now we step in and change the course of a major battle. What happened to all that butterfly wing bullshit?"

"I know this much," Kyle said. "If Early doesn't move fast, the South will probably lose this battle. Then who knows what happens. Maybe history gets all screwed up." Kyle gave it some thought, and checked the time. "We give Early another fifteen minutes to get moving. If he doesn't — I tell him."

"Now I'm not being facetious," Carter said. "How do you tell him? You'll sound like a complete whacko."

"I'm not sure. He suspects something is different about me. I guess I play off that."

They waited fifteen minutes and then walked to Brigade headquarters. Kyle spotted Early sitting under a large canvas covering eating lunch by himself, with his large tin cup in hand. Yesterday, Early had loaded that cup with whiskey— and probably now as well.

As they approached, Captain Edwards spotted Kyle and rushed over. "This is not a good time for a visit. I've never seen the Colonel so upset. He thinks we've probably lost the battle."

"Captain, it's not a social visit. I have some important information for the Colonel. I need to talk to him immediately. It could save this battle."

"All right, but don't say I didn't warn you. I'll go tell him you're here."

Edwards headed over to Early, then turned and motioned Kyle over.

"It's not too late," Carter suggested, "we can still walk away."

Kyle ignored Carter and headed for Early. As he approached, Early scowled and took a big sip from the cup.

"O'Brien, you picked a shitty time for a visit. I'm in no mood for casual chitchat. Speak your mind and get the hell out of here before I shoot you."

"Yes sir. This is important or I wouldn't be here. I have information that requires you to act fast, to leave now for Henry Hill. If you do, you will save this battle."

Early took another sip from the cup. "How did you come by this *important* information?"

"I can't tell you, sir."

For a few seconds Early stared at him, and then jumped to his feet. "You think I'm a fucking idiot? I'm going to send my troops charging into battle on your orders? Who the hell do you think you are?"

"Colonel, call it intuition, call it the ability to predict the future. I don't care what it's called. *I know* it is your destiny to play a major role in this battle. And, I'll stake my life on it. Hold me and my friend as prisoners. If I'm wrong you can shoot me."

"Hell, I'll hang both of you and watch you squirm before you die." Early reached over, grabbed a map, and slammed it on the table. "This better not be bullshit." He unrolled the map. "Show me."

After studying the map for a moment, Kyle pointed to Henry Hill. "This is where General Jackson is right now and he desperately needs your help."

"Is this where the firing's coming from?"

"Yes, sir."

Early studied the map. "In this heat it will take at least three hours to get there. The battle will be over."

"Not if we leave immediately and move fast. The battle will rage back and forth for the next three hours." Kyle pointed to the map. "At about 1600, Colonel Oliver Howard's brigade will be ordered to slip in behind Chinn Ridge."

"How do you know Howard?"

"I don't know him, but I know he will be making a move around the Confederate left flank. If you aren't there in time he'll probably be successful."

"I know Howard. He's a damn fine soldier, even if he is a Yankee. I heard he was leading a brigade against us." Early rubbed his chin and studied the map. "If I line up right here," he pointed to small hill next to Chinn Ridge, "I can move in undetected, catch him by surprise and roll up *his flank*."

"That's right, Sir. You'll have the entire Union army flanked."

For a few moments Early studied him, and then pointed his finger at Kyle. "If you're lying to me—you're a dead man."

"I know that."

"Yeah, I forgot. You're a fucking fortune teller." After a quick sip from his cup, Early slammed it down on the table. Whiskey spilled over the map. "Let's do it! I've been waiting all day to kick some Yankee ass."

Early rushed out from under the canvas and yelled for Captain Edwards. "Captain, I want four of your best men as guards on these two men. If they try to escape, shoot to kill."

It took half-an-hour to round up the troops and start the march. Kyle discreetly checked his watch—at least thirty minutes late.

Can they make it? I'm not sure.

The guards threw Kyle and Carter in a wagon with their hands tied.

Early rode up to the wagon and look down at them. "If you're right about this battle, I promise I'll make it up to you. If you're wrong—we're both in deep shit." He turned and rode away.

After a few minutes, Carter spoke up. "Have you considered we might be wrong?"

Kyle gave him a hard look. "That is no longer an option."

CHAPTER

38

*K*yle checked his watch — 1500 hours. They still had an hour to go. The hot, humid afternoon sun blazed down. It had to be at least ninety degrees on the narrow dirt road.

Over the last eight hours some 10,000 Confederate troops, plus thousands of horses and wagons had plodded along Sudley Road. A fine pulverized dust rose high above Early's 6th Brigade. It penetrated the eyes, ears, noses and, most importantly, the mouths and throats of every soldier.

The water from farm wells along the way had long ago dried up. An hour earlier the brigade had crossed a small brook. Frantic for water, the men made a wild dash for the stream, but by this time only muddy puddles remained. The more desperate fell to the ground and drank from the filthy, brown pools. Within minutes even that foul water had disappeared.

The previous troops had ignored the blackberry bushes bordering the road. Now Early's men constantly broke ranks to strip the bushes of berries and provide some relief for their thirst. The berry raiders could be easily identified by their teeth and lips — all stained a dark blue.

Even under a layer of dust, Carter's face shone a bright red. His lips were parched and cracked. Four of the troopers who were unconscious from heat exhaustion now shared their wagon.

Carter gave Kyle a glance. "How are you holding up?"

Kyle licked his bone dry lips. He attempted to spit the grit out of his mouth—but no moisture remained. "My mouth feels like it's full of cotton, my head hurts like hell, and this wagon's only making everything worse."

"Remember," Carter said, "Two days ago you were in the hospital with a concussion. No wonder your head's pounding. You need R&R, not a hot, bumpy wagon ride."

"Yeah, tell me about it." Kyle brushed the fresh scab on his forehead. "It's now Sunday afternoon and I'm supposed to be in Atlanta playing golf with my prospective father-in-law. How's that for R&R, sitting in a golf cart on a lush, green golf course, with a cold beer in my hand?"

In the distance, the rumbles of massive nonstop artillery fire filled the air. The Henry Hill battle still raged.

Kyle checked his watch again. "Now, back to reality. This was a bad idea. We're way behind schedule. I don't think we're going to make it to the battle by 1600."

Out front, Colonel Early galloped up and down the formation, pushing the troops hard, many of them exhausted and collapsing beside the road. Some of the men refused to move, while others continued marching but couldn't maintain the steady pace. A long line of stragglers followed the column.

The officers on horseback spent all their time shouting at the men to stay in formation and *keep moving*.

Once, while riding through the bushes to herd the berry eaters into ranks, an officer knocked over a wasp nest. It caused a ten minute halt while troops scattered in all directions and hundreds of hot, enraged wasps buzzed to the attack.

Confederate soldiers fleeing the battlefield started appearing on the road, many with bloody wounds, others with no visible injuries, only blank, dejected stares. This didn't help the spirits of Early's men, most of them marching into battle for the first time.

Captain Edwards appeared out of the haze and trotted up beside Kyle's wagon. "Not much farther now. Colonel Early just met with General Johnston's aide. We're heading for the left flank of our line, right where you said we should go."

"How are your men holding up?' Kyle asked.

"This forced march has cost us at least three hundred men. But we've still got well over a thousand ready to fight. We should be there in less than half an hour."

Carter glanced at Kyle. "That should make you feel better."

"Yeah, it does." Kyle closed his eyes. Despite the thirst, heat, and a pounding head, he dropped off to sleep.

"O'Brien, get up."

Kyle jerked awake.

Early sat on his horse, smoking a cigar and smiling down at him. "We're about exactly where you predicted, just off Sudley Road, with Chinn ridge in front of us. I've got Jeb Stuart's Cavalry on our left, and the 4th Brigade on my right. I thought you might like to get off your ass and watch the charge?"

"You bet I would." Kyle held up both hands and beamed. "Hard to enjoy the moment if you're tied up."

Carter stood beside the wagon with his hands already untied. A soldier untied Kyle and he climbed down. "I'm no longer under arrest?"

"I got a ton of questions about these *intuitions* of yours," Early said, "But that can wait until later."

Early handed him an eye glass. "You might want to watch our attack. I spotted Howard's Brigade on the ridge. You called it correctly."

Kyle held the glass piece up to his eye. Less than a mile away, a long, disciplined line of probably a thousand blue-uni-formed Union soldiers extended across the field. What an impressive sight they made, with the stars and stripes and numerous battle flags held high. They were attacking Henry Hill in an attempt to surprise the Confederate forces–exactly as he had described to Early at noon.

As far as Kyle could see to his right and left, Confederate troops were lined up and ready to charge across the field and surprise the enemy. The Confederate flag hung limp in the still air.

Mounted Confederate officers galloped up and down the front line, yelling orders. "Fix bayonets! Fix bayonets! Hold the line. Hold the line. Wait for my command to attack."

Colonel Early rode to the middle of the column, turned and faced the troops. He stood tall in the stirrups, pulled his sword from the scabbard, and waved it high above his head.

The line of troops went silent and stared at Early. He pointed his sword at the enemy and shouted, "Charge! Charge!"

A tremendous yell, an ear-piercing, hysterical screech, rose deep from over three thousand parched throats. That scream, which would later be known by the enemy as a rebel yell, continued as the troops surged forward in a long straight line.

To get a better view, Kyle jumped onto the wagon and watched the charge through his eye piece. The Union troops didn't stand a chance. He could imagine what they must be feeling. The Northern battle line stopped and turned to watch a massive wave of screaming men appear out of nowhere, all across their flank. They were outnumbered by at least three to one.

As he watched, Kyle had to keep reminding himself that those were his country's troops being attacked.

Most of the young, raw Union recruits fired once, hesitated, and then turned and ran. The officers galloped along the line, yelling at the men to rally and fight, but it was hopeless. Within minutes it changed from an organized battle line into a stampede for the rear. Union soldiers started throwing away their muskets, knapsacks, ammunition pouches, even their canteens, hats and uniform jackets. Nothing would impede their desperate dash to safety.

The collapse of the Union Army of Northern Virginia had begun.

CHAPTER

39

*T*he battle sounds rumbled across the field from the west. Union General Daniel Tyler sat on his horse, listened intently, and pulled out his pocket watch. Four o'clock. *I've sent two messengers to McDowell and still no answers. What the hell's wrong with that idiot?*

Earlier in the afternoon Tyler had tried an ill-fated advance along the Warrenton Pike. His troops had been soundly pushed back. For the last hour he had moved his men through ravines and dense forest. Now they were in the perfect position to surprise the rebels with an attack on the enemy's extreme right flank.

In the distance Tyler spotted Colonel Keyes galloping toward him.

Keyes reined in and saluted. "General, the first Brigade is aligned and ready to advance. My scout reported back from the battlefield. The rebs are located less than half-a-mile in front of us and have no idea we're on their flank. Our charge will catch them completely by surprise."

Tyler motioned to the west. "In the last few minutes the artillery has stopped firing. "I hope we're not too late. It would be a damn shame not to play a major role in this victory. Get your troops moving as soon as possible."

"Yes, sir." Keyes pointed down the hill. "Is that Lieutenant Upton from McDowell's staff?"

Tyler watched the man gallop toward them. "Yeah. It figures." He shook his head in disgust. "Four hours we've been waiting for orders. Now when we're ready to attack, one of McDowell's lackeys shows up."

The lieutenant raced up to them and came to a quick halt. "General. I've been looking all over for you. Our army is in full retreat toward Bull Run and Centreville."

"What do you mean?" Tyler shouted. "Our scouts informed me two hours ago that we were winning the battle! My troops are in position to make a huge difference. We need to attack."

"General. I saw it with my own eyes. This battle is over! General McDowell orders you to move your men back across Bull Run and to form a defense on the opposite bank. This prevents the rebels from using the bridge to cross and attack our rear."

Tyler shook his head in disbelief. "This can't be true. I've got two brigades ready to fight."

The lieutenant pointed to a nearby ridge. "From that hill we should be able to see Bull Run and the approach roads. Follow me and see for yourself."

"OK, but let's make it fast."

Tyler, Keyes and the lieutenant galloped up the ridge. It gave them an excellent view of Sudley Road, the Warrenton Pike and the approaches to Bull Run. Tyler pulled out his field glasses for a better view.

"My God! I don't believe it," Tyler gasped. "This is not a retreat. It's a stampede. A disgrace." Thousands of men, horses and wagons filled the roads in disorganized, chaotic confusion, all of them desperately running for Bull Run and the safety of the Centreville fortifications. "How the hell could this happen?"

"The rebs out flanked us. They caught Howard's brigade on our right by surprise. Once his troops started running, the whole army panicked and followed."

"Didn't the officers try to stop them?"

"We tried. Those men are desperate, They've been marching since the middle of the night and fighting most of the day. It didn't take much to set them running, especially for the cool water of Bull Run."

Tyler turned his attention back toward the battlefield. Except for scattered musket fire, the noise of battle had stopped. Through the smoke and haze Tyler spotted a hill littered with bodies. *I can't believe it. Somehow that idiot McDowell has managed to turn victory into defeat.*

On the Warrington Pike, Tyler spotted rebel cavalry riding toward the stone bridge. "This battle is lost." Lowering the binoculars, he turned to Keyes. "We could get trapped on this side of the run. Move your men across the bridge as fast as possible, but like professional soldiers. We will do it in an orderly fashion, not like a desperate mob."

For the next hour the brigades moved across Bull Run. Tyler stayed with the rear guard and crossed over the stone bridge near the end of the column. Rebel scouts had harassed them, but no serious attack had been launched.

Tyler cast one lingering look at the bridge–it had taken all morning to clear the obstructions. *If only McDowell had let me cross the bridge early this morning. We would be at Manassas Junction, with the rebs running back to Richmond.*

Tyler turned to his aide and pointed to the hill where they had fired the first three rounds early that morning. "We'll set our artillery up on that ridge. After all our troops cross the run, start retreating toward Centreville. I'm going to find General McDowell."

CHAPTER

40

*C*IA Officer Stan Jackson glanced up from his desk and checked the wall clock in his Quantico office. Normally he would be home on a Sunday afternoon with his wife and two kids.

But not today. Kyle and Carter were now into their fifth day back in time and he still had no word from Evan Chao on finding a wormhole for them to travel through. Chao had promised Stan a call by noon. It was now four o'clock and still no call. He considered calling Chao—even as his phone rang. Stan grabbed it immediately.

"Hello, Stan here."

"Stan, Evan Chao."

There was shouting in the background and Stan found it difficult to hear. "Evan, I was about to call you. What's all that racket?"

"The team's celebrating. I've got great news. Your men are coming back tonight."

Stan sprang from the chair. "Congratulations! You've found one of those damn holes."

"Kind of," Chao said. "Actually we don't search around and find wormholes. It's not like an Easter egg hunt. It's complicated. We use mathematical formulas in differential geometry to calculate the tangent vectors of the hole. In this case we got lucky. We'll be using a *perfect* traversable Morris-Thorne wormhole. I couldn't have asked for any better."

Stan rolled his eyes. "I'm not going to even ask what the hell all that means. When and where does all this mumbo jumbo take place?"

"Tonight, between eleven and midnight, they'll return to the Quantico warehouse, same spot they left from."

"That's eight more hours! Can't you speed it up?"

"No. I won't go into all the reasons. All I can tell you now is that the timing has to be perfect."

"OK, OK. Will we have any health issues? Since they've been back there five days?"

"None regarding time travel," Chao said. "We called The Center for Disease Control down in Atlanta. The CDC has some concerns regarding a few of the diseases from the 1860s. They want us to quarantine them for at least two days."

Stan checked his watch. "Right. I'm on it. I've got work to do. We'll need a complete medical team standing by—just in case. Let me know if any problems develop."

After finishing with Chao, Stan immediately called the CIA Director.

"Stan, what have you got for me?" the Director asked.

"Good news, Sir. The scientific team has worked out all the details." He wanted to say *finally*, but let it pass. "The two men will be transported back to the Quantico warehouse late this evening."

"Well it's about damn time."

"Yes, it is, sir, but good news anyway." *I'll be so happy to get this guy off my back.* "They checked with the CDC and the men will be quarantined for at least two days. I'll let you know if any problems develop. This should brighten the day of the people over at Defense, plus of course, the President. Do you want me to notify Secretary Evans?"

"No, no. I'll call Evans and the President. By the way, Stan, an hour ago I finished a review on this time travel shit. That project's going on hold until we get a definite answer as to what the hell went wrong. Nobody goes back in time again until I give the word."

CHAPTER

41

$\mathcal{K}$yle and Carter stood in the wagon bed and watched Early's troops dramatic charge over the crest of the ridge.

"Wow! Now that's something," Carter said.

"Yeah." Kyle stared in disbelief. "Never in a million years did I imagine I'd be watching a fixed bayonet charge of three thousand screaming soldiers — led by a half-crocked Colonel, riding a horse and waving a sword."

After a quick check, Carter said, "Maybe this would be an opportune time to get the hell out of here. Our guards must have gotten caught up in the moment. They seem to have disappeared."

"No. We can't leave yet." Kyle shook his head. "Things are too confused right now. We could be mistaken for deserters, or enemy soldiers and shot. Let's hang close to Early's Regiment. We'll leave tonight."

"OK," Carter said. "Tonight the Confederates are going to be doing some heavy duty celebrating. With their guard down it would be the perfect time to steal some horses and head west."

In the distance the artillery fire had stopped, but the sound of small arms still peppered the air.

Kyle pointed at the two unconscious men on the bed of their unhitched wagon. "Let's see if we can help these guys."

Carter checked the pulse of both soldiers. "They're both dead. They must have died from heat stroke."

"A burial detail will find them," Kyle said. "I'm afraid we're going to see a lot of dead men today. We can't bury them all."

They climbed out of the wagon, and Kyle pointed to a small brook near the road. "That stream probably heads down near Henry Hill. I think Early will bivouac near there tonight. Let's try to hook up with him."

"He should be happy to see us," Carter said. "Today your information made him a hero."

"Yeah, and I'm afraid he's going to want more information about where we came from—which is why we get out of here tonight."

When they reached the streambed, only a small trickle of brown water still flowed through it. Carter motioned up stream to a dead horse that lay sprawled across the water. "If we don't get some fluids in us we'll die of dehydration like those two men in the wagon."

Kyle sighed. "You're right. The least we can do is move up above that dead horse before we drink."

Farther into the woods and upstream they found a small pool.

"This stream is being fed from that ridge and away from the battleground." Kyle dropped to his knees, cupped water in his hands and took a good look and sniff. "It's clear, it doesn't smell, and it's from a flowing stream."

Carter joined him. "You know what they say in survival training. It may look clear, but it could be loaded with bacteria. We've got two options. We start a fire, make a filter to remove the sediment and then boil the water for at least seven minutes. When it cools we'll drink it. That could take at least an hour or more. Second option—we drink it and hope for the best."

"We need water now." Kyle scooped up another handful and took a small sip. "It tastes OK. I say we go for it."

With cupped hands, they took long drinks.

Once finished, Carter stood up and wiped his mouth. "Man, that's good. I'm starting to feel better already."

Kyle took a last, long gulp. "Let's hope our organs feel the same way." He stood up. "Both of those men in the wagon had empty canteens. Let's grab them and fill them here. We'll have a tough time finding drinking water at Henry Hill."

They filled both of the tin canteens and headed downhill through a grove of tall pine trees. The crackle of musket fire finally came to a halt.

Kyle tried to prepare himself for the sights he knew would greet them. After four intense hours of battle by over 15,000 troops, in an area slightly larger than a square mile, he knew the casualties would be terrible. They found a path and headed down through the thick forest.

"What's that noise?" Carter asked.

They stopped and listened.

"I don't know," Kyle answered, "it's kind of a murmur. Sounds like the distant hum of traffic on a busy highway. That can't be possible."

With each step the sound grew in intensity.

Carter stopped. He listened carefully. "It's not traffic. It sounds almost human." They took a few more steps. " I know that sound—it's the cries of men."

They moved out of the forest and onto Sudley Road. Directly across from the Henry house.

"My God, look at this." Kyle viewed the battlefield. The gates of Hell could not have been worse. From the thousands upon thousands of cannon and musket rounds fired, a thick haze of grey smoke hung in the still air. It blocked the sunlight and cast a red, fiery hue across the field. Not a leaf remained on the stately old oak trees lining the road, with most of them being reduced to stumps. The Henry house leaned precariously, with large holes blasted through the walls and roof.

More than a thousand men and horses lay sprawled across the battlefield, some dead, some screaming in pain, and some pleading for help and water.

The stench hit Kyle immediately. He recognized the sweet, horrible odor of fresh blood – he had sniffed it often in Iraq and Afghanistan. Directly in front of him, along the edge of the road, a group of ten Union soldiers lay dead in the blood-soaked sand. In the intense heat their bodies had already started to bloat. Fly's swarmed around the pools of blood.

"My God!" Kyle exclaimed. From the look of the mangled and torn bodies it appeared they must have been killed by an exploding cannon ball. Both of them stared in disbelief as the screams, cries and pleas for help rose from across the road.

One of the soldiers Kyle had assumed to be dead, rose on his elbow and weakly waved. "Water. Water."

Kyle rushed over and grabbed the man's hand. "Lie down. I don't have any water, but I'll try and find some." Kyle noticed the man had a massive wound across his chest. He probably didn't stand a chance.

At least I can quench his thirst. Kyle rushed to a nearby dead soldier and checked his canteen . . . empty.

Kyle felt for the prized canteen on his shoulder and then rushed back to the fallen man. "I have water."

The man didn't respond. Kyle checked – no pulse. He sat beside the man, held his hand and stared out over the field. The screams of injured troops and the agonizing screeches of wounded horses filled his ears.

What can we do now? I see a few men out on the battlefield helping with the wounded, but not nearly enough. There has to be an aid station set up somewhere on the field. We could move to the aid station and offer our help. To hell with those damn butterflies. I'll try and save as many lives as I can.

Kyle jumped to his feet and searched for Carter. He had also gone to the aid of a Union soldier alongside the road. Kyle hurried over to him.

"He's been shot in the leg," Carter pointed at the man. "I put a bandage on it to stop the bleeding. I think he's in shock."

Kyle looked into the man's eyes. He had a blank stare. "You're right." He leaned down and placed the lip of the canteen to the man's mouth. The soldier looked up at Kyle, gave a weak smile and grabbed the container. Kyle stood and looked around. "I'm going to search for a field hospital. They must have one somewhere near here. See what you can do to help these men."

Carter nodded and moved to another wounded man.

A Confederate soldier on horseback raced up the road next to them.

Kyle flagged him down. "Where's the nearest medical station?"

"I don't know." The Southerner pointed down Sudley road. "I seen some men haulin' stretchers to a house down by the Warrenton Pike."

"Thanks." Kyle moved over to the side of the road and climbed up on a picket fence. Farther down the hill he spotted a two-story stone house circled by wagons and horses. He remembered visiting the stone house on his tour. It had been turned into an aid station after the battle.

Out across the field, Kyle spotted two men loading a body into a wagon. He ran toward them. Both men stopped working and stared at Kyle. One of them picked up a rifle and pointed it at him.

Kyle stopped, and held both arms high in the air. "Don't shoot," he yelled, "I'm not armed."

"Slow down, keep your hands in the air and walk to me," one of the men yelled.

Following orders, Kyle slowly moved forward. Approaching the wagon, he recognized one of the men.

"Doctor Daniels. I'm Kyle O'Brien. I was your patient two days ago."

Kyle reached the wagon and the doctor gave him a blank stare. *Poor man, I'm sure he's completely overwhelmed by this.*

"Remember me?" Kyle said. "I was in your hospital with a head wound."

The doctor stared at him. "Yes, now I remember. You cautioned me about the number of wounded we would have." He spread his arms over the field. "How right you were. Look," his voice quivered, "we can't handle this horrible mess."

"How can I help?"

Daniels glanced around. "There are probably more than a thousand injured soldiers on this field, both Union and Confederate. Some need help immediately or they will die. Others will die even with our help." He pointed down the hill. "A field hospital's been set up at a tavern down there. Do you know what triage means?"

"Yes." Kyle nodded. "You prioritize the injured for treatment."

"That's what we need to do. We're sending teams on to the battlefield. You stay here and start selecting patients. We need all the doctors and medical attendants back at the hospitals. Wagons will be sent out for the seriously wounded. The first to be loaded are major leg and arm wounds. Next are shoulder and hip wounds. That's about all we can handle right away. Leave the serious abdominal and head wounds for now. There's not much hope for them."

Kyle looked over the field. The cries and screams of suffering men grew louder by the minute. "I'll go get my friend and we'll start right away. If you can find water, bring it out in the empty wagons."

Daniels climbed on to the wagon. "Be careful. Some of these men still have loaded muskets. One of the Union soldiers tried to run me through with a bayonet when I tried to pick him up."

CHAPTER

42

*K*yle left Daniels and searched for Carter over the rows of knocked down corn stalks. More than a hundred Union soldiers littered the nearby field, most of them dead, their faces etched in agony. From the intense heat their exposed skin had started to blacken. Those still alive cried and pleaded for help and water.

One of the wounded reached for Kyle's hand. "Help me. I don't want to get captured by the rebs."

Kyle noticed blood streaming from the man's shoulder. He knelt and examined the shrapnel wound. To keep the man alive he had to stop the bleeding, but with what, he thought. He had no bandages, no antiseptics, no medical supplies whatever. He spotted the shirt on the lifeless man next to him. Although dirty and bloodied, it would at least act as a compression bandage for the gaping wound.

"Water, please water," the man pleaded softly.

After applying the tourniquet, Kyle answered, "I'll look for water and be right back."

After checking the canteens of three bodies, Kyle found a half-full one hanging around the neck of a lifeless man. He gripped the strap.

"Halt, you dirty bastard!" Six feet away another Union soldier lay on the ground with a musket pointed at Kyle.

"Don't shoot!" Kyle dropped the bottle and raised his hands.

"You're going to hell for stealing from the dead," the soldier yelled.

"I'm getting a wounded man some water."

The corporal aimed at Kyle's head. "You God damn reb!" He pulled the trigger.

Kyle jolted back.

The musket's hammer snapped down.

Nothing happened.

The soldier franticly pulled the hammer back again.

Kyle rushed over and kicked the weapon out of his hands.

With a gaping wound the size of a baseball on his right calf, the man tried desperately to crawl for his musket.

"Stop." Kyle jumped on top of him. "I'm not a rebel. I'm helping the wounded."

The man swung a fist at Kyle's face.

"Listen to me." Kyle pinned his arms to the ground. "Quit fighting and I'll bandage your leg."

With wild eyes, the corporal thrashed about. "Leave me alone, you filthy reb!"

Jumping up, Kyle grabbed and inspected the Springfield model 1855 musket. It had already been fired. A ramrod jammed in the barrel. "For the last time—do you want me to take care of you?"

The soldier reached out with his good leg and tried to kick Kyle. "Get away from me, you son-of-a-bitch."

Kyle pitched the musket across the field. The soldier gave him a dirty stare. Blood poured from his wound. Long before help arrived, he would bleed to death.

"Have it your way," Kyle said. *I can't save them all. Hate is going to kill this man.*

Kyle turned, retrieved the canteen and rushed back to the man with the bandaged shoulder.

He lay on the ground with his eyes closed. Kyle placed the canteen to his lips. The man's swollen eyes opened as he grasped the container and gulped down the water. After a quick smile and a mumbled thank you, he drifted into unconsciousness.

Many of the soldiers nearby had mangled bodies. Unidentifiable hunks of flesh and limbs lay on the ground. This must be the area where Stonewall Jackson had concentrated his shrapnel bombardment.

What a difference. After being shot in Afghanistan, a chopper with a medical team aboard whisked me away from the combat zone. In less than an hour I lay on the operating table in a germ-free hospital surrounded by surgeons. I would have died here today with those same wounds.

Kyle scanned the field and spotted Carter a few rows away. He sat on the ground. Blood covered his shirt and hands.

"You've been shot?" Kyle cried out while running to him.

Carter pointed to the man on the ground next to him. "No. I tried to help this poor kid. He died in my arms before I could stop the bleeding. Where the hell are the doctors and medics? Don't they give a shit about these men?"

"They're overwhelmed. I ran into Doctor Daniels. He needs help. It'll take a while before the army stops chasing Yankees and starts tending to the wounded. But we can help now."

"What about that butterfly bullshit?"

Kyle motioned across the field. "Look at this. These are real men suffering and dying. I don't give a shit about time travel. Right now we start saving as many lives as possible."

After a single nod, Carter jumped up. "Hooyah, Colonel. Let's get going."

They both returned to the wounded—concentrating on the men with treatable injuries, soldiers from both armies. Kyle noted other men moving into the fields to help.

Within half-an-hour, Kyle heard his name called. Doctor Daniels stood atop one of two open wagons on Sudley Road. With the help of attendants they moved six wounded men into each of the wagons.

"We've got more carts and men heading out to help," Daniels said. "That should make a difference. I'm assigning you four slaves. They'll be here shortly. You tell them what to do."

Most of the soldiers had gunshot and shrapnel wounds requiring some form of compression bandage to stop the bleeding. Kyle ripped clothes off of dead men to use for bandages. He hated placing dirty clothes on an open wound—but better than watching men bleed to death.

Kyle glanced up as four black men approached. All barefooted with ragged clothes.

One called out, "The doctor told us to see you 'bout helpin'."

"You two go help that man." Kyle pointed across the field at Carter. He turned to the two remaining men. "You men can start by checking all of the dead around here for water bottles. The wounded are desperate for water."

One man looked familiar. "Aren't you Jacob, the cook for Lieutenant Squire?"

"Yes, sir. They loaded all the slaves in wagons and moved us over to help with the wounded, and to bury the dead."

"Do you know anything about dressing wounds?"

Jacob nodded. "I used to take care of the sick on the plantation."

"Good. You can help me apply compression bandages. Watch and see how it's done."

Jacob proved to be a big help. The two of them worked as a team. Kyle wrapped the wounds and Jacob moved ahead of him, locating men with serious leg and arm wounds, and finding cloth to be used as bandages.

With the additional help, within an hour Kyle and Carter were able to load four more wagons with wounded.

While Kyle dressed a wound, Jacob ran to him. "Sir, someone you know needs help."

Kyle glanced up. "I know somebody here?"

"He guarded you this morning. Remember, I gave him some extra jonnie cakes."

"Oh, the young private from Mississippi?"

"That's him." Jacob nodded. "He needs you now."

Following Jacob, Kyle rushed fifty feet through the field. He immediately recognized the boy, who sat on the ground tightly hugging another solider. Kyle noticed half of the other teenager's head had been blown away. Blood, bits of bone and brain covered both of their shirts.

Jacob whispered, "He won't let loose. I tried, but he holds on real tight. I found him like this."

Kyle dropped beside the boy. "Do you remember me? We met this morning."

The private, red-eyed and trembling, gave Kyle a puzzled stare.

Kyle remembered he had mentioned a cousin. "Is that your cousin?"

The private gave a slight, confused nod.

"Why don't you let him go? I'll take care of him."

"No, no." The boy held tight and fiercely rocked his head from side to side. "There's nothing wrong. He's resting. He'll do fine."

Kyle placed a hand on his shoulder. "He's not resting. You know that."

The private sobbed. "It's my fault. I saw the cannon ball. It landed bout ten feet in front of us and took a big bounce. I shoulda yelled, but I didn't."

He burst into tears and hugged tighter. "I just ducked. Billy Ray didn't see the ball. It caught him upside the head." The boy closed his eyes and cried, "I shoulda' yelled!"

Kyle glanced at a nearby grove of oak trees. "It's hot in the field. Let's move Billy Ray under those trees and out of the sun. That's a nice spot for him."

The private nodded. "Put him in the shade and give him some water. That'll make him better."

They moved the body underneath an oak tree. Shrapnel had shredded most of its leaves and branches but it provided a little shade.

Kyle motioned Jacob aside. "I need to get back to the wounded. You sit here and try to talk him into returning to his unit. Right now he needs friends. Tell him you'll take care of the burial. If you aren't successful, come and get me."

Jacob moved in next to the boy. "You remember me? I gave you jonnie cakes this morning."

"I remember," The private nodded. "Billy Ray's got um. They're still in his knapsack. He's saving um for later."

Kyle heaved a big sigh. *I wish the leaders of both sides could witness this scene. War's not so grand for this poor kid and his cousin.*

Kyle could see Carter and his two helpers about fifty feet away. They had a make-shift stretcher and were moving a man to the wagon on the road. Kyle joined them. "How's it going?"

"We're making progress," Carter said. "I noticed more men helping with the wounded. Hopefully we can get most of the living off the battlefield before it's completely dark. Can you imagine being left out here all night with the dead?"

"Yeah, and there's no way all the dead will be buried, not for days," Kyle said. "Remember the hospital I was in two days ago? The wounded are going to be stacked up in that field hospital. They're so understaffed that most of the injured won't get proper care for days, maybe weeks –If they live that long. It's going to be worse than hell."

After checking to make sure the workers weren't listening, Carter whispered, "Are we still out of here tonight?"

"Yes. After dark. Everything is so disorganized we'll have no problems. I'll be glad to leave this mess." Kyle noticed Jacob heading toward them. "How's the boy?"

"Better. He knows his cousin's dead. He wants to bury him under the tree. Says it's a pretty spot—looks out over the valley with plenty of shade. All we got is a bayonet to dig with." Jacob pointed to the Henry house. "I saw a shovel near the road. I'm gonna to give him a hand."

Kyle wondered how many dead cousins and brothers were on this field today.

"Mr. O'Brien, Mr. O'Brien!"

Kyle searched the field. In the distance a man on horseback waved to him. As he galloped closer, Kyle recognized Captain Edwards, who had another horse tethered behind him.

"Mr. O'Brien, I've been looking all over for you. Fortunately, I ran into Doctor Daniels. He said you've been helpful."

"What's the problem, Captain?"

"Colonel Early is anxious to find you. He's got four men out searching. The army headquarters has been moved to Portici, a nearby plantation house." He held up the reins of the second horse. "I brought a mount for you."

After a quick look at Carter, Kyle answered, "Captain, can we wait until tomorrow morning? As you can see, there are wounded all over the battlefield. We're helping save lives."

Edwards slowly shook his head. "Sorry, you'll have to come with me. Colonel Early can be really hardheaded and demanding." He glanced at Carter. "Mr. Weston can stay and help."

"I can't go like this." Kyle looked down at his filthy, bloody clothes.

"Let's get to headquarters and then we'll see about clothes. I suspect you'll meet with Colonel Early and maybe General Beauregard. Major Thomas, you remember him, the ex-Pinkerton guy. He's been asking a lot of questions about you and also wants a meeting." Edward's voice sounded stern. "My orders are to bring you in, Mr. O'Brien."

Kyle swung back to Carter. "Keep working. I'll try to get back as soon as possible."

"OK." Carter nodded. "We'll work until dark and then head to the field hospital down the hill."

Kyle pulled Carter to one side and whispered, "This meeting could be trouble. If I don't come back by midnight, leave without me. That should give you plenty of time to clear the Manassas area before daylight." Kyle tried to remember cities to the west. "Head for Lexington, Kentucky. Find the fanciest hotel in town and leave a message for me."

"Be careful, sir," Carter whispered. "This doesn't sound good."

Kyle mounted up and rode off.

CHAPTER

43

*T*he ride to Portici took Kyle and Captain Edwards up Henry Hill and directly between the thirteen cannons of General Stonewall Jackson, and the eleven just-captured artillery pieces of the Union forces. The guns were quiet now, scattered in disarray across the field—with smashed caissons, busted ammunition chests and broken wheels. For over three hours they had blazed away at attacking troops and each other.

Hundreds of dead and wounded soldiers and more than three hundred horses, most used for hauling artillery and munitions carriages, covered the battlefield near the cannons. Mortally wounded horses rolled on the ground in agony, legs kicking, wide eyed and snorting in pain.

A Confederate cavalryman rode across the field with a pistol in hand. He stopped, aimed and fired.

Edwards shouted at the rider. "Corporal, who are you shooting?"

"Shootin' horses, Sir. I'm with the First Virginia Cavalry. Colonel Stuart rode by and couldn't stand the sound of suffering animals. He ordered me to kill all the seriously wounded."

The cavalryman glanced across the field. "I'd say I got at least fifty to go."

"You're not shooting wounded Yankees are you?" Edwards asked.

"No, Sir." The man reined in his mount. "But look around, there sure as hell's enough of them sufferin' too. They might welcome a bullet."

The horseman turned and renewed his grim task.

Kyle and Edwards continued the ride up the hill in silence, trying to ignore the carnage surrounding them.

"Did you hear about General Bee?" Edwards asked.

Kyle knew what to expect. "No. I did meet him last night with Colonel Early."

"He led a charge on this hill and died a few hours ago. Colonel Early took the news real hard. Bernard Bee was like a younger brother to him."

"I'm afraid there's going to be a lot more dying before this war's over."

"Maybe not," Edwards said, "those yanks might just decide we know how to fight and leave us alone."

"Do you believe that?"

Edwards took a few seconds and then heaved a sigh. "No. I guess not. It could be a long war."

Once they crested Henry Hill, Portici appeared less than a mile in the distance. Kyle could see why General Johnston had picked this spot for his headquarters. The imposing, two-story Georgian mansion sat on a knoll with commanding views of Bull Run and most of the approaches to the battlefield. On both sides of the white, two-story, wooden house stood a massive red brick chimney. A number of outbuildings and slave cabins also surrounded the plantation.

Kyle stared in wonder. He remembered visiting this site in Manassas National Park. At that time, which now seemed like a life time ago, only the foundation of Portici remained. A historic marker, located near where they now rode, had a photo of the house and information on its use as the Confederate headquarters during the battle. The owner and his family had fled south at the start of the battle. In 1862, after being occupied by Union troops, the mansion burned to the ground. The owners returned after the war to find absolute devastation. The glory days of the antebellum south had passed forever.

They rode closer to the mansion and Kyle spotted hundreds of wounded troops spread across a manicured front lawn the size of a football field. A few tents had been erected, but most of the wounded lay exposed on the ground.

"It looks like it's been turned into a field hospital." Edwards said. "Colonel Early told me it would be used for army headquarters."

Upon reaching the front portico of the house, Edwards yelled to one of the Confederate officers. "Where can I find Colonel Early?"

"General Beauregard and General Johnston are holding a meeting inside. Colonel Early may be there."

They dismounted to the sound of thunder rumbling across the sky. Edwards glanced up. "Those are nasty looking dark clouds. It's going to be a wet night. What will they do with all these wounded?"

Kyle thought of the soldiers they had passed on the ride over Henry Hill. In their hurried retreat the Union had left behind most of their wounded. The Confederacy, unprepared for its own thousand or so injured, would now care for close to an equal number of Union troops. Plus, the South had captured over eleven hundred Union Prisoners of War. Where would they spend this night? He had no idea. But it would probably be in the rain, on the ground, and without food.

They reached the front door of the mansion and met Major Thomas walking out. He had managed to find a major's uniform, but on his small frame it looked several sizes too large. Thomas gave Kyle a surprised look. "O'Brien, what are you doing here?"

Edwards spoke up. "Colonel Early wanted to see Mr. O'Brien."

"Early is finishing up a meeting." Thomas turned back to Kyle. "What happened to the guard that I assigned to you?"

Edwards answered again. "Once the battle started, I ordered the guard to return to his company. We needed all our manpower for the battle."

"I'll make that decision in the future, Captain." Thomas wheeled back to Kyle. "Since our last meeting I've done some checking on you. My staff in Richmond can find no information about the sinking of a French ship named *Calais* in the Chesapeake Bay."

"Really?' Kyle looked surprised. "Remember, that only happened last week. I'm sure there's confusion in Virginia right now. Keep checking and you'll find it."

Thomas sneered and tilted back his head. "We most assuredly will. And fortunately, with today's modern inventions we were able to telegraph the sheriff of Ocala, Florida. There is a family there named O'Brien . . . but no son named Kyle. Nor have they ever heard of a Kyle O'Brien. How do you explain that?"

He must have spoken with my Great-grandfather . . . or would it be my Great-great-grandfather? All I need is one more night. I just have to stall this haughty little ass a bit longer.

"Sir, there must be some mistake. That must be another O'Brien family. My parents have a farm on Fort King Road five miles outside of Ocala. Please check that again."

"I will most assuredly." Thomas gave an exaggerated nod, then turned to Edwards. "I suspect O'Brien is a spy." He eyeballed Kyle as he spoke." I wanted him and his friend placed in custody until we get answers to that question. But General Beauregard would have none of that. So, a reliable member from my staff will be assigned to guard him until this is all cleared up. Captain, you will not dismiss this guard."

"Yes, Sir," Edwards said. "Where can I find Colonel Early?"

"He has just finished a meeting with General Beauregard and General Johnston. They are in the dining room." Thomas gave Kyle an exaggerated bow. "Good day, O'Brien. We shall talk again."

Thomas headed down the stairs.

Kyle watched him leave. That clinches it. *I must leave tonight, no matter what.*

"What a pompous ass," Edwards said. "Let's go find the Colonel."

They entered Portici through the double front doors. A large entry hall extended the length of the two-story dwelling. Two large sitting rooms, with sofas and chairs were on both side of the entry way. Further along the hall way was a dining room with table and chairs for at least twenty. A group of eight senior Confederate officers and a civilian were leaving the room.

Edwards nodded and whispered toward the civilian. "That's the President of the Confederacy, Jefferson Davis. He just arrived this afternoon."

Kyle watched the group pass. *Jefferson Davis.* The thin, almost emancipated man, with a gray mustache and goatee looked much old than his fifty-three years. Kyle remembered reading that he had reoccurring bouts of malaria. At war's end he would be highly criticized by other members of the Confederate government, and by its generals. Ultimately he would be captured and imprisoned for over two years, but released without being convicted of a crime.

Edwards spotted Early and motioned him over.

Most of the men leaving wore new Confederate uniforms, with polished brass buttons and ornate swords. Early wore the same ill-fitting gray coat, now even dirtier, with no insignia on his shoulders or sleeve.

Early spotted them and smiled. "Mr. O'Brien. It's nice to see you." He looked around. "Let's go outside where we can have a little privacy."

They moved to the front porch and sat in rocking chairs.

Early motioned across to the front yard at the wounded still filling in. "Do you remember our conversation a few days ago about the terrible casualties in Europe?"

Kyle nodded. "Yes, at the Battle of Magenta."

"This war will be much worse. We just received the first estimates of casualties from the battle. It's staggering."

Early stood, walked to the edge of the porch, spat a stream of tobacco juice, and used a brown, stained sleeve to wipe his lips. "Look at those poor souls out there. This won't be the last battle, and the next one will be even worse."

How right you are, Kyle thought, if only I could tell him about those battles.

Early turned and faced them. "Mercifully it's been decided that we won't follow up tomorrow morning with another attack. Our troops are exhausted. So are the yanks." Early gave a smug grin. "They'll limp back to Washington with their tail between their legs. Hell, I heard we captured a Yankee congressman today. He came down from Washington *to cheer the troops to victory.*"

And it will just make the U.S. more determined, Kyle wanted to say. But he kept his mouth shut and nodded.

Early tilted his head and gave Kyle a hard look. "You played an important role today. I told Beauregard that you made some valuable suggestions, but I didn't give him all the details. We need to talk later in private about your *special talents.*"

General Beauregard came charging through the doorway with an entourage of four aides. He noticed Kyle and zeroed in on him. "Ah, Mr. O'Brien, has Colonel Early told you the good news?"

"What news, sir?"

Beauregard nodded at Early. "The Colonel informed me of your help today. You have a valuable insight into modern military strategy. Your country needs you. I have decided you will join my staff." Beauregard reached over and shook Kyle's hand. "Congratulations, you are now a Major in the Army of the Confederate States of America."

That's just great. We should have left during the confusion of the battle. How could I have been so stupid?

"Sir, have you talked to Major Thomas? He thinks I'm a spy."

"Don't worry about Thomas." Beauregard beamed. "He's just doing his job. Finding spies is important." He patted Kyle on the shoulder. "I'm sure the information you gave him will check out. Just consider the guard he assigned as your aide."

Beauregard walked to the rail and gazed at the wounded men on the front lawn. "We're turning this home into a field hospital. I'm moving our headquarters back to the Weir plantation. Please join us tonight, Major O'Brien. We'll celebrate the victory—and you joining the army. We'll be joined by President Davis, General Johnston and possibly General Robert E. Lee."

Shit, how the hell can I get out of this?

Kyle nodded and smiled. "It would be my pleasure, sir."

CHAPTER

44

*K*yle **walked back to** the front porch of Portici. After a quick wash with a cold bucket of water, a change of clothes, and a bite to eat, he felt much better. He rubbed the five day stubble on his face, and wistfully contemplated the luxury of a nice shave and standing under a hot shower for half an hour. He didn't know when that would happen — maybe never.

At least the beard would help him blend in with most of the Confederate soldiers.

A light sprinkle fell on the front lawn and helped clear the air of hazy smoke and the acrid smell of gun powder. Thankfully the temperature and humidity had also fallen. It would be dark soon and the staff of General Beauregard and General Johnston would be heading back to the Weir mansion, located about eight miles farther east. Kyle had been ordered to join them, and Colonel Early made it clear he didn't have a choice.

The severely wounded men were being moved out of the rain and into the mansion. The main house, a large barn, and all of the slave quarters would be converted to field hospitals. These plus the two hospitals being set up along the Warrenton turnpike would still not be enough.

The general staff continued to count, but Kyle already knew: the number of wounded and dead would reach over three thousand. Until now, the United States of America had never experienced a battle with so many casualties. The numbers had a sobering effect on the victory celebration at Portici.

Second Lieutenant Benjamin Davis, a newly commissioned young man from western Virginia, stood beside Kyle. Assigned by Major Thomas, Benjamin had the dubious task of being both Kyle's aide and guard. He seemed like a nice young man, but very inexperienced.

Kyle still planned on making an escape when the opportunity presented itself. The second lieutenant shouldn't be a problem. Somehow, before midnight, Kyle would find a way to discreetly disappear and meet Carter at the Warrenton Pike Hospital.

From his spot at the porch railing, Kyle watched the wounded being carried into the mansion. Most were in horrible condition, some unconscious, others with bone-chilling screams.

Davis sighed. "I never thought war would be this bad." He glanced over Kyle's shoulder, stiffened, snapped to attention and saluted. "Good evening, General."

Kyle turned to see General Stonewall Jackson standing behind him. As with most of the men, he had a full beard, with long hair down to his collar. In contrast to General Beauregard's brass buttoned, spotless uniform, Jackson wore a frayed blue Union Army jacket, probably a leftover from his U.S. Army days. His finger had been bandaged and blood stained the front of his uniform. Jackson moved to the railing next to Benjamin as soldiers hauled by an unconscious man with a missing arm and leg.

"That's not a pretty sight, is it lieutenant?" Jackson said. "I pray this war won't last long."

"Were you shot, General?" Benjamin pointed to Jackson's finger.

Jackson nodded and held up his right index finger. "It's broken, and only a nick. The man that shot me must have been a terrible marksman. I finally got it to stop bleeding." He stared at the stretcher being hauled into the house. "Nothing like that poor soul."

Jackson's attention turned to Kyle. "Who are you, sir?"

"Kyle O'Brien, General. I was just appointed to General Beauregard's staff."

"Oh yes, I heard Jubal Early speak of you in our meeting. Early's Brigade saved my flank this afternoon." Jackson held out his hand. "Welcome to the Confederacy. We need all the help we can get, and God's blessing."

"Thank you, sir." Kyle noted Jackson's eyes, a penetrating deep blue. Even with the beard and long hair he looked young, and he was—only thirty-seven. Too young to die, Kyle thought. But he would inevitably die in another year, mistakenly shot at night by a Confederate patrol. Before dying he would rise to the rank of a three star general and become Robert E. Lee's trusted advisor.

Kyle asked, "Will you be going to the Weir mansion tonight, General?"

"No. I'm not much for celebrations. My brigade took a lot of casualties today, more than any other. I got wounded men to look after, and I haven't said my Sunday prayers." Jackson glanced at the sky. "Looks like heavy rain heading our way. I better get moving. Goodnight, gentlemen."

Kyle watched Jackson walk down the carriageway. *I would love to spend hours talking to that man. I should be careful what I wish for, I might get that chance.*

"I had a good friend who attended Virginia Military Institute," Benjamin said. "Last year he had Thomas Jackson as one of his teachers. They called him old Tom Fool. Says his class on artillery was the most boring course he ever took. Jackson had his lectures memorized and he recited them to the class."

Kyle smiled. "His artillery knowledge came in handy today. General Jackson just might be an important man in this war."

"You think so?" Davis said. "Rumor is that Jackson didn't have a future in the union army, resigned and taught at VMI for nearly ten years. Everybody there was surprised when they appointed him a colonel, and now look, he's got a star."

In the distance Kyle saw a black man waving his arms and running toward the mansion. As the man moved closer, Kyle recognized Jacob, who charged up to the front porch gasping for breath. "What's wrong, Jacob?"

After a few deep gulps of air, Jacob answered, "You got to come quick, sir. Your friend's been shot."

"Carter's shot? How serious?"

"It's plenty bad. Shot with a pistol in the arm, up above the elbow. Doctor Daniels says they gonna have to cut his arm off."

"Amputate his arm!"

Jacob nodded. "The arm that's got a fancy bracelet on it. They got him at the hospital down the hill. He won't let nobody touch his arm. He's in terrible pain and yelling for you. You need to come now."

Kyle ran down the stairs, hesitated, and turned back to Benjamin. "I'm leaving now. You can follow later if you want." He turned to Jacob. "Hop on the back of my horse. Show me the way."

Benjamin ran down the stairs. "I've been ordered to stay with you."

"There's not room for three on this horse. Go tell Early what's happened. I'll be down the hill at the field hospital."

Jacob hesitated. "Slaves don't ride on horses with white men."

"They do now." Kyle mounted the horse and reached down for Jacob's hand. "Get on the back. Let's go."

Jacob climbed on and they headed over Henry Hill, as Davis stood and watched. The drizzle became a heavy rain and turned the fine dust on the road into a soupy sludge. Thousands of Confederate troops and hundreds of wagons heading back to their campsites were mired along the road.

Kyle yelled over his shoulder. "What happened to Carter?"

"I was there when it happened," Jacob said, "He reached down to help a wounded Yankee and the man pulled a pistol and shot him. Some of them wounded men startn' to go crazy from pain and lack of water."

"Did Doctor Daniels say he would wait for me before amputating?"

"Yes, sir, he did. But he says he can't wait long cause Mr. Carter's arm needs fixin'."

With the road a quagmire of mud and men, Kyle headed off into a cornfield. "We've got to get there before they amputate. We can move faster in the fields."

They still moved at a slow pace through the rows of corn, made more difficult as darkness closed around them.

Kyle couldn't image Carter without an arm. If only they had left during the battle this wouldn't have happened. It was Kyle's decision and his fault. He had to get there before the doctor took Carter's arm. He took a deep breath and increased the pace. Hopefully his mount would hold up.

Finally they reached the bottom of the hill and the hard-packed Warrenton Turnpike. In the dim light Kyle would have missed the modest, two-story, red sandstone structure had it not been for the lanterns shining through the three first floor windows.

Kyle had toured this same Stone House on one of his visits. It was one of the few pre-civil war buildings still intact in Manassas National Park. During the civil war area it had been described as a small tavern on the turnpike, a place where hard men drank hard liquor. The basement served as a storage-room and kitchen, the first floor as the bar and dining room, and the second floor as living quarters for the owners.

In the darkness Kyle could barely see, but he clearly heard the moans of wounded men. Hundreds surrounded the tavern, with most of them lying on the wet ground in the rain. As they rode into the yard, Kyle noticed a few canvas lean-tos had been set up next to the stone exterior of the building for the severely wounded. Near the picket rail fence in front of the house, a ten foot line of dead men lay two deep. No one had bothered to cover them.

Kyle and Jacob dismounted. Jacob pointed to the building. "Carter's inside. So's the doctor. I'm going out to the battle-field to help bury the dead."

"Thank you." Kyle said. "Without your help I wouldn't have known about Carter."

"You're a good man, sir. I hope your friend makes it." Jacob headed across the road.

Kyle couldn't resist and called out to him. "Jacob, hold up." Jacob turned around and Kyle yelled. "In a few years you're going to have your freedom, I promise. Have a good life."

Jacob nodded, waved, and disappeared into the field.

I hope he makes it out of this mess alive and enjoys that freedom.

Kyle headed for the front door of the tavern. Against the outside wall stood a large pile of amputated legs and arms. *Is Carter's arm in there? I hope I'm not too late.*

Portici Mansion. Built in 1820. It became the Confederate Headquarters during the First Battle of Bull Run, and after the battle used as a field hospital. After the Second battle of Bull Run, Portici was burned to the ground and never rebuilt.

General Thomas J. "Stonewall" Jackson (1824-1863) A CSA General during the Civil War. He became the most trusted commander serving under General Robert E. Lee and played a major role until he was accidentally shot by a Confederate picket. He died May 19 1863 at the age of 39.

The Stone House. Built in 1848, the two story house functioned as a residence, toll stop on the Warrenton turnpike and at times as a tavern and lodging. During both the first and second battles of Bull Run it would be turned into a field hospital. One local described it as a horrible place loaded with dead and suffering men from both armies. The stench of death could be smelled far down the turnpike.

CHAPTER

45

*G*eneral Tyler watched in disgust as the Union soldier tossed his musket and ammo pouch alongside the Warrington Turnpike. The teenager had his head down, his face a mask of dejection. Yesterday, Tyler would have ordered the private arrested. Under the Articles of War, section 52, he could have taken it a step further and ordered him shot for discarding a weapon in battle. But not now, not with muskets, ammunition, haversacks, blankets, shovels, even wagons and cannons littering the road.

A lightning bolt lit up the gray sky, followed by the sharp crack of thunder. Tyler glanced west as ominous dark clouds rolled in. The rain would start anytime now and make a horrible situation even worse.

The twilight accentuated the faces of the thousands of troops moving up the road and away from the rebels. Earlier it had been a look of terror as they ran for their lives. Now they trudged along with despair and exhaustion showing. He had given up trying to organize them. Yesterday they were an army, today a bunch of desperate men trying to stay alive.

Tyler leaned back in his saddle and turned to his aide. "What a difference. A few days ago, when they marched out of Washington, they had a bounce to their step, bright smiles on their faces, and loads of confidence. In all my forty years in the military and later in business, I have never experienced defeat. It hurts far worse than I imagined."

"Sir, we'd better get moving to Centreville or we'll miss General McDowell's meeting."

"I hate to ride past all these troops," Tyler said. "They'll think I'm like them . . . just trying to outrun the enemy."

Tyler's ride back to Centreville had been slow and wet. Hundreds of discarded wagons and cannon caissons lay mired deep in what had been a dirt road, but now a crowded, muddy morass.

Finally, as Tyler and his aide made it to army headquarters, the downpour stopped. Nearby, a group of officers sat huddled around a campfire.

After dismounting, Tyler stretched. The nearly eighteen hours on horseback had been hard on the sixty-two year old general. Holding his back, he slowly walked over to the circle of men. Most of the division commanders were already there.

"Where's David Hunter?" Tyler asked.

General Heintzelman looked up. "General Hunter was wounded this morning. Shot in the neck. He's being transported back to Washington."

"And McDowell, where's he?"

Heintzelman gave a quick motion toward the tents. "McDowell's over there. His aide said he would be out shortly. That was thirty minutes ago."

Tyler glared at the men around the fire. "What happened out there today?"

No one answered. Finally, Colonel William Sherman, who stood on the other side of the fire, spoke up. "We got our butts kicked, General. That's what happened. I lost thirty percent of my regiment."

"Any reports on casualties?" Tyler asked.

"Yes," Heintzelman said. "First report shows some two thousand of our men captured, wounded or dead. We know a lot of those shown as captured are probably lying dead on the battlefield. It's too early for accurate numbers and we have no idea how many the rebs lost."

Tyler shook his head. "Two thousand. This will be the bloodiest battle our nation's ever fought."

"Yeah, and I just found out," Heintzelman said, "The rebels also captured a member of the U.S. Congress, Representative Alfred Ely. He came here today to cheer the troops to victory and got a might too close to the action. I'm sure President Lincoln's not going to be happy about that."

"So, what happens now?" Tyler asked. "Do we make a stand here? Or do we head back to Washington?"

Heintzelman pointed at McDowell's tent. "That's what our leader's mulling over right now."

Just then the flaps on McDowell's tent flew open. He lumbered out to the fire with a map rolled up under his arm. He looked drained and slumped into a chair. After a glance around the group, McDowell spotted Tyler and scowled. "It's about time you got here."

Tyler glared back. "It's hard traveling that road, General. It's full of abandoned equipment and deserting soldiers."

McDowell ignored the comment. "I've been studying the map. I'm trying to determine if we should form a defensive position here at Centreville."

Tyler glanced at the road, fifty feet away. "General, see those men over there? They've been streaming past for the last three hours. They've already made that decision with their feet. They are headed for Washington and safety. Look at them—they are exhausted and dejected. It would take a miracle to turn them around and get them organized. And, General McDowell, *Sir*, you're no miracle worker. "

Heintzelman joined Tyler. "I agree. We've got the Potomac River and good defensive positions around Washington. We move behind those barriers and protect our nation's capital. Centreville is of no importance."

"I also agree." McDowell glared at Tyler. "This is entirely your fault. If you had moved faster this morning we wouldn't be in this mess"

"General McDowell." Tyler glowered. "If you had attacked a day or two earlier, or this morning at the stone bridge—we would be on the road to Richmond right now. I venture to say you'll be out of a job in a few weeks. Maybe even a few days."

McDowell pointed at Tyler and yelled. "That, General, is insubordination."

"Enough of this bullshit." Tyler ignored McDowell and addressed the other officers. "I'm going back to my troops. I suggest you do the same. Gentleman, we've got a busy night and a long and bloody war on our hands."

CHAPTER

46

*K*yle stepped into the stone house and the smell hit him like a hard punch on the nose. A horrible odor of blood, urine and dirty bodies filled the steamy, hot room. Holding down a gag, he raced back out the door. After a few deep breaths, he covered his nose with his palm and reentered the tavern.

Nearly thirty wounded men lay scattered across the hard-wood-floor of the bar. Moving man to man, Kyle searched for Carter, scanning each face in the dim light provided by two oil lanterns.

In the middle of the room a staircase led to the second floor. A woman, her hair wrapped in a scarf, walked down the steps. She wore a light blue gingham dress, spotted in blood. Once she reached the bottom step, Kyle recognized, Mary Beth Collins, the young woman he'd met at the Weir mansion.

Kyle rushed to her. "Miss Collins, I'm Kyle O'Brien, do you remember me?"

She stepped back and gave him a bewildered stare.

"I met you and your mother last night," Kyle said, "with Colonel Early and General Bee."

"I do remember." She nodded and gave him the same deep dimpled smile she had the night before. "We talked about France. I'm sorry I didn't recognize you." The smile disappeared. "That seems so long ago. So much has happened since yesterday."

"Yes," Kyle said, "you planned to remain with your mother at the Manassas Junction rail yard and help the wounded troops."

"That's right. But no one knew the magnitude of the injuries. They needed immediate help on the battlefield and I volunteered." Mary Beth held out her arm and motioned around the room of wounded soldiers. "Very different from last night's elegant mansion, isn't it? And poor General Bee, I heard about him dying today." A tear appeared. She straightened sharply. "What are you doing here Mr. O'Brien?"

Even in this horrible place, Kyle thought, she had a certain poise and confidence. "I'm searching for a wounded friend, Carter Weston. Doctor Daniels sent for me."

"They're both upstairs. The doctor is using one of the bedrooms for operating." Mary Beth headed back up the stairs. "Follow me, I'll take you to Mr. Weston."

"Does he still have his arm?"

She paused half way up. "Yes, he does. I should warn you, Mr. Weston received morphine for his pain. The medication has caused some confusion. He's talking about disappearing into black holes in the sky, and he keeps shouting about someone stealing his cell phone. Do you know anything about these holes and this cell thing?"

"I have no idea. It must be the morphine."

If he keeps talking like that it could be trouble for us.

On the top stair Mary Beth stopped and pointed across the room. "Mr. Weston's over by the wall. And one more strange thing, he keeps talking about seals coming out of the sky to rescue him. It's common for patients to see imaginary spiders and other insects climbing the walls but he's the first to mention *flying seals*. Does he mean those sea creatures?"

"Yes, I suppose so, Miss Collins."

The second floor was the same size as the first, with a living room and two small bedrooms. The furniture had been piled in the corner and wounded men filled the remaining space.

Immediately Kyle spotted Carter. He lay on his back, his left arm bandaged and slung across his chest. The transponder was still attached to his wrist. "Can I wake him up?"

"Yes." Mary Beth added, "You see that bracelet on his arm? I tried to remove it, but he got very upset."

Kyle moved over and knelt beside him. "Carter. Wake up."

Carter opened his eyes and smiled. "Hooyah, Colonel, it's good to see you."

After a quick glance at Mary Beth, Kyle said, "No, Carter, it's me, Kyle. Remember me?"

"Yes, of course I do, *Kyle*. They want to cut off my arm. You've got to help me." Carter tried to get up. "Call in a chopper and let's exfil outta here. They can save my arm."

Kyle grabbed his good shoulder and gently pushed him down. "Take it easy, Carter," he said softly. "I'll get you out. Lie back and relax. I'm here now."

"I'm so glad to see you." Carter closed his eyes, and then popped them open. "Don't forget, we've got that mission in Iran."

It took a few moments for Carter to settle down. Kyle remained beside him until he dropped off to a restless sleep.

"You see what I mean?" Mary Beth said. "Did you understand any of that? He's very confused. Morphine does that sometimes."

Kyle stood up. "No, I didn't understand. It's the drugs talking. How long will you keep him on it?"

"Without morphine he would be in unbearable pain. He should stay on it at least a month." She frowned. "They say we'll run out in a few days. I don't know what we'll do without it."

Kyle remembered that both morphine and opium had been used extensively throughout the Civil War, both as a pain killer and to cure diarrhea and dysentery. So much so that as many as 200,000 men came out of the civil war with a new ailment known as *the soldiers disease,* or as it is known today—drug addiction.

"Can I speak to Doctor Daniels?" Kyle asked.

"Of course. He's operating on a patient. I'll bring him over when he's finished. The doctor has worked eighteen hours straight. He needs a break."

While waiting for Doctor Daniels, Kyle wondered what to do about Carter.

No doubt Daniels will recommend amputating the arm. If I could only get Carter back to Quantico, military doctors have the experience and the technology to probably save his arm-—and his life. If the operation's done here and now, Carter will lose his arm and possibly die. Stalling this operation as long as possible and being transported back is Carter's only hope.

After a few minutes a very exhausted Doctor Daniels returned with Mary Beth. He wore a blood spattered oilcloth apron and his hands were also stained with blood.

"Mr. O'Brien, I'm so sorry about your friend." Daniels gave Carter a grim look. "We must remove that arm. The bone is shattered. Amputation is the only option."

"Doctor," Kyle said, "can't we postpone the operation for at least a couple of days?"

Daniels adamantly shook his head. "No. Every hour we wait, Weston gets weaker. In two days he'll die from the trauma of the operation."

"When will you operate?" Kyle asked.

"He'll be moved to a larger field hospital at the Sudley Church. The best surgeon in the army's there. I will insist he operate on Weston tomorrow morning. That's the most I can do to repay you and Mr. Weston for helping today."

Kyle looked down at Carter and heaved a sigh. "Go ahead. Operate tomorrow morning."

"I'll make sure he's in good hands," Daniels said.

"Doctor," Mary Beth placed a hand on his shoulder. "You're exhausted. Three attendants are looking after the wounded. We'll wake you if there's a problem. Mattresses are set up on the basement floor and the other two doctors are down there sleeping. Join them and get some rest."

Daniel's shoulders dropped. "I will. Wake me at five tomorrow morning. We'll start moving to Sudley Spring at daylight. Goodnight." Daniels headed down the stairs.

Mary Beth turned to Kyle. "Mr. O'Brien, there's nothing more you can do for Mr. Weston tonight. There's room in the basement for you. I'll wake you early and you can help us move the troops, including your friend."

"No." Kyle shook his head. "I'll stay here, in case he needs me."

"You're not going to get any sleep here. This is a noisy place, and there's no room. Go to the basement." She held up an open palm. "I promise you I'll look after Mr. Weston."

After looking down at Carter, who now slept soundly, Kyle turned to Mary Beth. "I'll do that. Thank you. You know, you'll make a terrific doctor."

Again, she gave him the dimpled smile. "Thanks for the compliment. Now go get some sleep before you collapse."

"Goodnight." He headed down the stairs and out the front door for a breath of fresh air. The rain had stopped and a bright moon shown down. Across the road a Confederate unit was setting set up camp.

Fires burned as the troops settled in for the night.

Kyle remembered those nights after major combat. You had gone through hell, adrenaline surged through your body and it felt exhilarating just to be alive. He could hear the troop's voices and laugher. They would live to fight another day.

Kyle checked his watch. He could get at least five or six hours of sleep before the move started. He filled his lungs with the cool night air and headed back inside.

The basement of the tavern consisted of one large room with a dirt floor that had been used as a kitchen and storage area. Currently the kitchen supplies and furniture lay piled in half the basement. Six single mattresses covered most of the remaining space.

With help from the dim light of a wall-hung oil lantern, Kyle found an empty mattress and collapsed on it. The day had been long, hard, and filled with the horror of war. He was exhausted and should have immediately gone to sleep, but not tonight. He tossed and turned while considering their terrible situation.

They had about ten hours before Carter's operation. According to those brilliant assholes at the CIA, they should have been transported back on the fourth day. That day had come and gone. With every hour their chances of being rescued probably diminished.

What happens if Carter survives the operation? Kyle considered his options. We can't pick up and move west. It will be months before he can travel. By then that little creep, Major Thomas, will probably have me in jail, or shot for spying.

I can't leave without Carter.

Twice he went upstairs and checked on Carter, who continued in his morphine-induced sleep. On his second visit Mary Beth joined him.

She patted his shoulder. "He's doing just fine. Doctor Daniels told me about you and Mr. Weston helping with the wounded this afternoon. Thank you. Now go to bed. Mr. Westin is safe in my care."

He returned to the basement and dropped into a worried sleep.

Kyle sat up with a start. Something hit his arm. He gave a quick check. The other three men were sound asleep.

He lay back down and closed his eyes.

Another jolt to his arm. He inspected the transponder. No vibration as on his last time travel.

A soft ringing started in his ears. A harder punch hit his arm.

The transponder began to lightly vibrate. No doubt, it's vibrating. Well I'll be damned, we're going home!

He jumped up and headed for the stairs. He wanted to join Carter. The ringing grew in intensity, as did the vibration.

Kyle reached the first step, but black mud covered it. He tried lifting his foot but it didn't budge. The ringing pounded in his head.

I need to get Carter.

The mud now oozed up around his knees. He pulled and twisted but his legs were stuck. He watched, helpless, as mud advanced up his body.

The black sticky substance now covered the entire basement and reached his neck!

Kyle closed his eyes and took a deep breath. The warm mud closed around his head.

How long can I hold my breath?

CHAPTER

47

The loud ringing stopped.

*K*yle gasped for air and opened his eyes. He couldn't see. The lighting was dim and his vision blurred. Could he still be in the tavern basement?

He rubbed his eyes and waited a moment. It didn't look like the basement. No mattresses on the floor, and a hallway with a counter directly in front of him. A single light bulb glowed softly from the ceiling–an electric light bulb.

It's the Quantico warehouse. I'm home!

A voice rang out from a speaker on the wall. "Kyle, this is Stan. Welcome back. I'll be there in just a minute. Do you see that surgical mask on the counter?"

"I see it," Kyle yelled.

"Put it on."

Kyle grabbed the mask. "Is Carter here? Where's Carter's mask?"

Stan went silent for a moment. "There's no one else here."

"There should be." Kyle searched the room. "Where's Carter?"

"Kyle, I can't come in the room until you put on the mask. Then we can talk."

"OK." Kyle slipped the mask over his mouth and nose.

"Thanks. I'm sorry about the mask, but the medical staff insists you put it on. We don't know what type of germs and diseases you may have picked up from the 1800's. I'm coming in now."

A moment later the door sprang open and Stan rushed into the room. "It's great to see you. I'd give you a hug—but they won't let me. Are you OK?"

Kyle rubbed the scab on his forehead. "I was grazed by a bullet." He paused. "But I'm fine."

"You were shot? I'm anxious to hear the details, but first . . ." Stan motioned to the man entering the room. "This is Doctor Roger Hampton from the Center for Disease Control out of Atlanta. The CDC is part of the team that will be checking you out."

"How soon do you transport Carter back?" Kyle asked.

"Once we get you out of here, we'll talk. So let's move."

Doctor Hampton stepped up. "Colonel O'Brien, we have a helicopter waiting for you in the field outside. You're going to be flown to a secure hospital where you'll be quarantined and given a complete examination. This will take a couple of days, or longer if we detect anything. Sorry about the inconvenience."

Stan added, "I'll come down in a couple of days and do the debriefing. We'll cover everything."

"No. I'll wait for Carter," Kyle looked from man to man. "Why didn't you ask about Carter's health? He's been shot in the arm. The bone's shattered and he needs immediate medical attention."

"We've got that covered," Stan said. "There's a complete medical team in the warehouse. Now, we need to get you on that chopper and out of here."

Kyle frowned. "Why are you rushing me? I'm not going anywhere until Carter Weston arrives. And I'll ask again, when does he get here?"

"Calm down." Stan walked over and opened the door. "Let's move into the warehouse."

Kyle walked into the warehouse and spotted ten people in medical garments gathered around a table. Nearby they had a stretcher, oxygen tanks, and mask, plus other medical equipment.

Stan headed for the exit. "I'll check on the chopper and be right back."

Doctor Hampton walked over to Kyle. "Have a seat, Colonel. Can we get started while you're waiting? First thing I'm going to do is hook you up to an IV. I'm sure you're familiar with the procedure."

Hampton motioned to one of the men, who wheeled over an IV stand with an attached plastic bag full of a clear liquid.

"Of course I know what it is. But I don't need an IV." Kyle checked his transponder. "Where is *Naval Petty Officer Carter Weston?*"

"It shouldn't be long." Hampton held the needle in his hand. "The IV contains a saline solution and nutrients. I'm sorry, but it's hospital policy. It's required before we can admit you."

"No." Kyle pushed the doctor's arm back. "Get the fuck away from me. You're not putting that thing in my arm." Kyle shouted, "This is starting to piss me off. Carter left with me and he should have returned with me."

The attendant, who had brought over the IV, rushed up to Kyle and grabbed his arm.

Three other men standing near the table charged him.

Kyle broke away—-kicked the attendant in the groin, and watched him drop to his knees.

The other three men all reached Kyle at the same time. He caught one in the throat with his fist, and shoved another aside. The remaining man darted behind Kyle and stuck something into his shoulder.

It felt like a pinprick. Kyle turned and faced the man, his legs began to buckle. The man watched as Kyle staggered back. He tried to lash out.

The room began to spin.

"What the fuck?"

CHAPTER

48

Kyle opened his eyes. He lay in a bed with an IV taped to his arm, the arm that used to have a transponder attached. This didn't look like a hospital room, more like an upscale hotel room. Sunlight shone through the windows and he could see green hills in the background.

He sat up and carefully swung his legs over the side of the bed. He wore one of those awful hospital gowns, the type with the open back. His head hurt. It felt like he'd been on an all-night binge.

The door opened and a middle-aged, heavy-set woman in a nurse's uniform walked in. She remained twenty feet away from the bed. "Good morning, Colonel. How do you feel?"

"I feel hung-over. How long have I been here?"

"You arrived yesterday." She checked her watch. "You've been asleep for about twelve hours."

Kyle shook his head. "Not asleep. I was drugged."

She smiled. "When you arrived you were medicated. But that wore off at least six hours ago."

"Do you have a Carter Weston in this hospital?"

"Mr. Jackson said you would ask that question. No, we don't. He also asked to be notified when you woke up."

"Stan's here?"

"No, but he's close by." She slipped on a surgical mask and gloves. "I notified him before I came in. He'll be here in

296

about an hour. Let's pull that IV out of your arm and get you cleaned up."

Kyle took a sip of coffee and leaned back in his chair. He had enjoyed a luxuriously long, hot shower, a shave, and best of all, instead of using his finger, he'd brushed his teeth with a real toothbrush and toothpaste. He had also changed into pajamas provided by the nurse. Now he looked down on three fried eggs, bacon and hash browns.

The meal was served at the kitchen table in Kyle's suite, which consisted of a bedroom, small living room and kitchenette. He had never seen a hospital with accommodations like these. After eating he felt much better. But he couldn't get his mind off Carter.

Any time now Stan would show up. Hopefully, he would have good news—-that Carter had returned and they had saved his arm.

Deep in Kyle's gut he knew something was wrong. They'd left together and they should have come back together. Possibly Stan had the answers. No . . . Stan damn well *better* have the answers.

Kyle had finished half the meal when the door opened and Stan came into the room.

Stan smiled. "You're not going to kick me in the balls are you?"

"If I do, you won't see it coming," Kyle said. "And speaking of a kick in the balls, thanks for the great homecoming you gave me. What the fuck was that all about?"

Stan walked to the table. "I'm sorry. I had no idea it would happen. We didn't know what kind of shape you'd come back in. That's the reason for the medical team."

"I understand medical. But those four goons weren't medical."

"No," Stan said, "they weren't. They were included at the insistence of my boss. He felt that after your five days back in time you might become hysterical or uncontrollable. Those men could handle the situation. It just got out of control."

"How are the two musclemen I punched?"

"They'll live. But the guy you kicked in the gonads has balls the size of grapefruit. He's not a happy camper."

Stan smiled, poured a cup of coffee and sat down. "But *I'm* happy. It's great to have you back, despite that greeting."

"Isn't one of us supposed to be wearing a mask?" Kyle demanded.

"While you were sleeping they ran you through all sorts of scans and tests. Everything checks out. You made it safely through space with all your organs in the correct location and no diseases. They're still waiting on a few more tests. Meanwhile, we need to do some serious talking. So screw the mask."

"Good. Now a simple question . . . where the hell is Carter Weston?"

Stan gave him a sad expression. "I'll give you a simple answer. And you're not going to like it." He took a deep breath. *"There is no Carter."*

"Bullshit." Kyle shoved his plate away. "You met him, gave him a briefing and reviewed his records. You were there when we went back in time together. Is this some kind of cover-up? The CIA screws up and loses a man somewhere in time and now you're saying he doesn't exist."

"Kyle, I know this with absolute certainty. Carter Weston was never a part of this team. I have never met him, and he didn't go back in time with you. You went by accident and by yourself. That is the truth."

Determined to stay calm, Kyle took a sip of water and a deep breath. What was going on? Were the spooks trying to force him off the Iranian mission by screwing with his mind? Of course he could prove Carter existed. The Navy would have his records. The CIA couldn't destroy every record. *Could they?*

"Carter Weston is real." Kyle stared directly into Stan's eyes. "He was here in Quantico. You know it as well as I do. He's a Navy SEAL and he's been in the Navy for ten years. He served with me in Iraq. Hell, I saved his life in Iraq. He was born in Aniston, Alabama, and his family lives there. That is the truth!" He paused. "Come on, Stan, I need you to tell the truth—you can't deny his existence."

"I'll check again." Stan held his hands out and shrugged. "I'm on your side. But, I can't make a person appear who has never existed."

I think Stan believes he's right. Could we both be right?

Kyle considered the conversation he'd had with the scientist in charge of the time travel project. "Stan, do you remember our conversation with John on the Butterfly Effect and the Grandfather Paradox?"

"Yeah, I remember. You think maybe something happened while you were back in time that caused this Carter person to disappear?"

Kyle nodded. "It's possible. I can't think of another reason."

"Well, let's find the cause." Stan reached into his briefcase and pulled out a small recorder. "Let's start the debriefing. You tell me every detail of what happened to you while you were back in time. Maybe we can figure this thing out."

Kyle sat up straight. "OK, let's go."

Stan turned on the recorder. "This is Stan Jackson. I am debriefing Marine Corps Lieutenant Colonel Kyle O'Brien on his recent five-day mission involving time travel."

Stan glanced at Kyle. "Colonel, what is your first memory upon being transported to Virginia on July 17, 2011?"

"I stood in an open meadow," Kyle said. "Carter Weston stood next to me. We had no idea where we were . . ."

299

The debriefing took six hours to complete. At times Stan interrupted with questions, but mostly Kyle talked. He left nothing out, including Carter's suggestion that they escape during the battle. He felt drained at the finish.

Stan turned off the recorder. "Man, that's one hell of an experience. It must have been ghastly seeing all those helpless, wounded men."

"It was. I've seen wounded and dead in both Iraq and Afghanistan. Neither comes close to the suffering that Carter and I witnessed. And he's still there and now one of the suffering. You should have seen him in that horrible hospital." Kyle leaned over with his head in his hands. "This is my fault."

Stan said, "You think you did something that made Carter disappear?"

Kyle slowly shook his head. "Since I've returned it's all I've thought about. Maybe one of those guys we saved should have died. By not dying, history gets changed and somehow Carter disappears."

Stan frowned. "You think that's what happened?"

Kyle throws up his hands. "I don't know. Maybe when Carter was shot, it destroyed the nerves running down his arm and the transponder didn't work. I do know this . . . if we had left earlier when Carter suggested, he would not have been shot."

"So, what do we do?" Stan asked.

"Send me back," Kyle said. "Remember the purpose of time travel. If a mistake is made we can go back and fix it. I'll go back and get Carter. Damn hard to say he doesn't exist when he's standing right in front of you."

Stan adamantly shook his head. "No. We can't do that. The program's been shut down until we can figure out what went wrong. Hell, we're not even sure how to accurately transport someone back to July, 1861. The most we've ever done for a human is fifteen minutes."

"That's not true. We went back to 1861."

"Yeah, by mistake. And *we* didn't come back—-only *you*."

Kyle went silent for a few moments. "Good point. How long before they finish this research?"

After a big shrug, Stan said. "A year at best, maybe two years, who knows."

"What's the battery life of the transponder?"

"I think one year. I don't know, I've never asked." Stan turned off the recorder. "I'm heading to Langley to drop this off on my boss's desk. I have no doubt he will play it for the CIA Director, and possibly to your favorite psychiatrist, Doctor Hurst."

"I hope they believe me." Tense and keyed up, Kyle stood, headed over and opened the refrigerator. "Two bottles of Gatorade? I need a beer." He slammed the fridge and turned to Stan. "So what's next?"

"I'll head to Langley and pass the debriefing along to the brass. We'll meet tomorrow ten o'clock. I'll call if there are problems."

"Speaking of calls," Kyle pointed to the phone on the kitchen counter. "I want to phone my girlfriend, Jennifer."

Stan hit his forehead. "Shit, I forgot. A woman, Jennifer Brown, has called numerous times. She was insistent on talking to you."

"I stood her up last weekend."

"Ah, I remember, you were going to a wedding in Atlanta."

"That's right. She's got to be really upset. Can I call her?"

"No. The CIA thinks you're confused and at risk to divulge time travel information." Stan shook his head. "But that's chicken shit. I'll arrange it on your phone. But no discussing time travel. What are you going to tell her?"

"I have no clue."

Stan stood up and grabbed his briefcase. "When my wife's pissed, I send flowers, works every time. Give me her address and I'll have a dozen roses sent. They'll be delivered tonight and you can call tomorrow. Trust me, it works."

"Thank you. Send the flowers. But as mad as she's going to be, I may need a truck load of roses."

Stan shook his hand. "Kyle, I'm sorry about the way you've been treated. I'm really sorry about Carter. If, after reviewing the debriefing, the director agrees there *is* a Carter, I'll propose sending you back again to 1861 — immediately."

CHAPTER

49

On Wednesday morning as Kyle ate breakfast, Doctor Hanson entered his suite.

"Colonel O'Brien, how are you?"

"You tell me, Doctor." Kyle motioned to a chair. "Have a seat. Although my accommodations are luxurious, I'm hoping to leave today."

"I'll stand. This won't take long. It's good news. We've reviewed all the tests and your health is almost perfect." Hanson pointed to the scab on Kyle's forehead. "You do have a slight concussion. So, take it easy for a couple of weeks. But it's nothing to worry about."

"Then I'm good to go?"

Hanson hesitated. "Well, that's not my call. We handled all the medical testing. The CIA will provide the psychiatric review. You're released to them."

"I can't leave without CIA approval?"

"That's correct. When I called and gave them your test results, they told me a psychiatrist had been assigned."

Kyle shot up. "No one's mentioned that. Not a word. Did they give you the doctor's name?"

Hanson thought a moment. "It's a woman."

"Madeline Hurst?"

"Yes. That's it. You'll be under her care." Hanson reached over and shook his hand. "Pleasure meeting you, Colonel."

He walked to the door, unclipped the ID from his coat pocket, inserted it in the lock and turned back to Kyle. "Have a nice day."

Oh yes, a wonderful day. His last meeting with that dragon lady had been an unmitigated disaster, which ended with Kyle storming out of the room. *And now she's in charge of determining whether I'm of sound mind.*

Kyle had noticed that Hanson used his ID to leave. He went to the door and checked. Sure enough, it was locked. He looked closely at the thick window panes. None of them opened.

This is not a fancy hospital room—it's a fancy jail cell. I'm in the psychiatric ward.

He banged on the door. Moments later the door opened and his nurse came in with a big smile.

"Is there anything you need, sir?" she said, in a chirpy voice.

"Yes. I need civilian clothes and this door unlocked."

The smile disappeared, as did the chirp. "Sir, there are orders I have to follow. The door is to remain locked and you must stay in hospital attire. I'm sorry. Is there anything else?"

"Yes, what about the telephone? Does it work?"

"Dial the operator. She can help you with an authorized call."

Kyle glared. "Authorized call?"

"Yes. I believe one number is currently authorized."

"One more question," Kyle said. "I have a ten o'clock appointment with Mr. Jackson. Has that been canceled?"

"No one has informed me, sir." She backed out, and the door closed with a solid click.

Kyle slumped to the couch. They had him isolated. No one knew where he was except the CIA—-unless they had informed the military, which he doubted.

He checked the kitchen clock—still time to call Jennifer before Stan arrived. The flowers should have been delivered last night. He knew it would take more than roses to calm her down, but hopefully they paved the way. He remembered

Carter joking about his calling Jennifer. "Tell her the truth. You traveled through space and ended up a hundred and fifty years back in time. The telephone hadn't been invented, so you couldn't call. She'll understand." Carter, the nonexistent man, had a sense of humor.

What he should do on the call, he thought, was humbly apologize and take the heat.

Kyle picked up the phone and dialed the operator. He gave her the number, she hesitated a moment, then put the call through. It rang five times. He could picture Jenn, franticly searching for the cell phone in her oversized bag.

"Hello."

Her voice sounded great. "Jenn, this is Kyle." Silence on the other end. He waited a moment. "I know you're upset that I didn't call you before the wedding. You have every right to be."

"Kyle, upset is a gross understatement. And a dozen stupid roses is insulting. You think I can be bought off with flowers?"

So much for that. "Jenn, you remember, I got that new assignment? Something happened that I can't discuss. I couldn't call you. I still can't tell you."

"How convenient. A minute, that's all it would have taken. I didn't need a reason, just one lousy minute to tell me you weren't coming. You stood me up in front of my entire family and close friends. Well, I don't have to give you a minute. Goodbye."

The line went silent. Kyle stared at the phone. He heard the hurt in her voice. He hung up, and glared at the empty TV screen. He didn't want this relationship to end. He really did love her.

After ten minutes or so, Kyle grabbed the TV remote and turned it on. The Jerry Springer Show popped up. A three hundred-pound bald guy with a tattooed head, had a huge bearded guy in a headlock. Jerry and a screaming woman missing her front teeth watched while the crowd stomped and cheered.

Kyle mindlessly sat and watched. Jenn didn't care enough to even listen to explanation. He couldn't let it end like this. He would try again.

Someone knocked at Kyle's door.

"Come in," he yelled, and turned off the TV. It must be Stan.

The door opened and Madeline Hurst stuck her head in. "Mr. O'Brien, am I interrupting anything?"

Her tinny, haughty voice sounded the same.

"No. Come in. I was waiting for Stan Jackson. We have a ten o'clock appointment."

Hurst pointed to a chair. "May I sit?"

"Of course."

Hurst's outfit looked similar to the one worn at their last meeting, a dark brown pantsuit with a beige, high necked blouse and dark brown, flat shoes. Her short brown hair had a touch of gray around the edges. If she had on makeup, it wasn't working.

Hurst folded her arms across her chest and gave Kyle a sweet smile. "Well, Mr. O'Brien, a lot has happened since our last visit."

She reminded Kyle of a snake found in the swamps near his home in Florida. The cottonmouth moccasin appears harmless enough with its plain, brown colors. The snake's not colorful, it has no fancy bright stripes, and no unique rattles to warn you away. When challenged, the cottonmouth simply coils-up, hisses, shows its venomous fangs, and strikes with lighting speed. By the time you realize you're in trouble, it's over.

"Yes, *Ms*. Hurst. A lot has happened." Kyle noted she gave him an annoying glance when he called her Ms. "Where's Stan?"

"The Director of the CIA has decided I could better serve your needs." She leaded forward with a distressed look. "Mr.

O'Brien, I have listened to your debriefing, it's disturbing. What a horrible experience you must have gone through."

"*We* went through—-remember *Ms*. Hurst, I wasn't alone. Carter Weston was also there."

She scowled at him. "My undergraduate, Medical School and medical residency were all achieved from Harvard University. I am an American Board of Psychiatry and Neurology certified psychiatrist, plus I have many additional years in practice. I deserve to be called Doctor."

Kyle nodded. "No problem, Doctor Hurst. Do you realize during our first meeting, and in this one, you have called me, Mr. O'Brien. I have twelve years of service in the Marine Corps with three tours of combat duty in Iraq and Afghanistan, where I served with distinction and was wounded twice. I deserve to be called Colonel."

Again, Hurst gave him the sweet smile. "Of course, Colonel O'Brien. Thank you for correcting me."

Immediately a scowl replaced her smile. "Now, let's talk about your friend, Mr. Weston. The CIA has conducted an investigation for Carter Robert Weston, including all government records. There's no Social Security Card, no Naval record, there's nothing. We also checked the name Weston in Alabama—no relatives found. You also described Weston's attendance at Quantico during the training, which lead to your unfortunate time travel. You are the only one who remembers him."

After another sweet smile and tilt of the head, she said, "Weston does not exist."

"You couldn't be more wrong. He did exist." Kyle spoke firmly. "I have spent the last two days considering nothing else but Carter's disappearance. It has to be something we did while back in time. History has been changed. I will agree that Carter does not exist in current time."

She nodded. "I'm encouraged. That's a good first step."

"Yes," Kyle said. "And the second step is to send me back to 1861, to correct the mistake and save Carter."

Hurst heaved an embellished sigh. "This is very distressing. You don't understand. The only place Weston has ever existed is in your mind. Have you heard of the term Paracosm before?"

"No."

"How about the term Imaginary Friend?"

Kyle gave her a furious look. "You mean like, little kids? My cousin, when she was six or so had an imaginary friend named Broccoli. You're suggesting that Carter Weston is my Mr. Broccoli?"

"Paracosm is more common than you might think, and is found in more than just young children. Many seniors who have lost loved ones have experienced Paracosm, as have war veterans. But only while no one else is around." Hurst gave him a knowing grin and nods, then said very softly. "As in your case."

"Bullshit!" Kyle stood and paced across the room. "This is ridiculous. What are you trying to do?"

"Sit down," she snapped. "When you walked out of the last meeting you weren't *my patient.*" The smile returned. "You are now. I can request a straightjacket if you keep this up . . . *Colonel.*"

Kyle sat down, rubbed his chin and stared at her. She had him and there was not a damn thing he could do about it. Nobody but the CIA even knew where he was.

"Think it through," Hurst said. "You arrived back in time all by yourself. You mentioned in your debriefing that at first you didn't know what century you were even in. How did your mind cope? By inventing another warrior to help you through the crisis. Our minds are creative that way. Now that you are back it will adjust."

I don't have a choice. I'll play along with her. "So what do you suggest, . . *Doctor?*"

"Very simple. You don't even have to agree with my diagnosis. Acknowledge that there is no Carter Weston and remain silent. My report will never be seen by the military and never be entered in your records."

"I get it." Kyle nodded. "The CIA has informed no one, including the Secretary of Defense and the President, that your highly acclaimed, extremely expensive, Hindsight Project, sent two men, by mistake, back in time a hundred and fifty years. And you lost one of them—forever!" Kyle pointed at her. "You're blackmailing me. To save my career just write off Carter."

"Weston exists only in your *mind*!" Hurst sprang to her feet. "Prove otherwise." She slammed a file on the table. "This diagnosis makes for very interesting reading. I think the Marine Corps will find it troubling. I'll give you until tomorrow to make a decision."

She stomped out the door.

CHAPTER

50

*I*n disgust, **Kyle slammed** the Hurst report back on the table. He had spent the last three hours working through the twenty pages. He had to admit, Madelyn Hurst had done her homework. She used case studies of military personnel who had suffered from Combat Post-Traumatic Stress Disorder, and then distorted the information to imply they may have also suffered from Paracosm.

Hurst stressed that Kyle's three combat tours and injuries had set the stage—his tipping point being the traumatic trip back in time, which pushed him over the edge and into Paracosm. His fellow warrior and kindred spirit, Carter Weston, became a mere imaginary crutch to lean on in troubled times.

The report also included Hurst's impressive resume, which mentioned over ten years of dealing with PTSD cases.

In one regard, Hurst was correct. Kyle had no way of proving Carter existed. All current day traces of Carter Weston had been erased. Kyle's only hope was to be transported back to 1861, with a chance to correct those mistakes.

Kyle considered his options. He had to convince the CIA and the military that Carter was real and Hurst was wrong.

Actually, he could forget the CIA. They would stand firmly by the Hurst report. Obviously they were the instigators of the report and covering their asses had become more important than the truth.

The military—his Marine Corps—remained Kyle's best hope.

But if the Hurst report ended up in their hands, his chances weren't much better. Once they read the document, he might not even *have a* Marine Corps career. Would they trust an officer who invented an imaginary friend, one who materialized when needed to help Kyle through difficult times?

All of these problems would go away with a simple look the other way. Just admit that Carter Robert Weston did not really exist—a mere fabrication. Then the Hurst Report gets buried by the CIA and Kyle gets a free pass back to the Marine Corps.

Simple as one, two, three . . . if you didn't mind eliminating a decent, honorable and loyal human being from the face of the earth.

He went to bed that night continuing to weigh his options. Between Carter's disappearance, Jennifer's rejection, and Hurst, this had been one of Kyle's worst days, right up there with the mission in Afghanistan and the tragic loss of his four men.

At 2:00 a.m. the night nurse gave him a pill and he finally drifted off to sleep.

The next morning a different nurse roused him.

"Mr. O'Brien, you have a visitor. You need to wake up."

Kyle checked the time—ten a.m. He'd never slept this late. His mouth tasted like a herd of goats had grazed through it. His groggy and dazed head pounded like hell.

Slowly he sat up. The visitor was probably the dragon lady, back for the final knockout, and here he was, too numb to talk.

"Who is it?" he painfully slurred.

"It's Mr. Jackson. Do you want him to come in?"

Kyle tried getting to his feet, but collapsed back on the bed. "Could you get me some coffee, please?"

The nurse smiled. "I checked. The night nurse gave you a potent medication. You must have had trouble getting to sleep last night?"

He nodded.

"What about Mr. Jackson?" she asked. "He says it's important."

I don't know if I can handle any more bad news.

"Send him in. And please, don't forget that coffee."

While waiting for Stan, Kyle eased out of bed, wobbled to the table and fell into a chair.

Stan entered the room with a steaming cup of coffee in one hand and his briefcase in the other.

He handed Kyle the coffee. "You look like shit."

"Thanks for the compliment. I figured I looked worse than that." Kyle took a sip. "What are you doing here? I thought the dragon lady replaced you as my confidante?"

"I thought so too. But early this morning I got a call from my boss. Yesterday all hell broke loose. The dragon lady has been shoved back in her cave." Stan beamed. "And we are both rising from the ashes."

"Well, Stan, it's nice to have you back, even if you're mixing metaphors. What do you mean by all hell broke loose?"

"We'll get to that later." Stan popped open his case. "I can't wait to show you these. It'll blast those cobwebs from your fuzzy brain. Without my boss's knowledge I've had CIA research working on this all night."

Kyle took a sip of coffee as Stan handed him a photo. "Stan, this better be good. My head is throbbing so loud you can probably hear it."

"It's not good, it's great!" Stan said. "They've scanned thousands of Civil War photographs, and guess what?" He pointed to the photo. "Do you recognize anyone in this picture?"

Kyle studied the photo for a few moments. It showed three men standing beside mounted cannons. Both white men wore Confederate Officers uniforms—the black man wore a ragged shirt, pants and no shoes.

"I don't believe it." Kyle shook his head. "That's Carter on the left! Next to him is a man we met, Charles Squires, who became friends with Carter. The black man standing behind them is Jacob. He helped Carter after he was shot."

"Read the caption below," Stan said.

Kyle squinted and read out loud the small hand written caption. "Lieutenant Colonel Carter Weston and Major Charles Squires, First Louisiana Artillery, General Early's 2nd Corps, CSA. Battle of Cedar Creek, Va. October 19, 1864." Kyle pointed to the photo. "Poor Jacob didn't even get a mention."

"You're sure that's Carter?" Stan asked.

"You bet it is!" Kyle vigorously nodded in agreement. "That's him alright. He's got a beard and much longer hair, but no doubt . . . *that's Carter.*" Kyle studied the photo closer. Though he'd known they would amputate, it hurt seeing Carter without an arm.

If only I could have transported him back. That arm could have been saved.

Kyle held up the photo. "Hey, I see a problem. Carter's arm is missing, which I knew would happen. But this shows him without his right arm. He was shot in the left."

"Check this out." Stan passed him the second photograph.

Two soldiers stood in front of a row of cannons, one man in a Union uniform, and the other, who was missing a left arm, in a Confederate uniform. The caption underneath read, "Lt. Colonel Carter R. Weston, surrendering his artillery to Lt. Colonel Henry A. du Pont, 5th Artillery Regiment, General Sheridan's Army of West Virginia, April 12, 1865."

Kyle held both photos and compared them. "It's Carter in both pictures. So, in six months he grew a right arm and lost a left—or someone doctored the photos."

"Our researchers were puzzled with this too," Stan said. "Until someone pulled out a magnifying glass and checked the first photo. The insignia on the Confederate uniform reads backwards, ASC, not CSA. The film negative had been reversed. That's really his left arm."

Kyle studied the photos again. In both Carter looked tired and sad. They'd shot the second photograph right after the surrender. That meant Carter had survived the amputation and the end of the Civil War.

I wonder how he ended up fighting for the South? What did he do for the rest of his life? Did he have a good life?

"I'm having a tough time with this," Kyle said. "Last week Carter was a happy, dedicated SEAL ready to face the world. Now I'm looking at a photograph taken a hundred and fifty years ago of the same, but different man."

"I know what you mean," Stan said, "this time travel shit messes with your brain."

"We can use these photos as proof that Carter does exist."

Stan frowned. "It helps. But remember, the Director of the CIA has decided it's best to handle this by making Carter disappear, and you keeping your mouth shut. Two photos don't change that."

"How about showing these to the Secretary of Defense?" Kyle held up the photos.

"It might work. They're kind of like Ying and Yang. What one likes the other hates." Stan checked his watch. "We'll discuss this in the car. You've got an important appointment in Quantico this afternoon."

"I'm leaving this prison?"

Stan smiled. "You're a free man. I've got your uniform in the car. I'll get it and check you out. You go stand under a cold shower and then eat something. Maybe you'll feel and look, human again."

"How did you manage my release?" Kyle asked.

"I'll explain it all on the ride to Quantico."

CHAPTER

51

*K*yle's hospital, located near Front Royal in the foot-hills of the Blue Ridge Mountains, was more than an hour's drive from Quantico.

As they pulled onto Interstate 66, Stan said, "Say, what happened with the call to your girlfriend yesterday? Did the roses help?"

"No. She dumped me."

"I'm sorry. Believe me—I've had plenty of experience with pissed off women. Wait a week, send twenty-four roses and call again. If you really care about her, don't give up. Wait another week and keep increasing the roses. She'll realize you mean it . . . plus she'll get damn tired of smelling roses. After about sixty-four roses they call and you make up—or they call the cops."

"I'll give it a try." Kyle said. "She's worth a truck load of roses."

Along the side of the Interstate, Kyle noticed a man on horseback. He watched the man gracefully trot along a trail. Three days ago, he thought, or a hundred and fifty years ago, however you wanted to view it, everyone walked or rode a horse.

"You know, Stan, I was only back in time a few days, but it's had an impact. In 1861, this short trip we're on would have taken days on horseback."

Stan grumbled, "Yeah, well they didn't have to worry about traffic, the Virginia State Troopers, and speeding tickets, either." He hesitated for a moment. "Yesterday did you call anyone other than Jennifer?"

"No. Remember, that's all I was *authorized* to call."

"Well, somebody has been making calls about you." Stan said. "Is James Simms your attorney?"

"No. I've never heard the name before."

Stan gave him a puzzled glance. "You really don't know him? Simms has been making phone calls for the last three days, desperately trying to set up an appointment with you. He says it's very important."

"I know nothing about it," Kyle said.

"He started by calling the Marine Corps. They referred him to the CIA. We gave him the runaround and referred him back to the Marines. He didn't stop there. His law firm, one of the largest, oldest and most respected in the nation, has plenty of clout in Washington. Simms called both the chairman of the House and the Senate Armed Services Committee. Apparently, the Senate Chairman used to be a partner in his firm. Simms told them the CIA was giving him the runaround about a highly decorated Marine. Then he called the Defense Department and told them the same thing. All hell broke loose with those calls."

Kyle slowly shook his still-pounding head. "I don't have a clue about any of this. Maybe he's suing me?"

"We checked him out. He's a Senior Partner in the firm's head office in Philadelphia. He handles estate planning and trusts for the mega wealthy."

"Hey." Kyle chuckled, "my dad's a retired butcher. I'm a Marine. Not much need for estate planning. What the hell does he want with me?"

"Well, you'll soon find out. You're meeting Simms at two o'clock. I'll warn you, if he says anything about time travel or The Hindsight Project, don't say a word. Get up and leave."

Stan checked his watch. "Simms has a conference room reserved at the Marriott. We'll be there in a few minutes."

"Speaking of missions," Kyle said, "am I still the leader? It's still good to go?"

"No. Remember we thought they might move the nuke assembly operation out of the cave. Three days ago they did just that. Neither of our assets has a clue where they moved it. The mission's cancelled until further notice."

Kyle slowly shook his head. "Shit. We lost a good man for nothing."

Stan didn't answer. They drove for a few moments in silence.

"What about Carter?" Kyle said. "I'm not backing off. I want to go back and get him."

Stan pulled off the Interstate and into Quantico. "While you're meeting with the attorney I'll do some checking at Langley. Maybe the photos will make a difference. I'll find out and we can talk later."

They pulled up in front of the hotel and Kyle got out.

"Any problems, I'll be in the lobby," Stan said. "remember, no discussions about time travel or Iran."

Kyle checked at the front desk and was given a room number on the second floor. On the way he tried to figure this out. Why would anybody, especially a bigwig from a law firm, go to all this trouble? He knocked on the door.

A man in his late fifties opened it. He wore the typical attorney uniform: a dark, expensive, tailored suit, with a conservative striped tie and white shirt. He was tall and trim, with a perfect smile.

"Colonel O'Brien." He held out his hand and flashed a smile. "I'm James Simms, from the law firm of Barrett, Wills and Ryan. Please come in." He pointed to a table with coffee, soft drinks and sandwiches. "Would you like something to eat or drink?"

"Maybe coffee." *What the hell does this guy possibly want from me?*

After walking over to the table, Simms poured two coffees. "Colonel, I've been reading the background information my firm has put together on you. Very impressive. Thank you for your service."

They moved across to a conference table that seated ten. A briefcase lay on the table with two neat stacks of paper in front.

"Please, have a seat." Simms motioned to the chair across from him. "I've had quite a task tracking you down. I apologize for all the excitement, and I'll explain the reasons once we get into the information."

Kyle chuckled. "Yes. I understand you caused quite an uproar at the CIA.

"Colonel O'Brien. I've handled estate planning for the firm's clients for thirty years. Yours is the most unique and challenging that I've faced in my career. I've been looking forward to this meeting."

"My estate? I have maybe ten thousand in savings, a four-year-old Toyota and a government pension when I retire. This is a big mistake."

"It's no mistake. Your financial situation is in for a major change." Simms reached over and slid a large envelope across the table. "Sir, this is part of the last will and testament of a man who died in 1908. He had no next of kin. His wife preceded him in death and also had no living relatives. This will definitely not be contested."

"What's this person's name? Is this some distant O'Brien that I'm not aware of?

I'll get to that in just a moment. You have been named as executor of the estate, and it's a sizeable holding. How he knew your name or where you would be located—when he died *one hundred and three years ago*—is a complete mystery to me. He also was very specific about the date on which we were to notify you—July 26, 2011."

"That's today," Kyle said.

"Yes, it is. We figured it must be an important date. Now you know why I've been trying to move heaven, earth and a bunch of bureaucrats to locate you."

From the large manila envelope in front of him, Simms pulled out another paper envelope. The flap was sealed with red wax and the paper yellowed with age. "This is from Carter Robert Weston, regarding his will and testament. He wrote the letter and sealed it in this envelope on September 10, 1908—one week before he died."

He pushed it across the table. "It's addressed to you, Colonel O'Brien."

CHAPTER

52

*T*he envelope lay in front of Kyle. He was alone in the room. Simms had volunteered to leave and give him privacy. As of today, according to the will, Carter had been dead for one hundred and three years. And yet after all, it had only been four days. The image still vivid of Carter, lying on the floor of that tavern in agony and pain.

Kyle cracked open the brittle wax seal and slid the letter out of the envelope. The sheets were faded and stiff in his hands; the ink appeared on the hand-written paper a dark brown.

Dear Kyle,

Even after all these years it's still an effort not to address you as Colonel. Where do I start?

I guess it's best to start at the end. The year is 1908. I am now seventy-seven years old and in what the doctor calls declining health. That's a nice way of saying, 'You're about to kick the bucket.'

I've thought about this letter for forty-four years and it's damn time to get my ass in gear and my life in order.

By now you have been contacted by the law firm that handles my affairs. They will explain the terms of the will and all that legal crap.

This is a letter between us. My lawyers have no idea what's in it, and have never heard of time travel. They think I'm a doddering old man. They can't believe I'm leaving my estate to someone a hundred and three years in the future. To someone I've never met. Little do they know that someone is you, and you saved my life.

I hope you survived the mud effects of time travel, and you're in Quantico and back in training for the Hindsight Project. I'm sure you'll be able to line up another explosives expert. There's plenty in your century, not so many in mine, which has made me a valuable asset.

I keep reminding myself that in your world only four days have passed. And here I sit, an old man about to die with a lifetime of experiences behind me. I know you are probably feeling guilty about the loss of my arm and my being left behind.

It's not your fault!

When I woke up to find you had disappeared, I had no doubt you had been transported back. Immediately I checked my wrist; the transponder was still attached. But I had no feeling in my arm, the nerves were shattered. I'm sure that's the reason I didn't go back with you. When I finally came to my senses four days after the operation, the transponder had disappeared, along with my left arm.

Everyone assumed you had escaped to avoid being arrested by Major Thomas. I went along with them. Fortunately, once Thomas discovered I had been shot and in critical condition, he forgot about me. Only Colonel Jubal Early remained skeptical of your disappearance, by the way he would later become a three star general. He continued to quiz me about where you had gone and why. Twenty-five years later at a soldiers' reunion he cornered me again with more questions. He knew something was strange about us, but he died never knowing the answer.

Please don't feel guilty—I've had a fulfilling life, a loving life, a rewarding life. With that said, there are a few things I miss—the comradery of the SEALs, my mother and father, my Ford F150 pickup and Alabama Crimson Tide football games. Oh yeah, how could I forgot—I really, really miss my cell phone.

I'll start with the loving part of my life: my wife. I'm sure, since you saw her only a few days back, you remember Mary Beth Collins, my beautiful, caring nurse. She has reminded me many times that her last words to you were, "I promise I'll take care of Mr. Weston." Little did she know her vow would last for forty-two years. Five days after they amputated my arm she kept that pledge and had me transferred to her father's hospital in Charlottesville, Virginia. The arm had become infected and for months both Mary Beth and I fought to save my life. I finally recovered after a long and difficult convalescence. Without her I would have died at Manassas in the squalor of an army hospital.

In the fall of 1862, I recovered enough to join the Confederate Army. Even though I was missing an arm, General Early, helped in arranging for my appointment as an artillery officer in his newly formed army division. I guess he figured he owed us a favor, and he did, big time.

Joining the Confederacy was a difficult decision and hard to explain. It was made easier by the fact that after a year, I realized that something had gone wrong with time travel. I would never be transported back to modern times. I needed to make a life for myself. My support system was all southern, and my skills all military. Without an arm I had few choices.

The three years of war were horrible, made even worse by the fact that I knew the South would ultimately be defeated. I fought in many battles during those three years, with Gettysburg being the worst. It was the only time I tried to change history. I pleaded with General Early to persuade

Robert E. Lee to halt the charge of Pickett's Division up Cemetery Ridge. Early tried, but Lee wouldn't be stopped.

The saddest day of my life was watching those twelve thousand men prepare for the march up the Ridge. They laughed and joked, with the bravado men have before going into battle. But I knew half of them would be casualties of that useless charge.

Whenever possible I would return to Charlottesville and a visit with Mary Beth. We married one month after the surrender.

In 1867, Mary Beth became one of the first female doctors in America and she proudly practiced medicine until her death of typhoid fever in 1905. My life has been empty since then, but I am comforted in the fine memories we had together. Many times I've thought of what would have happened if I had been transported back. My thoughts always turn to Mary Beth—she would not have been part of that life. I can't imagine an existence without her.

On our twenty-fifth wedding anniversary I informed Mary Beth about time travel and of my life in the twenty-first century. It took some convincing but finally she believed me. For all those years she had suspected I held a disturbing secret back from her. She was relieved and overwhelmed with my story. Now she understood why you had disappeared in my time of need. And why, when discussions turned to my family and the past, I fell silent. Time travel remained our little secret. Mary Beth took that secret to her grave—as I will in the very near future.

As the war ended in April 1865, I surrendered my artillery battalion to the Union Army. To my good fortune, I handed my sword over to Lieutenant Colonel Henry du Pont. He was a few years younger than me and although we fought as enemies, we soon became fast friends. You may recognize the name. Yes, he was a part of the du Pont family involved in making explosives in Delaware. I impressed him with my knowledge of explosives . . . Gee, I wonder why! He found a job for me at the du Pont gun powder factory in Brandywine, Delaware.

For the next 40 years I would live in Delaware and work for the du Pont family. I helped in developing dynamite in the 1880s, and later convinced them that plastic would be the product of the future. When the DuPont Company reorganized in 1902, in appreciation for my efforts, I was given one thousand shares of stock in the newly formed Corporation. I continue to hold those shares and the attorney will discuss this with you.

My dream and your task will be to establish a non-profit foundation that will spearhead the research efforts in limb prostheses. For over forty years I've lived with one arm, and dreamed of two. I want those veterans returning from war to have limbs as good as their own—and a better life. I wish I could have done this for all those poor returning Civil War veterans.

I know that DuPont remained a successful public company in modern times. But I've never been interested in business and don't know how successful. I'm hoping my stock, now worth a little over a thousand dollars, could possibly be worth ten million in modern times. This will give you a good start for the foundation.

Kyle, I think there is a special bond established when someone saves another person's life. You saved mine by risking yours. I will never forget it. Consider this that big one I owe you.

I trusted you with my life and I know I can trust you with my dream for the future.

Have a wonderful life and God Bless.

Kyle placed the letter on the table. He stared at it and tried to comprehend what he had read.

Carter was dead. He had died over a hundred years ago. *Should I feel happy that Carter had a good life? Should I feel sad that Carter was left behind, fought in a horrible war, lost an arm and remained in the 1800's? Maybe both.*

A knock at the door interrupted his thoughts.

The door opened and Simms stuck his head in. "Can I join you?"

"Come in. I just finished the letter."

Simms sat down across the table. "I hope the letter answers some of the questions you may have. When I took over as executor of this estate twenty-five years ago, I wondered who this Kyle O'Brien could be? More importantly how did Mr. Weston pick you out over a hundred years ago? Maybe after reading the letter you can answer that question?"

Kyle smiled. "Mr. Weston was in the Civil War with a relative of mine. I think my relative saved his life."

After giving him a puzzled look, Simms continued. "Yes, but how did he know your name and that you could be found at the Quantico Marine Base? I researched that. There was no marine base here in 1908."

"I can't." Kyle shrugged. "I guess we'll never know."

Simms stared in bewilderment. "Well . . . anyway, after some difficulty, we have found you. That's what's important." He reached into his briefcase and pulled out a large file. "So, let's get started. Each year a CPA firm has audited the records of Mr. Weston's estate and trust. This is last year's audit. I'll summarize the information and leave the documents for you to study."

Kyle interrupted. "The letter mentioned he was giving me a thousand shares of DuPont stock to establish a foundation."

"That's correct. But DuPont over the years has had numerous stock dividends and splits. For example, the first split was in 1926. A two for one stock split, so your thousand shares became two thousand. We were also instructed to buy additional stock with the dividend payments."

After studying a sheet of paper for a moment, Simms said, "Over the years there have been a total of seventeen stock splits, plus hundreds of dividend payments. The Trust now owns over a million shares of DuPont stock.

Kyle gave him a stunned look. "Really? So how much is the estate worth?"

Simms grinned. "If you weren't sitting down I would have suggested you take a seat. As of the close of the stock market yesterday, the estate is currently worth over three hundred million dollars."

"Three hundred million!"

"That's correct." Sims glanced down at the paper. "Three hundred and eight million and change to be exact. Mr. Weston picked a good company. I don't know if Mr. Weston mentioned this in his letter. He has willed that ninety percent of the estate is designated for a non-profit foundation, and ten percent to Kyle O'Brien." Simms grinned. "Congratulations Mr. O'Brien. You are now worth over thirty million dollars, plus that four year old Toyota you mentioned."

Lieutenant Colonel Henry A. du Pont (1838—1926). The grandson of the
founder of the E.I. du Pont de Nemours and Company, in modern times
referred to as DuPont Chemical Company. Henry A du Pont graduated from
the U.S. Military Academy in 1861 and immediately joined the U.S. Army.
He fought as an artillery officer and was a Lieutenant Colonel
by the end of his career in 1875. He was awarded the Medal of Honor
for action during the Battle of Cedar Creek.

CHAPTER

53

*F*or the next two hours Simms spelled out the current status of the estate and the necessary legal and financial disclosers that would be required for the courts and the U.S. government. He suggested Kyle immediately find a tax consultant and financial advisor to help with the myriad of tax and investment issues facing Kyle. They agreed to meet in two days at the law firm's offices in Philadelphia to continue discussions.

Kyle left the room dazed, and with two large folders under his arm. He walked through the empty lobby and headed for the restaurant and lounge.

At the end of the bar, Stan sat on a stool with a drink in his hand, the room empty with the exception of the bartender.

With a wave of his glass Stan motioned Kyle over. "It's a good thing I'm a slow drinker or I'd be smashed by now. What took so long?"

Kyle climbed onto a stool. "I need a drink. After that I'm going to tell you a story you won't believe."

It took almost an hour to give Stan the details of the will, and to let him read Carter's letter.

"Holy shit. Three hundred million. That's a lot of new legs and arms." Stan pointed to Kyle. "And you—you're a multimillionaire!"

"So, what do I do about Carter?" Kyle asked.

"I'll make that decision even more difficult. Chao called me an hour ago. They've discovered what caused the problem that sent you back to the wrong time. It was a miscalculation."

"You mean that sent *us* back in time. What happened to all that electrical storm bullshit?"

"Nothing," Stan said, "simply a human error, and it's been corrected. We can send you back to 1861, to any day you request." Stan put his hand on Kyle's shoulder. "If you wish, you can go back and save Carter. Or if you say forget it, the CIA will most gladly oblige."

Kyle picked up Carter's letter and studied it for a few minutes. "If I go back and save him, he'll have no idea what his future would have been like in the 1800s. No Mary Beth Collins, no devoted wife or loving marriage, no rewarding career."

"But he'll have both arms. Who knows, maybe he'll have a good life." Stan laughed. "He'll have his Ford pick-up, he'll have Alabama football."

Stan gave him a hard look. "How about you? No DuPont stock. *No thirty million dollars.*"

"I've already told Simms that most of that money goes back to the foundation. When Carter set it up he thought I'd get a couple of a million or so. That's what he intended, so that's what I'll take."

Stan had ordered bourbon. He picked up the glass, swirled the ice around and took a sip. "You're the man, Colonel. What's it going to be?"

"Twice Carter wrote exactly what he wanted—to stay back in time." Kyle studied the letter. "He had a great life—he wanted to remain in the 1800s. How could I face him, knowing I'd taken that away?"

Kyle remained silent for a few moments. Then said with a determined look, "This is what I'll do—take that money and form the Carter Weston Foundation. I'll turn it into a renowned center for limb prosthetics. Carter may not exist in this world, but his name will be on the lips of thousands of amputees who have had their dreams turned into reality."

Stan nodded. "Carter would like that. And I suspect you'll like making it happen." He held his glass high. "A toast to the Carter Weston Foundation."

Kyle stood up, finished his drink and slammed it down on the table. "As Carter would say, 'Hooyah, let's get to work.'"

THE END

CPSIA information can be obtained
at www.ICGtesting.com
Printed in the USA
BVHW06s2250081018
529576BV00004B/93/P